TITLES BY D.N. SIMMONS

THE
KNIGHTS OF THE DARKNESS
CHRONICLES

DESIRES UNLEASHED
THE GUILTY INNOCENT
THE ROYAL FLUSH
HOSTILE TERRITORY
THE LION'S DEN
UNHOLY ALLIANCE

UNHOLY ALLIANCE

KNIGHTS OF THE DARKNESS CHRONICLES

BOOK SIX

D.N. SIMMONS

RUSHMORE PUBLISHING

FIRST EDITION

This is a work of fiction. Names, characters, places and incidences either are the product of the author's imagination or are used fictitiously and are not to be construed as real in any way. Any resemblance to actual persons, living or dead, business establishments, events or locales is entirely coincidental.

Copyright © 2010 by D.N. Simmons
Edited by H.I.Gantt
Rushmore Publishing 2012
ISBN-13: 978-0615677910
ISBN-10: 0615677916

Dedication and Acknowledgments

I would like to dedicate this novel to my absolutely wonderful, loyal, understanding and *truly* patient readership. Your unwavering support has meant the world to me. Writing these books for you has been one of my greatest pleasures and I am thrilled to have you all as readers. I only hope that I can continue to entertain you for years to come. I love you all.

I'd like to thank my mother for being the wonderful, supportive and loving person you are, honestly, I wouldn't be here without you. I'd like to thank my father for his encouragement, sense of humor and advice given, that has guided me on my life's journey. May he forever rest in peace in the loving arms of our Lord and Savior. Last, but not least, I'd like to send a special "thank you" to all of you who have supported me in life and in my career.

Author's Note

Although this may be the last Knights of the Darkness Chronicles novel, it may not be the last time you see these characters. You never know what the future may hold. :D

Love Always
D.N.

CHAPTER ONE

The door closed behind the two men with an audible clink. To Warren, it was an ominous sound, almost like the clinking of sliver chains that he hoped wouldn't be slapped around his wrists in the next few minutes. The two men looked around at all the pairs of eyes that were staring back at them. There was a slight hush around the lobby as the other S.U.I.T. officers regarded the two men who were missing and many were shocked to see that they finally came in to the precinct. For several days, they all felt that both Warren and Matthew were hiding something.

Warren looked around, feeling extremely uncomfortable. "Jeez, the last time I had these many eyes on me, it was because Adrian pulled my pants down in gym class as a prank in junior high," he whispered to Matthew, who chuckled uneasily.

"Well, we decided this was the best course to take, let's follow through," Matthew said, leading the way to the captain's office with Warren following behind. He knocked and waited for her to allow them in. When he heard her give the "okay", he opened the door and they walked inside.

"My God, where have you two been?" the captain asked, shocked. She jumped up from her seat, raced around her desk toward her door, slammed it shut and locked it.

"Sorry to be so out of touch, Captain, but we had a lot of shit to deal with. What's going on around here?" Warren asked.

"The shit's really hitting the fan. I don't know how much of this you've already heard, but it's ugly, guys. It really is. The S.U.I.T. organization has lost a total of twenty-seven officers, some of them were shape-shifters and the others were their human co-workers who tried to arrest them.

Some officers who we suspect are shifters have simply avoided contact with the S.U.I.T. all together, while others have come in willingly to face whatever is coming," the captain said, bringing them up to speed.

"That's why we're here now. There's no point in us trying to lie our way out of it this time. We heard about the tests and figured our best bet would be to just come in, surrender," Matthew said.

Michelle Lawrence, Captain of the Illinois division's Supernatural Unit Investigation Team, placed her fingers to her temple, trying unsuccessfully to quiet all of the noise in her head that was giving her the worst migraine she'd ever had. "God, I hate this."

"It's not your fault, Captain," Warren said, trying to console her. She was always fair, honorable, and he respected her a great deal.

She shook her head. "This entire debacle is ridiculous. Those sons of bitches in Washington have no idea what they're doing. Instead of condemning supernaturals for joining the S.U.I.T., they should be praising you for jobs well damn done."

"I'm not going to argue with that," Warren agreed. He'd much rather prefer to get a pat on the back for helping to save countless lives, than the kick in the balls that he was getting at the moment.

"In a way, I really wished you two hadn't come in, but I know why you did," Michelle said.

"Why do you say that?" Matthew asked, wondering if they made the right decision to come clean.

"Well … shit, I don't know. I don't know where this is going, or what's going to happen to you guys. It may not have mattered if you tried to wait until the smoke and dust cleared or not. The outcome might have been worse if you had. So I guess it's best that you did come in."

"So, what is going to happen now?" Warren asked.

"If I follow protocol, you will take the test. If the results show that you're either shape-shifters or vampires, then you will be immediately relieved of your official duties and placed under arrest." She looked down, as if she was too ashamed to face the two detectives.

"It's always nice to feel appreciated for your hard efforts protecting citizens from danger," Warren mumbled, feeling his anger boiling within. Then he thought about something she'd said. "Hey, are there any vampires on the S.U.I.T., I didn't think it would be possible for them to pull off that charade."

Michelle shook her head. "So far, we haven't discovered any vampires, and I don't think we will. At this point, though, the big wigs aren't leaving any stone unturned."

"Okay, so we take this test, the results *are* going to come back positive, we get booked and charged … then what?" Matthew asked.

Michelle exhaled a long sigh. "You'll get a trial to determine if you'll have to spend any more time in jail."

"How much time? When will we get our trial?" Warren asked.

"At least seven days from today …" Michelle's eyebrows creased as she shook her head. "The penalty could be up to ten years in prison."

"Ten years for telling a little white lie?" Warren shook his head, disgusted with the government entirely.

"We're going to need Darian's lawyer," Matthew said. Warren nodded.

"I hate to ask you guys, but I have to … what about your case, this vampire coven, what's going on with them. We've been trying to monitor their activity, but there hasn't been any as of late," Michelle asked, looking from one man to the other.

"Well, I guess the only good news you'll be hearing today is that they're dead," Warren answered.

"They are? How? When?" their captain asked, shocked and relieved.

"Two nights ago, our Packs combined with more supernaturals took them out. As you can see, we both want the same things; to live in peace. When will humans understand that?" Warren said his eyebrows creased in his irritation.

Michelle shook her head solemnly. "I don't know. I know the human race owes you a great amount of gratitude. Not just for this case, but for all of the others."

"Not just gratitude, but debt, as well," Warren clarified.

Michelle nodded in agreement.

"Should we schedule a press conference to announce the good news about that coven being killed?" Matthew asked.

"Oh, yes, we will. I just don't know how I want to go about it. You two have always been the ones to break the news to the media, but with you two turning yourselves in as supernaturals … The S.U.I.T. organization is going to want a human face to present to the world." Michelle turned walking toward her desk, sitting down on the edge.

Warren chuckled harshly. "Ain't that peachy? All of the detectives who were on the case are or were changed into supernaturals. You mean to tell me someone else is going to take *our* credit? All of the shit we went through to solve this case? We lost members of our Packs; our fucking friends are dead! Our families slaughtered! What the fuck?" He turned sharply hand raised to punch the wall, but he stopped himself. Instead he put his face in his palms, struggling to control his rising temper.

Matthew walked over to Warren, rubbing his back, trying to help him calm down. "Let's just take this one step at a time, Warren, okay?" he asked, hoping to keep his lover focused.

Warren nodded as he slowly removed his hands from his face. With his finger and thumb, he wiped away the tears that had gathered from the memory of his fallen family and friends.

"All right." He kept his back turned toward their captain, not ready to face her yet.

Matthew looked at Michelle. "If we can't address the public personally, then we'd like you to."

Michelle nodded. "I can do that."

"Let's just get this shit over with. Let's take this fucking test," Warren said, turning around to face her. He wanted to move on, so that he could know what his next step was going to be.

"Are you ready?" Michelle asked.

"No, but we need to get this over with," Warren answered.

"Very well, follow me." Their captain led them to a room that used to be the lounge, but had recently been transformed into a makeshift testing lab fully equipped with cotton swabs, ultraviolet lights and silver stamps. There were several people in the room, some were doctors, and others were S.U.I.T. officers fully armed just in case matters got out of hand.

Warren looked at his fellow S.U.I.T. officers, their guns in their hands. He began to feel his anger boiling inside again, stronger than before. He *knew* these officers, had worked alongside of them for *years*. Now they stood there, looking at him suspiciously. Three of them were staring at him and Matthew with a hint of disgust in their expressions. One of the doctors approached them holding a small tray with the necessary testing equipment.

"Good morning, Detectives. Now, I'm just going to conduct a simple test and record the results. If the test proves negative, you're free to go. However, if the test proves positive, we asked that you place your badge and gun on the table right here." The doctor pointed to a white table. "Next, we asked that you follow these two officers to a containment unit to await further processing."

Warren snorted. "A 'containment unit'? Don't you mean cell, the kind with ultraviolet lighting and silver bars?"

"Yes." The doctor picked up a silver stamp. "If you would please extend your hand," he requested.

Both Warren and Matthew obliged, knowing full well what was going to happen next. The doctor pressed the silver against the palm of Warren's hand. The skin sizzled and blistered instantly under the silver stamp. Warren inhaled sharply and winced through the pain. The doctor removed the silver, his eyebrows raised in amazement as the video camera recorded the results.

"I guess this is the end of my career as a cop, huh?" Warren asked, sarcastically as he removed his badge and his gun placing both on the table. A S.U.I.T. officer walked up to him; reinforced silver handcuff dangling from his hand. "You're not going to need those, I'll go with you."

"It's protocol," the officer shot back. He was disgusted to discover one of the best cops, whom he *had* admired, was a supernatural.

"It's not necessary," Warren insisted, not wanting to suffer unduly. The silver on his wrists would be extremely painful.

"Just following my orders," the officer said as he reached for one of Warren's wrists.

"Like he said, Officer, it's not necessary," their captain spoke up, stopping the officer from locking the silver around Warren's wrist.

"Yes, Captain," the officer said, finally relenting. He placed his handcuffs back on his belt and led Warren away, to the holding cells. There were eight cells in the large room, four on each side. Clear

Plexiglas over bars separated each cell, and the bars were made out of silver. Overhead, the ceiling was equipped with ultraviolet lighting and the newest addition was a sprinkler system, which released a spray of silver nitrate and ultraviolet liquid if triggered. The holding cell was designed to keep supernatural creatures neutralized or eliminated if they tried to escape.

There were two other S.U.I.T. officers there awaiting their trial. The officer opened the door to the adjoining cell and lightly shoved Warren inside, locking the cell door behind him. Warren turned, looking at the officer, who gave him a scornful glare before walking away.

"Hey Warren, welcome to the doghouse," Fredrick Benton said. He was one of the top officers on the Infiltration Team, second only to Christine McKenzie, the IT team leader, who was sitting on the top cot.

"The humans finally caught onto your asses, I see," Christine joked sarcastically.

"Yeah, I wonder what took them so long," Warren joked back, although his tone held not a glint of humor. "I see they haven't gotten to Henry in accounting."

"Nope, although he did quit the day they started conducting the test. I guess he thinks he can avoid incarceration by quitting, but that won't work. He still lied while on the job," Fredrick said, plopping down on the cot below Christine's.

Warren nodded, then turned as he smelled Matthew enter the holding area accompanied by another officer. His cell door was opened and Matthew was directed to go inside, which he did.

The officer closed the door behind him. He looked at Warren and Matthew.

"I can't believe you two were shifters." He shook his head, shocked.

"I was born this way, Markison. All I ever wanted to do was help," Warren said in his defense.

"I know. I want you to know that I'm on your side, a lot of the fellas are." Derrick Markison simply nodded at them and walked away, returning to his post.

"Do you believe that?" Christine asked. "That he's on our side?"

Fredrick snorted. "Yeah, in theory, but in reality, what is he doing to help us?"

"Well, at least he didn't shove you inside like Wilson did me," Warren said, referring to Officer Wilson's behavior.

"That's probably because he was too scared to pull that stunt. I could smell his fear of me a mile away," Matthew said, taking a seat on the bottom cot in their cell. "So, when do we get our one phone call?"

Warren shrugged. "Probably within an hour, after they've finished their 'processing'."

"Ah, yes, the 'processing'," Matthew mumbled. He looked down at his hand, rubbing the sore spot, which was healing quickly. He knew in a matter of seconds, the skin would be flawless. It was one of the things he had grown to love about being a shape-shifter--the strength, power, speed and above all, the ability to heal almost instantly.

"I guess I'll tell Xander what's going on, he'll be able to make all the necessary arrangements from his end," Warren said. He went to lean on the bars, and jumped back the moment his bare skin made contact with the cool silver. "Ah shit! Fuck!" He looked at the damaged skin on his forearm. The blisters were already starting to heal.

"Why don't you come and sit by me," Matthew suggested.

Warren nodded, taking a seat beside his lover. "We get Darian's lawyer on our case and hopefully we'll just lose our jobs. I don't want to spend any more time in jail than I have to."

"I don't want to lose our jobs. I love what I do," Matthew fussed.

"Our jobs are already lost, Matt. Humans saw to that when they made up the laws."

"Are you starting to turn on the humans too, like Adrian?" Matthew looked at him.

Warren shook his head. "No, but this situation is their fault. If they knew what we go through to keep them safe, I wonder if they'd be a little more appreciative. I know that there are some humans out there who are protesting this and let's just hope some good comes out of this bullshit."

Matthew nodded slowly, acknowledging he understood his lover's

sentiments. "How long have you two been in here?" he asked
Christine and Fredrick.

"Two days," Fredrick answered.

"I still can't believe they took you two off the case. I mean, there's
still this crazy ass vampire coven out there killing people, does the
Captain really have time, or for that matter, the resources to bench
the best on the S.U.I.T.?" Christine fumed. "By the *best*, I mean us,
too."

"That's just it, the coven is dead. My Pack and friends took care of
them. But I'm guessing that's a story these radical humans don't
want to hear. They want to believe that their beloved S.U.I.T.
organization made up of all humans was able to take them out and
keep the city safe. They want the fantasy," Warren said.

"Yeah, because the reality would prove that they need us more
than they want to need us," Fredrick agreed.

"How are Barry and Gabe doing?" Christine asked.

"Fine, I guess. They still have a great deal to learn. They've been
accepted into a lion Pride and we'll just have to see how it goes,"
Warren answered.

"Well, I for one am relieved to know that those sons of bitches are
dead," Christine said, referring to Marcus and his coven.

"I think we all are. It wasn't easy either. We lost friends and family
when we were attack by them. It's a long, sad story, and I really
don't want to get into it," Warren said.

Christine nodded, letting it drop. The four former officers sat
talking, discussing anything that would help keep their minds off of
their predicament. After an hour passed, an officer came into the
holding room.

"You've got one phone call each," the officer announced. He slid
the handset through the silver bars and Warren grabbed it. "Okay,
you give me the number, and I dial. You know how the system
works, what's the number?"

Warren never knew how emotionally painful it felt to have all of
his rights so restricted. He had to admit that even he felt a little
remorse for the supernaturals that he'd tossed in the very same cell
he now occupied, not caring how they felt, because he knew they
were guilty. Still, going through what he was going through, he was

starting to feel a little sympathy now, especially for the supernaturals whose crimes were misdemeanors.

"I don't get to make this call in private?" Warren asked.

The officer smirked. "You know how the system works. You've got three minutes and you're wasting one of them right now."

Relenting, Warren gave the officer Xander's cell number. The officer dialed the number as he held the base of the phone firmly in his arms. The telephone rung twice before Xander answered.

"Hello?" Xander asked, not recognizing the number on his caller ID.

"Xander, it's Warren. I don't have much time. I'm in jail right now. Matt and I took the test and failed. We had to surrender our badges and guns. We're going to need representation because they're talking more jail time, like ten fucking years."

"Were you harmed in any way?"

"No, but I don't feel the least bit comfortable in these cells. I don't want to spend any more time here than necessary."

"Can we post bail for you?" Xander asked.

"No. There is never a bail set for a supernatural who's been incarcerated."

"So the only way to get you out of there legally is to go through the trial process?"

"Yes."

"When is the date?"

"They haven't set it yet, but I'm guessing seven days from today, well six days, because today counts as one."

"Your three minutes are up," the officer informed him before pushing the dial button down disconnecting the call.

"You son of a bitch!" Warren cursed the officer. "You know that wasn't three fucking minutes, you asshole!"

"Just following protocol," the smug officer said with a smirk.

"Yeah, right." Warren snarled at the officer, which made him step back a few feet.

"Watch it, freak! Just hand the phone over to him, let's get a move on."

"Who are you calling a *freak*?" Warren asked. His lips were twisted in a menacing sneer. He went to move forward, but Matthew grabbed his shoulder, stopping him.

"Just hand me the phone, Warren. The quicker he gets out of our sight, the better off we'll be," Matthew said, hoping to calm Warren down.

Warren never took his eyes off the officer as he handed Matthew the handset. Matthew took the phone and gave the officer a number to dial. He waited for Richard to pick up on his end.

"Hello?" Richard greeted.

"Hi Richard, it's me. I'm being held in jail along with Warren. We kind of knew this was going to happen. Warren called Xander so that he could get Darian's lawyer," Matthew said in a rush of words, hoping to get the most out of his so-called "three" minutes.

"I see. Have you been harmed in any way?"

"No."

"Good. I've sent Ignacio there to speak with this Marshall Galen; I'll contact Xander as well. I take it there's no bail set?"

"You'd be right. Not for us, there never is."

"All right, so can you receive visitors?"

"Yes."

"I'll be there shortly, once I touch base with a few people."

"All right, see you when you get here."

"Be strong, in seven days, you will be free."

"I know." Matthew had every confidence his friends and Alpha would get them free.

"Your three minutes are up," the officer announced.

"Okay, hey Richard, I have to go."

"I heard. Take care." Richard ended the call.

Matthew slid the handset through the bars, being very careful not to let his flesh touch the silver. "Here." The officer took the handset, putting it back in its place on the base and left.

"Isn't he the *sweetest* person in the world?" Christine asked, being very sarcastic.

"Almost as sweet as a pile of shit," Warren commented. "I swear I wanted to ring his neck for that bullshit he pulled."

Matthew chuckled lightly. "It's best that you didn't. The less violence we have in here, the better our chances are of getting out of here alive."

"So, I wonder what Richard is going to say when he gets here," Warren speculated.

"I don't know. Whatever it is, I hope it's good news." Matthew sat back down on the cot, making himself comfortable. Warren joined him and both men waited for the next phase.

CHAPTER TWO

Ignacio strolled up to the front desk, placing his hands, palms down on the counter. "Hello, I'm here to see Marshall Galen." The desk cop looked up from his morning paper. "Sign in right here," he pointed to the sign-in sheet. "And place this on your shirt front." He wrote the word "visitor" on a white sticker and handed it to Ignacio, who took it.

Ignacio filled out the sheet and placed the sticker over his left pectoral. "You'd think with all the advanced technology you guys have, you'd have something a little more hi-tech or flashier for a visitor's pass other than this," he commented.

"Sorry if flashy visitors' passes aren't in our budget. We put our well-spent tax dollars where it counts. I guess you'll just have to settle for our antiquated technology," the desk cop retorted with laden derision.

"So much for the small talk. Now, do I go to him or does he come to me?" Ignacio asked, ignoring the cop's snide attitude.

"You can wait there, I'll call him." He pointed to the metal bench against the far wall as he picked up the telephone.

Ignacio walked over toward the bench, taking a seat. After a few minutes, a slightly tall, thin man rounded the corner. He was wearing black slacks, a white button up shirt and a lab coat. He cleaned his glasses with a handkerchief, stuffing the white cloth back into his pocket once he was done. He looked at the desk cop, who pointed in Ignacio's direction. Marshall approached Ignacio, who rose to greet him.

"Hello, they told me you're here to see me?" Marshall greeted, shaking Ignacio's hand firmly.

"Ah yeah. Is there some place we can speak privately? I'm a friend of Matthew and Warren," Ignacio said, ending the handshake.

"Ahhh, I see. Yes, we can go to my office." Marshall turned, leading Ignacio toward the morgue. The two men entered the cold room. "So, you say you're a friend of Matthew and Warren?"

"Yeah, I don't know how much they told you, but I want to know how much you're supporting them." Ignacio stated, getting right to the point.

"I like that you don't beat around the bush. I heard that they turned themselves in earlier today. It was a smart decision. I'll tell you what I told Warren. I'm fully supportive of supernaturals being members of the S.U.I.T. organization. I think many people are alive today because they have supernaturals to save them," Marshall said as he sat down at his desk, picking up his breakfast sandwich and taking a bite.

"I suppose my question should be; how far does your support go? If need be, will you be a witness for them when their trial comes? Will you protest them losing their jobs?"

Marshall nodded as he swallowed the food in his mouth. "I understand. Some people can say they're supportive of you, but never step up to the plate to help. I'm not one of those people. I think what's happening is a travesty and a true dark mark in history. I will be there for them, even if it means *my* job. See, this is bigger than Matthew and Warren; it's bigger than the S.U.I.T. ... People out there need to understand that supernatural beings are an important part of our world and we can't live without them, just as supernaturals can't live without humans. Once we begin to realize how much we need the other, times like these can finally be a thing of the past." He took another bite of his sandwich.

Ignacio was in awe of the man. Never had he heard a human being speak so profoundly about the co-existence of humans and supernaturals. "I agree with what you said. It's nice to know that's the way you feel."

Marshall swallowed and took a sip of his coffee. "I've known the cops on this force for a long time now. Warren and Matthew have shown more humanity and a thirst for justice towards humans than a great deal of the human cops we have here. They really care and want to help. This is a political battle we are in right now, riddled with ignorance and prejudice. I honestly don't know what's going to happen next, but if I'm called as a character witness to attest to their contribution to the organization, I will be proud to do so."

Ignacio nodded. "Thank you for your time. I'll leave you to enjoy the rest of your meal." He turned to leave, when Marshall called out to him. He turned around. "Yes?"

"You never told me your name," Marshall prompted, keeping eye contact.

"Oh, I'm sorry about that. It's Ignacio."

"Are you a Pack brother of Matthew?"

"They really told you everything, didn't they? Yes, I am." Ignacio gave him a slightly crooked smile.

"Not everything, but enough. I had known the two were shifters for a while now."

"Yeah, about that … I thought it was pretty cool of you to keep their secret."

"I take it your Alpha wanted to know the extent of my support?"

"Yes, he did. For all of the reasons you've stated. He'll be happy to know that you'll be there for them."

"All the way."

Ignacio nodded. "Take it easy."

With that, he left the morgue. On his way towards the exit, he met up with Richard who was coming through the doorway. He smiled to himself as he took in Richard's appearance. His Alpha was impeccably dressed in black from head to toe. He knew he wore that whenever he wanted to make a certain kind of impression on people. Richard's brown eyes locked on Ignacio's as the two came closer.

"Did you get a chance to speak with this, Marshall Galen?" he asked.

Ignacio nodded. "Yeah, he's definitely pissed about what's going on?" He went on to tell him everything Marshall told him.

"I see. Very good. I've spoken with both Xander and Elise and we decided to follow the human course of action during this time. Xander will call Darian to get the number of his lawyer …" Richard snorted. "I think we're all kicking ourselves for not doing that earlier."

"We'll it's not like it's too late," Ignacio pointed out.

"That's true. When Darian awakens this evening, we'll get the number from him. I'm sure his lawyer works evenings and we'll be able to touch base with Warren and Matthew tonight." Richard stepped around Ignacio making his way towards the front desk. The clerk looked up, his eyes widening slightly as he stared at the man with a beautiful chocolate complexion; smooth freshly shaven head, standing over six feet tall, donned in black, staring back at him with a no-nonsense expression.

The desk cop cleared his throat. "How can I help you?" he asked in a low steady voice.

There was something about the man in front of him that sent chills down his spine and made the hair stand up on the nape of his neck. The expression in the man's eyes unnerved him and there was something else about his very presence that sent vibrations through his being.

Richard's voice was low and calm when he spoke. "I'm here to see two prisoners, Warren Davis and Matthew Eric."

"Sure, if you can just sign in here. Someone will take you into the holding area." The desk cop pointed to the same sign-in sheet that Ignacio had signed earlier.

Richard gave the officer another look then he signed his name. Meanwhile the officer called for another one to escort Richard into the holding area. Once Richard had finished signing in and pasting the little sticker over his chest, he was approached by another officer who took him to the holding area. He followed the officer's instructions and stepped through the metal detector, after removing all of his metal belongings. Once that step was done, the officer read him the rules. Once that was done, he was allowed entrance and was taken directly to Warren and Matthew's cell.

"You have fifteen minutes, no more than that," the officer informed.

"That's all of the time I'll need. You may go." Richard gave the officer a dismissing wave of his hand.

The officer nodded and then returned to his post, relieved to be out of Richard's powerful presence, if only for fifteen minutes.

"Man, am I glad to see you!" Matthew declared as he approached the cell bars. Warren followed, standing beside him. Matthew looked at his Alpha's attire. "Damn, don't *you* look menacing?"

"That's the point," Richard answered, flashing his pearly whites.

Matthew chuckled. "I'm really glad to see you."

"You've said that already." Richard chuckled. "You've only been here for about two hours. Do you think you can survive seven days?" he asked with a hint of humor.

"I hope so," Matthew replied, slightly joking.

"If Darian could, I know I can, too," Warren stated.

"Well, it's not as if you have a choice otherwise." Richard looked at the bars, shaking his head. "My, my, my … what a monstrosity. It would be impossible for you to break out of here without the help of a vampire and vice-versa. They really did cover their bases when they constructed this place, didn't they?"

"Yeah, they wanted this system to work and that meant creating a prison to keep supernatural criminals locked inside," Warren said.

Richard looked at him. "Is that what you are? A 'supernatural criminal'?"

"I did break the law, we both did." Warren looked down at his hands.

"So does that mean you feel you should face your penalty for the crime you committed?" Richard asked, wondering what the young shifter was thinking about.

"If it was fair, the penalty would fit the crime. When people lie on their job application or cheat on urine test, they get fired. Lose their pension, and possibly mar their record. They don't, however, go to jail for ten years."

"Ah, so would this mean that all of the supernaturals who you have arrested might have faced an unjust penalty for their crimes committed?" Richard's eyebrows were raised now, intrigued.

"I see what you're doing. You're trying to talk me into a hypocritical hole. It's not going to happen. The supernaturals that were put in here deserved the punishment they got. Matt and I did our jobs well. We never arrested anyone who was innocent, never," Warren said, standing by his conviction.

"Can the same be said about the other officers here? I'm only getting you to question the justice system you vowed to uphold. See, Warren, this system has never been fair. Is it fair to kill a supernatural simply because they lost control and fed on a human or hunted off sanctioned grounds? Humans do not execute every human who kills. They even have gradations of crimes to charge each other with. First degree, manslaughter, accidental homicide, this list goes on. They even believe in rehabilitation for these harden criminals, but where is that compassion for us?" Richard asked, waiting silently for his response.

Matthew turned towards Warren, also curious as to what his answer would be.

Warren shrugged. "I'm not saying that our system was perfect and I'm not saying that this situation isn't frustrating. I just know that I've felt justified with everything I've done for the S.U.I.T., the same as I feel for what I've done for my Pack."

Richard nodded, understanding the younger shifter. "Let us hope your faith in these humans don't prove to be fruitless. I've spoken with Xander; he said he'd be here to visit you later today after he makes a few phone calls. I on the other hand have to contact some of my political connections to see if I can pull some strings to get your trial date rushed so that you don't have to spend any more time in here than necessary."

"That'd be very nice," Matthew said. "Think you can arrange that?"

"Of course. That's not a problem. The only difficult part of this is your trial. Will a jury of your peers judge you? Or is the judge the sole decider of your fates?" Richard asked.

"Wow, Richard ... you really know how to make some shit sound ominous," Warren commented.

Richard gave him a sly smile; a slight parting of his full, luscious lips enough to show a slit of his pearly whites. "I'm just trying to get a clear understanding of how this system works."

"The judge has the final decision. He or she will view the evidence, listen to character witnesses and any other testimony and then give their verdict," Matthew answered.

"Is there a judge you have in mind who you believe will be lenient?" Richard asked.

"Yeah, but only two. Allison White and Margaret Hillington, they've been known to give light sentences or even to release supernaturals with only probation," Warren said.

"This is good to know." Richard nodded.

An officer entered the cell area. "Your fifteen minutes are up, you'll have to leave today, but you can come back tomorrow."

Richard sighed. "Very well. I'll return soon when I have more news for you," he told the two men, who nodded. He left the precinct with Ignacio following behind him.

"How are they?" Ignacio asked, concerned about his Pack brother and friend.

"They are in good spirits, hopeful," Richard said as walked to his Anaconda Quest SUV, opening the door.

"That's good to hear." Ignacio climbed into his Boa sports car. He was going to drive back home, get Ryan and return for a visit. "Where are you going?" he asked his Alpha before he could drive away.

"I'm going home to make a few more telephone calls."

"Oh, okay, I'll see you there, then."

The two men drove off, heading in the same direction. Ignacio stopped off along the way to pick up something to eat before going home. When he met up with Ryan, he asked her if she wanted to go back with him to visit Warren and Matthew and she agreed. The two drove back to the precinct to chat with the two men, hoping to help keep their spirits up.

***

Richard sat in his soundproofed office that he had designed a year ago because he was impressed with the one that Xander owned. The younger Alpha had impressed him from the moment they had first met on the battlefield. As time passed, the two men had become very good friends and both enjoyed long conversations about days passed. As he scrolled through his Rolodex, he marked off the cards with important contacts on them. He was going to have to pull some strings for his Pack member and Warren. He knew that he had more political contacts than Xander. Politicians who gave a sympathetic ear to supernaturals, not to mention the most important of his contacts who was a shifter he wished he didn't have to call. He knew it was unavoidable if he was going to help Warren and Matthew. He settled on the first number and dialed. The telephone rung four times before the man's secretary picked up.

"Senator Beasley's office, my name is Samantha, How may I help you?" the secretary greeted.

"Good afternoon, Samantha, I'm calling to speak with Senator Beasley," Richard said.

"I'm sorry, but the Senator is unavailable at the moment, I can take a message."

"Very well, please give him this message promptly. Tell him that Richard Stevenson is trying to get in contact with him."

The secretary wrote down the message. "All right, sir, I have your message and will give it to him as soon as possible."

"Immediately, please." Richard tacked on the "please" to soften the urgency of his demand.

"As soon as I can, sir." The secretary didn't take too kindly to demands, but she would give the message to the senator as promised.

"Thank you." Richard gave her a polite "goodbye" before ending his call and moving on to the next person on his list. He called another senator and was able to speak with her directly.

"Ah, Richard, how nice to hear from you," Senator Elaine Baker cooed over the receiver. She remembered Richard very well … intimately as a matter of fact.

Richard chuckled, sending deep, seductive vibrations over the inner shell of her ear. "Likewise, my darling. I am calling for a reason, though."

"Please, let's not talk over the telephone, it's been such a long time, I want to see you."

"You're in town?" Richard asked; surprised to find her in Chicago instead of Washington D.C. where he had hoped she would be.

"Yes, I'm here on business."

"Who granted you permission to enter this territory?" Richard asked, a bit too accusatory.

"I'm a U.S. Senator, I dare any supernatural in this country to deny me access into their territories," Elaine said. "Speaking of, you sound very disappointed that I'm in Chicago, is there a problem?"

"No," Richard said, making sure his tone was neutral. "I didn't intend for my words to sound so defensive. I apologize. It's just that you didn't call to let me know you wanted to visit."

"Is that all … your feelings are hurt? Well, for a minute I thought you had forgotten about the secret arrangement. The last thing we need is a lot of ruckus and territorial disputes exposing us, now wouldn't you agree?"

After learning that she was in his territory, Richard had forgotten about the "arrangement" made between the Council and every supernatural leader in the country that allowed other supernaturals in high-ranking politics to travel back and forth whenever they needed to without incident. This protocol was customary throughout the world, as well.

"No, we wouldn't want that to happen. I understand the importance of having our kind in politics," he said, hoping to disguise his blunder. "That is actually the reason why I'm calling. So where should we meet? Perhaps, the *Rooftop Gardens*?"

"I'd prefer to meet at the *Rosette Café*."

Elaine purposely selected the café located on the first floor of the *Xavier* Hotel. "Hotel" being the target location. It had been well over sixty years since the last time she saw Richard and she was sure he'd look just as delectable as he did then, now.

Richard suspected Elaine was trying to maneuver him into a predicament that he knew would be almost impossible for him to get out of, but what choice did he have? He needed a favor from her, not the other way around. "I'll meet you there at two, then?"

"Until then." She ended the call, knowing she had him where she wanted him.

Richard placed the handset back onto the base just in time for the telephone to ring. He answered it. "Hello?" he greeted.

"This is Senator Beasley, may I speak with Richard Stevenson?"

"Dave, it's Richard."

"Hi, I was kind of surprised when my secretary told me you called. It's been a while," Dave said, happy to hear from his old friend. Not only had Richard saved his life from a shifter attack when he was a ten-year-old boy, but he helped put him through college and funded his campaign when he decided to run for Washington state senator. Needless to say, he owed Richard big time.

"Yes, time has passed by quickly. Listen Dave, I have a favor to ask of you, it's quite urgent," Richard began.

"You sound serious enough, what do you need?" Dave inquired.

"I have a Pack member and a friend who were S.U.I.T. officers who are now under investigation and they may face charges which could lead to incarceration."

"That's a big problem, do you need a lawyer?"

"No, I have one already."

"Really? Who?"

"I believe Darian said his name was Howard Langston."

"Ahh, then your guys are in good hands. Howard is one of the top defense lawyers in the entire country. And he isn't cheap; it's good that you're rich." Dave chuckled. "Okay, well, what do you need from me?"

"I need you to expedite the trial date. I don't want them held for the extent of seven days."

"Wow, that's one hell of a favor you need. I don't even know if I can pull that off."

"How many days do you think you can eliminate from the standard seven?"

"Richard, I don't think that I can. Don't get me wrong, I have a lot of pull, but this whole S.U.I.T. debacle combined with all that's happened has raised a lot of concerns. Everything is moving so fast and heads are literally rolling over in this revelation. I mean, is there a reason you don't want them in there for seven days? … It's just seven days."

"I think it's safe to say that I don't trust the system or those other officers for that matter. Have you seen this torture contraption they call a 'containment unit'?" Richard asked.

Dave chuckled sadly. "Yes, I have. You think some overzealous cop will press the panic button and kill them instantly and then claim they tried to escape?"

"In a matter of the words, yes. I'm sure many feel as though they betrayed them by being shape-shifters on the force. In the time they must stay imprisoned, these officers may decide to take matters into their own hands and deal out their own brand of justice. It's not as if it hasn't happened in the past."

Richard was going to do what he felt was best. The human race was out of control as far as he was concerned and he didn't trust them one bit. As a matter of fact, to use the phrase "*as far as he could throw them*" would be giving them too much trust, considering he could throw a human pretty far.

"Yeah, I don't blame you for being concerned about their safety. This reminds me of what happened when the world discovered supernaturals were real. The witch-hunts that ensued were frightening. Listen, I'm going to pull as many strings as I can, but I can't make you any promises," Dave said, making sure Richard understood that he wasn't a miracle worker.

"I understand, please just do what you can," Richard said.

"All right, let me make some calls, see what I can do. I'll call you back later to let you know if I had any success."

"Thank you, Dave."

"Sure thing."

The two men ended their call and Richard looked at his watch, knowing he had agreed to a meeting with Elaine. He left the house driving toward the *Xavier Hotel* and when he arrived, he made his way toward the café; there he saw her, as beautiful as ever. Elaine sat in a booth against the wall under a sparkling chandelier. Her dark brown curls were short at the top and trimmed low on the sides and along the back to the nape of her neck. Her hazel eyes locked on Richard as he made his way over toward her. He admired the way the light glimmered over her smooth chocolate skin. As he drew closer, feelings he thought he was over with began to bubble up, re-igniting his desire for her. This little meeting was going to be more difficult than he had expected.

"Hello Elaine," Richard greeted as he took a seat in the booth on the other side of the table.

Elaine smiled to herself as she noted the distance Richard was trying to keep between them. "How nice to see you again, darling. It's been a while; we shouldn't let so much time pass between us again."

A waitress came to the table and politely handed them menus and glasses of water before walking away, but not before announcing she would return in a few minutes once they've had a chance to look over the menu. Both thanked her before she left.

Elaine looked at Richard over her menu. "How are things going for you and your Pack? Are you still with, what's her name ..." she paused as if in deep concentration, struggling to remember a name. "Katrina?"

Richard chuckled softly as he flipped through his menu. He recognized a "game" for what it was and he knew Elaine loved playing games.

"No, I am no longer with her. As a matter of fact, my Pack is the reason why I wanted to speak with you," he said, getting right to the point.

"My, aren't you all business?" Elaine placed the menu on the table.

Richard did the same, deciding on what he wanted to eat. "Well, it's important. One of my Pack members worked for the S.U.I.T. and now because of the controversy the S.U.I.T. is under, he's been exposed as well as his partner. Now, I asked them which judge they would prefer to preside over their trial and they mentioned Allison White and Margaret Hillington. The favor I wanted to ask of you is can you arrange it so that one of these judges officiates their trial?"

"Wow, you're in a predicament, aren't you?" Elaine asked, leaning over seductively toward him across the table.

"Can you help?" Richard asked, trying his best to keep the conversation and their meeting, platonic.

"Maybe. It *would* be in their best interest to have either of those judges on their side. Both are known to be extremely lenient, almost to a point of suspicion. There are some people who believe they are supernaturals, but they aren't. I know these two women personally."

"So, can you arrange this?" Richard asked, getting more specific.

"It depends."

"On what?"

"On whether or not we can cut out the idle chat-chat and make our way upstairs to the room I have reserved for us, just like old times," Elaine said, smiling seductively.

Richard sighed. He was really hoping to avoid this situation. "Elaine, I'm involved with someone now."

"Who? I know for a fact you don't have true committed relationships within your Pack."

"Doesn't matter who, we can't … we just can't."

Elaine sat back, with the toes of her left foot, she began to lightly stroke Richard's inner thigh.

"I don't believe in the word 'can't', especially with so much at stake." There was a definite air of threat to her words.

Richard glanced down at the perfectly painted and pampered toes that were now rubbing against his groin, enticing him. With his hand, he pushed her foot away before she could feel his hardness growing, although he was certain she was able to sense his arousal.

"Oh Richard, must we play this game?"

"I don't want to play any games with you, Elaine. I'm simply asking you for a favor, can you do it?"

"And I *told* you, it depends." Elaine sat up straight, looking at the younger shifter directly "I want you. I have always wanted you, and if I have to play dirty to get you, so be it."

"But you told me before, you don't want a relationship."

"There's a certain *kind* of relationship I want with you."

"My answer is no. I'm not going to sleep with you. If there is another favor I can do for you, than I will. Now, I need to know, will you help me, one old friend to another?"

Elaine's expression grew hard, her eyes narrowed into slits and her nostrils flared slightly. "As a friend, I wish I could help you, but as a scorned lover, I simply *can't*." She rose from the table, snatching up her purse at the same time. She looked down at Richard. "Oh, I think you should know. The judge that will be presiding over the trial now is Thomas Shelton, and from what I've heard about him, your boys better start preparing themselves for the long haul."

Richard reached out, grabbing her arm. "You're being irrational!" He struggled to keep his voice down.

"Let me go!" she demanded, almost hissing the words in her anger.

"You're one of us, why would you turn your back on your own kind?"

"What part of 'scorned lover' didn't you grasp? You seem to think just because I'm like you that I should be the heroine for supernaturals everywhere. I didn't make it to where I am today by being a bleeding heart. They knew the risks they were taking when they joined the S.U.I.T. It's time for them to take their medicine." Elaine looked at him, her expression softening slightly. "Now, unless you plan on taking me up on my offer, let go of my hand."

Richard looked at her for a few more seconds, before he released her, knowing she was stronger. The last thing he wanted to do was make a scene. He released her without saying another word.

"You know where to find me if you change your mind. Remember, a worthy Alpha knows how to make a great decision," Elaine commented.

"Why would a woman of your standards lower yourself to sleep with a man whom you've coerced into bed?" Richard shot back.

"Some say I'm a bitch and maybe I am. I didn't write the rules to playing hardball, but I'm a master at the game. By the way, I'm not lowering my 'standards' as you say. I know you want me as much as I want you. I can smell your *lust* for me as strong as your expensive cologne. Besides, I don't play fair, sweetie. You know this about me." She gave him a winning smile and walked away, leaving the restaurant.

Richard decided to stick to his original plan to eat since he was already there, ordering two twenty-ounce steaks with double the delicious side dishes. The waitress nodded and took his order to the chef. He sat in his seat, thinking about what had just transpired. A few seconds later, his cell phone rung, he answered it.

"Hi, Xander, anything new?"

"I would say so. The Captain of the Illinois S.U.I.T. division just held a press conference in which she gave complete credit of closing the case to Warren and Matthew and the other detectives who risk their lives to solve the crimes Marcus and his coven created," Xander informed.

"That could only work in their favor," Richard replied.

"Indeed. Unfortunately, she also mentioned that their Packs, Prides and a local vampire coven were also responsible for killing Marcus. I believe her intent was to prove how useful supernaturals were to the world."

"Ahhh, I see."

"I'm fortunate that Warren kept a home separate from the main manor," Xander said, feeling relief that he could look outside his window and not see one reporter or camera.

"Likewise. But now we have to make sure no one follows us home," Richard said, not at all looking forward to the extra exposure.

"Indeed. However, I'm willing to guess reporters are already banging down Darian's door, as she did mention his name as the local 'vampire coven'. He does seem to stay in the news," Xander said, chuckling in spite of himself.

"I'm sure he knows how to handle the reporters. Even though I'm willing to bet that's attention he doesn't want or need."

"Who does want that kind of invasion of privacy? It's fortunate for him that he can simply erase memories as well as plant some of his own. Ah, to have that ability," Xander said thoughtfully.

"That is an asset. Listen, Xander, I'm trying to arrange it so that both Warren and Matthew's trial date is expedited, but also, I'm trying to insure that a certain judge presides over their case. Do you know of anyone you can contact who can arrange that?" Richard asked, hoping to have a backup plan, not wanting to give himself to Elaine.

"I've made some calls on my own with little success. I know of a politician who has a lot of influence in congress, but I have no ties to her–"

"Elaine Baker?"

"Yes, that is her name. Do you know her?"

"Intimately, and that's the problem."

Intrigued, Xander decided to pry. "*Really*, in what way?"

"You do know you're behaving as if you're a nosey teenager trying to gather lunchroom gossip."

"As they say these days, 'so sue me'." Xander allowed himself to be a bit mischievous.

Richard exhaled with a sigh. "Very well, I'll tell you. She's the only person I know of who can arrange to have a more lenient judge handle their trial, but she won't do so unless … well, let's just say she wants to rekindle our old relationship."

"Ahhh, I see. Nice friend you have there."

"She used to be."

"So, what are you going to do?"

"I don't know yet. I'm hoping Darian can in some way mentally influence the judge they will have officiating." Richard was going to make the request to Darian later that day.

"I wouldn't count on Darian being able to attend the hearing. They tend to turn on the ultraviolet lighting to keep vampires out of the courtroom for fear they will try to alter the minds of the judges and witnesses," Xander said.

"Shit," Richard said dryly.

Xander chuckled, not meaning to, but his sentiments were the same as Richard's. "I've sent Adrian to the precinct to check on them, anything you want him to pass on?"

"Just tell them we're still working on it."

"All right. I'll keep in touch with you."

Both men ended their conversation. When Richard's meal arrived he ate it quickly then left the restaurant after leaving a handsome tip. When he got home, he took a nap, hoping to clear his mind.

CHAPTER THREE

A drian had just finished signing in and pasting the white visitor's sticker over his chest and was now being led to the holding cells. After clearing the detectors at the entrance he walked toward the cell where Warren and Matthew rose to greet him.

"Don't you two look haggard. Shit, you've only been here a few hours," he joked lightly.

"I've got to tell you, this is pure hell. I'm not used to being on this side of the bars. What's going on out there?" Warren asked.

"Pure chaos. Your Captain gave a press conference announcing that three S.U.I.T. officers and their Packs and Prides, along with the help of Darian's vampire coven, destroyed Marcus and his coven. She also gave credit to the other officers who were working with you," Adrian informed.

"Shit, she did! Lawrence must have lost it. The S.U.I.T. specifically wants a human face behind this success, not a supernatural one," Matthew stated, still shocked by the news.

"Apparently she believed in giving credit to where credit's due. Xander thinks that may help your case. The bad news is; I have to make sure no one follows my ass home. The last thing Xander wants is unwanted media attention," Adrian said. "Darian's ass is screwed, but he can handle it."

He reached over to grab one of the bars to lean on and before Warren could warn him otherwise, the silver seared the skin of his palm.

"Fuck!" He snatched his hand away, shaking it. "Shit! What the fuck?" He looked down at his blistered and reddened flesh.

"I was trying to stop you before you did that," Warren said apologetically.

"I forgot they had this place rigged up like this, fucking humans!" Adrian cursed.

"That's just the beginning of it." Matthew told Adrian about the other features of the holding area.

"It's always nice to know where my tax dollars were spent," Adrian remarked after hearing about the new sprinkler system.

"What else is going on?" Matthew asked.

"Oh, well, Richard and my Dad are trying to contact a few of their political connections to see if they can get your trial date moved up and if they can get one of the nicer judges to get you two released, hopefully with a slap on the wrist and nothing more," Adrian said.

"I'm relieved to hear that," Matthew said, smiling.

"What if they can't?" Warren asked.

"I heard on the news the judge that's supposed to come to your trial and probably theirs too," Adrian said, nodding his head in the direction to the next cell where the other two shifters were standing, listening to every word spoken. "I think they said his name was Thomas–"

"Oh fuck!" Fredrick cursed. "Not that son of a bitch! He hates supernaturals!"

"Him and his brother, Cornelius," Christine added. "Last year a shifter was arrested for eating a stray dog on a full moon and Thomas sentenced him to death stating he was a danger to society. They charged him with obstruction of justice, attempted murder in the first degree, animal abuse and cited him for hunting off sanction grounds."

"What the fuck, who?" Adrian asked. His handsome features contorted in both rage and disgust.

"Two asshole cops on the force, Lance Wilson and Kyle Ronen, they get off on taking down supernaturals," Christine answered.

"Oh, I've had the misfortune of meeting those two motherfuckers a few days ago," Adrian said with a snarl. He remembered how the two officers treated them, especially their total disrespect for Daniel. "Well, our Alphas are going to do what they can to get you two out of here."

"Thanks Adrian."

Adrian nodded, than he looked over at Christine and Fredrick. "Do you have a Pack or Pride?"

"No," the two said in unison.

Adrian shook his head. "I don't mean to sound heartless, but I've got to throw this out there. It really pays to belong to a Pack or Pride. You two should think about it. I'm guessing you'll benefit from what we do for them."

"I'm starting to see that," Christine said, feeling a bit jealous by all of the support Warren and Matthew seem to be getting. Both she and Fredrick had been in their cell two days before them and had only received a hand full of visits from family who knew what they were and a few friends who had to find out on the news. They all gave the two of them well wishes and prayers, but could do nothing more for them. Christine's mother vowed to get her a great lawyer, but with limited funds, she was hoping for a miracle.

"I don't mind tagging along on your bandwagon if it gets me the hell out of here," Fredrick said, silently wishing he had a Pack with "connections".

Adrian turned back toward Warren and Matthew. "So, how are they treating you in here?"

"Like we're a bunch of criminals and not their co-workers. Galen came by, gave us support. Told us he had spoken to Ignacio earlier. But there hasn't been much going on, I'm still waiting for them to serve us lunch," Warren said.

"Can we bring anything in?" Adrian asked.

Matthew shook his head. "No. Contraband will be tossed out. They'll feed us; it's the law. They'll just feed us when they think we should be ready to eat."

Adrian bit his tongue, fighting down the urge to "go off on someone's ass" as he liked to call his tangents. He took a few long breaths to help himself calm down. "We're going to get you out of here, don't worry."

"I know, Adrian." Warren smiled.

"Your fifteen minutes are up," the officer announced.

"I thought this was a conjugal visit?" Adrian joked, tossing the officer a look. "I'm going to need access into their cell and a hell of a lot more than fifteen minutes."

Warren and Matthew laughed aloud; it felt good to them to laugh that way after so much stress. Adrian turned away from the guard, chuckling as well as the other two shifters in the next cell.

"Once you're in that cell, that's where you'll stay. Still got jokes for me?" the officer shot back.

Adrian grew serious. "You want me in that cell then put me there. I'd like to see you try."

Warren reached out, taking hold of Adrian's arm. "Hey man, calm down."

Adrian turned toward him to see his best friend shaking his head, silently urging him to back down. He nodded, his nostrils flaring in his anger. The officer had taken his gun out of his holster and was now switching the safety off.

"I'll see you two later," Adrian said.

"I don't think so. You've proven to be a threat and we can't allow you back in here. Now you need to leave before I place you under arrest for obstruction of justice and threatening an officer of the law," the officer warned.

"Adrian, just go," Matthew urged.

Adrian agreed, lest he'd try to kill the cop who was now pointing the gun at him as he passed by toward the exit. Adrian left the precinct, immediately calling his father on the way home. He made sure no one was following him, although the lobby and around the entrance of the S.U.I.T. precinct was surrounded by media sharks. When Xander answered his cell phone, Adrian rattled off everything that has transpired at the precinct.

"Adrian, you have to keep your temper. I can't afford to have both you *and* Warren under fire," Xander said, after hearing about his son's behavior at the precinct.

"I know, Dad, but that asshole just pissed me off. They were completely rude and I don't even understand why … wait, I do understand. They hate what they fear and they fear us. Doesn't matter that Warren and Matt worked alongside of them for years. Doesn't matter that they were supposed to be a team. I swear, Dad, I wanted to break in there and just kill them all," Adrian admitted.

"Well, I glad that you did not. If we are going to get them out, we are going to have to play by their rules as much as possible. Now, you mentioned two other supernaturals were being held?"

"Yeah, one coyote and the other is a hyena."

"Really? The only Hyena Pack I am familiar with is in Indiana. I know there are more Packs in other states, but I do not have connections with them. Do they have a Pack I can contact?"

"I don't think so. They're orphans or pariahs. I told them they would probably benefit from what we do for our own. I also suggested they join a Pack."

Xander chuckled softly. "It's not always that easy to join a community, Adrian. Most Packs and Prides don't want any new members and often times, shifters seeking communities are killed."

"Are you seeking new members?" Adrian asked his father, curiously.

"Not really, in all honesty, I have enough members in my Pack. However, I do not mind other shifters inhabiting my territory as long as they obey my rules. In the case with this S.U.I.T. business, I will help these other shifters in the name of justice. I believe what is happening is unfair."

"Should I relay this information to them?"

"Not you, no. I do not want you to go back to the precinct again. After what happened today, they might try to use it against you. I will send Nagesa."

Adrian pouted slightly. He was disappointed in himself that he had angered his father. "All right. Sorry Dad."

Xander sighed. "You really have to learn how to control your temper, my son. Keeping a level head in every situation is how great leaders rule. Remember that."

"Okay. I'm on my way home now. Is there anything you want me to do before I head in?"

"If you can, pick your mother up some strawberry ice cream. She has been craving some as of late."

"Craving?"

"She is *not* pregnant."

"Oh, and here I was hoping for a little brother."

Xander rolled his eyes, smiling to himself. "I will see what I can do."

Adrian laughed. "All right, Dad, I'll pick up a few gallons of ice cream." The two men disconnected their call and Adrian did what he said he was going to do before going home.

***

After his nap Richard decided to do a little research on the judges who presided over the S.U.I.T.'s trials. He stared at his LCD flat screen monitor reading the biography of Judge Thomas Shelton. He had already read the glowing biographies on the two female judges and it was true. They were very lenient, Allison almost to a fault. She was currently under fire, having released the group of vampires and a shifter who had vandalized a series of businesses in the Human-Only district. As it turned out that very same group of supernaturals were responsible for murdering a woman a few days ago. Warren and Brian had killed them, ending their killing streak before it got out of control.

He wanted Margaret Hillington to preside over Warren and Matthew's trial. She was someone whose judgment wouldn't be so easily challenged. As his eyes traveled over the words on the screen, he could see that having Thomas Shelton presiding over the trial would be a mistake. To Richard, the man hated supernaturals and used his high position to punish them.

Ryan came into his office, coming up behind him and massaging his shoulders.

"Wow, you're tense," she commented as her fingers kneaded his tight muscles.

"This ordeal with the S.U.I.T. is becoming more problematic than expected," Richard said, exhaling as he allowed himself to relax.

"What's wrong?"

"The judge who is slated to preside over Matthew's trial is, for lack of better phrasing, an asshole. He hates supernaturals. I've read his trial history and not one supernatural has escaped his brand of punishment. He's also responsible for sentencing many to death. The very fact that he's presiding over their trials is a message from the government to our kind. They're making an example out of these ex-S.U.I.T. officers."

"What? We can't let him do the same to Matthew and Warren. We have to get a different judge," Ryan insisted.

Richard smiled sadly. "I tried, but ..."

Ryan looked down at him, confused. "But what?"

"An old friend of mine, well she's a … I should say … an old lover of mine. She's the one who can pull the strings to arrange for another, more supernatural-friendly, judge to preside, but …" Richard hesitated again.

Ryan was beginning to worry. It wasn't like Richard to be so evasive or uncertain.

"But what?" she asked again, eyebrows creased.

"I turned her offer down."

"What was her offer? Richard will you *talk* to me; stop being so damn cryptic."

"Very well. She wants to sleep with me again. If I bed her, she'll make sure Warren and Matthew get the judge they want."

"What a bitch!"

"She seems to take great pride in being known as one, yes."

"Ugh," Ryan groaned as she turned away from Richard, walking toward the window. She looked through the clear glass pane, staring at a couple of birds flapping around in the ornate, marble bird pool. "What are you going to do?" she asked softly, thinking he was going to do whatever was necessary to save his Pack, even if it meant sleeping with a *manipulative shrew*.

Richard rose from his seat, walking over to her, wrapping his arms around her waist. "Don't worry. I realized that I couldn't do this on my own an hour ago. I'm going to find out who's in charge of arranging the judges, and then ask Darian to, as they say, work a little of his mental mojo."

Ryan smiled, liking that option much better. "That sounds like a great idea. I didn't want to share you anyway."

"Keep in mind this is only an option. If Darian can complete the task, that would be great. If not …"

"I know, you'll do what you have to do to save your Pack," Ryan said, finishing his thought.

Richard nodded. "Right now, I'm waiting to hear back from a friend to see if we can get the date moved up."

"Are you hungry?"

"No." He sat back down in his leather-bound chair.

"Are you … other things?" Ryan asked imploringly. Simply looking at Richard dressed in black was sending her into a sexual frenzy. She gazed lustfully at his powerful body hidden underneath the fabric. She ran a fingertip over his smooth skin, feeling the muscles that flexed under her touch.

Richard flashed his sexiest smile, knowing full well the effect he had over her.

"Well, I am a bit tense." He grabbed her by her waist, pulling her closer to him and sitting her down on his lap.

"Ooohhh," she purred as her hips moved seductively over his growing erection.

Her finger began undoing the buttons on his shirt, one after the other exposing the beautiful chocolate smoothness of his well-developed torso. Her hands instinctively found his nipples, playing with them between her fingers and thumbs, causing him to moan. Richard gripped the firm mounds of her luscious ass before pushing her skirt up exposing creamy, soft skin. He groaned as the scent of her arousal filled the office making him ache to be inside of her. Fervently, he slid his fingers beneath the thin, lacy fabric of her panties, ripping them from her in his haste. Ryan removed her shirt along with her bra baring perfectly plump breast and nipples eager for Richard's attention. With a hunger he could barely contain, his mouth closed over her breast as his tongue expertly teased, sucked and nipped her sensitive flesh causing her to moan and beg for more. He obliged, bringing her to the crest before finally pulling away. His favorite thing was to tease and seduce until the moment came when he could no longer hold back. When he had to have her... all of her.

Richard began kissing her throat, running his soft lips over her flesh, tickling her. She ran her hands over his broad shoulders as he lifted her, and at the same time freed himself. Gently, he slid Ryan over his hardness causing them both to shudder with intense pleasure. She gripped his muscular shoulders, bracing herself against his powerful thrust. He moaned again as he relished the heat that surrounded him. The pleasure of her body so satisfying as it drove him to the point of no return. Their lips met in a passionate kiss as the two rocked together, stroking each other's inner fire until the burning inside of them erupted, spilling over them with wave after wave of intense ecstasy. They sat content, joined together, trembling and panting as they waited for the calm to take effect. Moments later,

Ryan sat up, brushing her long, dark hair from her eyes.

She smiled down at him. "I love you," she whispered sweetly.

"I love you, too." He held her still, his hands resting lightly on her hips. "I really did need to relax. You're always looking out for me." He smiled again.

"Well, someone has to." Ryan giggled.

The two sat together until the telephone rang.

Richard answered it, giving the person on the other end a charming greeting in spite of being annoyed by the interruption.

"Hi, Richard, it's me. I was able to arrange it so that Warren and Matthew's court date was moved up to Wednesday, instead of Friday," Senator Dave Beasley said.

"There was no earlier date?" Richard asked, slightly disappointed.

"I did the best I could. That was the earliest date I could get them, just short of busting them out myself."

"I appreciate what you've done. I know it wasn't easy. I certainly hope all goes well until the court date."

"I'm sure it will. I wish I could do more, but–"

"You've done enough, thank you, Dave."

"You're welcome."

The two men ended the call and Richard sat back in his chair. Ryan rose from his lap, shivering slightly as he slid out of her.

"Well, that's some good news," Ryan said as she pulled on her shirt and adjusted her skirt.

"It is. Once I speak with Darian, I think their trial may be an easy one. I can't say the same for every supernatural who's been arrested, though." Richard tucked himself in before zipping up his pants.

"Let's hope so. I want Matthew home where he belongs." Ryan finger-combed her hair putting each strand into place as best she could. "I'm going to make lunch."

With that, she left his office, heading for the kitchen. Richard sat at his desk, more relaxed than he was before. He hoped that Darian could do them the favor, but if he couldn't, he would do what he must.

CHAPTER FOUR

W hat the hell was that?!" Milton Cunningham, the Director of the S.U.I.T. Organization bellowed across the room, after storming into Michelle's office.

"The truth. The S.U.I.T. didn't take out that coven, local supernaturals did. The public needed to know that much," Michelle said in her defense.

"*You* don't get to decide what the public *needs* to know." Milton was outraged over the press conference. Not to mention he was getting heat from the big wigs who signed his check.

"I did what I thought was right. I'd do it again, too," Michelle replied.

"And just who are these masked superheroes?" Milton questioned sarcastically. His voice was laced with contempt so thick Michelle could feel it wash over her like molten lava.

"The two S.U.I.T. officers who are currently being held in our prison and their Packs solved this crime, along with Darian Alexander and his coven. I felt it was important for the people to know that the very same officers we have arrested are the ones responsible for saving their lives." Michelle had expected to be berated by the Director of the S.U.I.T. Organization. The man was a politician in every sense of the word and, to Michelle, politics and the need to "serve and protect" didn't go hand-in-hand.

Milton huffed. "How noble of you. While you were off being Humanitarian of the Year, this very organization our government has invested millions if not billions of dollars in, ends up looking like a waste of fucking money. Tax payers' money!"

"Then tax payers should be relieved to know that their money is well spent. They should be happy that the S.U.I.T. officers who are supernaturlals really do go far and beyond the call of duty to protect them," Michelle said, putting things into perspective. "I did what I felt was the right thing to do."

"You've said that already as if that's supposed to mean something. It means nothing to me. Simply put; what you did was disobey a direct order and talked yourself out of a job."

"You can't fire me over this." Michelle argued incredulously.

"The hell I can't. You were insubordinate. I told you what to say and you decided to go off on some heroic tangent without any proof to substantiate your so-called 'truth'. I never wanted to appoint you Captain. I knew there'd be a problem with putting you in charge of the S.U.I.T. division. You're too damn emotional, you're not a team player and you're prone to making rash decisions."

"That is the biggest pile of bullshit I've ever heard. I've earned my position here."

"So you say, but the truth is, you had friends within the organization and Chandler had a soft spot for you... *I* on the other hand don't. Clean out your office, your termination takes effect immediately."

She stared at Milton Cunningham, secretly wishing she could shoot him right between his beady little eyes and not feel bad about it afterward. Men like Milton, who felt as if they controlled the world, annoyed her tremendously. His utter gall didn't cease to amaze her. But still, it was hard for her to accept what she was hearing after all of her years of dedicated service. She felt she deserved better. At that moment, she thought about Gabriel and Barry and how they felt after she had to tell them they were fired only a few days earlier.

"I hope I don't have to repeat myself, Ms. Lawrence," Milton said, one eyebrow cocked.

"I heard you loud and crystal clear. You know, Chandler wasn't the most honest man, but at least he had some measure of integrity," Michelle commented.

"I'm giving you the opportunity to leave with some of yours. Now, I'm a patient man, but even I have my limits. Pack your stuff or I'll have you escorted off the premises and your belongings mailed to you." Milton crossed his arms over his chest.

"May I have a chance to gather my things and put them in boxes?"

Milton nodded. "You have fifteen minutes." With that, he walked out of her office, leaving the precinct to address the media frenzy that awaited him outdoors.

Michelle cursed under her breath as she looked around her now former office. She had worked tirelessly behind that desk, making sure she kept the city safe and at the same time, make the S.U.I.T. look good. Often times, she'd only get about three hours sleep in a day's time when crime was up. Out of all the S.U.I.T. divisions in the country, there were only five who had female captains, a position they had to work twice as hard to keep. They were always under scrutiny, not only from other male captains, but from the officers under their command as well. She thought she held up her end tremendously. However, she knew the risk she was taking when she decided to tell the truth and had already prepared for the inevitable. She pulled two boxes from underneath her desk and began loading her personal belongings, filling the boxes to the brim. Once she was finished, she took one box to her car then returned for the other. When she got to her office, there were two officers standing in front of her door.

"Please tell me the rumor isn't true?" Monica asked. She was a member of the Infiltration Team. Furthermore, she had nothing but the utmost respect for Michelle, not only as a female, but as a Captain.

"If the rumor is that I've been canned, then it's true," Michelle confirmed.

"Fuck," cursed Rodney, another officer on the IT. "Why? Because you told the truth about Warren and Matt?"

Michelle nodded. "Apparently, that was not in the S.U.I.T.'s best interest."

"This is bullshit," Monica fumed as she pouted, eyebrows furled.

"If the S.U.I.T. didn't solve the crime, then we shouldn't be trying to take credit. Not one of us can say how we took out that coven if we're asked," Rodney said.

"I know, but that wasn't the spin I was told to put on it," Michelle said. "Listen, I want you all to do your jobs. People out there still need protecting."

"Shit, you ain't got to tell us. What's going to happen to Warren and Matt?" Monica asked.

"I don't know. However, if I'm called in as a character witness, I'll support them. Right now, I have to go." She patted her two loyal officers on their shoulders before heading into her office to gather her last box.

"I've got it," offered Rodney as he took the box from her hands, assisting her as she made her way to her car.

"Thanks," Michelle said as she closed her driver's side door.

"Listen, Monica and I were talking about starting a petition to get you back into your position, will you support it?" Rodney asked.

"That's very sweet, but I don't know how much good that will do. Once the S.U.I.T. decides to fire someone, there really isn't a chance they'll get their job back."

"We'll see," Rodney said with an air of confidence.

Michelle offered him her sweetest smile before igniting the engine and driving away. Secretly she was honored by their determination, or at least the promise of their support. She had wanted to see Marshall before she left, but her fifteen minutes were up and she didn't want to take the chance that Milton wouldn't have followed through on his threat that he'd throw her out instead of letting her walk out on her own. As she was driving home, her cell phone started ringing. Checking the caller ID, she saw that it was Marshall.

"Hi, Marshall," she greeted.

"Michelle, I heard about what happened, why didn't you tell me?" Marshall asked, disappointed to find out about his girlfriend's termination from gossip in the hallway.

"Because I didn't have enough time to tell you at the precinct, Marshall."

"I can't believe they fired you for that."

"I know! I kind of figured it would happen. Milton Cunningham is living up to his reputation of being a world renown asshole."

"I know that there are a couple officers here talking about striking if Warren and the others aren't reinstated back at their jobs, you too," Marshall informed.

"Really? I mean, I don't really want a strike because that would leave the city vulnerable. Regular cops can't handle what we do—hell, we can barely handle it. It's just, well–"

"–Nice to know people care that much, right? I get it," Marshall finished her thought.

"Yeah, it is."

"I think this exposure is letting people know just how important it is to have supernaturals working on the S.U.I.T."

"That was my intentions when I told the truth. Listen, baby… I'm tired and really pissed. I just want to go home, take a nice bath and go to sleep."

Marshall chuckled. "I wish I was there to help you relax," he said imploringly.

"I swear, if people knew just how freaky you were in the bedroom, they'd never look at you the same way again," Michelle said, laughing. It felt good to laugh after so much drama. That was one of the reasons why she loved Marshall. He could always put a smile on her face and brighten her day even under the gloomiest of circumstances.

"Sometimes, I'm too cool for myself, I know." Marshall laughed softly. "All right, I'll be there later on today. Take care of yourself until then."

"I will." The two ended their call just as she pulled into her driveway. Michelle really was looking forward to that nice long bath after the last couple days she'd had. After keeping her word to herself, she settled down for a nice long nap.

***

Marshall decided he was going to visit Warren and Matthew to find out more about how they went about killing the coven of vampires and the shifter. Maybe if they had proof, that would help all of their cases. He finished filling out some of his paperwork, then he made his way toward the holding cells. The officer at the desk let him through without any resistance. He walked over to Matthew's and Warren's cell.

"My, my, it is so strange seeing you two on the other side of these bars. I don't like it. This is not where good cops belong," Marshall said, frowning at the silver bars.

"Shit, tell me about it," Warren agreed.

"Listen, I came here mainly to ask you about the coven you killed.

Do you have any proof that they are dead?" Marshall asked.

"Well, they first attacked us at Darian Alexander's mansion. The damage has probably been cleaned up by now. They work fast to cover up shit like that," Warren said.

"The rest of the proof is in Rome. That's where you'll find the corpses of Marcus, the coven master and his two female companions," Matthew added.

"Well, that's good news. We can contact the local police there in Rome, and have them confirm that. At least that will be solid proof of what you all did. It may also help Michelle get her job back," Marshall said.

"Michelle's been fired? What the fuck? Why, 'cause she told the truth?" Warren asked. His eyebrows were tightly creased together in his anger. He was growing more incensed by their situation with each passing hour.

"Yes. Milton Cunningham paid her a visit and told her to clean out her office immediately. I've got to say, I'm proud of her for sticking to her guns." Marshall tapped a tune on the silver bars with his fingertips.

"Who's taking her place?" Matthew asked.

"I don't know. Cunningham's calling in a temporary replacement and if he likes this person, I suppose they'll have a more permanent position here. My guess is, he's probably going to be a company man, if you catch my drift," Marshall stated.

"Yeah... someone who's going to kiss his ass, inside and out." Warren snorted.

Marshall chuckled. "That's the point."

"Look, Marshall, I know you want to have proof of what we did, but is that evidence going to incriminate us as well?" Warren pointed out.

"Hmmm, I hadn't really thought about that."

Matthew nodded. "Perhaps, just Captain Lawrence mentioning our communities' involvement may have already incriminated us."

"Would it matter? You were both acting as S.U.I.T. officers at the time. Well within your jurisdiction to execute that coven," Marshall said.

"Yeah, but we did so in Rome where they don't have a S.U.I.T.

organization. Not to mention we were way out of our jurisdiction at the time and there it would be considered murder. Supernaturals may not have the same rights as humans in Italy, but they are still considered citizens," Warren pointed out.

"It's not like you could have extradited them," Marshall said. "You did what you had to do."

"True, but the law is the law. At that point, we became vigilantes," Matthew said.

"It's somewhat of a double edge sword, isn't it?" It was a statement more than a question. "I wouldn't worry about the incrimination anyway. What's important to the people now is that the threat is gone. I don't think they care too much about the why, how or where."

"Yeah, now the witch hunt is on us," Warren said.

Marshall nodded. "You know, if Michelle had given full credit to the S.U.I.T. you two would have gotten credit as S.U.I.T. officers and the organization would have gotten more funding and positive press, but it wouldn't have been the truth. To tell the truth would prove how much supernaturals are needed to protect humans against other supernaturals, that the human S.U.I.T. officers aren't enough. Ultimately, the truth breaks down the façade."

"It's a double edge sword, all right and someone's ramming that fucker up my ass repeatedly. I swear, I don't want anything to do with this bullshit," Warren fumed.

Marshall burst into a fit of laughter.

"What's so damn funny?" Warren asked, slightly agitated.

Marshall waved his hand as if to excuse himself. "I'm sorry, it's just… you really had to be inside my mind to get the mental image I saw when you said that."

"Knowing you, I bet I was bent over my desk with my pants down around my ankles and Milton Cunningham was standing behind me with a huge, jagged-edged sword jamming it up my ass while laughing the entire time. Am I close?" Warren looked at the other man, one eyebrow cocked.

Marshall chuckled again. "Except in my vision, Milton Cunningham had a thin bad-guy mustache and there was music of impending doom playing in the background."

This time it was Warren's and Matthew's turn to laugh.

"Okay, back to more important matters. Are you saying I shouldn't look for the evidence?" Marshall asked.

"At this point, I don't know what to do. I don't know what's a bad idea or a good one," Warren admitted.

"Well, if the cat's out the bag, maybe it will help our case, because truth is, the media *will* be looking for the evidence," Matthew said.

"Yeah, but do we really want to involve Kysen in this?" Warren asked his lover.

"No, and we may not have to," Matthew answered.

"Who's Kysen?" Marshall asked.

"An extremely powerful vampire, who would not want to be bothered with any of this, he's the one who took out Marcus and two of his vampires in Rome with the help of my Alpha and a few of our friends," Warren said.

"Ah, I see. Okay, why don't we do this? We'll just wait and see what your Alphas do for you. I'm sure they are working on something right now," Marshall said.

Matthew nodded. "They are."

"Even if it means going above the law?" Marshall asked.

"Especially that. They aren't going to let the human world judge us for too long and I don't think they're going to accept any human punishments either," Warren said.

"Then we need to make sure we get you the hell out of here as soon as possible," Marshall stated, not wanting to see the extent of their Packs determination.

Warren nodded. "That's the plan. Hopefully we'll get Allison White or Margaret Hillington as our judges. I also hope that our trial date can be moved up so we can get out of here sooner."

"All right, then... I'll leave well enough alone," Marshall said.

"We really wish we could help out Captain Lawrence," Matthew added.

Marshall nodded. "Who knows what will happen. We might be able to get her job back in a way that won't affect you any further."

"What about staging a strike?" Christine asked.

"From my understanding, a few officers are discussing that possibility now. However, I know that Michelle doesn't want a strike. She doesn't want the city to be vulnerable while the only officers who can help are refusing to. Now, whether or not they go through with it against her wishes, or if it works, is up to fate," Marshall answered. "Let's keep our fingers crossed. I have to get back to the grind. See you all later on."

The shifters said their goodbyes to Marshall and watched as he left the holding cell area.

"Man, that's fucked up. I can't believe the Captain was fired," Fredrick fumed.

"I can. She dared to defy the Director of the S.U.I.T.. That son-of-a-bitch is worse than Chandler," Christine commented.

Both Warren and Matthew gave each other knowing looks, remembering the last time they dealt with Chandler. As a matter of fact, the last person to see Chandler was Darian when he drained him dry.

"Yeah, I guess Chandler wasn't as bad as Cunningham, but they're both assholes," Warren stated.

"So, do you think we're going to get Hillington or White for our trial?" Fredrick asked, clearly concerned about his fate.

Matthew nodded. "I'm willing to bet our Alphas are going to look out for you, too. Don't worry."

Fredrick nodded as he exhaled a long breath, slightly relieved that they were going to get the same help that Warren and Matthew were. "Thanks a lot."

"Besides, Adrian kind of said that already, don't worry man. You being nervous makes me nervous," Warren said, hoping to keep the other two Packless shifters calm.

"So I guess we sit here and continue to play games until our trials, eh?" Fredrick said.

"I guess. Okay, I'll start. I spy with my little eye, something that begins with the letter 'A'," Warren said, kicking off another game. They had already played concentration, but it wasn't as fun for them since there was no alcohol involved for penalty shots. So the four shifters decided to stop playing right before they got a visit from Marshall.

Matthew looked around the room for something that began with the letter 'A', he pointed at a circular round device attached to the ceiling. "I've got it: alarm."

Warren shook his head. "Nope, that's not what I was looking at."

"But that's the only thing in the whole damn room that beings with the letter 'A', Warren," Matthew protested.

"Not true, keep looking." Warren lay back on his cot, hands resting behind his head.

After another minute, Matthew snorted. "Oh, I think I know where you were going with that," he said, rolling his eyes. He pointed at the guard standing post at the doorway. "Asshole."

The four shifters chuckled.

Warren laughing a little harder than the others, his shoulders shook as he struggled to breathe. "Right!"

"You know, you're too old for this shit," Matthew joked as he laughed harder at his lover.

The four shifters continue to keep each other entertained to pass the time away *and* to keep from worrying.

***

Adan finished sweeping the last of the broken glass and debris into the dustpan, dumping it into the trash can. He ran the back of his hand across his forehead, wiping away the beads of sweat that had leaked from his pores. He looked around the mansion, his Pride, along with members of Elise's Pride and Xander's Pack were finishing up their assigned duties. Darian's home was almost restored to its original state, except for the windows that were damaged. In their place were oak plywood boards. The door that was blown in was replaced by two thick redwood doors Adan had purchased from *Home Décor*. He sat down on one of the comfortable leather chairs in the living room, finally allowing himself to relax after a hard day's work. After fifteen minutes, his Matron, Danielle joined him, sitting on the armrest.

"Are you all right?" she asked, as she ran her fingers through his soft curly locks.

Adan nodded. "I'm fine. I'm just happy we've managed to clean up Darian's home. I don't want to leave though, until I know that Warren and Matthew are going to be all right. I saw on the news this morning they were being held at the S.U.I.T. precinct pending a trial."

"I know. I saw that on the TV while I was cooking breakfast. I can't believe they would be treated like that. All they did was try to do the right thing," Danielle said as she shook her head, disgusted.

"From what I can tell, this entire fiasco is just humans puffing up their chests, trying to re-establish control, or at least the façade of control," Adan stated.

"It does seem that way. I heard on the news the S.U.I.T. Captain revealed that local supernatural communities were the ones responsible for solving the case. I was actually surprise to see the credit go to us instead of them."

Adan's eyebrows rose in slight amazement. "That was unexpected. I thought for sure they'd claim this as a S.U.I.T. victory in the same way they did everything else."

"I did, too."

He looked toward the door. "That would also explain the reporters waiting outside."

"It does."

"I'll try to help in any way I can," Adan said as he leaned more comfortably against the soft cushions of the expensive suede sofa.

"Well, I'm sure Darian can handle the reporters. I'm also certain Richard and Xander are working on getting their members back home safe and sound. Those are two very powerful and well-connected Alphas. I'm sure everything will work out," Danielle said, rising from the armrest. "Are you hungry?"

Adan nodded. "Starving. All of this activity has really worked up my appetite."

"Okay, I'll make you a plate. I just finished cooking steaks, potatoes, corn and my broccoli casserole."

"Make my mouth water, why don't you," Justin said as he plopped down on the sofa. "'*Feed* me, Seymour.'"

"You're stupid," Devin commented, chuckling. "That's from that movie about that man-eating plant, right?"

"Well, yeah. Also, her last name is 'Seymour'," Justin clarified.

"Double pun." Devin smiled.

Danielle shook her head looking at the two men. She didn't know them that well, but she could tell they were kindred spirits. She also suspected they were best friends by how well they seem to bond with each other. She thought they were both adorable.

"Well, I'm going to need a hand setting the food out on the table," she implied.

"Awww, I just sat down," Devin whined.

"Me too," Justin added.

"All right, I know two hungry shifters who won't be eating my famous casserole," Danielle teased.

"Threats are so unbecoming. All you had to say was 'get off your lazy asses and help me set the table'," Justin joked.

Danielle laughed as she rolled her eyes. "Come on." She beckoned them to follow her into the kitchen.

As they were setting the table, the doorbell rang. Adan ignored it, as it was the twelfth time in the past hour the bothersome reporters outside had pushed the little button hoping someone would open the door and answer their meddlesome questions. They wanted to speak to the extremely well-connected, rich and publicized vampire, Darian Alexander, who they all suspected along with the S.U.I.T. to be the master vampire of the city.

"My God, won't these people get a life!" Carmen fussed, annoyed by the horde of reporters outside the mansion.

"Don't these idiots know that vampires sleep during the day?" Adan stated.

"Darian's always in the news for one thing or another. Besides, they can't get to Xander, Richard or Elise. Darian's their best bet for their story." Carmen peaked at the mob through a slit between the curtains. One of the photographers saw her and snapped a quick photo. "Damn it!" she cursed, pulling back as she repeatedly blinked her eyes, forcing them to focus once again.

"The cameras are bright, aren't they?" Adan asked, laughing at her reaction.

"Yeah! Man, I wanted to go home after cleaning up the mess. Now, I don't know if I can. I don't want any of these jerks following me home. Hell, now I wished I had parked my car in the garage. At least that way they couldn't be taking down my license plate," Carmen said, wishing she had the foresight to see this happening.

"I would suggest you call Elise and let her know what's happening. I'm sure once Darian awakens, he can address them and make them leave just as quietly as they came," Adan said, settling back into his chair.

"So, we're like, held hostage here until sunset?" Devin asked as he re-entered the living room.

"Looks like it," Carmen answered him. "Unless you want to take the chance of having your face plastered all over the news and the media following you home."

"Naw, that's okay. I'll stay here." Devin thought about how angry Elise would be if he led a trail of reporters and photographers back to her peacefully quiet mansion. He looked at Justin when he stepped up next to him. "I dare you to go outside and get attacked by the photo mob," Devin said.

"Don't tempt me. I ought to go out there and moon their asses," Justin joked.

"And break all of their cameras? …You know, that's not a bad idea," Devin remarked, smiling at his own jest.

"Oh I see you've got a bag of jokes, well, I've got a five-knuckle sandwich just for you," Justin playfully threatened holding up his right fist.

"Threats are so unbecoming," Danielle teased, giving Justin back his own words. "Lunch is ready."

"Oooh, she got you good," Devin said as he turned making his way toward the dining room.

"Shut up," Justin shot back, following behind him.

All of the shifters made their way into the dining room, taking their seats. Adan was the first to make his plate and the rest followed suit. They ate their lunch and settled comfortably in the den after they washed the dishes. To past the time away, they watched television and played video games waiting for the sun to set. Soon, Darian would do away with the media who was still waiting outside and they would be able to go home.

CHAPTER FIVE

The sun began to set, igniting the horizon in a blaze of red, purple and gold as day turned into night. Darian's eyes opened once his body relinquished its resting state. He focused on his surroundings, quickly realizing where he was. He turned, seeing Xavier resting beside him. Reaching over, he brushed a few strands of Xavier's dark brown locks from his face to gaze at his lover's exquisite features.

"How beautiful," Darian whispered as he looked at Xavier's long dark lashes brushing his cheeks. He ran his finger over the length of his lover's bottom lip, feeling the soft, yielding skin. He thought back to the day he found Xavier dying in a puddle of his own blood. The first thought that came to his mind was how much of a crime it would have been to let such beauty rot away. He had no idea of knowing how much Xavier would complete him as a companion. Furthermore, he had no idea that Xavier's love for Natasha would pull him even closer to her. He hadn't expected he'd love the both of them as much as he did. He was relieved that they had survived their latest ordeal.

Rolling over, Darian climbed out of the bed. On his way to the bathroom, he stopped to gaze at himself in the mirror. *Still perfect*, he thought to himself. Kysen's wise words helped him cope with what had happened. Although he hated what he went through, he knew that his young coven members endured so much, even loss, as well. He wanted to be there for them, when they were ready. He entered the bathroom and turned on the shower. Running water was one of his greatest luxuries. And he rarely missed an opportunity to indulge, especially with his newly remodeled bathroom. The six shower heads released a steady jet stream of hot water over his body, causing him to moan in pleasure. The spray of water tickled his flesh as it helped relax his muscles. After his shower, he dressed quickly in a pair of black slacks and a red ribbed v-neck t-shirt and black, leather shoes. He glanced out the window, seeing that the sun had completely set and now the sky was a darker shade of blue.

Darian looked at Xavier still resting. "You'll be up soon," he said aloud.

He wanted to see Natasha and knew Xavier would want to see her, too. He understood why she didn't want to stay in the mansion last night. He wouldn't have wanted her to anyway. The carnage that was left by Marcus was not what he wanted her or his son to be around. He trusted Billy to take care of them. As he waited for Xavier to rise, he knew that his home was surrounded by reporters and photographers waiting to ask him questions he was not going to answer. He smiled to himself after reading their minds, discovering they knew he solved the case with Marcus and his coven. He would address them soon enough. Suddenly his cell phone began to ring. He answered it without checking the caller ID which was something he rarely did.

"Hello?" he asked.

"Hello, Darian, this is Richard. I need to speak with you. Well, actually, I need to ask a favor of you," Richard said.

"What is the favor?"

"Warren and Matthew. They turned themselves in this morning and are now being held at the S.U.I.T. precinct pending their trial."

"Ah, I see. Please, go on," Darian encouraged, curious as to what the favor was.

"I have managed to arrange for their trial date to be moved up, but I really need to have a specific judge presiding over their case. Unfortunately, my political contact kind of fell through in that regard."

"Fell through?" Darian inquired.

"I need your help," Richard said, purposefully ignoring Darian's curiosity. He'd already told Xander about the proposal Elaine had offered him and didn't really want to tell anyone else.

"Why did it fall through?" Darian probed.

Richard sighed. "It's kind of embarrassing."

Darian chuckled. "Well now, knowing that only piques my

curiosity even more."

"And…"

"*And*, now I want to know why it's embarrassing. Why did it 'fall through'?"

"You're worse than Xander, right now," Richard retorted with a sigh. "Very well."

He told Darian about the proposal.

"I see. So you want me to use my superior mental abilities to hypnotize Dominick Anderson to get him to arrange the switch?" Darian asked. He had to smile to himself. He knew for a fact that most shape-shifters hated having to rely on vampires to help out one of their own. However, this situation was different… *their* situation was different. Darian considered them his friends and if working his "mental mojo" (as Natasha liked to call his abilities) would save his friends, it was his pleasure and honor.

"That is the favor I'm asking of you. Can you do it?"

"Of course I can. I'll do it tonight, where can I find him?"

"All I have is his office information."

"Give me that."

Richard told Darian the information he had on Dominick Anderson who was the current Illinois Judicial Director of the S.U.I.T., he was in charge of assigning judges to supernatural criminal cases.

"I want to thank you for this, Darian."

"There really is no need. Tell me, how are they doing? I'm sure it's a devastating experience for them seeing that they are now on the opposite side of those silver bars?" Darian asked, remembering his own stint inside the notorious S.U.I.T. prison.

"I believe they are keeping in good spirits, but I'm sure they'd much rather be in their own beds tonight instead of those hard cots."

Darian chuckled. "Or each other's beds."

Richard sighed. "Yes, Darian, or each other's beds."

Darian snickered. "Don't worry… this will all be behind them in a matter of days."

On his own bed, Xavier began to stir as he took in his surroundings. He turned, looking at Darian talking with Richard on his cell phone, and smiled.

Darian tossed him a wink before bidding Richard a good night. He closed his cell phone. "I have to pay a visit to Dominick Anderson on behalf of Warren and Matthew this evening. So, I will meet you at the hotel."

Xavier creased his eyebrows. "What hotel?"

"Ah, that's right. You were resting by the time Natasha left. She didn't want to stay here, so she left for the hotel with Billy."

"Oh," Xavier nodded. "I can see why she didn't want to stay. Have the remains been removed?"

"Yes. Our friends did the disposal and clean up. Speaking of which, I need to thank them."

"That was nice of them to do that while we rested," Xavier said as he made his way into the bathroom.

"It was," Darian agreed. Then he sighed. "All right, I'll meet you there after I take care of some business—mainly getting rid of these uninvited guests on my front lawn and around my home."

"Yeah, I know. I'm not going to the hotel until they're gone," Xavier called out from the shower.

Darian chuckled as he left the room, heading down the ornate, wood-carved and marble staircase. He met up with the others in the den and thanked them all for their help.

"Don't mention it, we wanted to help," Daniel said. "But I am ready to go home."

"Ah yes, I'm aware that the media is on my front lawn. Apparently, they suspect I'm the one responsible for killing Marcus," Darian said.

"Well, they got it half right," Justin said.

"Don't worry, I'll take care of everything and you'll be able to go home," Darian reassured as he turned, making his way toward the newly replaced front door. He smiled approvingly, liking the new design. He opened the door and over a dozen cameras went off, flashing repeated, nearly blinding Darian with bright lights.

"Mr. Alexander, Mr. Alexander! Were you the one who solved the case with the mysterious murderers who were terrorizing the city over the past few days?" one brash male reporter questioned, shoving a microphone into Darian's face.

Before he could respond, a petite female reporter thrust her microphone forward, as well. "Mr. Alexander, what happened to your mansion? Were you attacked by this murderous vampire coven?"

"Mr. Alexander, isn't it true that you are the master vampire of the city?" another female reporter asked.

"Mr. Alexander, did the S.U.I.T. hire you to do their jobs?" another male reporter asked.

Darian stood there, waiting for all of the reporters to finish asking all of their questions. Once they were finished, he spoke and as he addressed the crowd, he mentally encouraged them to obey his command. "My involvement with this case was very miniscule, to say the least. I only assisted the officers assigned in the case with information I had gathered on my own. Nothing more." He saw the video cameras rolling and knew he had to form his words carefully. He continued. "The real heroes of this tale are now held prisoner behind silver bars at your local S.U.I.T. precinct, ladies and gentlemen. I'd suggest you rally around them and get their story. Good night." With that, Darian turned, walking back into his home, closing the door behind him.

"Do you think that will work?" Xavier asked as he trotted down the stairs, buttoning his shirt.

Darian couldn't help but to gaze at the exposed skin under Xavier's shirt. For a split second, he wanted to rip the shirt from Xavier's torso and run his tongue along his soft flesh, paying close attention to his lover's sensitive nipples. He smiled to himself as Xavier came closer.

Xavier cocked an eyebrow. "What are you smiling for?"

Playing it off like a pro, Darian responded. "Because I do believe it will work." He decided to answer Xavier's first question to avoid having to answer his second.

"Hmmm," Xavier still tossed him a suspicious look as he made his way toward the window, peeking through the curtain. "Well, you were right. Not one reporter or photographer is out there. Good."

"Finally!" Justin said, exasperated. "I can go home now."

"Is my home that horrible?" Darian asked, both eyebrows rising.

"What? No. It's just, well, I kind of felt trapped here. I would be feeling this way even if this was my house. I don't like that feeling, had enough of that over the past couple of days. Know what I mean?" Justin said in his defense.

Darian nodded, fully understanding his sentiments. "I would have to agree. All right, you are all free to go home now. Rest easy."

With that, everyone, except for Adan and his Pride left to go to their own mansions. Darian left to pay a visit to Dominick Anderson and Xavier climbed into his Viper RX20 on his way to the hotel named after him, to see Natasha and their son.

***

Darian moved so quickly, that Dominick hadn't even realized that he'd entered his office and had taken the seat in front of his desk. When Dominick finally looked up, he gasped and jumped in his chair. Papers he was holding flew up in all directions as he struggled to lower his heart rate and catch his breath.

"Jesus Christ! What the hell are you doing here? How did you get in here?!" Dominick asked, his voice going up and octave with each question. Once he had gotten over his initial fear, he felt ashamed that he'd shown any at all and now he was just angry at the intrusion.

Darian cocked his head as he gazed at the man in front of him whose chest still heaved from the surprise he'd given him. Dominick was actually handsome; time had treated him very well. His full head of black hair was dusted with gray at the tips and on his sideburns. His gray eyes glared at Darian as he waited for answers to his questions. He was clean shaven and for a man his age, he was well built. Darian could plainly see his toned muscular physique that was clothed in a designer black and white business suit.

Darian decided he would drink from this man, if only to share a moment of pleasure with such a handsome fellow. "I have a matter to discuss with you."

"What matter? Who are you?" Dominick asked, still incensed.

"My name is unimportant. You won't remember me ever being here anyway," Darian said, rather cockily.

"I'm calling security." Dominick reached for his telephone.

"No, you won't." Darian said, at the same time, he was mentally asserting his will over Dominick taking control of the man's mind.

Dominick placed the receiver back on the base.

"Good. You're going to come toward me, roll up your right sleeve." Darian smiled as Dominick did as he was told. "Offer me your wrist."

Dominick extended his right arm, wrist exposed. Darian leaned forward, gently taking hold of his arm. His fangs extended and he sank them into the bluish vein underneath the soft flesh. Dominick gasped and jerked from the initial pain. Instantly, he began to feel the most exquisite pleasure coursing through his body. He trembled as he leaned against his desk, barely able to stand on his own anymore. He began to moan and twitch in ecstasy as his body released in climax. Darian pulled away, partially sated from his feeding. He did have to admit, he enjoyed it when Devin or Justin offered him their blood. The experience was always more intense and satisfying. Licking his lips, he settled back into his chair.

"Wasn't that exciting?" he asked Dominick.

"My God, yes," the other man answered in a shaky, breathless voice.

"You should sit down," Darian instructed.

Dominick did as he was told, nearly falling into the chair beside Darian's.

"I have something I want you to do for me for the trials pertaining to all of the supernaturals in this country."

"What do you want me to do?" Dominick asked, still under Darian's complete control.

"I want you to make sure that every trial has the most lenient judge to preside in each state. For Illinois, I believe it's Allison White and Margaret Hillington."

"Yes, they are known to show compassion for supernaturals convicted of crimes," Dominick responded dully in his hypnotic state.

"Make sure that they handle the cases in Illinois. For all the other states, you know what I want from you."

"But I am only the Judicial Director for Illinois. I have no power over the other states."

"I see. Who do I need to get in contact with that can make that arrangement?"

"Her name is Elaine Baker. She has that kind of pull. She'd be able to arrange that easily."

Darian frowned. He now knew who Elaine was and what she wanted for her services. He wondered if he should even bother, knowing Richard wanted little to do with her. He decided to let it go, leaving the leaders of those other supernaturals to deal with their own individual problems.

"Very well. I still want you to do as I requested. If this is not done properly, I will return and I will not be pleased," Darian threatened.

Dominick's eyes widen, letting Darian know that he fully understood the meaning behind his words.

"Good." Darian, felt it was best not to enslave this man to him, but he would keep his connection. He erased the man's memory of him and just as quickly as he came, he was gone, leaving Dominick alone to tend to what he wanted him to do. He flew quickly to the hotel, landing softly on the balcony. Sliding the doors open, he quietly stepped inside. He could hear his two lovers chatting in the living room and walked toward them.

"Hi, Darian," Xavier greeted, knowing that he was there.

"Hello, Xavier... Natasha," Darian bent downward, kissing both Natasha, then Xavier full on the mouth, before taking his seat next to Natasha on the sofa. "Where's Billy?"

"He wanted to visit his family, so I let him go. He said he'd return before sunrise," Xavier informed.

"Ah, I see... very well. So, what did you do today?" Darian asked Natasha.

"Not much. I took care of our son, played a few card and board games with Billy, watched the news... I saw you on it," Natasha teased.

"Did you? What did you think?" Darian asked, smiling devilishly.

"I think you put the mental mojo whammy on those reporters and sent them on their way without the truth," Natasha answered, giggling.

Darian nodded. "You are correct. The last thing I want is media attention when it pertains to my personal life. I don't care if they want to run a special on the new college, or my businesses. Besides, the attention should be on the S.U.I.T. and their inability to protect the people they serve."

"I for one am glad you did that. I really don't like the media," Xavier said.

"Oh really, why not?" Natasha asked, curiously.

"I suppose I could tell you that story. I've had only one encounter with extremely pesky paparazzi. I believe the year was nineteen twenty-seven, I had spent the night with a certain celebrity."

"Ah, yes, I do remember this tale. Go on," Darian said, smiling.

"I bet you do," Xavier said, with a wink. "Anyway, this celebrity was pretty popular during those times and his personal life was always under scrutiny, so privacy was hard to come by. We were in his bedroom, enjoying ourselves, when I heard a rustling of leaves just outside of his window. Mind you, we were on the second floor of his mansion."

"The media is always trying to out gay celebs," Natasha said, grinning widely. "Who was it?"

"Well, it's all out in the open now, but back then, he was perceived as a 'lady's man'."

"Who was it?" Natasha asked again, more anxiously.

"Well, I'll give you a hint, he starred in that movie you like, '*Anxiously Awaiting*'," Xavier said.

Natasha gasped. "No! Really?! Wow, I would have never guessed."

"Yes, I wouldn't have guessed it either had his assistant not approached me at a party." Xavier smiled. "Well, anyway, I ran over toward the window to see a photographer running away towards his car. I didn't want to chase him naked as I was, so I decided I'd catch up with him later."

"You're so sweet, trying to help him keep his secret," Natasha commented.

"It really wasn't about him. He had taken pictures of me feeding in the throes of passion. That's something I didn't want publicized, if you know what I mean?"

"Well, why didn't you just hypnotize the man to get him to stop running?" Natasha asked.

"I tried, but it didn't work. Some humans are a little harder to control than others and I was a very young vampire still honing my skills," Xavier answered.

"Did the guy know you were a vampire?" Natasha asked.

Xavier nodded. "He was a groupie, among other things."

"Okay, so what else happened?" Natasha asked.

"When I finally caught up to the photographer, he threatened to expose what I was to the world. Well, as you know, I couldn't let that happen."

"Did you kill him?" Natasha asked... she almost didn't want to know the answer. She had grown accustomed to the fact that both of her lovers and all of her shape-shifters friends killed whomever they felt threatened them. It wasn't an easy truth to deal with at times, but she knew they did what they felt was necessary. Someone threatening to expose vampires to the world—Xavier in particular— was a serious problem.

"Would it bother you if I told you I did?" Xavier asked, curious as to why she wanted to know such a detail.

"I'm not sure. Sometimes it's weird when I think about that side of you, all of you," Natasha said, being honest.

"It's a part of what we are," Darian said.

"I know. And don't get me wrong, I understand fully why you have to be that way. It's just... well... there's a huge contrast to that side of you, and the one I'm seeing right now. It's just awkward." Natasha shrugged her shoulders.

Xavier chuckled, understanding her sentiments. "It's the predator inside of us. When we are turned, we become natural hunters... killers if you will."

"I know. Okay, so did you?" Natasha asked, getting back to the story.

"Did I what?" Xavier asked teasingly, flashing his smile.

Natasha playfully slapped him on his arm. "Come on, you know what I'm talking about."

Chuckling, Xavier shook his head. "No, I didn't. Having him near me, I was able to successfully hypnotize him into handing over all of the photographs he'd taken. I also made him forget about everything he saw. Then I left."

"That's it?" Natasha asked, slightly disappointed his tale wasn't more exciting.

Xavier blinked, shocked. "I'm sorry to have bored you with my tale," he sourly joked.

"You didn't bore me, it's just… I thought there would be more excitement."

"Are you disappointed that I didn't kill him?" Xavier asked, perplexed.

"Oh, no, I'm glad you didn't. It's just… I don't know. Seemed a little anti-climactic, is all." Natasha shrugged.

"You've grown accustom to our lives as of late. You know, we didn't used to have so many battles and kidnappings. Supernaturals were very secretive, we all kept to ourselves for the most part. After the exposure, we kind of expanded our communities. In some ways that's been a good thing and in others, as you've seen and experienced, it's been bad," Xavier enlightened.

"I see. How did we get to this part in the conversation?" Natasha asked.

"You brought up the fact that you saw Darian on television," Xavier reminded her.

"Oh, that's right. By the way, television did not add that extra ten pounds on you," Natasha told Darian, who only smiled.

"Did you visit Warren and Matt today?" Xavier asked.

Natasha shook her head. "I didn't have time. I was so tired; I slept a good portion of the day. Then dealing with our son and all his antics, by the time I wanted to go, they said that visiting hours had passed."

"You called? Or did you go down there?"

"I called."

"What time?"

"Around four, I think."

"They lied. People were able to visit until seven PM," Darian said.

"Ah, that's right. I remember now from when you were in jail, but I thought that was just because you were a vampire, you could receive late visits. I didn't think they would lie about it," Natasha said.

"Apparently, this exposure has given assholes an excuse to be assholes," Xavier said.

"Well tomorrow, I'm going to go down there and I'm smuggling in a nail file baked inside a cake," she joked.

"You don't seem all that worried for them," Xavier commented, noticing Natasha's candor.

She smiled. "What's to worry about? They have a ton of people working on their side. They'll be out of that place and back at home before the week is over with. Xander and Richard won't let anything bad happen to them, and I know you won't either."

"You're right. Richard arranged for an earlier trial date and he pulled a favor out of me, although I would have done it anyway," Darian said.

"What was that?" Natasha asked.

"He needed me to convince the Illinois Judicial Director of the S.U.I.T. to assign specific judges for their trial," Darian answered. "That was my concern as well, because if they were found guilty by a harsher judge, he could have condemned them to death, in which I'm not sure any of us could have prevented it."

"Because of the silver and ultraviolet precautions?" Natasha asked.

Darian nodded. "It's my understanding this trial will be held during the day as all trials pertaining to shape-shifters are."

"That keeps us vampires out of the mix," Xavier said.

"And without the ability to control the minds of others, a shifter is pretty much screwed, right?" Natasha asked.

Darian nodded. "I *could* plant a command in the mind of a human, but in my resting state, I can't control them to make sure they'd carry out my command."

"Which is why it's just best to have a good judge rather than a bad one, I get that." Natasha thought it was wise to switch judges now. She hadn't put too much thought in how they were going to protect Warren and Matthew; she just knew that they would. She had not realized that there might be a chance this could all go very wrong.

"Good news is, their trial date has been moved up," Darian said.

"Oh, that's good news," Natasha said, relieved. "I still can't believe they arrested them—they're heroes. They should be getting medals and praise, not Miranda Rights and handcuffs."

"Some people don't care about that. Even more so, they don't want to credit those kinds of accomplishments to supernaturals," Xavier said.

"I don't know about that. The Captain of the S.U.I.T. gave credit to all of us for killing Marcus," Natasha stated.

"That was an anomaly," Xavier said. "I'll be happy when this dies down. Let the humans have their human police force if that's what they want. You know what they say, 'be careful what you ask for, you might just get it.'"

Natasha nodded, knowing what he meant by his words.

"I'm surprised I haven't heard from Xander tonight, requesting my lawyer," Darian said.

"Maybe he has one of his own," Natasha said.

"I don't think Michael can defend Warren and Matthew," Xavier said.

Natasha frowned. "Why not, he's a defense lawyer, right? Besides, he's their Pack brother, he'll help them if they need it."

"That's not what I meant. Being that he is a shifter, he's automatically not allowed to defend them," Xavier clarified.

"Damn, that's right. I kind of forgot about all that. God! I hate this. It's so not fair, they aren't even being judged by a jury of their peers," Natasha fumed.

"Apparently, that doesn't seem to matter to our human government," Darian said, a second later, his cell phone rang. He checked the caller ID. "Well, speak of the devil." He answered his cell. "Hello, Xander."

"Good evening, Darian. I'm calling to take you up on your offer. Do you think your lawyer will be willing to assist us?" Xander asked.

"Of course. He'll do it because I want him to, but furthermore, it's high-profile. He would want to bathe in the flashing lights of the media as he destroys the prosecutor's case. He feeds on that," Darian said, with a bit of humor.

"That's good to hear. Thank you, Darian."

"Don't mention it."

"I'll have him contact you soon to go over the details and payment arrangement," Darian added.

"Oh, you aren't paying for this?" Xander asked jokingly. "I wasn't aware."

"I'm making you aware now," Darian said, chuckling softly at Xander's joke.

"Of course, I didn't expect you to pay."

"I know. It was a cute joke. I'll contact him right now."

"I'll leave you to that. Have a good night."

Xander ended the call and Darian contacted his lawyer, telling him what he wanted him to do.

"The prosecutor's case is weak, at best. These men are heroes and it would be my honor to defend them. Don't worry, they'll be free soon enough," his lawyer assured him.

"That's what I want to hear. Oh, and you may send your bill to an Alexander Peterson," Darian gave his lawyer Xander's telephone number so that he could make financial arrangements.

"Ah, thank you, that was going to be my other concern. I'll contact him right now. Take care."

Darian closed his cell phone, slipping it back into his pocket.

"You know, you could have paid the bill," Natasha stated, giggling.

"Why? It is Xander's Pack member needing the defense. It seems only right. Besides, I'm sure he'd make me pay if our roles were reversed," Darian said, smiling cleverly.

"I guess," Natasha said, having no choice but to agree with Darian's statement.

"There's one more phone call I have to make," Darian said, pulling out his cell phone again. He called Richard and waited for the Alpha to answer.

"Hello, Darian," Richard greeted.

"Hello, Richard. I just wanted to let you know that I spoke with Dominick and the judges will be switched," Darian informed.

"That's excellent news. Thank you," Richard said, happy that things were looking better for his Pack member and Warren.

"It was nothing."

"Trust me, it was something." Richard was happy he didn't have to deal with Elaine.

"I understand." Darian chuckled. "I wanted to have it so that all supernatural S.U.I.T. officers who were under arrest could get the same deal, but apparently only Elaine Baker could arrange that."

"That was thoughtful of you."

"I thought so."

"So you don't want to pay a visit to Elaine?" Richard asked, knowing the vampire really didn't want to be entangled with the shifter if he didn't have to be.

"Is she as old as you are?" Darian asked.

"Older," Richard replied.

"Then I wouldn't be able to compel her to carry out my commands without using physical force. There is also no guarantee she'll do as I ask even if I threaten her."

"I wouldn't want you to do that," Richard said. Even though Elaine had angered him, he still had feelings for her. He wouldn't want to see her harmed by his friend.

"I didn't think so," Darian replied.

"She isn't an easy woman to deal with, that's for certain. Again, thank you for your help."

"Not a problem. Take care."

"You too." Both men ended the call.

The three continued to spend time with each other talking about various subjects and watching television. When their son woke up, the two vampires played with him as Natasha slept. They put him in the bed beside her before sunrise. Xavier stayed with Natasha, while Darian returned back to the mansion to rest for the day.

CHAPTER SIX
THE GAME

The next day, Dominick Anderson sat in his office looking over the upcoming court schedule. The night before, he had made certain that Margaret Hillington was going to be the judge presiding over the Illinois S.U.I.T. trials. He couldn't remember the reason why he wanted to remove Thomas Shelton from the case, but he knew it needed to be done. He sat back, satisfied with his decision. He went about his workday, tending to his daily business until his secretary informed him that Ms. Elaine Baker was on the line waiting to speak with him.

He took her call. "Good morning, Elaine," he greeted.

"I'm going to cut right to the chase," she said by way of a greeting. "Why did you switch the judges for the upcoming trials?" Elaine asked, her words were filled with venom. She didn't know how Richard was able to make this arrangement, although, she had her suspicions. She already didn't appreciate that fact that their court date had been expedited. Nevertheless, she was not going to let him have his way completely if she could help it, not without meeting some demands of her own, at least.

"Margaret Hillington is a well-respected judge, I don't see a problem with her presiding over the case," Dominick answered.

"There was already a judge in place," she shot back.

"With all due respect, Ms. Baker… I don't see why you are so upset? I'm simply doing my job."

"I don't have to explain myself to you. If you want to continue to do your job, I suggest you reinstate Judge Thomas Shelton before the trial date, because if I have to do it myself, I'll look for your replacement at the same time." Elaine wanted her way and she knew this was the only card she had to play.

Not wanting to lose his high-ranking position he'd kissed a lot of ass to attain, he decided to give into her *suggestion*. "All right, Ms. Baker, I am changing the judges as we speak."

"That's reassuring. Looks like I picked the right man for this job," Elaine said, ending the call. She checked her computer, viewing the court schedule. It was done, Thomas Shelton was back in place. She smiled to herself before picking up her telephone. She dialed Richard's cell phone and waited for him to answer. When he did, she informed him of the new change. "Hello Richard, it's Elaine. I just wanted to call you up and let you know that your boys still have Judge Thomas Shelton to deal with."

"What are you talking about?" Richard asked, agitated.

"You do play hardball well, but this is my playground, darling. Nothing happens within this system that I don't know about. Changing the judges behind my back wasn't a smart idea. Don't try that little stunt again," Elaine said.

"I don't have time to play your little games, Elaine. Don't piss me off–"

"Don't threaten me, Richard," Elaine interjected. "We both know who'd win in a fight between us, don't we?"

"I don't want to fight you, Elaine. I wanted your help, but you refused."

"It's not my refusal that's hurting your Pack right now. It's yours. What I ask for isn't life threatening. As a matter of fact, I recall you enjoying the pleasures of my body on many occasions," Elaine said imploringly.

"That was nearly a hundred years ago."

"Time only makes the heart grow fonder."

"Elaine, we've been friends for a long time, don't ruin a great friendship over something so trivial." Richard tried his best to reason with her.

"What can I say, I'm selfish that way. It's really simple, darling."

"Actually, it's not. I'm in a serious relationship with someone, as I've told you."

"And as *I've* told *you*, I don't care. I thought you were an Alpha, in charge of your own Pack. Who runs it, her or you?" Elaine said, striking a blow to Richard's domineering nature.

Richard laughed, seeing her strategy for what it was. "My God,

Elaine. What happened to you?"

"I've learned to go after the things I want with a take-no-prisoners attitude. Be glad that I did, or you wouldn't have a supernatural friend in such a position to help you out when you needed it."

"If a human had your position, I wouldn't be talking to you right now," Richard pointed out.

"If grandma had balls, she'd be grandpa. What difference does it make? Enough with this pointless conversation, you know what I want. What is your decision?" Elaine asked, getting down to the nitty-gritty.

Richard was silent for a few moments, thinking about his situation. He didn't want Darian to threaten her, although he suspected the vampire would do so if asked. Not only that, he knew that Elaine would be so stubborn, it would force Darian to have to harm her and even then, there was no guarantee she'd do as he wanted, as Darian stated. Besides, he really didn't want to put Darian in that position when it was his mess to deal with. Then he got an idea, one that would completely turn the tables on Elaine.

"I'm not going to do this thing with you. You want me to betray the relationship I have with my mate, and that's not going to happen," Richard said, laying down the gauntlet.

Elaine huffed, taken aback by the Alpha's resolve, although, his attitude did entice her. "You forget whose side of the court the ball's in, Richard?"

Thinking about what Darian had originally wanted he decided to ask for that. "I'm done playing with you. As a matter of fact, I want you to make sure that the most lenient judges in every state preside over the cases of the ex-S.U.I.T. officers."

"Don't be ridiculous. That's going to look like a controversy in and of itself."

"This is bigger than your lusts, Elaine. It is bigger than my friends currently incarcerated. Can you imagine what's going to happen if any more supernaturals are killed because of this scandal?"

"That's not my prob–"

"Before you say it's 'not my problem', let me point out how much of a problem it could be for you. Imagine hundreds of supernaturals taking revenge against the judicial system which abused its' power.

Can you imagine supernaturals killing S.U.I.T. officers out of anger? Think about that last couple of days and multiply that by infinity." Richard hoped he was getting through to her.

This time, it was Elaine who was silently thinking on the other end of the line. After she gave it some thought, she answered him. "A convincing scenario you've presented. However, think about this. If judges all across the country are all of a sudden switched for more lenient judges, something that's never happened before. It's going to look like a plot supernaturals created in order to free their members. It will mock our judicial system and anger a lot of people in high positions. Not to mention, bring a shitload of heat down on me."

"I guess you're going to be taking all the risk now, eh, Elaine?" Richard said.

"You don't get to bargain here, Richard. It's the original deal or no deal at all," Elaine was trying to regain control of their game.

"There is no 'deal'."

"Richard, you would allow your members to suffer for your pride?"

"I'll rain hell upon the S.U.I.T. if they try to extend imprisonment or kill my Pack and I won't be alone when I do." Richard was feeling the ball coming into *his* side of the court with every counter-argument he gave.

"You won't be able to stop them if they did, Richard. With all the anti-supernatural equipment the S.U.I.T. has, you'd die if you tried," Elaine said, showing her first signs of worry for her ex-lover.

"The rest of the precinct isn't as fully equipped as the holding cell area is. I'll start there and work my way through and only God will have mercy on them if they harm my Pack in any way." Richard made sure that his voice was steady, but forceful, letting her know he meant every word he's said.

"If I do this your way, it could bring unwanted media attention to me. They'll want to know why I wanted to be so lenient toward supernaturals. It may expose me, Richard."

"Either way, you're going to get burned. You might as well choose the least painful option—the one that won't lead to countless deaths."

"It could ruin my career!"

"That's not *my* problem. Now, I have told you what I am willing to do for my Pack. I'm sure I'm not the only leader willing to go that route. You spin this the right way, you may not have to deal with any controversy at all, but that's only if you go about this peacefully."

Finally backed against the wall and seeing her advantage gone, she decided to give in. "You think you've won this, don't you?"

"I did and you know it. It would be in your best interest to change the judges."

"I knew you were a smart man, what I didn't expect was for you to play so dirty. Well done, by the way." Elaine ended the call, getting in the last words. She sat at her desk, looking at the telephone, now on its base. She knew he had turned the tables on her. Instead of him taking all of the risk, it would now be her taking the biggest risk of all. As it was, she had underestimated the younger shifter, allowing him to outsmart her. She wouldn't be making that mistake again. She decided that it was in her best interest to give into his demand, knowing a bloody war between supernaturals and the S.U.I.T. was going to be worse than the controversy that may follow by switching the judges. If she played her cards right, she might be able to avoid any negative feedback all together.

She picked up her telephone, dialing Dominick. When he answered, she told him to switch the judges once again, putting Margaret back into place.

"What's going on, Ms. Baker? First, you want me to change them, now you want me to change them back. What game are you playing?" Dominick asked, confused.

"I thought about your decision and I fear I didn't give you credit for making such a wonderful choice. You were right to have Margaret preside over the upcoming S.U.I.T. trial," Elaine said, hoping to stroke his ego enough that he'd stop asking questions.

Surprised that *Elaine Baker* actually gave him a compliment, he decided not to question her decision to have him switch the judges. "Well, I thank you for that, Ms. Baker, and I'll reinstate Judge Hillington right away."

"Thank you, Dominick," Elaine said, ending the call. She decided to email the other Judicial Directors, giving them her order to assign the most lenient judges to each S.U.I.T. case only. Although, she made sure to word it differently, requesting each judge by name and giving credentials to support her decision. After sending the email, she sat back in her chair, frowning, having been defeated at her own game. Her day was not going well and after it all, she still didn't get a chance to sleep with Richard.

***

Richard walked onto his balcony, taking a seat on one of the reclining chairs. He knew that Elaine was beyond livid after having control stripped away in her little game of seduction. He didn't care. Had she'd done what he asked when he first came to her, she wouldn't be in this predicament now. Ryan joined him, taking the chair beside his.

"How are you doing this morning?" she asked.

"I'm doing very, very well, sweetheart," Richard said, still basking in the glow of his victory.

"I see. Well, what has *you* so cheerful today?"

"Elaine Baker called me this morning to inform me that my plan to have the judges switched failed."

"That bitch! You know, I'm getting sick and tired of her ass, sorry-ass, desperate bitch trying to trick my man into sleeping with her. You're too good for her," Ryan fumed.

"She tried, but−"

Ryan interjected. "Don't sleep with her. I don't like how she's trying to manipulate you. She knows you don't want her, so she's using Matthew and Warren against you."

"I know, but−"

"No. Listen to me, baby. We have to help out Warren and Matt, but we have to get around her ass to do it," Ryan said. "I know I said that I would stand by you, no matter what… but we can't let her have her way."

Richard didn't say anything for a few seconds, only sat still watching her.

"Why are you looking at me like that?" Ryan asked.

"I'm just waiting for you to get it all out of your system before I try to speak again," Richard replied.

"Oh, I did cut you off a few times, didn't I? Baby, I'm sorry… I'm just so angry!"

He chuckled. "I know. But you don't need to worry. Elaine lost at her own game. I informed her that I would raise holy hell if anything bad happened to my Pack. I gave her two scenarios then told her to choose the one without the body count."

"Oooh, you did? I love when you take charge like that. It's so sexy. Will she take your advice?"

"If she knows what's good for her, she will. If she doesn't and I'm forced to attack, the backlash will hit her hardest as she's the one who's in charge of the S.U.I.T. organization. Elaine may have changed over the years since I've known her, but she's ambitious. She's not going to ruin the career she worked so hard to get."

"What if the judge you want still finds them guilty?" Ryan asked.

"I did a lot of research on this judge and she seems reasonable enough to make a sound and just decision. I honestly believe that she will let them go. If not, I'll do what I have to do, still."

"All right, baby. Man, I bet Elaine probably hates having to change the judge for Matt's case—"

"Not just Matthew and Warren's trial, but every ex-S.U.I.T. officer who is now awaiting their trials."

"Wow! I bet she wasn't expecting you to drop that on her."

Richard laughed. "No, she didn't. I have to admit, it was originally Darian's idea."

"It's a good idea," Ryan said, settling back into her chair. She was quite for a while then she thought about something. "Honey, if you did have to sleep with her, would you have told me?"

Richard turned toward her. "Of course I would have. You deserve to know something like that. Besides, infidelity isn't an activity supernaturals indulge in. There's no way we could hide such a thing anyway, which is why most of us have honest, committed relationships or very open ones."

Ryan nodded. "That's true." She slipped her hand into his, smiling to herself. She loved Richard and was happy he loved her.

CHAPTER SEVEN
WEDNESDAY AT NOON
THE TRIAL

A ll four shifters stood by the silver bars as the judge took her seat behind the podium. Two lawyers stood behind their own podiums, ready to present their cases. Only a few news stations were allowed inside the holding area to cover the trial. There were no other friends of family members allowed inside the holding area as a precaution. It was a concern that if they were to allow the relatives of the accused inside the holding area, they might try to cause a commotion or attempt to free their loved ones. This was the case especially if that relative was a supernatural. There were no vampires allowed in the area at all. It was a rule that had angered many who had to face the judge. Many who never got a chance to say "goodbye" to their family and friends.

Warren looked around the room, wishing he could see his Pack supporting him, but knew why none were present. He was however, pleased to know that Xander had acquired Darian's lawyer for their defense, and he was even more pleased to see Margaret Hillington presiding over their trial.

The judge looked over the paperwork before her, making sure everything was in order before she began. She looked up, eyeing the four supernaturals. She felt sorry for them, having to be locked away like that after dedicating their lives to save others. It angered her greatly that so many supernaturals had been arrested and killed. She thought it was unfair and ungrateful.

"I am very familiar with your cases and I will be presiding over each one. It's my understanding that you all have the same lawyer, is this correct?" Ms. Hillington asked.

"Yes, Your Honor," each shifter and their lawyer replied.

"Very well, I don't think any of us want to be here all day hearing the same argument from both lawyers four times over, am I correct?" the judge asked.

"I would agree, Your Honor," the defense lawyer said.

"Yes, Your Honor," the prosecutor agreed.

"Good. Now, the crimes they've been charged of are identical, am I correct?"

"Yes, Your Honor," both Lawyers answered.

"This is my courtroom today, and it's my decision that we have one mass trial, Now, are there any objections?"

Both lawyers looked at each other, Howard Langston turned toward his clients to discuss the motion. "Do you agree with that?"

The four shifters looked at each other and nodded, knowing their stories were the same.

"All right." Howard turned back toward the judge. "Your Honor, that is acceptable."

"No objections here, Your Honor," Prosecutor Wayne Harrison agreed.

"Excellent, there are no objections. All right, let us begin. Mr. Langston, how do your clients plead?"

"Not Guilty, Your Honor," their lawyer, Howard Langston stated.

The judged nodded. "All right, state your case."

"Thank you, Your Honor." Howard Langston began his argument, pointing out many facts and opinions to support his defense. The two lawyers battled it out in the courtroom/holding cell area, each one giving their best counter-arguments.

"Your Honor, these officers broke the law. Regardless of what their intentions were, we can't ignore the fact that the law has been disregarded," the prosecutor, Wayne Harrison declared.

"I will now refer to Mr. Langston," the judge said, alternating the floor between both lawyers allowing them to fairly state and argue their cases.

"Your Honor, it's true. The law has been broken. Documents have been forged, and there have been some slight deceptions. But more importantly, lives have been saved, countless lives, because these supernaturals took it upon themselves to put their lives on the line to protect the humans. They knew it was the right thing to do." Howard went on to explain the sacrifice and trouble each shifter had to endure in order to serve their country.

"I will now hear the rebuttal from the prosecutor," the judge said.

"That wasn't their decision to make, Your Honor," the prosecutor said, getting right into his counter. "The S.U.I.T. is an organization that prohibits supernaturals from joining for a reason. There's no telling how these officers have abused the system. How many of their fellow supernatuals have they allowed to live because they were of their kind?"

"Objection, Your Honor. He's making allegation without substantiated evidence. This is all just outlandish speculation," Howard countered.

"That's just it, Your Honor, we *don't* know what other illegal tactics these supernaturals have done using their power as S.U.I.T.. They have even pled the Fifth Amendment when inquired about who is the person responsible for changing their test results. They can't be trusted," the prosecutor pointed out.

"Your honor, it's not against the law to take the Fifth Amendment. The people who assisted them are not on trial today, my four clients are. Three men and one woman, each of which their record with the S.U.I.T. speaks for itself. Warren Davis and Matthew Eric hold the record for the highest arrest and or executions in the entire precinct. This proves that they've shown no favoritism to other supernaturals who've broken the laws they've sworn to uphold. Christine McKenzie and Fredrick Benton have saved the lives of many members on their Infiltration team. I don't think anyone can argue that if they were human, those same men and women who are alive today would be dead."

"*Now* who's speculating?" commented the prosecutor.

"Gentlemen, I will have order. The floor does not recognize you, Mr. Harrison," the judge reprimanded.

"My apologies, Your Honor," Wayne said.

"Your Honor, these supernaturals only want the same chance as their human colleagues, the same opportunity to save lives and keep the peace," Howard said. He paused in his argument to give the prosecutor a chance for a rebuttal.

The judge kept the peace, alternating between both lawyers.

"Your Honor, the defense is trying to argue that the end justifies the means. These supernaturals became vigilantes with badges. If we allow them to get away with it, maybe we should just reinstate the *Slayer Manifesto* again," Wayne said.

"That's going way into the extreme, Your Honor. The prosecution is trying to build a case based solely on outlandish speculation. 'Why if we let the supernaturals get away with lying about who they are… then what's to stop humans from taking the law into their own hands and killing their neighbors again.' Your Honor, people have felt safe because the law that's supposed to protect them was enforced. Supernatual criminals have been removed from the streets and lives have been saved. The only crime here is a rule that prohibits supernaturals from saving lives as officers of the law." Howard stepped away from his podium. "The crime doesn't fit the punishment, Your Honor… and that is the bottom line."

The judged looked at the two lawyers. She was impressed by both of their arguments and soon she would have her decision. "I understand that you both have character witnesses you want to bring to the stand?"

"Yes, Your Honor," both lawyers said in unison.

"Very well, the defense may present their first witness."

"Thank you, Your Honor." Howard turned motioning for the officer to allow Forensics Pathologist, Marshall Galen into the room.

The officer did as requested, allowing Marshall to walk pass him. Marshall looked around the room. Somehow, it looked so different to him with the podiums in place. He glanced at the four shifters standing behind bars and he smiled at them, hoping to give them some reassurance. He stood before the bailiff and swore on the bible to "tell the truth and nothing but the truth," then he took his seat beside the judge's podium.

"Your witness, Mr. Langston," the judge said.

Howard approached him. "Mr. Galen, how would you describe the four people in those cells?" He pointed at the four shifters.

Marshall looked at the four shifters again. "I have nothing but the utmost respect for those four officers right there. I've seen their dedication with my own eyes. I've watched how they've worked tirelessly and endlessly, giving everything they had to give to save lives and keep the streets safe. There are human officers within the S.U.I.T. who don't have an ounce of their integrity or loyalty. They believe in the law, they believe in justice. Quite frankly, the S.U.I.T. needs them."

"Objection, Your Honor," Wayne called out. "The witness isn't here to determine new protocol for the S.U.I.T. organization."

Howard turned toward the judge. "Your Honor, the witness is here to prove how having shifters on the S.U.I.T. has only been beneficial to the organization. He is also here to attest to the character of these supernaturals. That's really why we are in court today anyway, isn't it?"

"Sustained. I'll allow it," The judge told the prosecution. "Go on, Mr. Langston."

Howard nodded and turning, gestured for Marshall to continue.

"Your Honor, these past few days have been nothing by an eye-opener for me and *should* be for every human being on the face of the planet. The S.U.I.T., for all its resources was completely powerless against the coven of vampires who terrorized not only *this* city, but also many others. It was not the S.U.I.T., who in the end brought them to justice, but supernaturals."

"Mr. Galen, would you agree that only supernaturals could have stopped the recent wave of crime?" Howard asked.

"Objection… leading question," Wayne interrupted.

"Objection sustained," the judge said. "Mr. Galen, please continue."

Marshall answered the question. "Had it not been for those very supernaturals behind those bars, there's no telling what would still be happening today. It is pure arrogance to think an all-human police force can take on superhuman criminals. It is egotism and stupidity. I see the bodies of the victims that come across my table, trust me… we're no match."

Prosecutor Wayne Harrison huffed. "Your Honor, may I point out that these supernaturals weren't the only ones with arrest records. Their human co-workers have been just as successful in apprehending the supernatural element."

"Duly noted." The judge gestured for Howard to continue his line of questioning.

"Marshall Galen, do you think these four officers should be punished for their crimes?" Howard Langston asked the pathologist.

Marshall shook his head. "I do not. I'm going to put my own career on the line—"

Howard held up his hand. "May I suggest you don't do anything rash, Mr. Galen."

"It's okay. Whatever happens will happen. I've known about Mr. Davis and Mr. Eric being shape-shifters for a while now and I've said nothing to my superiors about it, because I knew they needed to be here. This bureaucratic bravado posturing will only weaken our defense, not strengthen it." Marshall looked at the prosecutor. "You think you're defending the people here, you're not. All you're doing is condemning them to a life of fear and uncertainty. You speak about the human officers arresting a few, young and immature supernatuals and you think that's the solution." Marshall scoffed. "You didn't see the mutilated remains of a five-month old infant posed in a department store window. You didn't get to see the dismembered remains of four innocent children stuffed inside an ice cream truck freezer. You and your political friends didn't get to experience the sight of two children disrobed, skinned and sexually assaulted and left exposed as if their lives meant nothing!" Marshall sat back, forcing himself to calm down. He took several deep breaths while everyone watched, transfixed by his demeanor. He was normally so cool and relaxed, he took everyone by surprise. Apparently, the last few days took a bigger toll on him than they had realized.

"Go on," the judge encouraged.

"These shape-shifters are heroes. We shouldn't be here." Marshall ended his statement.

The Judge nodded. "Does the prosecution want to cross-exam the witness?"

"No questions, Your Honor," Wayne said, not wanting to give Marshall any more leeway than he already had. His testimony had been damaging to his argument and he didn't see any weakness in the man's integrity that he could exploit. He felt it was best to have Mr. Galen leave the courtroom as soon as possible. He had seen the telltale signs that the judge was sympathetic to the defense.

The judge dismissed Marshall and asked if the defense had any other witnesses. Howard answered, saying he had seventeen character witnesses willing to speak up for the four shifters on trial.

"Objection, Your Honor, certainly we don't need to hear seventeen biased testimonies from the friends of these officers," the prosecution argued.

"As judge presiding over this trial, I believe I'll decide what testimonies we should hear, Mr. Harrison," the judge reprimanded. "The prosecution is sustained."

"Of course, Your Honor, my apologies."

Howard chuckled. "Your Honor, one of my witnesses is the former Captain of the S.U.I.T. precinct. Surely her testimony should be heard."

The judge nodded. "I'll allow it."

Wayne stood behind his podium growing more agitated by the second. He had five officers who were willing to speak on the state's behalf. He hoped that would be enough for the judge to see things his way. The bailiff walked Michelle Lawrence to the chair, had her swear an oath on the bible then walked away as she sat down.

Howard approached her. "Ms. Lawrence, is it safe to say that you were fired from the S.U.I.T. because you spoke the truth about how the supernaturals solved the last case."

Michelle nodded. "That's correct. I was instructed to say that the officers within the S.U.I.T. precinct took down the vampire coven and shifter that had been attacked Chicago citizens. I could not tell such a bold-faced lie with a clean conscious. I felt the people needed to know who really saved their lives. It is a decision I would make again, even knowing the consequences."

"I have one question. Do you believe these officers should be punished for their crimes?" Howard asked.

"No, I do not. Personally, I don't believe they've committed any crimes. They broke a protocol, disregarded a rule—"

"Objection. The witness is misleading. They broke the law, Ms. Lawrence. You *do* remember what that is, don't you?" Wayne interjected.

"Your Honor, the witness is not on trial here," Howard pointed out.

"Your objection is overruled," The judge told the prosecution, who nodded dejectedly. She looked at the witness. "You may continue."

Michelle nodded. "They were the best officers on the force. I always knew the job would get done when I assigned it to them. They never had a complaint filed against them, never a report of abuse, unlike some of the officers within the S.U.I.T.. They upheld the law with honor and integrity. I can only imagine how well other supernatural officers across this country have done doing the same."

"No further questions." Howard ended his examination and walked back to his podium. Wayne stepped forward, approaching her.

"Ms. Lawrence, did you know that they were supernaturals before they turned themselves in?"

"I had only found out they were supernaturals a few days ago when Marshall Galen informed me after I couldn't get in contact with them," Michelle answered.

"You couldn't get in contact with them? Did they abandon their duties? What was the reason why you couldn't get in contact with them?" Wayne asked, hoping he found something to use against the shifters.

Warren and Matthew watched the trial, completely nervous, seeing it could go either way. The prosecution had a good case against them and they were willing to bet he was going to hit away at their shield until he made a crack then he'd really get relentless. On the other hand, they were so touched and honored by what Marshall had said in their defense and seeing Michelle before them, supporting them, let them know how well they were respected.

Michelle answered the prosecutor. "They didn't abandon their duties. They were avoiding the silver and ultraviolet test we were administering at the precinct. They didn't want to be exposed before they could capture the vampire coven."

Wayne nodded. "They seem to have a penchant for breaking the rules when it so suits them, don't they?"

"Objection, prosecution is making an accusation," Howard declared.

"Sustained." the judge said but she turned toward Wayne. "I'll have you chose your words more carefully, Mr. Harrison."

"Yes, Your Honor," Wayne said. He turned back to Michelle.

"Please answer the question?"

Michelle smirked. "Only the rules that don't make sense, as it would seem, the rules that prevent them from doing their jobs effectively."

This time, Wayne smirked as he turned away from Michelle. "I have no more questions for this witness, Your Honor."

"Very well." the judge sent Michelle out of the room, allowing Wayne to bring in his witness. Officer Kyle Ronen stepped through the door.

"Oh shit, not this motherfucker," Fredrick murmured.

"I know," Warren agreed.

Kyle took his seat after swearing in.

Wayne approached him. "Officer Ronen, how would you describe the four supernatuals in those cells?"

Kyle looked at his ex-co-workers. "I always knew something was up with them. But the Captain always showed them favoritism, giving them most of the cases that came through our precinct. Frankly, I don't have any respect for anyone who thinks they should take the law into their own hands or who think they're above the law."

Wayne asked Ronen several questions about his own success within the S.U.I.T., hoping to prove the employment of supernaturals unnecessary. "Well, it looks as though you have had a very successful career. I have no further questions." He returned to his podium.

Howard stepped forward. "That was quite impressive, Officer Ronen. That's quite an arrest record you have there. Almost as impressive as the list of complaints you have from people who claimed you've abused your power. Arresting supernaturals without just cause, not reading Miranda Rights and falsifying your own police documents."

"Objection! Your Honor, point to line of questioning," Wayne called out.

"Your Honor, I'm simply pointing out the witness's own questionable character. It's not as if I'm making this up. I hold in my hand a stack full of complaints from family members of supernaturals and supernaturals themselves who've felt that this particular officer took the law into his *own* hands. His file is filled with reprimands and at least one suspension. It would seem that Officer Ronen has an extreme distaste for supernaturals based on this evidence."

"Your Honor…Your Honor, my witness is not on trial here," Wayne stated.

"But he is, if he's to be a witness against my clients," Howard replied.

"Order!" Judge Margaret Hillington said, hammering her gavel. Once the room quieted, she went on. "Do you have any more questions for the witness?"

"No, Your Honor," Howard said, he felt that he'd been successful in discrediting the officer's character well enough.

"Good." She dismissed Kyle and he left the courtroom. "Does the prosecution have any more witnesses they'd like to present?"

Wayne thought about the other officers who had volunteered to bad-mouth the four shifters, and thought it be a bad idea to bring them forward. He knew Howard Langston had done his homework. He knew their personal records were as questionable as Ronen's. He couldn't afford to weaken his case anymore than he already had by letting Officer Ronen take the stand.

"Not at this time, Your Honor."

"All right, then. Please gentlemen, present your final statements." The Prosecutor went first.

Wayne walked toward the cells, taking a good look at the four shifters inside. "You may have wanted to do what you thought was the right thing. You may have even saved the lives of countless humans. You may even be considered the best officers on the S.U.I.T.. However, that doesn't take away from the fact that you broke the law. You lied time and time again to protect yourselves. You betrayed the judicial system and the people of this country. We cannot overlook the crimes you've committed in your quest for justice. If you truly respected the law, you would have never done what you did." He turned to face the judge. "No matter what motivates a person to take the law into their own hands, we as a civilization cannot accept vigilante justice. The government may not be perfect, but it's the only system we have in place that can keep order. It must be respected and obeyed, or there will be chaos. The Prosecution rests its case." With that, he walked back to his podium.

Howard looked at the judge. "My clients may have broken a law, this is true. An antiquated and ill-conceived law that didn't take into consideration how dangerous supernaturals can be and that maybe having some on the S.U.I.T. would be a good idea. When you look at the grand scheme of things, there really is no comparison. Would you go back and erase all of their accomplishments. Would it have been better to let people die horrible deaths for the sake of upholding a biased law? The love and respect these supernaturals have for the sanctity of human life compelled them to do what was necessary. History has proven that sometimes it takes breaking laws to get justice. Set these heroes free, Your Honor... they don't belong here. The defense rests."

Margaret had to admit, both lawyers performed in the court on this day. She called for recess and went to her chamber to make her decision.

Howard walked over to his clients. "Are you nervous?"

"Can you tell?" Warren asked.

Howard smiled. "I've never lost a case and I don't plan on doing so now. I wouldn't be worried," he said reassuringly.

After ten minutes, the judge returned, taking her place behind her own podium. The lawyers did the same.

"I've reviewed everything in this case and I've made my decision," Judge Margaret Hillington said, pausing.

All four shifters held their breaths as they waited for her to continue.

"Although these four supernaturals broke the law, I don't believe a crime has been committed. I find them Not Guilty of the charges. Therefore, they are free to go. Bailiff, please release them."

"Thank you! Oh my God!" Warren exclaimed, so thrilled to be free again.

The prosecutor shook the hand of Howard Langston. "It was an honor to battle it out with you."

"Likewise. If you ever get tired of working for the state and want to make some real money, give me a call." Howard handed him his firm's card.

Wayne took the card and nodded. He did have to admit, there was no way he could afford the designer suit Howard was wearing on his salary. But he wasn't ready to turn in his lead prosecutor title just yet. He left the courtroom, heading back to his office.

The bailiff opened the cell doors and the four shifters rushed out, each hugging Howard and shaking his hand thanking him for his services.

"Don't mention it. It's what I do. Once I read over your case, I knew I had to take it," Howard said. "Hey, you're free, go home. That's got to feel great."

"Man, you don't know how great this feels! You have to come over to our house for dinner sometime," Warren offered.

Howard smiled. "Your Alphas paid me quite handsomely for my representation. There's really no need to−"

"Still, I want to thank you," Warren said.

"Will you be doing the cooking?" Howard asked.

"Ah, well… I, ah… really can't cook that well, so no." Warren chuckled.

"We'll see, thank you." Howard patted him on the shoulder before taking up his briefcase and leaving the precinct.

Warren turned toward Matthew. "I can't believe it's over and we're free. Let's get the hell out of here."

"Finally, something I've been wanting to do for a while now," Matthew said and both men left the holding cell area. Outside, their fellow S.U.I.T. officers who supported them applauded as they walked by.

"I was hoping she'd set you free. Thank goodness something good finally happened," Officer Alice Gains said.

The four shifters thanked their friends as they made their way through the S.U.I.T. precinct.

"We should go out and celebrate," Officer Mike Betty suggested.

"I'd love to, Mike, but all I want to do now is go home, take a shower and a nice, long nap," Matthew said, respectfully declining the offer.

"Don't sweat it, I get it, sure. Another time, then?" Mike asked.

"For sure," Matthew agreed.

After getting past the overjoyed mob, the four shifters exited the precinct. Standing outside, were Richard, Xander, Ignacio, Adrian and Sergio.

"Man, am I fucking happy to see you!" Warren exclaimed as he made his way to his Pack and friends. Matthew did the same, hugging Richard and Ignacio, then the others.

"We came just in case we had to open a can of whoopass on these people," Adrian said.

"I was all game to tear this place apart," Sergio said. "Elise kept calling me, giving me tidbits about the trial. How was it in there?"

Warren laughed. "Shit, it was rough. It really could have gone either way. You wouldn't believe how the prosecutor made us look like a bunch of crazy ass vigilantes."

"Was he good?" Richard asked.

Matthew nodded. "He was… although I think he made a mistake putting Kyle's ignorant ass on the stand." He laughed.

"Oh yeah, I knew Howard was going to rip him apart on his cross-examination," Warren said.

"How was Howard?" Xander asked. He didn't doubt the lawyer's skill; he'd hoped he could live up to his reputation *and* price. He was glad to see that he had.

"Oh man, Howard was amazing! That man has a mouthpiece on him. I bet he cost you an arm and a leg to defend all four of us," Warren said.

"Oh, you noticed my missing limbs, did you?" Xander joked. "Indeed, he was pricy, but having you free and back where you belong is priceless. Besides, Richard and I split the cost."

The two Alphas smiled.

Warren then remembered something. He turned, looking at Christine and Fredrick standing behind them, remaining silent. "Oh, where are my manners. Come on." He gestured for the two shifters to come closer. "This is Christine McKenzie and Fredrick Benton."

Christine shook the two Alphas' hands. "I really want to thank you for helping us out. I know you didn't have to, but you did. I can't tell you how much that means to me."

Richard nodded. "Don't mention it. We have to stick up for our kind. It's how we stay strong."

"I'm with her, thanks for everything," Fredrick said, releasing

Xander's hand.

Xander looked at the two Packless shifters. "What are you going to do now?"

They looked at each other, shrugging. "Hadn't really had time to think about it. I was so worried I'd never see the light of day again… that was my only priority," Christine said.

"You may want to look into joining a Pack, simply for protection," Richard suggested.

"Who would have us?" Fredrick asked.

Both Richard and Xander looked at each other. Adrian turned away, smiling to himself, thinking about what his father had said earlier about not wanting to accept any new members.

"Well?" Ignacio asked, putting both Alphas on the spot.

Richard tossed him a look that said, 'shut the hell up'.

"It's okay, we don't want to impose, but it's the reason why we don't have a Pack," Christine said.

"I would be lying if I said I wanted new Pack members, however, I'm not going to eliminate the possibility," Xander said.

Richard chuckled. "How about you come over to…" He paused, looking at Xander. "…How about you come over to Xander's home?"

The other Alpha turned sharply, looking at him. "*My* home?"

"Why not? Tatiana can make us all a wonderful dinner and we can discuss the issue of accepting new members with our respective Packs," Richard suggested, smiling deviously.

Xander was at a loss for words. He narrowed his eyes as Richard's smile widened. "Very well." He turned toward the younger shifters. "Please, do come to my home. I will have Warren contact you, but it will be in a few days. We will discuss your predicament then, how is that?"

Both Christine and Fredrick smiled and nodded. They had wanted to be in a Pack. They knew it was safer and better to be in one, but they didn't know where to go and the Packs they did approach had rejected them. In the end, they ended up being their own sort of "Pack".

"It's settled then," Richard said. "We should get going. Everyone is waiting to see you both."

"I'm all for that," Warren said. He and Matthew said 'good-bye' to Christine and Fredrick then climbed into their own car heading back toward Xander's mansion with the others.

"Do you think Xander is going to accept any new members?" Matthew asked.

Warren shrugged as he steered the car. "Who's to say? Both he and Richard already protected them. Christine and Fredrick are good people. Besides, Richard could use a larger Pack."

"I don't think he wants a bigger Pack. Remember, he had a big Pack and he was going to leave them," Matthew said.

"Well, one more coyote with Fredrick's skill can't be a bad thing. Besides that old Pack of his had too many assholes. I'd want to leave them, too, if I were him," Warren said, thinking about Katrina and the other members of Richard's old Pack they'd killed in Florida.

"I guess. It's up to Richard anyway," Matthew said.

"How would you feel about Fredrick becoming your Pack brother?" Warren asked, looking at his lover.

"I'm okay with that. I've always gotten along with Fred. He never exposed us, and I respected him for that."

"I agree, although, it wouldn't have done him any good to do so."

"True, but he's still a stand-up guy, Christine, too." Matthew paused. "Boy, if feels go to be free," he said as they drove back home.

CHAPTER EIGHT

At Xander's mansion, the rest of Richard's and Xander's Packs, Elise and her Pride, along with Adan and his Pride and Natasha all welcomed Warren and Matthew back home. They hugged and patted the two men on their backs, a few like Natasha, gave them kisses on their cheeks.

"I'm so happy to see you," Natasha said, stepping back from the two men.

"It's great to be back. You have no idea how much we missed all of you. It was awesome how you came to visit us, though. That really meant a lot and made the days go by faster," Warren said.

"Geez, you pussy, you were only in there for five days," Adrian teased.

"One hour felt like a whole day, trust me, it sucked," Matthew said.

"I bet. It's good we got you out of there before the *Lunar*. I'd hate to see how many eyes would have been on you then," Sergio said.

"I know, three more days and they would have gotten a show, that's for sure," Warren agreed. He was very pleased to have been freed before his ex-co-workers could see one of his most intimate moments.

They all began to calm down and settle more comfortably around the mansion, chatting with one another about all of the events that took place over the past couple of days.

Xander turned towards Richard. "Ah, yes, there was something I meant to ask you."

Richard looked at him. "What's that?"

"Why did you invite those shifters to my home?"

Richard laughed at his friend. "Because your mansion is much larger than mine."

Xander raised one perfectly shaped, dark eyebrow. "Is that the *only* reason?"

Richard shook his head. "Well, with such a huge dinner, I knew Ryan wouldn't want to do the cooking. Not to mention the clean-up afterwards."

"Oh, but I do?" Tatiana interjected.

Ryan laughed, but nodded.

"You have help. Also you're used to cooking for a lot of people," Richard said.

"I'll tell you what, Ryan can come by and assist me, how about that?" Tatiana asked.

"How did *I* get mixed up in this?" Ryan asked, pointing at her chest.

"Because you thought it was funny. Now, either you help me prepare this meal *your man* arranged, or I'm only making enough food to feed my Pack and you and yours can sit and watch us enjoy our meal," Tatiana said, with a wiggle of her neck, giving as much sass as she could.

"Man! Fine," Ryan pouted. "Why are we having the dinner anyway?"

"The two shifters who were incarcerated along with Matthew and Warren are without a Pack. Richard suggested we have a dinner where both of our Packs can decide if they want to accept either of the two after meeting them," Xander answered.

"Oh yeah, now I remember… One of them is a coyote, right?" Ryan asked.

Richard nodded. "He is. His name is Fredrick."

"Personally, I think you should take both, Richard. Two more members in your Pack can be a good thing," Xander said.

Richard pursed his lips, contemplating what Xander had said. He looked at Matthew. "What do you think about that? You know them, would they be loyal?"

"Yeah, they would be…" Matthew replied. "… And grateful."

"Chris and Fred are great," Gabriel added. "I had no idea they were shifters, but they've always been cool people to know. Funny, hardworking… they didn't partake in a lot of gossip around the precinct. They kind of kept to themselves."

"Knowing what they are, I can see why. Just like Matt and Warren used to keep to themselves a lot. I guess it was to keep unnecessary attention away from you, right?" Barry asked.

"That's true. Now that you're shifters, you can see how, in a public environment with so much scrutiny, you really just want to fade into the background," Warren said. "On *Lunar* nights, if I didn't work the morning shift, I'd have to take off. You really didn't want people asking questions about that, ya know?"

Gabriel nodded. "I never did notice that you and Matt weren't there on full moon nights. So you did a good job hiding that shit."

Warren chuckled. "Thanks." He then grew more somber. "Not that it matters now. None of us have our jobs at the S.U.I.T.."

"So what are you going to do now?" Devin asked.

Warren shrugged. "I don't know. The only thing I've ever been was a cop. The only thing I ever wanted to do was be a cop. At this point, I just don't know what I want to do."

Xander reached over, patting his adopted son on his knee, reassuringly. "Do not worry. Take your time."

"I don't even know what I'm going to do about my home. Without a job, I can't pay the mortgage," Warren said.

"Damn, you're downer," Adrian fussed. "We were all laughing and having fun and here your ass go with the gloom and doom."

"Adrian, shut the hell up," Warren shot back.

Xander chuckled at the two men. "Warren, you are of my Pack. This home is your home. You really do not need the other one unless you want to keep it. I must admit, I was happy you had your separate home when the media frenzy was at its height."

"Glad you didn't have reporters camped out on your lawn like Darian did three days in a row?" Matthew asked. Even though Darian has sent the first set of reporters and paparazzi away with a plausible story, new ones showed up to get their own version.

Xander and Richard nodded at the same time, relieved they never had to deal with them.

"Indeed. However, if you want to keep it, I will pay the mortgage off," Xander said.

Warren was shocked. "You'd do that?"

"Of course. I am the Pack Alpha, it is my honor and duty to make sure all of my members are happy and safe. Having this separate home is probably a good idea, especially since you seem prone to high-profile employment."

Warren smirked. "Thanks Xander. I really do appreciate that."

"Ah, Dad, since you're in a generous mood, there's this car I've been looking at. Now, don't let the three-hundred thousand dollar price tag intimidate you, it really is a thing of beauty," Adrian said, getting into his hustle.

"Adrian, my son, as Warren said earlier; 'shut the hell up'," Xander said.

"Oooh, that's cold as ice. Brrrrrr. Dang, Dad, what I do to deserve that?" Adrian laughed.

"You pestered me." Xander smiled at his son as he shook his head.

"Hey, you were the one boasting about how it's your 'honor' and 'duty' to keep your Pack 'happy' and 'safe'. All I'm saying is… The new Anaconda Sport XZ40 would make me *very* 'happy' and with its controlled power steering among many other state-of-the-art safety features, that car is bound to keep me 'safe' while on the road."

The others in the room went into a fit of laughter. Xander even had to laugh himself at his son's antics.

"You're a hot mess, Adrian," Natasha said, after she caught her breath.

"No, I'm not." Adrian smiled. "I'll let you think about it," he told his dad, who only shook his head, still chuckling.

"How kind of you," Tatiana said.

"So, how are things going with you and Adan's Pride?" Warren asked Gabriel and Barry, once the laughter had ceased.

Both men had only been shifters for a little over a week and were still having a hard time adjusting to all of the changes. However, Adan was patient with them and that was making the transition a lot easier for them to deal with.

"Things are going good, for now," Barry said. "It's still taking some getting used to."

"It's really hard to be around Shannon right now, because… well…" Gabriel began, but was too embarrassed to finish.

"She's in heat," Justin finished his sentence for him.

Gabriel nodded, his face reddening slightly.

"Adan wants you to be able to control yourself around her, 'cause as you know, he gets first dibs and if he doesn't want to satisfy her, then you could," Sergio said.

"Not only that, they just need to learn to control themselves. That's what's most important," Tatiana said.

Sergio nodded. "Well, yeah, of course, that, too."

"About him getting first 'dibs', Adan explained it to me. Being the King of our Pride, all other males must be subservient to him and I think that's probably one of the things that's hardest for me to grasp. I'm not used to bowing down to any man," Gabriel said.

"You were a cop, you should be used to following orders, especially considering your captain was a female," Devin pointed out.

Gabriel shrugged. "Well, I guess that's one way of looking at it. I have to admit, I didn't see it that way. Still, even as a cop, I felt I had more freedom. Not to mention that at the end of the day, I could go home and be the king of my own domain. I'm just not used to being told what to do twenty-four seven."

"Me neither, but you can't help but feel his aura and it kind of compels you, ya know?" Barry added.

Warren chuckled. "I get that. You two must challenge him a lot."

"Not intentionally," Gabriel said in his defense. "Just lately, wanting Shannon… it's hard to control myself. I guess you can say I've challenged him for her."

"He's had to beat your ass, hasn't he?" Adrian asked.

Gabriel rolled his eyes. "I wouldn't put it that way," he said, sarcastically.

"Yeah, I bet," Adrian continued to tease.

"I do have to say it's so weird how we're so much like what I've seen on TV watching animal shows," Barry pointed out.

A few of them nodded.

"It's in our nature, the animals we turn into control us even when we're in our human forms," Ignacio said. "So, did you mark Darian's house yet?"

A few of them laughed, some laughed more boisterously when they saw the two lions' face growing even more redder.

"He's going to kill ya'll's asses!" Devin blurted out.

"Shiiit, forget about Darian. What are you going to do when you move out to Montana with Kysen?" Adrian asked.

"It wouldn't be me. That dude is über-scary," Justin said.

"Did you all decide on that, already?" Elise asked.

Barry and Gabriel nodded.

"It's Adan's choice. I guess it's not a bad one," Barry said.

"I doubt if any other supernaturals are going to be fucking with ya'll on his territory. You could mark the whole state if you wanted to," Devin said.

"I can deal for as long as it takes me to learn what I need to know. From what Adan has told me, most lion Prides only have one male," Barry said. "Besides, I'd rather be with my wife and kids."

Gabriel was silent. His wife and kids were in Maine with his wife's mother. The last time he spoke with his wife, she told *him* she wanted a divorce. He told *her* he wanted joint-custody and the argument that followed was laden with harsh words filled with anger, resentment, feelings of betrayal, *and* him inadvertently admitting his extramarital affair. As far as he was concerned, if Adan was willing to keep him in his Pride, he wanted to stay. He felt more wanted and cared for being with the Pride in the past few days, than he had living with his wife over the past several months.

"What about you, Gabe?" Matthew asked.

Gabriel blinked several times as he came out of his reverie. "Haven't really given it much thought," he lied in a monotone voice.

The others didn't bother to press him, it was obvious that the issues surrounding his personal life were very painful to him and they didn't want to pry. The conversation switched to more lighthearted topics. It was at that point, both Matthew and Warren announced how tired they were.

"I'm going to bed." Warren yawned and stretched as he rose from his chair.

"Me too," Matthew said, following his lover out of the room.

"Have a nice nap, you two," Adrian said. He waited until they were upstairs and in their room before he added, "I bet they are going to f–"

"Don't say it," Sergio interjected.

"*Fffluff* their pillows pretty good before going to sleep," Adrian joked.

"By pillows, you mean di—Ow!" Devin was cut off by Sergio slapping him on the back of his head. "That hurt!"

"It was supposed to. You all know you take shit too far, sometimes," Sergio commented, not wanting to hear about any sexual conquest between his two male friends.

"And you're a pussy... pun intended," Adrian shot back. "But I'll let it go. I'm hungry, what are we going to eat?"

"I don't know what *you're* going to eat, my Pride and I are going home and picking up dinner on the way there," Elise said, rising to her feet. She had only come over to welcome her friends back home. She was now eager to return to her mansion and relax. Her Pride followed her lead, saying their farewells before leaving.

"I guess that's my cue," Richard announced as he rose to his feet.

His Pack left, heading toward their home. Gabriel, Barry and Natasha climbed into one car and drove back toward Darian's mansion. She had left her son with Danielle and was happy to see him when she came through the door.

"How's mommy's little baby boy?" Natasha said as she scooped her toddling son into her arms. She covered his plump little cheeks with kisses as the child giggled.

"He cried when you first left, but then he calmed down and played with us," Danielle informed her.

"Thanks so much for watching him, Danielle," Natasha said, giving the woman a warm smile.

"It was my pleasure." Danielle watched Natasha with her son, longingly. "One day, soon, I hope to have a child."

Natasha looked at her. "I'm sure you will, and you'll be a great mother."

"It's not that easy for shape-shifters to conceive, which is why some females may have one child. Or if they have more children, they are far apart in years," Danielle said.

Natasha nodded thoughtfully. "That explains a lot. Like Madeleine, she loves children, but she only gave birth to two and Sebastian is way older than Mia. And Adrian has over thirty years on his little sister."

"Exactly. Adan did manage to impregnate Amanda forty years ago. They have a son together," Danielle said.

"Oh really? Where is their son now?" Natasha bounced her son on her lap as the little boy giggled and clapped.

"Being a dominant male, he had to leave the Pride and search out one for himself."

"How does that work, by the way?"

Danielle sat up straight. "Well, there are a lot of lone male lions roaming around. Some seek their own Prides, while others choose to remain rogue. When they do seek their own Pride, there's almost always another male in control of it. The two fight; the victor inherits the entire Pride."

"And the women just go along with it?" Natasha asked, shocked.

Danielle nodded. "It is our nature. The victor has proven to be the strongest, therefore the more qualified to lead the Pride."

Natasha remained silent, thinking about their lives. "Can you leave if you wanted to?"

"That depends on the King. He may let you leave, he may not. He may choose to kill you if you tried, it would be within his right."

"That's kind of fucked up," Gabriel said. He and Barry had been leaning against the doorway listening to the two women converse. "It's almost like a pimp getting another pimp's prostitute stable after he shoots him in the street."

Danielle huffed. "We're *not* prostitutes."

"I know… I didn't mean it like that," Gabriel apologized. "I'm sorry."

Danielle calmed down. "I know you didn't, I'm sorry. I know you're still getting used to all of this. The thing is we are true to our animal nature. It is the way things have always been and will always be."

"I had a question about the *Lunar*," Gabriel began.

"Sure, what is it?" Danielle waited for him to ask his question.

"Where are we going to go?"

Danielle blinked, caught off guard, because she didn't have an answer. "I don't know. Let me ask Adan." She called out to her King, bringing him into the room.

"What is it?" Adan asked, entering the den, bringing along his powerful aura with him. He felt it necessary to display some authority because of the two new males within his Pride.

Both Gabriel and Barry straightened when he came into the room, their gaze lowering slightly to show submission. Adan took note of the behavior and smiled. He then toned down his aura just a bit to let them know he approved. Both younger lions looked up at their King but remained silent. Adan returned his attention to Danielle.

"Gabriel wants to know where are we going to go on the *Lunar* night?" Danielle presented him their question.

"We'll stay here. Darian has arranged for several wild animals to be shipped here for our hunt. His land is vast and blocked off," Adan answered.

"I'm surprised I didn't know about this," Natasha said, slightly irritated.

"Does this bother you?" Adan asked.

"As long as you don't try to bring half-eaten animal carcasses back into the mansion, I think I'll be all right," Natasha said.

Adan chuckled. "I'll keep that in mind."

"I'm confused, though. I thought you'd be going over to Elise's?" Natasha asked.

Adan shook his head. "I wouldn't be able to share the territory with another Pride... or Pack for that matter. Not when we're hunting. I'd want to claim her land as mine and I don't think Sergio would like that much." He laughed.

"Or Elise for that matter," Natasha said. "So, you'd get into a fight with her?"

"Quite possibly. And I wouldn't want to do that," Adan said. "But my instincts would take over and I'd have a hard time restraining myself in my animal form."

"King of the Jungle, right?" Natasha said, repeating the title most given to Lion kings.

Adan nodded. "Very much so."

"You should fit in just great with Kysen, then," Natasha said.

Adan laughed. "He called me today, pestering me about how long it's going to take me to come to Montana."

"What did you tell him?" Danielle asked.

"I told him we'd come after the funeral ceremony."

"Is he going to come to the ceremony?" Danielle asked.

"I don't believe he was planning on it," Adan said.

"Well, he should. If he wants us to move in with him, he should share in this moment with us. He needs to understand that we are a family. We do everything together."

Adan raised both eyebrows. "I'll ask him. What if he doesn't come? How would you feel?"

Danielle sat quiet for a moment then she spoke. "I already don't like the man, but I'd really not like him if he didn't show. To me, that's showing disrespect to you and your Pride."

"To tell you the truth, I hadn't thought about asking him to come. But because it means so much to you and you feel the way you do, I will *insist* that he come," Adan said.

"You sure you can deal with that man?" Natasha asked. "I mean, he doesn't seem like the kind of guy who would take kindly to being ordered around."

"He needs taming, that's all," Adan said, with confidence.

"Oh, and you think you're the one to do that?" Danielle asked with one eyebrow rising.

"Yes. He doesn't intimidate me the way you all think he should. Don't get me wrong… his aura is powerful, overwhelming even. And I know he could kill me without putting forth much effort. But I seriously doubt he'd be interested in me if I were to cower at his feet. He enjoys defiance, it quickens him, and I enjoy defying powerful men. I think our relationship will work out just fine," Adan said.

Gabriel shook his head. "This conversation isn't one I'm interested in hearing." He turned to leave the room.

"Are you prepared for the *Lunar*?" Adan asked him, stopping him in the doorway.

Gabriel turned toward him. "I don't think I am. I'm told that it'll be my first transformation and that it'll be extremely painful and longer than any other transformation. I'm not looking forward to that at all."

Adan nodded. "But once it's done, you'll be complete and free to hunt with your Pride. It's an experience you'll never forget."

Gabriel shrugged. "I guess."

Adan chuckled. The young lion intrigued him. His strength was admirable as far as he was concerned. What he had been through in the past week was harsh and a weaker person would have spiraled into depression. Gabriel didn't, both he and Barry seemed to have picked themselves up and dusted themselves off and got back into the game, as people say.

"Don't worry, I'll be there with you the entire time," Adan said.

Both Gabriel and Barry nodded.

"Are there any more questions?" Adan asked.

"I don't think so," Danielle said.

"Okay, good. I'm going back to watch *The Sampsons.*" Adan left, heading back to the bedroom Darian had given him.

"I forgot *The Sampsons* was on. Turn the channel," Natasha said.

Shannon turned the TV to the channel and the famous cartoon appeared on the screen. Everyone sat down to watch the hilarious antics of the characters. Natasha rocked her son to sleep, allowing him to take a nap so that he'd have energy to spend time with his dads when they rose that evening. Once the little child was sleeping peacefully in her arms, she put him to bed and went back to watch TV with the others.

CHAPTER NINE
THE LUNAR

G abriel and Barry stood in the yard of Darian's estate. Each
shifter was extremely nervous about their upcoming change.
The entire day, they could feel their skin tingling, their muscles
humming and they knew this day was a special one. Adan had told
them, this is how it would be every *Lunar*. That their body
recognized the moon's cycle and when the moment came, they
would have to embrace it. Gabriel turned toward the mansion, he was
expecting to see the vampires on the balcony, watching them and
was surprised that they weren't.

"Thinking we should have an audience?" Adan asked, seeing the
direction in which his young shifter was looking.

Gabriel turned toward him. "Well, yeah. I know I'd be out on the
balcony trying to see what I can."

Adan smiled. "This is a very intimate moment shifters share with
nature and each other. It's not really meant to be seen by others. That
is why most communities have their own private hunting grounds.
You should remove your clothes."

Gabriel looked down at his outfit, feeling a bit shy. "Am I'm going
to rip out of them?"

Adan nodded. "Besides, nudity isn't something you should be
ashamed of." He began to undress, stripping away all of his clothes.
He stood in front of Gabriel, naked.

"Man, this is going to take some getting used to. The only time
I'm naked around other men is in the locker room." He began to
remove his clothing, taking off his underwear last.

"How long will it take?" Barry asked as he stripped naked as well.

Adan looked up, his eyes closed as he inhaled deeply. "Soon. You
should be able to feel it even more acutely now. The sensations in
your body will tell you how long until we began our change."

Danielle and the other females joined the men, standing beside Adan. They had already undressed inside, hanging their garments in the closet. Both Gabriel and Barry couldn't help but give the nude females admiring looks.

Shannon winked at Gabriel. "You like what you see?" she asked.

Gabriel's mouth curved upward. "What are you trying to do, get me killed?" he joked.

"Good point, I'll stop teasing." Shannon giggled.

Adan watched his two Pride members joke with each other and smiled. He was happy they were getting along. They stood under the luminescent glow of the full moon for a few more minutes before Barry and Gabriel began their change. Both men doubled over, holding onto their abdomens, their faces were so contorted, a mere reflection of the excruciating pain they were enduring. They screamed in agony as they fell to the ground, rolling into fetal positions.

"This is all a part of your first change. Don't try to fight it, you can't, simply let the transformation happen," Adan instructed.

The others watched their two youngest members undergo their first change. As they stood there, they were beginning to feel their own transformations beginning. Being used to the process, they lowered themselves on all fours, allowing the change to happen. Their bones broke and reformed underneath their skin. The muscles moved, changing, getting stronger and more defined. Sweat poured from their pours as fur began to sprout. After a few more minutes of agonizing pain, their transformations were complete.

Adan shook himself, letting his black mane flow, declaring his dominance within the Pride. His females rubbed up against him first, licking his face as they purred. Then they rubbed up against Barry and Gabriel, who were still in a daze. Adan walked over to the two males, sniffing them. He nudged Gabriel, pushing him slightly. Gabriel leaned over, licking Adan, nose and ear. Adan pawed Gabriel's head; he leaned over licking Gabriel's muzzle. He did the same to Barry, wanting them to feel comfortable within their Pride. Adan stood back from the others and belted a ferocious roar, sending the intimidating sound echoing throughout the neighborhood. Danielle rubbed up next to him before sprinting off, searching for their meal. The females of the Pride followed her as she tracked down an elk. The large animal sensed he was in danger and tried to sprint off. The females were too fast for it, flanking the animal, pouncing on it, digging their nails into the flesh, and ripping the skin. The elk cried out and tried to struggle against his predators, but it was no use. The Pride brought him down, Danielle dipped her head under its neck and plunged her teeth into its throat, severing its spine and rupturing the elk's jugular.

The females stood around their kill as Adan made his way towards it. He began devouring the meal, as the rest of the Pride waited. After he had his fill, Gabriel and Barry ate. Once they were finished, the females of the Pride were allowed to eat what was left. Adan marked a tree, spraying it with his scent then he walked over to a man-made pond, and drank some water. After that, he lay down, watching as his Pride hunted another animal. After the females had eaten their meal, he watched as Gabriel and Barry sniffed around Shannon. He rose to his feet and ran over to the three shifters. With his large paw, he hit both male shifters, knocking them to the ground. Gabriel hissed, but made no move to challenge the King further.

Adan growled low, standing between the two males and Shannon. Gabriel and Barry walked away, losing their battle over Shannon, who had positioned herself to accept Adan. He sniffed the female, but he didn't mount her. Instead, he lay down beside her, protecting her. The other two males, circled her for a while longer, until they decided to play with the other members of the Pride. They frolicked for several hours until they tired themselves out. Eventually, they all ended up in a cluster, sleeping beside and on top of each other for warmth and comfort, their bond growing stronger. The morning came with their bodies changing back into their human state. The pain of their transformations woke them up as their bodies reformed. Once it was over, they sat still in the cool grass, basking in the heat of the sun's light.

After a few minutes, Adan rose to his feet, stretching. "That was exhilarating."

"That hurt like a motherfucker," Gabriel said, mocking Adan's tone. He climbed to his feet with easy, slow movements as his body went through the last effects of his transformation.

Adan laughed. "Yeah, but you'll get used to it."

"What do you remember from last night?" Danielle asked as she finger combed her hair, getting all of the dried leaves and tangles out.

Gabriel shrugged. "Not much."

"It's that way for shifters who are turned. Your memories are a bit fuzzy, whereas natural born shifters remember everything," Adan informed.

"I remember being really horny after I ate," Gabriel confessed.

"That's expected," Adan said. "Amanda, Gabriel, Barry and Lisa, I want you four to stay behind, make sure we don't leave a mess. The garbage bags are over there." He pointed to a bench beside the man-made pond where a stack of industrial-strength, black, plastic bags lay. `

"You want us to clean up?" Gabriel asked.

Adan nodded. "Yes. I don't want Darian to be taking a stroll on his property and discover the chewed up remains of our meals or anything else we may leave behind." With that, he began walking back toward the mansion, leaving the four members behind to clean up whatever mess they had made.

Gabriel looked at Barry. "Ain't that about a bitch?" he said once Adan was inside the mansion and a decent distance away.

Barry laughed. "I guess he feels we need to earn our keep."

"Besides, he's the King… delegating chores is his right," Lisa said as she began retracing their steps looking for remains left by them.

Gabriel shrugged. "I guess it's good to be the King."

"It is," Amanda said as she followed Lisa.

"About last night, I can't believe we went through that, can you?" Gabriel asked Barry, who shook his head.

"I'm still getting used to the fact that I'm not human anymore. I tell you what; I am *not* looking forward to these damn *Lunar* nights," Barry said.

Gabriel laughed, sharing his sentiments. The two lions jogged, catching up with the two women. They made sure the land was as pristine as it was before their *Lunar* night activities. When they were done, they decided to take showers before going back to sleep. The mansion itself was quiet except for the human servants who were wide awake and aware.

Billy looked at Adan when he entered the den; the lion King's hair was still damp from his shower. "Darian wanted me to give you a message," he said.

"Oh, what is it?" Adan asked.

"Kysen called again," Billy said then he took a sip of his coffee.

Adan chuckled. "Thank you. I'll give him a call." He walked into the bedroom he shared with Danielle. She was toweling off her hair when he entered. He sat on the bed, dialing Kysen's number on his cell phone. "Hello Kysen, have you given any thought to my request for you to come out here for the ceremony?" he asked when the vampire answered.

"I have." Kysen stated.

"And?" Adan asked, after a few seconds of silence.

Kysen sighed. "I realize if I'm going to have you be a part of my life, I'm going to have to accept your ways. I don't want to come, but I will."

Adan was actually surprised that the ancient vampire had agreed. "I really appreciate this, Kysen and I know my Pride will be very happy."

"After the ceremony, we return to my home."

"You know, you're worrisome," Adan said.

"I'm what?"

"Worrisome. You already have what you want, but you pester me constantly. Even calling during the *Lunar* when you should know I'm in my animal form and can't come to the telephone."

"I'll have you know, I called before the *Lunar*, but Darian told me you were busy training your new felines, so I simply left a message for you to call me," Kysen said. "I'm an impatient man, Adan, and you're infuriating me by making me wait."

Adan sighed. "You're an immortal being, Kysen, time has no meaning for you."

"I've waited ages for someone such as you. Forgive me if I don't want to wait another eight-hundred years. Now that that's been addressed; we'll be returning to my home after the ceremony, correct?" Kysen asked, although the tone of his voice indicated that it was more of a statement than a question.

Adan chuckled deep in his throat. "Yes. We'll return to *our* home."

"By 'our', I hope you mean, Montana." Kysen noticed the emphasis on the word "our".

"Of course. I only wanted to stay to make sure Warren and Matthew were going to be all right and for all of us to share in our farewell ceremony of our fallen members."

"That's good, because your old territory has already been taken over. No sense of you wasting time trying to reclaim that," Kysen informed.

"I figured as much. Besides it was decided my Pride was going to live with you anyway," Adan said.

Kysen moaned seductively, sending tingles down Adan's spine. "The way you sound right now... ahhh, quite frankly, Adan... I won't be satisfied until I have you in my bed." Kysen had turned on the charm, softening his voice even, seducing Adan over the telephone.

Adan blushed. He was actually happy they were having this conversation over the telephone, so that the ancient vampire wouldn't see the kind of affect his seduction had over him. Although, he figured the jig would be up once he moved in with him. "After tomorrow night, once the ceremony is done, we'll see if you can stand true to your words."

The vampire had been calling him—practically engaging him in what they call "phone sex" over the past several days—attempting to entice him. It had worked and he was greatly attracted to Kysen. He looked forward to spending time with him.

Kysen chuckled, his voice sending vibrations over Adan's skin. "I'll see you tomorrow night, then." He ended the call.

Adan slipped his touch screen phone back into his pocket. "He's so excited to finally have a mate again, he's beside himself. At least that's what Darian told me."

"What else did Darian tell you about him?" Danielle asked.

"That Kysen is very loving and giving and sweet... once you get past his callous, jaded and arrogant exterior."

"Oh, so he's like a jawbreaker, if you don't mind spending a lot of time trying to melt down the layers, lest you shatter every tooth in your mouth trying to quickly get to the sweetness. So in other words, one would need the patience of a saint in order to tolerate or even love that man," Danielle said.

Adan laughed. "My God! I am going to have to tell him you said that."

"Go on ahead and tell him."

"I will. That is a great analogy, in the end I suppose it means he's worth it."

"Only time will tell if that's true," Danielle said as she braided her hair.

Adan pulled her close to him, tickling her. She giggled and squirmed in his embrace.

"Stop! Let me go!" she laughed.

"Nope." He nuzzled her neck, causing her to moan.

She pushed his face away. "Stop it, you big tease."

Adan chuckled as he pulled away. "Speaking of tease, Shannon told me she wanted Gabriel."

Danielle cocked her eyebrows. "Oh really? What does the King say?"

"The King says if he's what she wants, I'm not going to stand in her way. I still want them to learn control, but they are consenting adults," Adan said as he lay down on the bed.

Danielle nodded. "I've been seeing them showing attraction towards each other over the past couple days, so I'm not surprised. Gabriel is getting divorced soon, so I suppose there's been no harm, no foul."

"If he wasn't, I'd never approve of it. The last thing I want is unnecessary drama within my Pride. This divorce business is bad enough, but at least it's going to be an ending to the drama." Adan stared at the ceiling. "I'm hungry, aren't you hungry?" he asked Danielle, giving her the tiniest hint in the sliest way possible.

Danielle rolled her eyes. "I'll go and prepare breakfast." She climbed off the bed and left, heading to the kitchen to do just that.

CHAPTER TEN
THE FAREWELL CEREMONY

Elise stood on the beach before her entire Pride along with all of her friends and their Prides, Packs and coven. She had prepared for this moment, even practicing her speech in private in front of the mirror. However, she hadn't prepared for the emotional strain it would have on her saying such heartfelt words in front of so many people who were sharing in her grief. Tears welled up in her eyes as she cleared her throat.

"I know we all suffered the senseless loss of our loved ones. Words cannot express the sadness I feel knowing I will never see Rachel smile again, or hear her laughter. I can only imagine what you all must be feeling as well. I do not know what waits for us when our time on this earth is done. However, I do believe that her soul is where it belongs, in a beautiful and wondrous place where the angels can enjoy what we've enjoyed. Her humor, her beauty, her mischievous sense of fun... her love, her childlike giggle and her smile will forever live on in heaven as it will on earth. We love you, Rachel," Elise said, ending her eulogy. She opened the urn containing Rachel's ashes. Turning the urn upside down, she released the ashes into the breeze that carried them off into the welcoming waters of Lake Michigan. All of the members of Elise's Pride and many of her friends cried as they watched the ashes soak into the soft, watery waves. Elise walked back into the crowd, taking her place beside Sergio, who took her hand into his. A comforting gesture and one that she was more than happy to accept.

Darian, who was dressed in black, like most of them looked at Miko. "Do you want to say anything about Annabelle?" he asked.

She shook her head, remaining silent. She was wearing a beautiful white, satin kimono, as was her Japanese custom.

Darian nodded and didn't bother to press her. He had figured she'd keep her feelings about Annabelle to herself, as she was never one to share emotionally. It had bothered him that members of his coven had died. It had never happened to him before and when he looked at Miko, at her sadness, he couldn't help but feel a bit of guilt, regardless of what Kysen had said to him before.

"Are you okay?" Natasha asked, looking at Darian.

He looked down at her. "I'm fine."

She nodded, but remained silent. He didn't *look* fine to her. He had an expression on his face that meant something was bothering him. She decided to ask him later, under different circumstances. She turned, facing forward again, as Xander, representing his Pack, finished giving their farewells to Philip. He stepped down, joining his wife, kissing her lightly on the cheek. Next Adan stepped up, standing where the others stood. He wasn't crying, although the redness in his eyes proved that he had already shed tears. Kysen had come, as promised. He kept quiet allowing the others to share and relinquish their grief in the manner they saw fit. He stood between Darian and Adan's Pride, watching as the leaders, human relatives and friends expressed their sentiments before casting the remains of the deceased into the calming waters of Lake Michigan.

Adan cleared his throat, and continued with his condolences to all. "I wish none of us had to be here... but we are. I wish many things hadn't happened... but they did. I only pray that the ones we lost will find themselves again and return to this world as beautiful and free-spirited as they were when they left. I want to thank all of you for being here with us, sharing in this moment. I may have only known many of you for only a short period of time, but I consider you my friends. Thank you," he said, ending his speech. He emptied the ashes into the water, as the other leaders had. Believing in reincarnation, he now hoped their new lives would give them even more pleasure and happiness than their last ones did. Once he was finished, he stepped back into the crowd, standing beside Kysen.

Phillip's family members had arranged for a choir to perform for the ceremony and they did, singing beautifully. After they were done, and the last person said their final words, they drove to Darian's hotel, where he had arranged for the grand banquet hall to be the location of their repast. They settled in, taking seats wherever they wanted. After a while, the waiters and waitresses began to bring out the food, setting platter upon platter of delectable foods on the tables. The shifters and humans began making their own plates, passing each platter of various meats, vegetables and pastas around the table.

"This was a good idea," Natasha said to Darian, who chuckled.

"I thought I'd spare the women the cooking this time around. And I thought it would be easier for everyone to make their own plates. Lord knows how these shifters can eat," Darian joked.

"Hey! I heard that," Devin said from across the room.

"Well, it's not like he's lying. Just look at your plate," John said, pointing to his lover's meal. "I think I see layers of food."

Devin giggled. "You do. These plates aren't big enough for what I want to put on them. Looks like I may have to make a second round." He scooped up some mashed potatoes with his fork and stuffed it into his mouth.

John chuckled as he watched his friends eat. He wasn't hungry, as he had fed from Devin earlier... which may have accounted for the shifter's ferocious appetite. He thought about Annabelle and missed her. She was warm, sweet and funny. He always thought her and Miko made a great couple. It hurt him to see Miko so depressed, Annabelle was the one person he knew who could bring out the giddiness in Miko and now all of that seemed lost forever, along with Annabelle.

"Are you okay?" Devin asked John.

"Yeah, just thinking about Annabelle. The house just hasn't been the same without her, know what I mean?"

Devin nodded. "I miss Phillip. I miss Rachel and Annabelle, too."

"I hate losing friends," John said.

A few of the others sitting at their table nodded in agreement.

At another table, Danielle looked at Kysen, who was sitting between Darian and Adan. "Kysen, I wanted to thank you for coming out here."

Darian discreetly pinched Kysen's leg under the table in his own way of encouraging the ancient vampire to behave.

Kysen tossed Darian a look then answered Danielle. "Contrary to what my young one sitting beside me may think, I do understand the depth of pain losing a loved one causes. I'm also aware of how strong the bond is between shape-shifters who share a Pride or Pack. Knowing that I want Adan and all of you to join me, I'd be remiss if I didn't pay my respects." He turned toward Darian. "Do not pinch me again, or I'll crush your fingers."

Darian flashed him his signature smile, showing off his dimples. "No you won't."

Kysen stared at his child for a few seconds, attempting to intimidate him but to no avail. He ended up succumbing to the overwhelming charm of the forest-green eyed vampire. He sighed. "You're despicable," he rolled his eyes, turning away, causing Darian to laugh.

Danielle looked at the powerful vampire, what he said made her feel better about moving in with him. The fact that he attended the ceremony meant a lot to her and the rest of the Pride. Life with Kysen may not be as bad as she was expecting.

"I have a question," Gabriel began, looking at Kysen, whom he was still very intimidated by.

"And that is?" Kysen looked at the young shifter, one eyebrow cocked.

"How do you feel about us marking territory?"

"Oh, what a *fine* conversation to have during dinner," Natasha said, giving Gabriel an aghast expression. The last thing she wanted to think about while drinking her chilled apple juice was a male shifter pissing on a tree.

Gabriel smiled slyly. "I'm sorry, seemed like as good a time as any to me."

Kysen watched the two of them exchange words, actually finding the repartee humorous. He cracked a smile. "To answer your question... I'm well aware of the nature of shifters. It is one aspect I'm not looking forward to, but as long as you keep the markings down to a minimum and nowhere near my mansion itself, I'll tolerate it."

Adan chuckled. "This is going to be an adventure in and of itself."

Kysen turn to him. "What is?"

"Getting adjusted to living with you. I'm used to being the dominate male in my household."

Kysen smirked. "I suppose you will have to get use to not being the dominant male anymore. But I'm sure you'll adjust just fine."

"Is this the part where you're taming him?" Danielle teased Adan.

"Taming me?" Kysen inquired.

Not being one to cower, Adan admitted he said the words. "I said all you needed was taming to calm down this rough exterior of yours."

"Like *The Taming of the Shrew*," Natasha said, followed by a fit of laughter.

Darian turned, hiding his face as he was laughing along with Xavier and several others around the table.

Kysen, however, didn't find the jest humorous at all. "Your human gets a little too personal," he said to Darian.

"She didn't mean it as a direct insult to you, Kysen," Darian said, hoping to calm his Maker down.

"Kysen, I've been meaning to ask you this, and I mean no disrespect. Why is it ancient vampires seem to be able to dish it, but they can't take it?" Adan asked, noting the vampire's rising temper.

Kysen sighed. "When did *I* become the subject of conversation at this table with all this buffoonery?"

"Point. In. Case.," Adan said.

"Fine, I'll humor you. It's not that we 'dish it'; it simply comes down to the fact that older vampires such as myself have little patience when it comes to nonsense. This conversation we're having, for example, is nonsense. You believing you can 'tame' me or that I need 'taming' is sheer nonsense. Her annoying cackling at her own foolish joke..." he pointed to Natasha. "...Is even more infuriating nonsense. So therefore, I feel compelled to express myself in a direct manner, as to not confuse you in regards to my sentiments."

This time, Adan sighed. "I just had to ask, didn't I?"

Kysen actually found what he said, funny. He laughed, which surprised those sitting around the table and a few of the shifters in the hall. Many had never heard him laugh; some didn't think he was capable of performing such an act. The ancient vampire could hear the whispers throughout the hall, pertaining to him.

"Yes, I do laugh… but only when something strikes me as humorous," Kysen said, hoping to clear the air.

"He also has a ticklish spot behind his right ear, you work it just right, you can get him going," Darian said, giving Adan a little advice.

Kysen turned toward his young child. "You don't want me to start revealing any of your little secrets, do you?"

Darian thought about all of the things Kysen knew about him, many which were very embarrassing, that he wouldn't want anyone else to know. "No. I'm done."

Kysen nodded. "I thought as much."

"Oh, now I'm curious," Xavier said, with a mischievous grin. "Please, do tell."

"I see someone wants to be on my bad side, tonight," Darian warned his young lover.

"Oh please, Darian, idle threats are so unbecoming," Xavier flashed him is most charming smile, the one he knew worked best on his lover.

Kysen laughed again, outright. He enjoyed seeing Darian getting as good as he'd given from his own young child. "Why not."

"Kysen, I beg you," Darian pleaded.

"But it's funny."

"What?" Darian asked, wondering which story he was threatening to tell.

"I was thinking about the time when my cook tried to kill you by feeding you poisonous mushrooms."

Darian grimaced. "How is that funny? I almost died. I remember being deathly sick for days."

"Indeed, but the things you were saying in your fevered state of delirium were just hilarious," Kysen said.

"Like what?" Xavier asked. Learning about Darian's history was always interesting and entertaining to him.

"Oh, all sorts of insane nonsense, such as he could hear a 'bird think.' He even went so far as to try to communicate with them using 'tweet' sounds. There was also that time when he declared he knew why the 'sun was black'. For three days, he babbled on. The only reason I didn't feed him my blood was because I knew he'd live through it and it kept me laughing."

Darian was shocked. "That's why you didn't give me your blood? You told me it was because the poison needed to work its way out of my system and that your blood wouldn't help me."

"I lied," Kysen admitted.

"Knowing the truth now, I'm glad I destroyed your favorite sheets," Darian said, frowning.

Kysen frowned as well. "That was unfortunate. We never could get them to come clean."

"Why did your cook try to kill Darian," Xavier asked.

"Because he was jealous of his beauty, and of the fact that I had chosen him to give the gift of immortality," Kysen answered. "He wanted to punish me by permanently removing Darian from my life."

"I suppose you took care of him," Adan speculated.

"Oh, indeed. He was Darian's first," Kysen said.

An awkward silence spread around the table, some of the others there didn't know what to say after Kysen's last comment.

"Well, don't everyone all speak at once," Kysen teased. "I had to make sure Darian's first victim would be easy to take. You'd be surprised how stubborn some newly turned vampires can be. Many hold onto the remnants of their flimsy human existence for dear life."

"I've learned from my own bitter experience how troublesome a new fledgling can be," Darian agreed.

"I didn't give you any trouble," Xavier said.

Darian chuckled. "No, you were a deviant, all too ready to raise havoc. I actually remember having to rein you in."

"I wasn't that bad. I just went after the mobsters who tried to kill me," Xavier said in his defense.

"No, you weren't that bad, but you were exacting revenge without finesse. I mean, it was just sloppy, Xavier. You'd leave bodies drained of blood without even covering your tracks," Darian said.

Xavier looked off to the side, slightly embarrassed.

"I had to come closer to this conversation," John announced, standing behind Natasha's chair.

"Oh go away, John. We're not even going to bring up your earlier days," Xavier teased.

"I don't care if ya do! I have nothing to be ashamed of. Besides, I've already told people my story, so now what?" John shot back, smiling.

"Whatever," Xavier said. "Enough of the embarrassing stories, all right?"

"Funny how you're done hearing embarrassing stories when they're about you," Natasha teased her lover.

"I know, I should be ashamed of myself, but I'm not." Xavier smiled.

Natasha shook her head. "You know what? I can't believe I just sat here and listened to a conversation about sloppy murders while eating my dinner as if we're talking about precious childhood memories. Ugh, I feel so corrupted."

"Our lifestyle is finally rubbing off on you," John teased.

"That must be it and what a damn shame that is," Natasha frowned, then shook her head again as she finished off the rest of her meal.

"Fine, we'll change the subject. I've been watching the news lately and for the most part, a lot of the supernaturals who were arrested by the S.U.I.T. were released and that's great," Natasha said, bring up current events.

"Yeah, I've been keeping track of that as well, they deserve to go free," Danielle said.

"Too bad a lot of people don't agree. There's been a couple of protests at the Judicial S.U.I.T. building. People complaining about biased judges and shit," John said.

"Sometimes people get on my nerves. They aren't even questioning the logic of their protests. It's in their best interests to have supernaturals on the S.U.I.T., you'd think getting murdered by Marcus would convince them," Natasha said.

"History has proven that people don't always look at the big picture. Nor do they embrace logic when trying to keep another group of people oppressed," Xavier said. "They'll justify their actions any way they can, regardless of how much sense it makes… or doesn't make."

"Can't argue with that. They still don't want shifter children to go to school with human children, as if it makes a difference," Danielle said.

"Denying supernaturals the same rights as humans only makes humans feel as if they're in control. We've been in the shadows for so long, that's where they want to keep us," Adan said.

"I hope one day they wise up and do the right thing," Natasha said.

"As long as supernaturals remain silent, I don't see that happening anytime soon," John said.

"You've got a point there. Let's hope the Council can clean up this mess," Natasha said.

Kysen only chuckled, but remained silent. He didn't have any confidence in the Council. They were politicians who focused on their agenda and if their agenda and the rest of the supernaturals were intertwined, then and only then, would the Council speak up.

They all discussed various topics of interest as they continue to enjoy their meals and companionship. Before the night was over, Adan and his Pride said their farewells to all of their new and old friends, then they boarded Kysen's jet, heading towards Montana to start their new life. The others went to their homes to rest and prepare for a new day.

CHAPTER ELEVEN
SEVERAL MONTHS LATER

S he's so *adorable*," Elise said as she nuzzled Natasha's infant daughter, Aria.

"Isn't she? She's so cute. But I swear, she looks so much like Matthew," Natasha said, taking note of her daughter's features.

Elise giggled. "She does, but she looks a lot like you as well. I love when children are this size. Look at her tiny little fingers and feet." She rubbed Aria's soft, tiny digits as the baby cooed.

"I know what you mean, although, I won't mind when they grow up because I want to know what kind of adult they will become."

"She does have a rather large head, though," Elise said.

"Oh, no you didn't. How are you just going to sit here and say that?" Natasha laughed. "You've gone too far, now. Don't be making fun of my baby's head. It's not that big."

"She must have split you in two coming out," Elise continued to tease.

"Give me my baby back, evil woman." Natasha giggled.

"No, I've got her now, she's all mine. Don't feel bad, both of my children had large heads. They're growing into them now, but whoooo! Besides, I remember you making fun of Cicero and Annette-Nate when they were little, too." Elise waggled her finger at Natasha, who smiled slyly.

"Well, I don't want to dwell on the past," Natasha said.

"Uh huh, I bet." Elise looked down at the precious baby in her arms. "So are you going to have any more?"

"Oh, hell naw! I've got a son and a daughter. That's more than enough. I'm not pushing any more big-headed-ass babies out of me any time soon." Natasha shook her head, thinking about the labor pains she had gone through during both pregnancies.

"I don't blame you," Elise agreed, thinking about what she went through during her own pregnancy. "So... I see her daddies are sparing no expense on their baby girl." She eyed the expensive diamond and sapphire earrings in Aria's tiny lobes.

Natasha nodded. "You're telling me, Xavier bought her the earrings. Darian's responsible for the anklet and matching bracelet. Not to mention all of the designer hand-made clothes in her closet and drawers. To me, it's kind of unnecessary since she's growing so fast, to spend all that money. But to them, I guess it doesn't matter."

Elise chuckled. "You know how daddies are about their little girls... and their sons for that matter." She thought about how much Sergio spoiled his children when they were little. She was happy that he knew when to spoil them and when to pull back. The last thing she wanted was bratty children.

"Everyone thought you'd be the one who would be lavishing gifts on them. Turns out we were all wrong," Natasha said. "I just knew you were going to have a matching feather, sequin and silk bathrobe for her."

"Oh, I do, but I'm not giving it to her until she's five and able to appreciate such exquisite things."

"From what I've seen of your pretty, pretty princess daughter, she's well on her way," Natasha stated, laughing.

"Oh, hush," Elise teased.

"Hey, did you hear that Ignacio and Christine are hitting it off?" Natasha decided to share a little bit of gossip.

"No, I didn't know that. Well, it was inevitable; I saw how he was looking at her at Richard's bar-b-que. They're in the same Pack, the chemistry there, it was bound to happen," Elise said.

"I'm surprised she didn't go for Fredrick," Natasha said. "He's handsome enough."

Elise arched a brow. "Yeah, but he's not Ignacio. Between the two coyotes, Ignacio just has that *je ne sais quoi*, wouldn't you agree?"

"You've got a point there." Natasha nodded. "I'm just glad that Richard decided to take them into his Pack."

Elise giggled. "I don't think Xander wants the extra responsibility. It takes a lot to control a shifter community, you know."

"Yeah, I can imagine," Natasha said.

The two women discussed their children further, bringing up all of the cute things they'd witnessed them doing. After a few hours, Elise left, going home to her own family and Pride. Natasha put her baby girl to sleep, knowing her two fathers would want to spend time with her when they woke up. The best thing about having vampires as parents, they were always willing to handle the nighttime feedings, which Natasha was extremely grateful for. She lounged lazily on the sofa, watching the television when the doorbell rang. A few minutes later, after Darian's staff had answered the door, Devin entered the den where she was.

"Hey Devin, what's up?" Natasha greeted.

"Nothing much, you know me, here to see my man," he answered. "How are you doing? How're the crumbsnatchers?"

"They're doing fine. I just put Aria to bed. Me, on the other hand, I'm still trying to lose this damn baby weight, but it's going well."

"Baby weight, where?" Devin asked, looking her up and down.

"Well, just about fifteen pounds, that's all."

"You can't tell."

"You flatter me." Natasha giggled.

"Is Aria's asleep or is she just dozing?"

"She's out cold and that's how I want her to stay."

Devin pouted. "Awww. I want to wake her up just to kiss her little cheeks."

Natasha smirked. "You do that and you're going to be the one responsible for putting her back to sleep."

Devin contemplated the trouble he may have putting a grumpy baby back into blissful slumber and decided he'd wait until one of her dads woke her up first and then he'd take advantage. "Well, you've convinced me not to disturb her rest." He sat down on one of the comfortable chairs, watching television with Natasha.

"How's the weather out there?" Natasha asked.

Devin shrugged one shoulder. "It's brisk but you'd probably think it's cold as hell… Is hell even cold?" he asked, one eyebrow rising.

Natasha giggled. "I'd be willing to bet hell is both hot and cold, because both in the extreme are hell to deal with." She sighed. "Now that I think about cold temperatures, I'm not looking forward to winter in Chicago, I'll tell you that."

"I just don't like driving in it. I can deal with the weather."

"I bet you can with your internal climate control capabilities." She rolled her eyes.

Devin laughed. "Jealous. Stop hating."

"Maybe a little." She smiled as she returned her attention back to the TV. As they were watching their favorite game show and participating along with the contestants, it was interrupted by a "breaking news" announcement.

"What's this all about?" Devin wondered.

The anchorman began to relay information about a tragic nuclear reactor explosion in the farming town of Hamilton, Kansas which managed to destroy the town's entire population.

"Oh my God!" Natasha gasped, shocked and sadden to hear of such total devastation.

"That's fucked up. I wonder if any supernaturals managed to survive that?" Devin speculated.

"Who knows, they said there weren't any survivors, I wonder how they'd know that?" Natasha asked.

"Maybe they made sure there weren't any survivors," Darian said, standing in the doorway watching the television from over their shoulders.

Natasha and Devin turned, facing him.

"You think they killed of those people to cover up something?" Devin asked.

"Isn't this the second incident that left a town without survivors in as little as a week?" Darian asked, one eyebrow rising.

"Natasha's eyes bulged out their sockets. "What? I didn't hear of another explosion."

"I did, but they said it was a terrorist attack that took out that town in Maine," Devin said. "The population was like five-hundred and seventy-three people, I think."

"What's even more puzzling and an insult to those who know this information, is that Hamilton, Kansas doesn't *have* a nuclear reactor," Darian said. "The closest one I'm aware of is in Burlington, Kansas."

"A cover-up," Natasha said.

"I would think so, and how big was the population in this city?" Darian asked.

"One thousand, seven-hundred and twelve," Natasha answered.

Darian huffed. "I don't believe in coincidences. Not of this magnitude."

"If it's a conspiracy, what do you think they are trying to hide?" Natasha asked.

Darian shrugged. "Whatever it is, apparently keeping it concealed is worth more than preserving human lives."

Xavier entered the den, his hair still damp from his shower. He was dressed in a black t-shirt and jeans, which hugged his body very well. Natasha's eyes panned over to Darian, noticing he was also wearing all back. A pullover cashmere turtle neck, slacks and shoes.

"Are you going out?" Natasha asked, sounding slightly disappointed.

Darian nodded. "Well, it is Friday, time to look over the club's finances." he lied. He was going to the first night of the *Tournament of Champions*, which he did every Friday night throughout the weekend.

Natasha cocked a brow. "You know what, Darian. You are so full of shit right about now."

Darian smirked. "Your meaning?"

"I know what you do on Friday, Saturday and Sunday nights." Natasha turned a little more on the sofa to get more comfortable as she confronted Darian.

"And that is?" he challenged, his Greek accent making each word sound seductive.

"I'd hoped you'd tell me on your own, but I see you won't."

"And that is?"

Xavier started to smile as he watched his two lovers square off. Devin only sat silently watching the interaction.

"You like to watch people fight to the death in that sick-ass tournament of yours," Natasha revealed.

Darian's smile broadened.

"So you're not even denying it, are you?" She looked at him.

"Why should I deny the truth? How did you find out?"

"About two weeks ago, when I was in the parking lot leaving

Desires Unleashed, I overheard some of your patrons talking about how great the fights were that night and how much money they'd made. I asked them about it and they were a little reluctant to tell me, but eventually, they did."

"And…?" Darian asked, waiting to see what she had to say on the matter.

"I'm disappointed that you never told me. I guess you'd thought I'd trip or something."

"Well, are you… '*tripping*'?" Darian asked, putting emphases on her slang term.

"No, I'm not tripping!" she paused. "You know what, I am tripping about it. Why would you do something like that?"

Darian cocked his head sideways, looking at her quizzically.

"Don't look at me like that."

"I'm sorry," he straightened. "I think sometimes you forget who and what I am."

"I know you're a vampire and a very ruthless and old one at that," she countered.

"It's more to it than that. You forget I grew up in a time where public battles to the death were common entertainment as well as executions. Where you could look out of your bedroom window and watch a war progress on the battlefield and see the mutilated remains of countless injured and dead soldiers strewn about with the notion that their deaths were brave and glorious. I walked the streets for over sixteen-hundred years and saw corpses of those left to die littered about. I've left trails of my own in my wake. Death doesn't have the same meaning to me as it does to you," Darian said.

Natasha seemed to reflect on his perspective. "I get that, it's just…" She was at a loss for words.

"I didn't want to tell you about the Coliseum because I knew how you'd react. With your humanity and gentleness, I knew you would instinctively be appalled. I'm not going to make any excuses. I enjoy the tournaments. I will not discontinue them because you find them distasteful." Darian's tone was more than absolute on the matter.

Natasha looked up, realizing it was her first time she'd gotten a taste of Darian's resolve. A chill ran down her spine and she began to understand why the other vampires didn't cross him. She cleared her throat. "I do find them distasteful, but I have to say that I wasn't surprised when I found out about them, just disappointed that you never told me. I don't know if I can ever look at *Desires Unleashed* the same, knowing what's going on in the bowels of that place."

Darian sighed. "Would you like for me to erase your memory of that knowledge?"

"Now you're just being a jerk."

"No, I'm not. If knowing about the Coliseum bothers you so, I can take that memory away and you can have peace of mind again."

She shook her head. "No, I don't want you to do that. I'd rather know about your weekend activities than not. If I can deal with you hunting and killing, I'll deal with this. It's just something new I have to accept. It's just this, though, right? You don't have any drag death racing going on do you?"

Darian smiled. "No darling, to my knowledge, this is it." He had hoped she would understand his sentiments and not be revolted by him or his opinion of what's "entertaining".

"I knew when I got involved with vampires it was going to be some shit I was going to have to get adjusted to. You're still a barbarian, though," Natasha commented.

Darian chuckled. "As are all of the patrons of the Coliseum, my dear. Can I go, now?"

"We all know I can't stop you and you've already told me it's your *thang*, so go. Have fun watching body parts get sliced off," she said sarcastically.

"That goes without saying." He turned, heading towards the front door.

Xavier watched him walk away, sucking in a deep breath. "I do believe that might have been your first official argument, Tasha." He turned, looking at her.

She rolled her eyes. "Were you cheering for him to win?"

"No. I didn't pick a side at all. Somehow, I knew you'd discover the truth about the Coliseum. I also wondered how you'd take it." Xavier stepped closer to the sofa.

"You could have told me yourself, ya know." Natasha pointed an accusing finger at him.

"I felt it wasn't my place to do so. It's one of the few things that bring Darian joy. No harm came to you by not knowing about it... why start trouble when it was unnecessary?" Xavier looked down at her, his beautiful gray eyes drinking her in, causing her to blush.

"Well, you do have a point." She turned back toward the television.

Xavier came around, sitting beside her. "Are you still mad at him... or me, for that matter?"

She looked at him. "No, not really. Like I said, I wasn't all that surprised when I found out about it. It kind of fits Darian's personality." She cocked her head to the side. "That's just fucked up when you think about it."

Xavier laughed outright, slapping his knee at the same time. "It quenches his bloodlust, that's for sure. It does fit him." He leaned over, kissing her softly on her temple. "If it's any consolation to you, the people who participate in the tournament are either there willingly, or they've pissed Darian off and he was planning on killing them anyway."

"Oh, that gives me all of the consolation in the world," Natasha said sarcastically.

Xavier smirked. "I thought it would."

Natasha huffed with a frown. Both of her lovers got one up on her this night and although she hated to admit it, she didn't like being on the losing end of any argument. Still, she knew when to throw in the towel, which she did.

"Are our children still resting?" Xavier asked.

She nodded allowing him to change the subject. "They'll be up soon, ready to play with their daddy."

"I should go hunt then." Xavier rose from the sofa.

"You could feed from me if you want to... save yourself the trouble," Devin proposed, secretly hoping the powerful vampire accepted his offer.

"You're addicted, you know," Natasha accused, exposing the young shifter's intentions.

"I'm a humanitarian. Xavier feeding from me spares some poor human," Devin joked half-heartedly.

"You just want to feel the pleasure of his bite," Natasha pointed out.

"So what if I do? Besides, it's not like him biting me isn't taking care of his hunger issue," Devin said in his defense.

"I bet if it hurt like hell to get bit, you'd be the last person to be so willing to be a meal," Natasha teased.

"Probably, but it feels so damn good, I'm first in line." He looked at Xavier, who had been smiling at the two of them going at it. "So, do you want some of my delicious, luscious, mouthwatering, rare and irresistibly satisfying shifter blood or what?"

Xavier chortled. "You drive a hard bargain, Devin. I must say."

"But you're turning me down! Man, is it because of Natasha?"

."No. As you know, we are predators—I feel the need to hunt."

"I'll be willing to run away from you if you want me to." Devin looked at him.

"Damn, Devin! Desperate much?" Natasha laughed, looking at the mischievous leopard. "You should be glad I'm not whooping your ass for trying to hit up on my man."

"Please, ain't nobody trying to hit up on Xavier," Devin retorted.

"Oh, so what, you're trying to say he's not desirable?" Natasha teased.

"See, *you're* just trying to start some shit. *I'm* just trying to feed my fellow man," Devin said with a devilish grin. He turned back toward Xavier. "So, what do you say?"

"John will be up soon–" Xavier began.

Devin cut him off. "I get it. Fine, go hunt."

"Don't worry, Devin… there will always be another time," Xavier said.

"Who says I'll be willing to feed you then?" Devin rolled his neck, giving him as much mock attitude as he could muster.

"Oh, like you're convincing anyone right now," Natasha said, leaning over, slapping Devin on the thigh.

"Fine, but I bet I taste better than anyone you'll eat tonight. Go on, have your TV dinner, when you could have had a gourmet meal," Devin said, waving Xavier goodbye.

"I want a gourmet meal," John said, entering the den.

"And you shall have one." Devin sprung up from the chair, approaching his lover. "Been waiting for you, let's go upstairs." He dragged John off by his hand, leading him to their bedroom.

Xavier watched the door close behind them and shook his head. "Never a dull moment around him, is there?"

"Nope. He's a trip." She kissed him on his cheek. "You should go so you can be back by the time the kids wake up."

"All right." Xavier kissed the top of her head before leaving. Natasha continued to watch the news, getting more detailed information about the "nuclear explosion," wondering if Darian was right about what happened. If so, who were "they" and what could "they" be hiding?

***

Xavier leaned against the brick wall near the opening of an alley. He had spotted his prey finally. A man who had just sold drugs to a pregnant lady, two teenage boys and a well-known politician who was now pulling away in his black-window-tinted Sidewinder sedan. Xavier scanned his prey's mind, seeing that there were no redeeming qualities left in him. He was deplorable, a ghastly blemish on the face of humanity and a most pleasurable future feast. Deciding to make his move, he crossed the street toward his prey. His eyes glowed red causing the man to panic and run.

Ah, yes, fear, that's the scent! It got the blood pumping, the heart racing, and the adrenaline rushing. Xavier licked his lips in anticipation as he closed in on his victim, catching him quickly before he could reach his car.

"Get the fuck off me, or I'll kill you!" the man said, pointing his gun at Xavier.

Xavier looked into the man's eyes, catching him in his gaze. "Drop the gun now," he said softly.

The man complied, letting the weapon slip from his hand onto the concrete. Smiling, Xavier released his control. He wanted his victim to know his fate. He wanted that fear to rise stronger when his prey would see his fangs extend right before he sank them into his neck.

"Please don't kill me, I didn't picket or nothing when that shit went down a few months ago," the man pleaded.

"That's only because you were too preoccupied with selling drugs to the children in your community," Xavier replied. With a speed too fast for the man to respond to, they were suddenly standing in a dark alley behind a dumpster. Xavier covered his victim's mouth with his

123

hand as he bent downward, locking his mouth to the man's neck, sinking his fangs into the plump vein he would feed from. Luscious, hot blood filled his mouth, instantly warming him, making his own heart beat in rhythm with his victim. With each hearty swallow, he could feel his body reacting, becoming alive and tingling all over. He loved this sensation, every night he relished the moment when he could fill himself with blood and come alive again. The flow started to trickle as his victim's heart ceased to beat. He pulled away, licking the remaining droplets from his lips. Biting into his tongue, he licked over the wounds, sealing them.

Darian would want him to dispose of the body, which he really didn't want to be bothered with. He never did. It was the one thing he hated about hunting. The messy clean-up afterward, but it was something he couldn't help. He needed to hunt. It was his nature. He picked the man's body up and walked back to the drug dealer's car. Taking the car keys from his victim, he placed him in the trunk, climbed into the driver's side, and started the engine. He drove the car to a remote location and climbed out. He walked to the back of the car, opening the trunk. On the way to the location, he stopped off at a gas station, filling up a container with a gallon of gasoline. He poured the contents of the container over the remains of his victim, and the interior of the automobile. Lighting a match, he tossed it, igniting the corpse and the car then he flew away.

It didn't take him long before he returned home, taking his seat beside Natasha once again. "Did I miss anything?" he asked, watching her breast feed their infant daughter.

"No, she just woke up actually." Natasha turned, looking at him.

"What?" he asked—perplexed by the look on her face.

"Was he or she a scumbag?"

"Oh, that." Xavier smiled slightly. "Trust me when I say humankind should be thanking me for my good deed tonight."

"I thank you. The police can't catch all of these people and there's far too many of them out there doing more harm to humans than any supernatural. I'm not shedding any tears over their demise," Natasha said somewhat coolly.

"I still find that amazing, that you don't seem to mind," Xavier said.

"It's not that I don't mind, it's more like I understand and I see the good that can come from it." She shrugged. "I've been through enough horrible situations with you all to know full well that evil needs to be put down no matter what form it comes in. I'm not that gullible."

"No, you're not that gullible." He smiled showing a row full of beautiful, even, white teeth.

"I know you're not hurting innocent people, you're saving them. I can live with that just fine." She ceased breast feeding her daughter and adjusted the baby so that she could burp her. Softly, she patted the infant's back, encouraging the baby to release the air in her stomach. After a few more minutes, both she and Xavier heard several tiny burps, pleasing them. "Good, if she pukes after that, at least it'll be on you. Here's your baby." Natasha said with a smile as she handed Xavier his daughter before closing the buttons on her shirt.

"You're just saying that because I laughed that time she spit up all over your shirt that day. You would have laughed if that happened to Darian or me… as a matter of fact, you *have* laughed when it happened to us," Xavier gave her a playful glare.

Natasha giggled. "It's funny when it happens to you… well, mainly Darian, because he has the most priceless expressions. You can't just sit there with a straight face when he's in that situation, now can you?"

Xavier smiled. "No, I guess you can't."

She watched him play, smell and fondle their little daughter.

Xavier leaned down, kissing her tiny chubby cheeks. "They're so amazing… little innocents, so dependent on us to protect, love and care for them."

"Yeah, they are. They're precious," Natasha agreed.

Christopher entered the den, taking the chair Devin had occupied earlier.

"I thought you were going to the club tonight?" Natasha asked.

Christopher shook his head. "Nope, I switched with Joseph. So I have the night off." He had given up on stripping at the club after the assault he endured at the hands of the powerful, ancient vampire, Marcus. Instead, he was now tending bar along with Tony, who still wouldn't teach him what was in his specialty vampire drinks.

"I can tell you haven't fed yet," Xavier said. "You look a little pale."

"I had some *Synblood*, to take the edge off. I'm hoping I can convince Devin to let me drink from him since he's here. Don't really feel like going out looking for a meal," Christopher answered.

Xavier shook his head. "I don't see how you can drink that stuff, not even to take the 'edge off.'"

"You drink it in Tony's drinks."

"Whatever he puts in his drinks takes the taste away or dulls it down enough for you not to be completely disgusted by it."

"You've got a point there. But I'm lazy tonight. Just want to chill."

"Do vampires even get tired or lazy like that?" Natasha asked.

"It's a mental thing, not physical," Xavier answered her. He was still concerned for the young vampire. He was coping well with what happened to him, but he was still dealing with the residual effects. He knew Christopher would eventually get back to his old self again... at least he hoped he would.

"Did you hear about what happened in Kansas today?" Christopher asked.

"Yeah, I did. Darian thinks it's a cover up to conceal something more devastating," Natasha said.

"It is odd that a terrorist attack destroyed a whole town three days ago, and now a nuclear reactor destroys a town too and there are no survivors." Christopher looked at Xavier. "Are there any Master vampires in those cities who may have survived the blasts?"

Xavier shrugged. "With the amount of fire and heat those blasts generated, I'm seriously doubting any supernaturals survived unless they can fly as fast as Darian can. I'll ask Darian to look into it, though. Good idea, Chris."

"Cool, cause I'd like to know," Christopher said.

"Matthew's awake now," Xavier announced and he rose from the sofa, leaving the room only to return three minutes later holding both his son and daughter. "He needed changing. I took care of it already."

"That was fast," Natasha commented.

"Vampire speed comes in handy." Xavier smiled.

The three of them were joined by John and Devin two hours later, at which point Devin did allow Christopher to drink from him. Afterward, they continued to watch television and chit-chat until Natasha grew sleepy and decided to call it a night.

"Sweet dreams, Tasha," Xavier said, returning her kiss. The others bid her goodnight as she left the room before returning to their conversation.

CHAPTER TWELVE
THE TRUTH

Another breaking news report interrupted Sergio's sports game for the second time within the same week.

"What the fuck now?" he wondered incredulously.

Daniel was just as agitated. He was enjoying the game and couldn't see why this news couldn't wait until ten o'clock. "This better be something that effects what I need to do within the next few seconds. They always do this shit when there's really nothing anyone can do about what's going on."

Sergio nodded. "The only time 'Breaking News" seems relevant is when there's a serial killer loose in your neighborhood or a tornado is plowing down your street. Other than that, it could wait."

It bothered them even more when the screen froze thanks to the new digital set-up all televisions had.

"Geez, I thought having digital cable was supposed to fix all this shit. Come on, already," Sergio fussed.

Finally the screen cleared up and a pretty anchorwoman was in the middle of her report announcing another explosion. This time, it was a science lab that emitted toxins into the air, killing thousands of people in the vicinity. Apparently, there were no survivors in Buffalo, Texas.

"What the fuck?!" Sergio exclaimed, leaning forward. "That's some bullshit. I know for a fact that toxins can't kill vampires so what happened to all of them in that city?"

"The government is definitely trying to hide something, and they are running out of plausible excuses," Daniel said.

"Elise knows the Queen of the Pride in Dallas, maybe we can get some information from her, since they aren't that far from Buffalo,"

Sergio said. "Elise!"

A few minutes later, Elise entered the family room with her two children in tow. "What is it?"

"Hey baby, we just heard that Buffalo, Texas has been destroyed." Elise's eyebrows rose in shock.

"Yeah, the news said a lab exploded, releasing toxins that killed everyone in town. Think you can contact the Pride Queen in Dallas to find out what's really going on?" Sergio asked.

"That's horrible! Of course, I'll contact Sylvia." She ushered her twins toward their father, who scooped them up into his arms.

"Daddy!" The two kids said in unison, which was music to Sergio's ears.

Elise sat down in a chair, picking up the telephone. She dialed a number and waited. "Hello Sylvia, I hope I'm not interrupting anything... no? ... Good. Listen, I called because I have a concern... Yes. You've guessed it." She nodded; a grim expression on her face. "Oh really. That's disturbing... I see. Well if you discover anything else, please let me know." She hung up the telephone.

"That just gives me more questions," Sergio said. He had heard every word of their conversation. Sylvia didn't know much, however she knew that it wasn't a lab explosion or killer toxins, it was a bomb —several bombs, for that matter—dropped from military airplanes that took out the city.

"What the hell is going on?" Daniel asked to no one in particular.

"Whatever is it, it's a big damn deal for them to kill thousands of people at one time," Sergio said. He turned toward the TV just in time to see a successful three-point shot put his team in the lead by one point in the fourth quarter.

"Hell yeah!" he belted out instinctively. Then he turned toward the others, seeing their confused expressions. "That kind of caught me off guard. Okay, we should find out what's going on, contact the other leaders in nearby cities where the 'explosions' took place."

"Nice to see you still have your priorities in check," Elise teased.

"You know how I am about my sports, but this is important," Sergio said.

He turned toward the television again to see the last few plays in the game. Both teams were tied with less than one minute on the clock. Getting excited to see how the game was going to end, Sergio leaned forward and right before the opposing team took a shot the game was interrupted again. However, this time, it wasn't by a TV news anchorperson. The man on the screen was someone none of them recognized. He was extremely handsome, almost unnaturally so. His long pale blond hair cascaded down past his shoulders. His ice-cold blue eyes pierced through the screen, holding the attention of all who were watching. He arched one perfectly shape blond brow as his lips parted in a wicked smile.

"Good evening," He spoke in a rich, masculine voice, his tone was even and there was a hint of an accent, though it was difficult for them to place it. "If you are not aware of it, this message is being broadcast on every television channel all over the world. I'm sure you are all wondering why there have been so many explosions as of late. No, it's not a terrorist attack, or a nuclear reactor or a lab experiment gone awry. That's just your governments' pitiful attempt at covering up the truth."

"Okay, this is fucked up, who's this guy?" Daniel said, gesturing toward the television.

"I'm guessing he's going to tell us really soon," Sergio replied.

The handsome man continued. "This is the truth, please observe very carefully."

The screen flipped to another video feed, showing a woman lying on what appeared to be a hospital bed, although it didn't look as though she was in a hospital room. The woman was extremely sick, she looked to be dying. Her skin was pale, sweaty and covered with greenish crusty clusters. She vomited a yellowish substance which spilled out of her mouth sliding down her cheek onto the sheets beneath her. Her eyes and nose were rimmed with redness and were extremely swollen. Her mouth was ringed in sores. Her tongue looked to have doubled in size and it was apparent that she had lost a lot of hair. Portions of her scalp were clearly visible. She was obviously in severe pain. Her body shivered as she struggled to inhale one deep breath. Then, she went still and—before the very eyes of everyone watching at that moment the world over—the woman died. Her eyes remained open, but they were empty. Void of all signs of life. The camera zoomed in on her grotesque face for a few seconds before the screen flipped back to the handsome man.

"Now you know the truth. Each town that has been eradicated was destroyed in an attempt to contain a serious viral outbreak." the man informed his captive audience.

"Jesus Christ!" Sergio and Daniel exclaimed in unison.

Elise called out to the others in the mansion. "Everyone come in here! Now!"

Within a matter of seconds, everyone who was home entered the den. She pointed to the TV and gestured for them to be quiet, placing a finger over her closed lips.

The man on the screen continued. "What I am about to tell you is very important and what you do will determine your futures. This is a warning to the human race. For far too long, we have sat back in the shadows, remaining silent while you've been allowed to thrive. At first, it was for the best. When humans didn't know about our existence, it made us free to roam around openly. Ironically, once we were discovered, supernaturals have been pushed back and told to disappear… to hide. No longer will we accept this treatment from such an inferior species. You've had freedom because we allow it. You lived because we allow it, and you've gotten drunk on your false sense of control, because we've allowed it. You have all overstepped your bounds and now we are forced to put you back into your place. You are *cattle*, food, lower beings whom are beneath us."

"Oh shit. I hoped something like this would never happen," Devin said.

"Shhh!" Elise said, quieting the younger shifter and anyone else who may have wanted to comment.

"There have been others of our kind who have only desired to be equal to you, to live freely. Yet, at every chance you get, you assert your false authority over them, condemning, oppressing and killing our kind!" The handsome man, who one could guess was a supernatural, took a deep breath, calming himself. He continued. "We kept quiet, allowing the Council to do something about it. We sat patiently, waiting for the human government to do the right thing, and yet nothing has changed. We've silenced ourselves long enough. We are no longer asking nicely for what we deserve. We are taking it by any means necessary."

The screen flashed back to the now dead woman lying on the bed, a horrible, ugly corpse. The image sent chills down Elise's spine and she was sure the others were feeling the same way. The screen then went back to the supernatural messenger.

"It's already too late for many of you out there. In various cities around the world, the virus has been released into the water supply. The water you are drinking has probably infected you." He laughed, no doubt imagining all of the people who were now tossing their glasses away from them in fear and disgust. "The beauty of this disease is this: it will only affect humans and we are the only ones who have the cure. Oh, and for any supernatural who tries to interfere with our plans, you will only receive one warning and it is this: if you, in any way, attempt to save the human race, you will wish you hadn't. We will find you and we will kill you. Remember humans, in our veins lies your salvation. In our mercy lies your future. You *know* what we want." The screen went black before returning to the network which was now airing the "Experiencing Technical Difficulties" message.

"Please tell me this isn't happening," Madeleine said.

"I wish it wasn't," Elise said just as her telephone began ringing. She answered it. "Yes, Xander, we were watching it as well. I have no idea what we can do. All right, I'll hold." She was quiet for a about a minute then she greeted the others on the telephone. "Hello, Richard... Darian. We have to make sure our children are safe, I agree. We need to know if this disease can enter the body through any means other than digestion .... All right, goodbye, Darian. ... Yes, I'm still here. I don't want to believe that humans brought this on themselves, but I will say they certainly didn't help the situation, especially after that whole S.U.I.T. fiasco." She was quiet for a few more seconds before she agreed to speak with them soon and ended her call.

"Do you think they can track us down and kill us if we try to help?" Carmen asked.

"I don't think they—whoever *they* are—would be the type to bluff. They must be very powerful," Sergio said.

"So what do we do?" Devin asked.

"What *can* we do? We don't know who they are, or where to find them or anything about them at all," Elise said.

"I hope this threat doesn't last long," Madeleine said, speaking her fears out loud.

"I need to call my son," Sergio said, dialing Sebastian's cell. He waited until he answered. "I need you to come home now," he demanded once his son answered. "You are? Good." He ended the call. "He's already on his way home. I want to test him when he arrives."

Several heads nodded in agreement.

***

Natasha came through the door with her two children, searching for Darian wondering why he had called her cell phone urging her to come home immediately.

Darian approached her, grabbing her by the shoulders. "Have you drank any water today?" he asked urgently, boarding on panicking.

His entire demeanor took Natasha by surprise, but she answered him. ."Y-yes. Why? What's wrong?"

Darian didn't answer her right away; instead he leaned forward, inhaling deeply. Still not satisfied, he took hold of her wrist, biting into the flesh.

"Ow!" Natasha yelped, but she didn't snatch away.

Darian released her after swallowing the mouthful of blood he sucked in. "You're safe." He exhaled a sigh of relief.

"Damn it, Darian, tell me what the hell's going on," she demanded finally.

"Supernaturals have released a virus into the water supply that only targets humans. They didn't say where or when they did so. There's very little we know about the virus except that it kills its victim very painfully and it's not at all pretty."

Natasha's hand went to her mouth. "Oh my God." Her knees grew weak, but Darian caught her, steadying her. "When did you find this out?"

"Not less than five minutes ago. That's why I called you and told you to come home right away." He looked down at their two children. One in Natasha's arms, the other holding on to her hand.

"Have our children had any water?" he asked.

"Matthew did, but not Aria."

He squatted down, taking his son's tiny hand into his. He looked into the child's eyes, sending him a gentle message not to be frightened. Then he cut a tiny wound into the palm with his nail, tasting the blood that bubbled up. His son released a tiny whimper, but quickly calmed down as his father sealed the wound. Satisfied, he kissed his son's forehead before rising to his feet.

Darian looked at her. "Natasha, you and our children are to avoid all contact with water, do you understand." It was a demand, not a question.

She nodded. "I will. What about bottled water?"

"I've sent my coven out to stock up on as much bottled water as they can. They should be returning soon. I don't want you to bathe in any water other than the bottled water, do you understand? Please remember to not drink any other water than the bottled kind, don't even rinse anything off in it. As a matter of fact, I'm going to have the water shut off so that you don't accidentally do so." He turned, calling for Billy, who came right away.

"Yes, Master?" Billy inquired.

"Have you had any water today?" Darian asked.

"Yes."

Darian huffed. "Gather all of my servants immediately. I want to test you all."

"Yes, Master." Billy walked away to complete his task.

Darian turned back toward Natasha. "You are not to leave this mansion until further notice. I want you to take the children, put them to bed. I have no idea if any other member in my home is infected. If so, I don't want you around. We have no way of telling if this virus is airborne or not."

Natasha nodded and without another word, she hurried upstairs, locking herself in the nursery with their children. She decided to call all of her friends and her parents, warning them of the threat in case they didn't already know. She wanted her parents there in the mansion if they were uninfected.

Downstairs in the foyer, Darian waited for all of his human servants to arrive. Once they all stood in front of him, he addressed them. "I need to taste your blood to insure that you have not been infected."

One by one, each of Darian servants extended their wrists to him and he bit, tasting each one. Satisfied with the results he then told Billy to shut off all the water. He also informed them that they were not allowed to leave the mansion then he dismissed them.

"Master," Billy called out as he trotted closer to Darian.

"Yes?" Darian replied patiently.

"My wife and son, sir. Can I bring them here if they are uninfected?"

"Of course, but only if they are uninfected. Do you understand?"

"Yes, Master. Who's going to test them?"

"When my coven returns, I'll send one of them."

"Thank you, Master," Billy said, satisfied with that arrangement.

Darian turned and made his way up the staircase toward the nursery where Natasha was, opening the door.

"Are you speaking with your parents now?" he asked, noting that she was on the telephone.

She nodded. "Yes, Mom, I know. So far, I'm safe. Listen, I want to send Darian or Xavier to you so they can test you and make sure you're uninfected." She paused. "Mom, they'll just need to taste a little bit of your blood to make sure. If you're okay, I want you to come here. We're stocking up on water and everything; you'll be safe here until... I don't know when this will be over, until there's a cure at least."

"I'll send Xavier when he returns," Darian told her.

Natasha nodded. "Okay Mom, expect Xavier to be there soon. I love you, too." She ended the call, looking up at Darian. "Why are they doing this?"

"According to their statement, they are upset in the manner in which supernaturals have been treated. They want to control this world or at least find some kind of common ground. It was somewhat difficult to say." He brushed a few strands of hair from her face, smiling sadly at her.

"Why did they have to go about it this way?" Natasha asked, clearly she was frightened and upset.

"Perhaps they felt as though they were pushed to taking such drastic measures, I don't know. I know I don't like what's happening. Unfortunately, it looks as though everything is depending on what the humans do."

"This is what happens when you oppress people, backing them in the corner with practically no options," she said.

Darian nodded. "It would seem so." He lifted his head up once he felt Xavier's aura coming closer. After a few minutes, Xavier entered the nursery.

"I managed to get as much water as I could from the grocery store. It was pure chaos there, too. Everyone was fighting for the water; one person was stabbed over the last bottle on the shelf." Xavier shook his head, remembering the vision of a river of blood pouring from the wound of the injured man lying on the floor.

"It's no surprise humans are panicking," Darian said.

"Not just humans, I had to fight off several vampires and shifters as well," Xavier said.

Darian nodded. "No doubt trying to protect their human lovers, servants and children." He turned toward Xavier. "I need for you to go to Natasha's parents' home. Test their blood, if they are free of disease, bring them back here."

Xavier nodded. "What if they are infected?"

"Give them your blood."

"Will do." Without another word, Xavier left the mansion, climbing into his car, heading towards Chicago.

The other vampires in Darian's coven began to come home. Darian told Natasha to stay put and he left to meet up with them. John and Christopher continued to bring in the bottles of water, lining the gallons up side by side. Their clothes were ripped and bloodied and their hair was tussled. Tony entered next carrying, two five gallon jugs of water, followed by April and Miko, who were also carrying several gallons of water. The vampires made several trips back and forth to their automobiles before they shut the door.

Darian stood before them, looking at all of the water, one eyebrow raised. "Was it difficult?" he asked, looking at their torn and blooded clothes... all except for Miko, who seemed to be untouched.

"Shit, it was tough as hell getting this water. I had to take down two vampires while Christopher loaded the car," John informed.

"They were trying to snatch them from my hands. You couldn't even pay for it. You just had to rob the stores."

"Yeah, if you stopped to pay for it, you take the chance of someone running off with your shit," Christopher added.

"At least *you* had a decoy. I almost got my ass kicked by this shifter and vampire team. Lucky for me, the other humans running for the water proved to be a bigger threat to them," Tony said. "That's when I took a much as I could from that company."

"I see Miko didn't have any problems, did you?" John asked her.

"They tried, but I took care of them," she said, tossing her long braid behind her back.

"You all did very well. For tomorrow night, I am going to ask that you all stay in," Darian said.

"How will we feed?" Christopher asked.

"Please tell me we don't have to drink *Synblood*," John pleaded.

"You will if you have to. However, I will see if Elise and Xander would be willing to spare some of their people," Darian replied.

"Master, can I ask what is the reason why we can't leave?" April asked.

"Because I have no idea how this virus is spread and I want to limit your contact with human exposure as much as I can. I have no idea if it's airborne once someone becomes infected. It was stated that it can't affect vampires, however, I don't know if vampires who've had tainted blood can infect an uninfected human. There's so much we don't know."

They nodded.

"Where's Xavier?" Tony asked.

"He's going to Natasha's parents' home, to test them."

"What if they are infected?" John asked.

"I've instructed Xavier to give them his blood. However, I would want to check him over before he enters this mansion afterward." Darian ran his hand through his long, black, wavy locks.

Again, they nodded.

"As a matter of fact, I want to test you all," Darian said, walking toward his coven. He took Tony's hand, biting the flesh of his palm, tasting the blood. Tony gasped, but remained silent and still. "You're all right." He repeated that process with them all and discovering their blood was uninfected.

"I thought it couldn't infect us," John said.

"I need to be sure," Darian said. "Forgive me if I don't want to take the mysterious and sinister vampire's word for it."

Again, they all nodded.

"I have a question and a request, Master," Christopher began.

"What is it?" Darian asked.

Christopher cleared his throat. "My family, if they aren't infected, can they come here?"

Darian nodded. "You may go to them, but if they are infected, they are not to be brought here."

Christopher nodded. "If they are, can I stay to help them any way I can?"

"If it comes to that, yes." Darian said. "Do you have anything else you want to ask me?"

"God forbid anything is wrong with Natasha's parents, but if there is and Xavier had the infected blood, what will happen to him?"

"If he's not infected himself, he'll be allowed to come inside. If he is, I will quarantine him on a different property of mine, as I will do with anyone who's infected," Darian said.

"Master, I don't mean to be a pest, but if it turns out that we can't be infected, then can we hunt?" April asked.

"I actually prefer shifter blood, I don't know about you. If Xander and Elise can send some over, I'm all for that," John said.

April thought about it for a few seconds. "Yeah, you're right, never mind."

"Besides, we don't need to take any unnecessary risks if we don't have to," Tony said.

They nodded.

"You may go now, Christopher. April, I'll have you go to Billy's family. Test them and if they are uninfected, bring them here," Darian instructed.

"Yes, Master," April said, then she left to carry out her duty.

"The rest of you put some of this water in the refrigerator and in the bathrooms then stock the surplus in the cellar," Darian ordered.

Christopher left to go to his family. One by one, the others began to do as instructed, taking away the bottles and gallons of water.

Darian walked away toward his study. He needed to contact Elise and Xander to ask for that favor. He made the call and both leaders were willing to send two people each to stay the duration with Darian until there was some kind of development or conclusion to the threat. He thanked them, ending the three-way call and waited to hear back from Xavier.

***

Xavier rang the doorbell of Natasha's parents' home. Her father, Mr. Hemingway answered.

"Hello, Xavier. Please, come in," he stepped to the side to allow his daughter's lover entry.

Xavier walked past him. "How are you this evening, Mr. Hemingway?"

"I'll be doing a damn sight better once I know if I'm uninfected."

Xavier nodded. "Please, get your wife, and I'll perform the test."

Mr. Hemingway nodded and led Xavier into the kitchen where his wife was sitting, knitting a scarf to keep her mind off the current threat.

"I'll test you first," Xavier said to Mr. Hemingway.

"All right. What do I need to do?"

"Just hand me your wrist."

He complied. Xavier took his hand gently, leaned closer and pulling his lip back, exposed his fangs. It was the first time Natasha's parent had ever seen them and they both gasped in shock. He didn't pause before sinking them into Mr. Hemingway's vein. After one swallow, Xavier jerked away, releasing his wrist. He walked over to the sink and he spit the rest of the blood into the basin. His first intentions were to turn on the facet and rinse his mouth out, but he thought better against doing just that. Instead he continued to spit as much of the blood he had gathered out of his mouth.

Mr. Hemingway could tell by Xavier's response that the news couldn't be good. He looked at his wife, holding her hand. Xavier turned around, wiping his mouth with the back of his hand. The taste of his blood was horrible and it still stained his mouth making him not want to even bother tasting Mrs. Hemingway, but he was going to.

"You're infected and it's not with any virus or disease I've ever tasted. Vampires can drink tainted blood, it doesn't taste the best, but it's still rather tasty. That's something completely different… revolting, even."

"Please, check my wife," Mr. Hemingway urged.

Xavier nodded. "Of course." He stepped closer, taking her hand and biting into her wrist. Immediately, he had the same response, causing him to gag. He went over to the sink, spiting the blood out as fast and as much as he could. Afterward, he used a paper towel to wipe his mouth before turning to face her parents. "Here, I'm going to give you my blood, this should cure you." He walked over to them, using his nail, he cut into his flesh. "This won't make you a vampire, so don't be squeamish, you'll need to drink–"

Mrs. Hemingway snatched his wrist, pulling it to her mouth, cutting Xavier off. She swallowed several times, until Xavier pulled himself free. She reached out for him again with bloodlust in her eyes. He pressed his hands on her shoulders pinning her to the chair until she was able to regain her composure. She blinked twice, clearing her vision, letting her eyes focus on the beautiful gray of Xavier's.

"All right, you're back. I need to test you to make sure it worked."

She gave him her wrist and he bit into it again. After two swallows, he pulled away. "It didn't. But it seemed to slow down the effects. Ugh!" He grimaced and reached for his stomach, immediately running to the sink in time to vomit her blood into the basin. This time, he did turn on the water, rinsing the blood away, spitting the rest into the swirl of liquid as it made its way down the drain. Once the sink was clean, he turned to face the two humans. "I apologize for that."

"It's not your fault. I didn't think vampires could get sick," Mr. Hemingway said.

"Not much can get us sick, almost nothing aside from too much alcohol in the blood. Listen, I'm going to give you my blood, because it seems to lessen the effects of the virus, but I think you should check yourselves into a hospital." He cut his wrist again, giving Mr. Hemingway his blood the same as he had with his wife.

Once he was done with that, he called Darian. When his Master and lover answered, he told him what happened.

"You said it made you physically ill?" Darian asked, perplexed.

"Very much so; it gave me an instant stomach ache and I vomited. Neither was pleasant. Not only that, but their blood tasted putrid."

"I don't understand why your blood didn't cure them."

"I don't either. It only slowed the workings of the virus. What do you want me to do now?"

Darian was silent for a few seconds, thinking about his options. "Natasha isn't going to take this well at all."

"No, she isn't."

"I doubt if the hospital has any vampire blood on hand to give to their infected patients."

"Do you want me to stay here?"

"No, I'll send Miko to look over them. Since my blood exchange with her that night, she's become a little stronger than you are. I'll share with her again tonight to give her even more strength."

"Very well, I'll inform them of that and I'll be home soon." He ended the call, then re-entered the kitchen where Mr. and Mrs. Hemingway stood holding each other's hands. Streams of tears ran down Mrs. Hemingway's cheeks. Xavier felt guilty that he couldn't help them and he was dreading having to see the look in Natasha's eyes when she discovered that her parents were infected.

"What did he say?" Mr. Hemingway asked.

"He's sending a stronger vampire than me to look after you. We're not sure, but this virus seems to slow with the ingestion of vampire blood. If you take in small quantities, it might not get any worse."

"But you're not sure?" Mrs. Hemingway asked.

Xavier shook his head. "No, but it's something."

The two nodded, their expressions − crestfallen.

It pained Xavier to see them that way. "I have to go, but Miko will be here shortly. Please do as she says."

"We will. Thank you." Mrs. Hemingway said.

"I wish I could do more."

"You've done what you could."

Xavier nodded then walked away, leaving their home and heading back toward his own.

***

"NO!!!" Natasha cried when Darian gave her the terrible news about her parents. "God, please no!" Tears ran freely down her cheeks as he held her in his strong embrace.

"We're doing everything we can to save them, Natasha," Darian said, hoping to ease some of her pain.

Natasha cried still, clinging to him as hard as she could. She couldn't believe her parents were sick. That they might die a death so horrible, she wouldn't wish it on her worst enemy, was unthinkable. "God, please don't let them die." she prayed softly over and over again.

Darian held onto her, rocking her gently until she was able to sit in a chair on her own. "Are you going to be all right?"

She shook her head. "No. I'm not going to be all right until I know my Mom and Dad are going to live."

"I understand."

"If it gets worse, will you turn them into vampires if they want it?"

Darian's eyebrows rose. "Are you sure that's what you want?"

"If they are okay with it, I'll be just fine."

"If they want it, and it's possible to turn them, I will."

"What do you mean, 'if it's possible'?"

"When Xavier drank their blood, it was vile, so much so, it sickened him terribly. He couldn't ingest much of it before regurgitating."

"Oh my God."

"As you know, we have to take in so much of *your* blood in order to give it back to you mixed with our own. The magic is in the process."

"I know," she said, looking even more hopeless.

"We'll see what happens, for now, Miko will keep them alive."

Natasha nodded. "I just want to be alone right now, is that all right?"

Darian nodded. "Of course. Call me if you need me."

She nodded as he closed the door, leaving her alone. He went into the den where the others were gathered.

"How is she?" John asked.

Darian rubbed a finger over his forehead and temple. "Not very well, all things considered." He sat down in his favorite chair, running his hands over his face.

No one said anything for a while, letting him gather himself. After several minutes, his door bell chimed.

Billy rose to answer it, returning a minute later. "Master, there are some people here to see you; they said they are from the Center for Disease Control and the Department of the Supernatural Civil Committee."

Darian's eyebrows rose again, surprised to hear that a member of the DSCC was visiting him. "Let them in. I can only imagine what they could want."

"Yes, Master." Billy walked away, returning a minute later with three humans.

Darian had dismissed the members of his household before they were allowed entry. He was currently alone, staring back at his three visitors. "I already know the reason why you are here, but I'd rather hear it from you."

The first person to speak was an older gentleman with graying hair, a slender build and what looked to be a permanent scowl. His blue eyes were visible behind gold-rimmed glasses. He stepped up to Darian. "First of all, my name is Dr. William Goldstein, this is Dr. Brad Conway." He pointed to an attractive middle aged man standing next to him with blue eyes and dark brown hair, who smiled and nodded at Darian. Continuing on with his introductions, he pointed to a third man with blonde hair, gray eyes. "This is DSCC Representative Bernard Dillinger."

Darian nodded at the three men, acknowledging them.

"Thank you for seeing us Mr. Alexander. As you may or may not know, we are in a State of Emergency. All of our attempts to contain the virus have failed. The hospitals across the country are overflowing with the sick and dying and we have no cure. We don't even have anything that could treat the symptoms enough to ease some of the pain these people are suffering," Dr. Conway said.

"Don't you have any vampire blood on stock from all of those volunteers in the past?" Darian asked.

"We did. Our stock of V-86 has been stolen from all of our facilities. Some of our buildings have been bombed to destroy what stock was left and the vampires who had volunteered refuse to help now because of the threat of death that was issued," Dr. Conway answered.

Darian ran his tongue along his bottom lip, moistening it. "And you're here in my home because…"

Dr. Goldstein pushed his glasses back on the bridge of his nose. "We have always suspected that you were the Master vampire of this city, hell, this entire state. With your influence, you could make younger vampires help, or you could help us yourself…" The man's voice trailed off when he saw the frosty glare Darian was giving him.

"You dare come into my home with such a foolhardy approach?" Darian gave each man a lengthy gaze.

They stood there in awkward silence, frightened and unsure if they would leave the mansion alive. They could feel the aura emanating off the Master vampire and it made them want to walk backwards out of the very same door they entered.

Dr. Conway cleared his throat. "Mr. Alexander, please forgive our approach. We meant no disrespect."

Dr. Goldstein shot him a dirty look. "I will not cower or beg this *vampire* for his help." He made sure to say the word vampire as if it were poison he spat from his being. "As an American citizen, he is expected to come to the call of duty when his government requests his services. If he doesn't he could easily be arrested and forced to do so."

Darian chuckled as he crossed one leg over the other. "You think so? You say you're not going to cower before me, but I can smell the fear dripping off of you … all of you." He let his hands rest on his lap, fingers interlocking, taking on a less intimidating position before continuing. "And it's that very same foolish arrogance that has gotten the human race into such a dilemma in the first place."

"It is *your* kind who is arrogant. You think we won't discover a cure?! We will! The human race can't be eradicated. Not by your kind, not by anything," Dr. Goldstein shot back.

Darian laughed outright, which seemed to anger the man even more. "I see I was mistaken. You're not an *arrogant* fool… you're just a *fool*. Leave my home. I'd rather not have someone such as yourself in my presence."

"I'm not going anywhere wh–"

Darian's hand around his throat interrupted his protest. The Master vampire moved much too fast for any of them to see.

"Please, Mr. Alexander, we come in peace," DSCC Representative Bernard Dillinger pleaded, hoping he could save his companion's life.

Darian looked at the other man. "You would do well to choose your companions better in the future." He returned his attention back to the human in his grasp, intensifying his gaze to put the human under his influence. "As for you, you will not remember me or that we had this conversation. You will leave my home and return to wherever you came from." He shoved the other man away, sending him crashing to the floor with an audible grunt.

This time, he didn't argue. He scrambled to his feet, running out of the mansion leaving the other two men there. Darian returned to his chair, crossing one leg over the other, bringing his hands together making an arch with his fingers. "I will not ask other vampires in this territory to risk their lives in order to provide you with blood," he said, somewhat confirming their suspicions that he was the Master vampire of that state without actually saying the words. He didn't want to commit to the role in front of them for a number of reasons.

"So does that mean you are the vampire Master of this territory?" Rep. Dillinger asked excitedly.

"It means I will not ask any vampire to risk their lives for humans. What I will do, however is give you one ounce of vampire blood for you to experiment on," Darian said.

"Will it be your blood?" Dr. Conway asked.

"No," Darian said. "I will have it delivered to your address, gentlemen."

"We're staying at the *Esquire Hotel*, room 1245," Dr. Conway said.

Darian nodded. "Very well, I'll send a sample there and it will be the only sample you'll receive from me. Understand, I have my own reasons for going this far, but I'm not willing to extend myself past this token of my generosity, do we have an agreement?"

The two men looked at each other then back at Darian. "We have an agreement. We will not bother you again. Thank you." Dr.

Conway smiled, pleased to be getting another supply of vampire blood.

"We'll leave you now," Rep. Bernard Dillinger said his farewell before turning to leave.

"Gentlemen," Darian called out. Both men turned around, giving him their attention. He stared at them, sending out his mental influence, making them forget about him, but not about the blood sample they were to receive.

"Only Dr. Conway needs to wait for the messenger. *You* may accompany the other man home, Mr. Dillinger." Darian turned his gaze on the other man. "Dr. Conway, you will believe that you were unsuccessful here. Within three hours, you will prepare to leave your hotel."

Both men nodded absently, letting Darian know he was successful in modifying their memories. Billy was called to escort both men out of the mansion. He made sure they joined the third man who was waiting in the car. Before he closed the door, he watched the red glow of their taillights fade into the darkness. He returned to Darian. "They're gone, Master."

Darian sighed. "I suppose I can't blame them for requesting the one thing they were told could save the human race."

"Are you going to give them your blood?" Billy asked, hoping he wasn't stepping out of line.

Darian shook his head. "Not my blood, but I will keep my word. You may go now, be with your family."

Billy nodded then walked away. Darian pulled his cell phone from his pocket, dialing the number of Antonio Costello, the mobster who John sired several years ago. After the third ring, Antonio answered.

"Yes, Master," he greeted recognizing the cell number.

Darian smiled to himself at the humble greeting. He remembered the time when the mobster wasn't so modest. "I want you to come here now."

There was a short silence on the other end and then Antonio spoke. "I'll be there shortly."

They ended the call. Darian could tell the other vampire was annoyed and he found it humorous. Thirty-three minutes later, the doorbell chimed. Billy answered and escorted the mobster vampire into the den where Darian was waiting with several members of his coven.

Antonio swallowed, remembering the last time he was in that room. He'd ended up dizzy with his back to the floor and his head smashed up against the fireplace. "Hello Master," he greeted Darian.

"Hello Antonio. I'm sure you're aware of the current crisis," Darian asked.

Antonio nodded. "I had to gather as much water for my humans as possible. One was already infected, so we've isolated him. I notice vampire blood seems to slow the death, but not cure it, which I don't understand. They said the cure was in our blood."

Darian nodded. "Perhaps our blood needs to be combined with something else in order to work, which is why I've asked you to come. I'm going to take an ounce of your blood which I will give to the Center for Disease Control to study."

Antonio took a step backward. "Why my blood, Master?" he asked, his voice hesitant.

"Because I said so. Now, give me your arm."

Antonio looked around the room at the other vampires. The last thing he wanted was to be humiliated again by disobeying. He extended his arm toward Darian who held his wrist over a thin tube. Darian punctured his vein with his nail and held the wound open, spilling the blood into the tube. The younger vampire winced, but remained silent as he watched his blood fill the tube. Once it was done, Darian released Antonio's wrist. The skin healed on its own in a matter of seconds.

"I want you to have one of your people anonymously deliver this sample to the *Esquire Hotel*, room 1245, care of Dr. Brad Conway," Darian instructed.

Antonio didn't argue or ask any more questions. He nodded, took the tube and left.

"He's totally different from the man who I turned," John commented, noticing Antonio's change in personality.

Darian chuckled. "He is still ruthless, greedy and egotistical. He just understands what his role is with me."

Several heads nodded, knowing full well what all of their roles where regarding their relationship with Darian.

Darian looked at his coven. "I want you all to gather more water, but make sure it's already been packaged and dated at least a month prior to today's date. Go to a water packaging plant if need be."

"Yes, Master," they said in unison and left to carry out their orders.

Darian sat down in his favorite chair, closing his eyes, and attempting to relieve some of the stress he was under. Under different circumstances, he would have never given the human race vampire blood. However, if they could find the missing element that might help save Natasha's parents, he was willing to risk it. He just hoped he wasn't making a mistake in doing so.

CHAPTER THIRTEEN

Dr. Brad Conway opened the door after the man on the other side told him about a package he had for him. The man stepped inside and looked around.

"Are you the only one here?" the stranger asked.

"Yes. My colleagues took an earlier flight home," Dr. Conway replied. "For some reason they didn't want to wait for me."

The stranger nodded then simply gave him the package without saying a word and walked away. Nervously, Brad looked down at the package in his hands, hoping it was the sample of vampire blood they needed and not a bomb. He closed the door and walked to the table setting the box down gently. He opened it tentatively and exhaled as he saw what it was. He smiled. This would be the first step in their fight against this virus. He called the office, letting them know to get the lab ready for experiments. He didn't wait until sunrise. At the speed this virus attacked the human body, time was of the essence.

He finished packing his bag and checked out of the hotel. He boarded the plane that was waiting for him, taking the new sample back to their main headquarters in Washington D.C. Five hours later, the sun had just risen over the horizon. He only had about three hours sleep, but he was energized enough to work on finding a cure. He entered the lab, dressed in his protective gear. The other scientists on his team were all waiting for him and the sample.

"To tell you the truth, Brad, I didn't think we were going to get a sample," Dr. Goldstein said.

"How *did* you get a sample?" Dr. Victor Summers asked.

"I honestly don't know. None of the suspected vampire masters were corporative. I was in the process of leaving the hotel when a man just dropped off the V-86," Dr. Conway answered. "He didn't say where it came from."

"Well, luckily for us, one of the vampires decided to help in spite of the threat," Dr. Renee Nelson said.

"Indeed." Brad did remember something from their quest for vampire blood and he gave the other man an irritated expression. "You were rude to so many of them. I'm surprised they didn't kill you. Had I known you'd make an ass out of yourself, I would have never brought you along."

"As if that was your decision to begin with. I'm as much invested in discovering a cure as any of us," Goldstein remarked.

"Not nearly, I didn't insult the vampire in Jersey or New York; that was you."

"They weren't going to help anyway and I wasn't going to beg them for something they should have given freely. They claim they want equality, well coming to the aid of the citizens of this country when your country needs you is the American way."

"From some of their accents, I can tell this isn't their mother country. Don't think the 'American way' matters to them much."

"These vampires are citizens, right? Pays taxes and all that? Then they should help when they're in the position to. It's not like we asked for much. They were lucky we didn't bring the S.U.I.T. with us. We should have for the bullshit that Jersey vamp pulled on me."

Brad looked up from his Petri dish. "You're a fool, Goldstein and you're lucky Mr. Fairfield-Price didn't kill you on the spot."

"Whatever," Dr. William Goldstein shot back. "Let's just work on trying to find a cure."

The team of scientists worked diligently for hours on what they hoped would be the cure. They mixed the sample of blood with various antibiotics when they realized, with unbridled shock, that vampire blood alone didn't cure the decease. Everything they believed would work was failing. So much had been riding on vampire blood being the only medicine needed as it was what they were lead to believe. In the past, vampire blood had cured everything they tested on it. AIDS, cancer, diabetes, lupus, even healing broken bones and damaged nerves that would have otherwise left a human being paralyzed.

Exhausted, the team took a break, drinking large amounts of caffeine and munching on sugary pastries in the employee lunchroom.

"What haven't we tried?" Dr. Leroy Sims asked the others.

"I don't know. I even tried using another virus to combine it with, but the vampire blood destroyed the virus," Dr. Renee Nielson said, rubbing her temples.

"We've got to think of something. These bastards said the cure was in their blood. We just have to find out how to work it right. We can tell from our experiments that this blood seems to be slowing down the virus, but it's not destroying it. I wish I knew how they created this super virus," Dr. Brad Conway said, putting his head down on the table.

"I need to use the washroom," Dr. Victor Summers said, rising to his feet and leaving the lunchroom. He walked past the men's washroom and right into the lab. He made sure to turn off the cameras before entering the restrictive area, pausing only to cover himself from head to toe in his protective gear. He walked over to the only sample of V-86 they had, now contained in several testing tubes.

Picking up a hand-held ultraviolet light, he exposed the blood to the rays. The blood bubbled then begin to smoke before catching fire. In a matter of seconds, the sample was reduced to a light dusting of ash in the tubes. Satisfied that the samples was destroyed, he left the lab and went to the men's room. After checking all of the stalls and making sure no one else was in the room, he pulled out his cell phone and dialed a number.

"Master, I've destroyed the sample," he informed when the other man answered.

"Excellent, Victor. Tell me, who was it who provided the sample?" the Master vampire asked.

"I'm not sure, sir. Brad kept this very hush-hush. I do know Brad and William when to Chicago, New York, Miami, Philadelphia, and New Jersey looking for vampires who were willing to donate blood," the servant, Victor, said. "Also, Master, they can't seem to remember the name of the vampire who gave them the blood."

"Hmmph. Well, in any case, that does narrow it down. I see some vampires aren't taking the warning seriously. I'll see that changed soon enough. You did well, make sure you aren't discovered."

"Don't worry, Master. I covered my tracks."

"Good." The Master vampire ended the call.

Victor slipped his cell back into his pocket and walked out of the washroom going back into the lunchroom with the others.

***

"I see we have a problem," the unnaturally beautiful vampire from the televised message said as he rolled over, looking at the vampire lying next to him.

"It would seem so," stated his equally handsome lover, who was wiping his eyes as he came out of his resting state.

"A vampire gave the CDC a sample of blood to work with. It's been destroyed, but it would seem we have a betrayer in our ranks." The Master vampire reached over, brushing several strands of blond hair from the other vampire's face. "You're so beautiful."

The younger blond smiled, but didn't respond. He was quite used to the compliment and its many variations.

"I want you to find out who this vampire is and take care of them," The Master vampire said.

"Do you want me to kill this vampire?"

"I'm trusting you to execute the worst punishment you can imagine. If death is that, then do so. If you find that punishing someone close to this vampire will be a better choice, do that."

"Leave it to me, I will not fail you."

"Oh, and Royce?"

"Yes, my Lord."

"Make sure you get it on camera."

Royce smiled. "Yes, my Lord." He left the room. It was going to take a little bit of research to find out who this mysterious vampire was. He was going to have to ask around, but he was confident that he'd get his answer soon enough.

***

Natasha stayed in bed with her two children, playing with them, hoping to keep her mind off of her parents. She wanted to see them, but she knew it would be a stupid thing to do. In doing so, she could expose herself to the virus. Also, Darian had forbade her to leave the mansion along with the rest of his coven. However, she did talk to them on the telephone for several hours. They prayed together and shared treasured moments. Both of her parents had told her how proud of her they were. They expressed how blessed they felt to have had a daughter like her and how much they loved her. It was one of the hardest conversations Natasha ever had. She couldn't stop crying the entire time. Finally, they both decided to end their phone call for the best.

Around one o'clock, Devin, Carmen, Adrian and Warren came by as promised. Soon, the vampires would be awake and they would be able to feed. Warren had knocked on her door earlier, trying to give her some words of comfort, but still, all she really wanted to be left alone. Nothing anyone had said to her could ease her stress and pain. The only news she wanted to hear was news about a cure and that her parents were going to live.

"That's your sister's little feet," Natasha said to her son, Matthew, who was playing with his sister's toes.

He looked up at his mother and smiled, showing his tiny baby teeth. Natasha leaned over, kissing him on his forehead, nose and both cheeks. She then did the same to her baby girl; only she nuzzled her a bit more, inhaling her sweet scent.

"This is a beautiful scene," an unrecognizable male voice said from behind causing her to jump and turn. Before she could scream, he was on her, his hand covering her mouth. "If you don't want me to eat your children in front of you, you'll do well to keep quiet." Royce could hear the other shifters in the mansion. He knew they couldn't sense his aura, as he was masking it; he didn't want to alert them to his presence. "Now, I'm going to take my hands from your mouth. You scream, you all die, do you understand?"

Natasha nodded.

"Good." He removed his hand as he sat down on the bed. "You're pretty, but not exceptionally so. I wonder what is it about you that has a Master vampire of Darian Alexander's caliber so smitten?"

"If you knew anything about Darian, you'd know that answer," Natasha said.

"I'll admit … I don't know him personally. We've never met, but from what I've gathered in the past two hours, he quite beautiful and powerful. Perhaps we'll meet eventually and I'll see for myself if the rumors are true."

"What do you want with me?" Natasha asked. Her voice was unsteady despite her efforts to keep it measured.

"I'm going to take you with me, but don't worry, I'll bring you back."

"Why?"

"I'll explain later." With that, he backhanded Natasha, knocking her unconscious. Lifting her up off the bed, he left through the same window he entered. He flew to an abandoned apartment building which he had made accommodations for her prior to her abduction. After tying her to a chair and binding her ankles and wrists he splashed cold water on her face to wake her up.

He was successful.

Natasha's eyes shot open as she shook the water off. "What do you want with me?" she demanded. The room spun a little as she struggled to gather her bearing, having been jolted awake from unconsciousness.

Royce stood before her pointing to the video camera he had carefully positioned on a table. "Unfortunately, your lover, Master and whatever else he is to you made the mistake of crossing us. We warned every supernatural about the consequences they'd endure if they interfered with our plans. Mr. Alexander decided to take it upon himself to give the Center for Disease Control a sample of vampire blood."

Natasha was terrified, but she refused to let this vampire see her fear. She refused to let him have that much power over her. They were the ones responsible for killing thousands of people and probably millions more. They were responsible for her parents' condition. She stared at him with all the hate she had in her heart. If looks could kill, Royce would be a pile of ash.

"Oh, such fire! Such strength! I think I'm beginning to see what

154

they might see in you. No matter though, Darian still has to pay for his actions. At first, I was going to kill him, slowly."

"You wouldn't be the first vampire who thought they could kill him."

"Oh, at my age sweetheart, he wouldn't stand a chance. Think about it. I'm up and about while he's sleeping the rest of a vampire who's really not worth my time. But I just can't let his actions go unpunished, so here we are."

"Whatever you're going to do, just do it already. I'll have peace knowing Darian will kill you regardless of how strong you think you are," Natasha said as proudly as she could.

Royce cocked an eyebrow. "You pathetic humans have no idea when to shut your mouths and when to speak. This brave act you have going on here is amusing at best. But there's nothing noble about it, considering if you enraged me enough it'll only take me a second to go and retrieve your children, bring them here and twist their tiny heads off in front of you."

That put something on Natasha's mind. She couldn't help what was going to happen to her, but she'd be *damned* if her actions caused the death of her children. "I'm sorry. I apologize for my outburst."

Royce smiled. "That's better." He reached into his pocket, pulling out his cell phone, dialing a number. After a few seconds, someone answered. "I'm ready. Good." He ended the call then turned the camera on; the red "recording" light glowed brightly. He began to walk toward her, taking his place behind her chair so that he was facing the camera. "Supernaturals the world over, you were warned of the consequences for your actions if you dared to meddle with our plan. There was one among you who didn't heed our warning, this is his punishment. Don't let something like this be yours."

Natasha began to tremble in her bindings as his clawed hand came closer to her face. With his nail, he sliced through her skin and she cried out. Blood seeped through the wound, staining her cheek. With his tongue, he licked the blood away, savoring her taste.

He slid his hands down the length of her arms, taking her hands into his. "These are the hands you love to touch your children with, are they not?"

Natasha didn't respond.

Slowly, he closed his fingers around her hands, applying pressure to the tiny bones. Natasha screamed in agony as her bones were crushed in the vampire powerful grip. Tears flowed freely from her eyes as she thrashed in the chair.

"I could stop your pain, Natasha. All you have to do is ask me to let you live. Of course, someone has to die in your place. Who will it be? Darian? Your children? Your other lover, Xavier? What about your parents, they are already dying a slow painful death as it is. The virus is working its way through their system as we speak. They don't have long left to live, even with that other vampire watching over them. Who will take your place?"

He squeezed her hands harder causing some of the tiny bones to puncture her skin. She screamed louder as she cried uncontrollably. Her chest heaved as she struggled to breathe between strained gasps.

"Do you want me to stop the pain?"

"Fuck you!" she shot back.

He released her hands. "I see you may need some extra convincing." He looked at the pajamas she was wearing. It was a blue night gown that came to her knees. Slowly, he began to slide his hand up her thighs between her legs. Natasha cringed and tried to press her legs closer together, but to no avail. His hand found her panties, and he slid his fingers pass the trim to the softness the thin fabric was covering. Natasha jerked as his fingers began to message the tender folds of her vagina.

"Ah, yeah, I thought you'd like that."

Natasha wanted to spit in his face, but in the forefront of her mind was his threat to her about what he'd do to her children. The fear of that was worse than anything he could put her through, so she kept her mouth shut and her saliva to herself.

Royce's fingers worked her over expertly; he could feel her responding in spite of herself and in spite of the intense pain she was feeling. He smiled, removing his hands. "Do you know why I did that to you?"

"I have a couple of ideas why but I don't think you'd want to hear them." She panted still with a mixture of pain and exhaustion. However, she was relieved that he didn't bring her to the brink as she had feared he would.

Royce chuckled. "Because vampires are extremely territorial and one thing they hate is for another to violate what is theirs, be it their humans or their territory. Trust me when I say, for Darian and Xavier … watching you go through what you're going through, it will be a fate worse than death for them."

"You'd be surprised what Darian and Xavier can handle."

"If they can handle your temperament, then I don't doubt they have formidable personalities. Nevertheless, this will be torture for them and a warning to anyone else who assumes we won't know when they betray us. Now, are you ready to stop the pain, or do you want to continue?"

"Kill me, because I'm never going to offer someone else in my spot." She looked up at him with an expression that said she meant every word and there would be no changing her mind.

"Admirable, indeed. Very well." Royce walked toward the table, picking something up, he turned revealing a syringe filled with a pink substance. Coming closer, he smiled. "Do you know what this is?"

Natasha swallowed hard. She could even hear herself swallowing and knew the audio on the camera picked it up as well. "I'm guessing that's not the cure."

Royce laughed. "You'd be right." He stood behind her and without waiting another second he plunged the needle into her arm. Natasha screamed as he injected the virus into her bloodstream then he pulled the needle out. "Remember, death was *your* choice." He walked away, turning off the camera. He began to pack everything back into his bag. "I've got to say, for a human, you were stronger than even I'd expected you to be. I knew for sure you'd give up someone else in your place. I mean, you have so much to live for. But as they say, 'life is a bitch and then you die.'"

"Why are you doing this?" she asked, tears in her eyes. She couldn't feel the effects of the virus yet, but she knew her time was limited.

"Because we were pushed to this. We've sat back and watched this little drama play out where humans thought they actually ran the world. For a little while, it was funny, entertaining even, but then you began to grow cocky. When we were exposed, humans took their arrogance to another level. The Council allowed you far too many freedoms. The Council betrayed the supernatural race. They should have been fighting for us instead of spreading their legs open for the human governments just for a few perks. Perks, mind you, that we could take if we actually wanted to. Anger continued to fester like an infected wound gone too long untreated. The longer things remained the same, the angrier we became. If you want to know the straw that broke the camel's back, it was when the S.U.I.T. decided to kill several members of our kind without just cause. Humans brought this predicament on themselves and humans are the only ones who can help themselves. That is the way we want it. Supernatural interference will not be tolerated."

"There was other ways of going about this. I refuse to believe you were pushed to this!"

Royce gave her a sad smile. "I know you're not like the rest of them and really, Natasha, I have nothing against you."

"I'm having a hard time believing that one, too."

"I'm sure you are, considering your current state, but it's true. I have no ill will against you, but I won't let what we've worked so hard for be derailed."

"Darian wasn't trying to betray you."

"Regardless, he did and he was warned." he walked over to her picking her up, chair and all, he flew out of the window so fast, Natasha couldn't even scream as the wind whipped around her. Suddenly the wind seemed to calm down and she was on the ground. She looked around, but the vampire was gone and she was in front of Darian's mansion.

Warren burst through the front door when he saw her. "Natasha, oh my God!" He ran toward her untying her bindings. "We've been going crazy looking for you."

"Do you know what happened to me?" she asked, sadly.

Warren's expression let her know he knew. He nodded solemnly. "Darian will be awake soon." He looked down at her damaged hands. "That motherfucker! I'll kill him!" His heart broke in a thousand pieces as he noted the severity of her injuries. Her hands were covered in blood with white bones jutting through the skin. She couldn't move them and he could tell by the way her body trembled, she was going into shock. "Jesus Christ. We have to get you to a hospital."

"No! They won't be able to help me more than Darian can and I don't want to put any more exposure on Darian than necessary."

"Natasha, that son-of-a-bitch broke every bone in your hands, you need medical emergency," Warren pleaded.

Tears ran freely as Natasha struggled not to think about the agonizing pain in her hands. "I know Warren, but I won't go to a hospital. Darian will rise soon. I can hold out until then, I know I can."

"At least let Sergio take a look at it, let him see what he can do to help ease your suffering."

Natasha nodded. "All right, let's do that. Oh, God, it hurts like hell." She tried to remain calm. She could feel her body growing cold and she didn't want to put herself in a worse situation.

"They won't get away with what they've done to you, we'll see to that."

"I don't know, Warren. This vampire was strong, if you can believe it or not, his aura felt stronger than Marcus'."

"Jesus," Warren hissed under his breath.

"I know. Plus we don't know how many are involved and who they are."

Warren ran his hand over his face. What Natasha was saying was putting him in an even deeper mood of anger and depression. Mainly because it was all true, especially if that vampire was stronger than Marcus. He looked at her. "We need to get you inside."

"I don't want to go inside where the others are. I don't want to infect anyone."

"Natasha, it's cold out here, are you sure?"

"Warren, my children are inside. If this is airborne, I won't risk getting them or anyone else infected."

Warren nodded. "All right. Why don't you sit in the car? At least you can run the heat and be comfortable."

Natasha nodded. Sounded like a good idea. Warren went back into the house, getting the keys to Darian's Anaconda Pavilion. Natasha climbed inside once it was open and he inserted the key into the ignition, turning on the engine and heater.

"All right, the heat should come on in a minute," Warren said.

Natasha nodded, tears streamed freely down her cheeks as she endured the pain she was in.

"We've taken care of your children, they're fine," Warren informed her.

"Thank you, Warren. Where are the others?"

"We saw the video feed; we recorded it even before we knew it was you the video was going to be about. When we saw it was you, we checked the bedroom and just saw your kids on the bed and the window open. After that, I called Xander and Devin called Elise and they been searching for you ever since."

"Let them know I'm back, would you please."

Warren nodded. "Of course, Natasha. God! I can't believe this bullshit is happening." He slammed his fist on the roof of Darian's car, denting it.

"Hey! Don't squash me in here." Natasha gave him a sideways glance.

"I'm sorry. I didn't mean to do that."

"I know."

"Natasha, I don't…" His voice trailed off as tears weld up in his eyes.

"I know."

"We'll find a cure, I swear."

"It's okay. Please go inside, protect my children."

"You still need medical attention," Warren said. He pulled out his cell phone, calling Sergio.

"Yeah, Warren, any news?" Sergio asked.

"Natasha's here, but she needs you right now."

"I'm on my way." Sergio ended the call.

"He's coming?" Natasha asked.

"Yeah, he'll be here in a few."

"Okay, please, Warren, my children."

Warren nodded and walked away to perform the task she asked of him.

Natasha sat in the car and watched as other automobiles began to pull up, her friends climbed out and ran toward her.

"Oh my God, Natasha, I don't know what to say," Elise said, tears in her eyes. She pressed her hands on the glass, feeling all of the pain that her friend was. "We have to take care of your hands, they must be killing you."

"Would putting them in a cast make the pain go away?"

"No, you'd still feel pain, but having them be supported will ease the pain. We need to get you to a hospital."

"Just have Sergio put a splint on them or something. Darian can take it from there when he rises," Natasha said.

"This isn't like when we were in Russia and you had a little cut on your hand," Elise urged, tears streaming down her face. "You can go into shock if you go on like this."

"But I'm not in shock and I won't go to the hospital. Not when Darian is so close to me," Natasha argued.

Sergio pulled up then and ran toward Natasha. "Let me see," he said as he opened the car door. He took a look at her injured hands and cursed. "It's really bad, Natasha. Frankly, I don't understand how you're still conscious right now."

"It hasn't been easy." Natasha exhaled a shuddering breath filled with all of the pain she was feeling.

Sergio nodded. "I can't do too much right now; I don't have much with me. I can give you a sedative that will help with the pain. I'll wrap your hands up as best as I can to keep them stable."

Natasha nodded and Sergio went to work, cleansing the wounds and securing her hands on wooden splints. She cried and flinched every time a nerve was struck and Sergio hated causing her even the slightest bit of pain after what she'd been through.

"That's all I can do right now. I wish you'd go to the hospital, but I know why you won't," Sergio said.

"You have at least an hour before Darian rises," Elise informed her.

"I know you all care about me, But I have my reasons," Natasha began, looking at all of the faces surrounding her. "Another thing I can't take right now is the look on your faces. I don't want everyone pitying me. I'm not trying to be some Super Chick or Warrior Woman or anything like that. I just can't deal with your pain, too. Elise, I'll wait for Darian all the same. Please, just go inside."

Elise looked away. It was hard for her not to cry as hard as her heart wanted to, knowing her friend was dying and that her death would be horrible and painful. She wiped her eyes and decided to be strong. Her tears weren't what Natasha needed, her strength was. "All right. Do you want anyone to stay out here with you?"

Natasha shook her head.

"Very well. I'm sure Darian will come get you soon." She turned to everyone else. "All right, let's go inside."

Reluctantly, they all went inside the mansion, even though they wanted to stay with Natasha. Elise decided she would check on her through the window as she closed the front door. Natasha sat in the heated car and waited for the sun to set behind the horizon.

***

Darian's eyes opened instinctively and he looked around the room. He knew right away that there were a lot more people inside his home then he was expecting and for some reason, he knew something was wrong, *very* wrong. In a matter of seconds, he was out of the room, down the stairs, out the mansion and standing beside his car outside looking down at Natasha.

"Natasha," he said calmly.

He had startled her still, but she regrouped quickly. He mentally unlocked the door, opening it then reached in, hugging her gently.

"I'm so sorry," he said, his voice was strained as he struggled to hide the guilt he was feeling along with the anger that boiled within knowing that someone dared to harm what was his.

"It's not your fault," Natasha leaned her head against his shoulder, hoping to ease his guilt.

"It is. I wasn't sure how far they'd take their threat, or if they would even know how to track down a supernatural who dared to help the humans. I took a chance and I should have been the one to pay the price."

"According to them, you are. Watching me die and watching what they did to me is supposed to be your torture. That's what the man said." Natasha gave him a small, sad smile as tears flowed down her cheeks leaving wet trails. "Darian, baby, I don't blame you. I know why you did what you did …" She took another painful breath and sniffed before continuing. "You're a *good* man and I knew you took the risk to help my parents and if other humans could benefit, that was worth it. I think what you did was very brave and selfless."

Darian turned away, the rage within him so powerful he could barely keep from unleashing it against anyone who was nearby. He looked at her then his eyes trailed downward. He saw how painfully swollen her hands were underneath the bandages and knew the bones had been crushed. He scanned her memory to see exactly what had happened. He knew that a mysterious blond vampire tortured and infected Natasha and she'd been so brave and so strong. She'd taken every demented attack the vampire gave and held her head up the entire time. Darian would see death come to this vampire if he had anything to do with it. Through gritted teeth, he spoke. "I need to take care of your hands."

"Please, the pain is so terrible."

He looked up at her, staring into her green eyes. "I will not let you die." He pulled the sleeve back off his wrist and with his nail, he cut into the flesh. "Here, drink."

Natasha did as she was told, drinking the blood that flowed into her mouth. She moaned in agony as the bones in her hands mended themselves. She continued to cry until her hands became whole again and the pain finally went away. She then became lost in the delirious and intense sexual sensation that always came with the drinking of vampire blood.

Darian pulled his wrists free then pressed his hands on Natasha's shoulders as she tried desperately to get at him, snapping and licking. After a while, her vision began to clear and her bloodlust faded.

"Good, it's done."

"I feel a little better," she said.

Darian's eyebrows rose, hopeful. "You do?"

She nodded. "Like I did before the virus was inside of me."

Darian took her wrist into his and cut a tiny hole in her flesh, just enough to get a tiny taste of her blood. He licked the dot of blood that came forth. He turned, grimacing in disgust.

"I guess I'm still infected," Natasha said sadly.

"Yes." He looked up at her. "But I *will* save you."

"Even if you can't, I was given the choice to save myself. I chose to keep those I love away from harm for a reason. I know even if I do die, my children will be loved, protected and cared for and their children and so on and on. I'm all right with this, Darian." She looked off to the side. "Okay, that's almost too full of shit for even me to believe. I'm not really all right with dying. It's the last thing in the world I want to do. But I have been happy knowing that you, Xavier and all of my friends will be the ones who would care for my children if or when I couldn't."

Darian took her hand into his, kissing it gently. He could smell the virus working on her immune system, destroying her healthy blood cells. He mentally cursed himself for giving the human race the blood, even if Natasha had forgiven him for it. "I won't let you die," he repeated himself.

"I love you," she said tenderly.

"I love you, too," Darian said. "We need to get you inside."

"I don't want to infect the house."

"I'll quarantine you in one of the rooms if that makes you feel better. We don't have to walk through the house to get there." He rose, extending his hand.

Natasha slipped her hand into his and Darian helped her out of the car, then holding her close, flew upwards. He mentally unlocked the window, opening it and flew inside. It was one of his guest bedrooms and it would suit Natasha well during this time as it was far enough away from the human quarters of his home and their children's nursery.

"You can stay here for now. You won't be near the other humans, besides, I'm going to send them away, along with our children," Darian said.

"I think that's best, thank you."

"I'll be back." He left the room heading to the den to address the others. All eyes locked on him when he entered and they waited for him to speak. Darian leaned against the door frame with both hands in his pockets. "Xavier has not risen yet, but he will very soon and he won't be in a good mood."

"No offense, Darian, but ain't none of us in a good fucking mood," Adrian said. He had wanted to kill someone ever since he saw the video feed on TV.

Darian nodded. "Fair enough. Elise−"

"Yes, Darian?" she answered, inadvertently cutting him off.

"Would you please take my human servants and their families with you along with our children?"

"Now?" she asked.

"Yes, please."

"All right." She rose from the sofa, several of her Pride members followed suit. The humans didn't argue they only walked out of the door, along with Elise. Madeleine and Miranda went to retrieve Natasha's two kids. Once they had them, they left as well.

"Don't ask me to leave, because I'm not," Warren said, daring for Darian to do just that.

"I wasn't going to ask you to leave." Darian walked to his favorite chair and sat down, resting his elbow on the armrest and his chin on his fist as he thought about his predicament.

"What are you going to do about Natasha?" Xander asked.

"I'm going to attempt to turn her, if she wants it and if it works. If it doesn't, at least my blood is powerful enough to stave off the effects of the disease until I can find a cure," Darian said. He turned when he heard Xavier coming down the staircase.

"I sense something's wrong, what is it?" Xavier asked immediately after seeing the worrisome expression on Darian's face.

"Xavier, Natasha has been infected with the virus as a warning and punishment to me for supplying the humans with a sample of vampire blood," Darian said, laying everything out for him … well not everything. Xavier didn't know about the video feed and torture.

Xavier fought the urge to race to Natasha's side when he saw the look of anguish flash across Darian's features in spite of the Master vampire's attempt to hide it. He knew his lover was suffering as much as he was and that understanding was what he needed, not condemnation. "I know you think my first response would be to blame you for this, because of what you did, but I don't. I know why you did it and I would have done the same thing," he said, forcing himself to remain calm and rationale.

"I should have heeded the warning," Darian said.

"You were trying to save lives, Darian. It was the right thing to do."

"I remember a time when I wouldn't have been so concerned about such trivial things as human life."

"Do you wish you were still so passé about it?"

"Human life is depending on me whether I want it to or not—our children, Natasha, her parents ... my servants. To be honest, I don't know if I'll ever be the vampire I used to be, or if I even want to be him," Darian said.

Xavier's mouth dropped open, shocked by Darian's revelation. "Well, I would gladly stand beside the old you and the current you any day."

Darian rose from his chair, walking toward Xavier. He stroked his lover's face tenderly and smiled. "Thank you."

Xavier nodded. "What about Natasha, we need to go to her."

Darian agreed. "She's upstairs."

"What are we going to do?" Xavier asked as he followed Darian up the staircase.

Darian told him about his plan to turn Natasha into a vampire. If that didn't work, he would have to think of his next option. The two vampires entered the room, Natasha turned, running into Xavier's rushing embrace. He wrapped his arms around her, holding her as tightly as he could without harming her. He kissed her several times as he ran his fingers lovingly down the side of her face, caressing her tender cheeks.

"We'll figure this out, Natasha. We won't let you die, don't worry," Xavier said. He hoped he wasn't giving a promise he couldn't keep, one that would soon rip him in two.

Natasha gave him a sad, and not so assuring, smile. It really was the best she could do considering. He didn't say anything, only held her close to him.

"Natasha, I want to ask you something," Darian began.

She peeked over Xavier's bicep, looking at him. "What is it?"

Darian licked his lips, and Natasha felt her heart skip a beat. Even knocking on death's door, she still felt passion for that man. Just watching the sensuous movement of his moist tongue running along his full-shaped lips nearly sent her into a sexual frenzy. No wonder Kysen had turned him.

Darian ignored the sensation of lust he felt emanating off Natasha, although he was surprised she was feeling that way at all. He had more important matters to deal with and so did she. "How do you feel about becoming a vampire?"

"I want to live, I know that much. I've thought about it, I have and I've been so up in the air about that decision. I've swept it under the rug so many times. But right now, I say go for it. I'll deal." She pulled away from Xavier and he allowed it.

Darian walked over to her, taking her by the shoulders. He leaned forward, looking her directly eye-to-eye. "Are you sure?"

"Darian, I'm dying. I'm sure."

"Are you sure we aren't rushing this?" Xavier asked as he looked at Natasha.

"Are you willing to wait for the human government to give into the demands of these vampires? Do you believe these vampires will give us a cure anytime soon?" Darian asked him.

"No, but once it's done, it'll be done forever." Xavier took hold of Natasha's shoulders. "If we do get a cure, it won't matter; you'll be one of us."

"Xavier, I know. I want to live and from what I know of the human governments, they'll let millions die before they give into the demands of supernaturals. And from what I know of these vampires, they'll let millions die before they turn back and give in. If we get a cure tomorrow, proving that I made this decision in haste, like I said, I'll deal."

"But will you be *you*," Xavier's voice cracked slightly and he cleared his throat. He hadn't meant to reveal his fear and the reason why he couldn't fully commit to turning Natasha even if it was against her will.

She took his face into her hands. "Look at me, Xavier."

He did, locking his gray eyes to her green.

"I will be satisfied with the decision I made, just like I was with the decision to be with the both of you. Life isn't avoiding risks, it's taking them and living with the conclusion of those risks, be them good or bad. Life is fighting to live. I'm all right with this, Xavier."

He was convinced as was Darian.

"Very well. Darian, make her strong," Xavier said as he stepped back.

Darian took Natasha into his arms and extended his fangs, leaning forward; he fastened his mouth over her jugular, sinking his teeth. She gasped and arched, but stayed still in his embrace. The first taste of her tainted blood hit his tongue making him gag in reflex, but he fought back, sucking more into his body. John burst through the door a second later, wanting to see Natasha, but Xavier's extended hand stopped him in his tracks. Darian's body jerked and shivered, forcing him to pull away from Natasha. Her knees grew weak, but Xavier caught her before she fell, He laid her down gently on the bed. Darian's face was a perfect mask of pain and sickness. He gagged and then vomited a violent gush of foul smelling blood onto the polished wood floor. He heaved several times until his stomach had expelled the rancid blood from his body. He stumbled, but John caught him, helping him steady himself.

"I need to sit down," Darian said. Both John and Xavier assisted him to a chair. He looked down, seeing his hands shake. "It can't be done, I can't turn her," he whispered to no one in particular.

John and Xavier gave each other a look then they turned toward Natasha who was a little weak from losing a pint of blood. Her eyes were open as she watched the three vampires, although she was feeling very hopeless at this point. John walked to the nightstand, snatching several tissues from the box. He went back to Darian, handing him the tissue, which he took, wiping his mouth clean of the spilt blood.

"I'll clean that up," John said, gesturing toward the vomit that covered the floor. He left the room, returning a few minutes later with a mob and bucket along with several cleaning chemicals. He began to clean up the mess.

"I'm fine now," Darian announced as his body regained its composure and his limbs stop shaking uncontrollably.

"This is a powerful virus," Xavier said, seeing how it affected a vampire as strong and resilient as Darian.

The Master vampire nodded. "It is … unbearable, even."

"What if you bleed me to the point of death then give me your blood?" Natasha asked softly from where she still recovered.

"Doesn't work that way, remember what I told you?" Darian

asked.

"Oh yeah, you need enough of my blood to mix with yours before you give it back to me," she said dejectedly.

"Correct, and my body rejected your blood instantly, hence." Darian pointed to the bloody vomit on the floor John was currently mopping up.

"What do we do now? We can't let her die," Xavier said.

"I don't plan on letting that happen," Darian said.

Xavier walked over to Natasha, sitting down on the edge of the bed. He leaned over her, licking her spilt blood from the tiny puncture wounds in her neck. He grimaced and wiped his tongue off with a tissue from the desk. Biting into his thumb, he rubbed his blood over the wounds, sealing them, before turning to look at Darian.

"Okay, from what I can gather, it seems as though the stronger the blood is, the more effective is it at slowing down this virus," Xavier said.

"Why do you say that?" John asked.

"Because I sampled both Mr. and Mrs. Hemingway's blood and Natasha's and my blood didn't slow down the effects as well as Darian's blood did on her."

"She had a more direct exposure as well," Darian noted, nodding. "We need to see Kysen."

"When do we leave?" Xavier was watching him.

"First I need to call him. If we want his help, I'm going to have to go about it the right way."

"He's your Maker, won't he help anyway? You're like his favorite, right?" Natasha asked.

Darian chuckled. "He's never told me in those exact words, but if I were to take a guess, I'd say so. Still, I owe him his respect."

"Please, make the call," Xavier said.

Darian nodded, leaving the room to go to his study. He called Kysen and waited for his Master to answer. He did.

"Yes, Darian," Kysen greeted, recognizing his child's number on his caller ID.

"Good evening, Kysen. I'm not going to beat around the bush, I need your help."

"Honestly, Darian, you are using up all of your favors at an alarming rate."

"Kysen, you know I wouldn't ask anything of you unless I really needed your help."

Silence on the other end. "I know that to be true, and I believe I know why you're calling me."

"Natasha–"

"–Is dying of the same virus a lot of other humans are dying from."

"I gave her my blood, but it didn't cure her, only slowed down the effects of the virus. Will you give her yours?"

Silence again on the other end. Darian was growing more annoyed and he really wasn't in the mood for his Master's attitude, but he'd endure it if he had to.

"I saw the video of her being infected as a repercussion for your actions. You really should have stayed out of it, Darian."

Damn it to hell! He knew it was coming. "Kysen, not now. Will you help me?" he asked, getting back to the point.

Kysen huffed "Very well, come. I'll give your human my powerful and ancient blood and see if that'll save her life."

"Thank you, Kysen. I owe you."

"Oh, yes, you do."

The two vampires ended their call. He went to the den where Natasha had gathered along with the rest of the members of his coven and several members of Xander's Pack.

"What did he say?" Xavier asked.

"He's expecting us. We should go."

"I want to go with you," Warren said.

"Me too," John said.

"I'm trying my best not to take an entourage with me. Only Xavier and Warren need accompany me along with Natasha," Darian said.

"But–" John began to protest, but Darian interjected.

"Those are my orders. This is not up for negotiation."

Dejectedly, John nodded.

Darian walked over to the sofa, reaching out for Natasha who he assisted to her feet. He turned toward Xander. "If you could stay here to make sure my coven is protected …"

Xander held his hand up. "Say no more. We'll guard them with our lives."

Darian nodded, giving Xander a slight smile. "Thank you."

CHAPTER FOURTEEN

The four of them left, heading for the airport. Along the way, Darian made arrangements for the flight so the aircraft would be ready and waiting for them when they arrived. Once they reached the airport, Darian and the others boarded the plane, making themselves as comfortable as they could.

"Kysen has arranged for a car to pick us up when we arrive," Darian informed the others.

"I'm happy he's going to help. With his powerful blood, it should be all Natasha needs. He may give us some to take to her parents," Xavier said.

"I'm sure he will," Darian said.

"It'd be nice to see Adan and the others while we're there," Natasha said, hoping to get her mind off of everything that was happening to her and those she loved, not to mention the rest of the world.

Warren and Xavier nodded. Darian only sat silently, his eyes staring forward in deep concentration.

"Natasha, why don't you try to rest, it'll be a few hours before we get to Montana," Xavier suggested.

"I don't think I can sleep, Xavier. I wish that I could."

"You should try." He was concerned that the stress that she was under would only exacerbate her body's deterioration.

"All right, I'll try," Natasha said, lying down on the sofa, closing her eyes.

Mentally, Darian calmed her enough for her to fall into a deep sleep. Gently he lifted her up and took her into the bedroom, placing her gently on the bed. He walked out of the room, closing the door behind him.

"I'm glad you did that, she needed her rest," Xavier said.

Darian nodded. "With what she's gone through today, I can't imagine what she's feeling. She never stops amazing me—her strength."

"I heard there was a video footage of what happened?" Xavier asked, looking around questioningly.

"There is, but I don't think you should see it." Darian said.

"Did you?" his young lover asked.

"I saw it through Warren's memories, and what I saw ... trust me when I tell you; let it be." Darian looked at Xavier, hoping he was convincing him to stay away from the video footage that would no doubt send him into an uncontrollable fury.

"You can't ask that of me, Darian. For some reason, I have to know what she went through in order to know how to help her. She needs us," Xavier protested.

Darian inhaled deeply, releasing the air slowly from his lungs.

"Xavier, are you sure?" Warren asked. He knew how much Natasha meant to her two lovers and watching her get tortured then infected would be as much torture for the vampire as it was for him.

"I need to know," Xavier said.

"Very well, I'm sure you could find footage of what happened online," Darian said, gesturing to the computer console located on the other side of the aircraft.

Xavier rose, walking toward the built-in computer. Sitting down, he turned it on. After a few minutes, he loaded up the internet, typed on a few keys then waited. Video footage showed up on the screen and his expression turned from that of disgust to anger and then finally something far more dangerous and indistinguishable than anger. He turned away from the computer, walking into the washroom, and closing the door. His entire body trembled with rage so blinding, he could barely make out his own image in the mirror.

"Should you go to him?" Warren asked Darian.

The Master vampire shook his head. "He needs to process what he saw in his own way. There's nothing I can say to him right now that will ease his suffering or his rage."

"I can't believe how bravely Natasha is handling this," Warren commented, thinking about how well she was dealing with everything. Being publicly humiliated and tortured worldwide, being injected with a killer virus, having her parents dying from the same. Warren couldn't put it into words how he really felt about her, but he knew for certain he'd always felt that she was one hell of a woman.

"I couldn't agree more," Darian said, having read his mind.

"You can stop doing that any time now," Warren said.

"I'm sorry, but your thoughts were screaming into my own mind, I couldn't help but read them."

"I'll try to think more quietly from now on," Warren settled back into his seat.

A few minutes later, Xavier emerged from the washroom, his face still a mask of complete rage. He sat down in front of Darian. "I want the vampire who did that to her."

"Easier said than done, Xavier. From what Natasha has told me, he may be stronger than Marcus was," Warren said.

"And where's he at now? Dead and rotting," Xavier shot back.

"Not by your hands," Warren reminded him.

Xavier shot him a *look* that said he'd better choose his next words carefully.

"Hey, don't look at me like that. I know what you're feeling, because I'm feeling it, too. But getting killed trying to get revenge isn't going to make Natasha feel any better about any of this, now will it?" Warren stared at the other man, before letting his gaze shift to Darian.

"What he did to her …" Xavier's voice trailed off.

"I know, Xavier." Darian placed his hand on his lover's shoulder. "Let's focus first on curing her and then we'll think about what we'll do next, all right?"

Reluctantly, Xavier nodded, sliding back into his seat. The three men were relatively quiet during the flight, not having much to say to each other at the moment. When the airplane landed in Montana, Darian went into the bedroom, picking Natasha up and carrying her off the plane. They got into the waiting SUV and drove to Kysen's mansion where the ancient vampire was waiting for them.

"Place her on the sofa over there," Kysen said, after greeting them. He pointed toward his comfortable suede sofa in the living room.

"Thank you for helping us, Kysen," Darian said.

Kysen looked at his child. He could see the fear and uncertainty in his expression, even though he was trying to hide it. "Let's not waste time unnecessarily, wake her up, please."

Xavier woke Natasha by shaking her gently. She opened her eyes and looked around.

"Are we there already?" she asked, shocked by how long she had slept and so peacefully, too.

"We are. Kysen's going to give you his blood. Sit up, please," Xavier said, helping her.

She looked up at the beautiful and powerful Egyptian vampire approaching her. "Thank you, Kysen."

He looked down at her. "There's no need, you're welcome."

She was kind of taken aback by how easily he accepted her appreciation. In the past, he'd always disregarded it as if she was insignificant. This time, he responded the way normal people do when they are helping someone else. She figured that must be Adan's influence … Hell, it had to be. Speaking of Adan, the lion King entered the room, coming closer to her.

"I'm so sorry this has happened to you, Natasha," Adan said, leaning down, he hugged her.

"I don't really want to talk about it," Natasha said.

"Of course, I apologize," Adan said, stepping back.

"It's all right." Natasha gave him a sad smile then she returned her attentions back to Kysen. "I'm ready."

Kysen cut into his wrist, creating a wound. He extended his bleeding wrist to her and she locked her mouth around the wound, sucking gently, then more fervently until Kysen pulled his wrist free from her frantic grip. Xavier held her down on the sofa until she rode out the final waves of her bloodlust which took a little bit longer than when she'd drank Darian's blood.

Darian looked at her. "Did it work?"

"She doesn't smell infected," Kysen said.

Xavier decided not to risk not knowing the truth. He took Natasha's hand into his own, biting the skin of her palm. She yelped and he pulled away, shaking his head and looking for a garbage can to spit the blood in. He found one near the doorway and he rid his mouth of the blood before returning to the others.

"It's not as potent, but it's still there," he said, crestfallen.

Darian sat down on one of the expensive, comfortable tan chairs. "They said the cure is in our blood … where?"

Kysen's eyebrows rose. He was as perplexed as they were. "I don't understand why my blood didn't work. It's ancient."

Xavier ran his hand through his hair. "It seems as though the more powerful the blood is, the more effective it is. Kysen, I know I probably shouldn't ask this of you–"

"–Then don't," Kysen said, knowing full well what Xavier was going to ask him.

"I can't *not* ask this of you, I'm sorry," Xavier straightened himself.

"You want me to help you seek out a stronger vampire than myself to see if their blood will heal your human?" Kysen asked.

"We have to do something, I can't lose her," Xavier said through gritted teeth.

"Kysen, please," Darian pleaded.

Kysen looked at his child. "Why don't you try to turn her?"

"I did, I couldn't. Her blood poisoned me. Maybe you could try, you're far more resilient than I am," Darian beseeched.

Kysen cocked one brow. "Poisoned you how?"

"I couldn't drink my fill before retching," Darian answered.

"And you want me to risk having that happened to me as well?"

"To save her life, I would ask that of you. I'd be in your debt."

"You're already in my debt. In fact, 'you're ass deep in debt,' as they say."

Darian turned away from his Master, clearly upset and frustrated. Kysen watched his child in silence as he thought about what Darian had asked of him.

"You could try," Adan suggested of the ancient vampire and his lover.

Kysen turned to him. "I don't fancy being sickened," he fussed.

"You'd let her die, knowing what your favorite child will lose because you're afraid of vomiting?" Adan asked, both eyebrows rising in amazement.

Kysen huffed. "It's not an experience I'd like to go through, no."

Darian turned back around. "Kysen, I beg of you, please help us in any way that you can. I don't know how to be any more humble than this in asking for your help."

Kysen smiled sadly at his child, caressing the masculine curve of Darian's jaw line. "You have always managed to get more out of me than any of my other children ... must be your green eyes."

"Yeah, because we both know it's not my winning personality, right?" Darian joked with a low chuckle.

Kysen responded in kind before leaning over, kissing Darian deeply. "I'll help you as much as I can," he said when he pulled back. Looking at Natasha, who was silent as her friends and lovers spoke for her. "I don't think I need to ask if you want this."

Natasha shook her head. "I want to live."

"Very well." Kysen knelt beside her, wrapping his hand behind her neck and pulling her to him. He extended his fangs, just one set, and sank them into her jugular. The room was silent as everyone listened to the barely audible sucking of Kysen's feeding. Then the noise stopped and Kysen pulled away, rising to his feet. "I can't ..." He grimaced, holding his stomach. Turning he left the room faster than the others could see.

They could hear retching noises coming from the other room, but no one went to his side, figuring he'd want to be alone.

Natasha began to cry. Tears welled in her eyes then flowed freely down her cheeks. She was losing hope and was wondering if it was just better to accept her fate than continue to chase a cure that didn't seem to exist. Xavier sat on the sofa next to her, taking her into his arms, as did Warren. Kysen returned, entering the room with an expression of sheer disgust on his face.

"That. Was. Horrible." He shivered, and then sat down in the chair opposite Darian's.

"What do we do now?" Warren asked.

"Adan, come here," Kysen said, beckoning to his lover, who came. In a movement too fast for Adan to see or react to, Kysen grabbed hold of his wrist, biting into the flesh. The shifter gasped, but didn't pull away, he moaned softly as his body felt the most exquisite ecstasy as the ancient vampire fed from him. His body quaked and his knees buckled sending him to the floor with his wrist still sealed to Kysen's mouth. Seconds later, his lover released him, licking his lips. "Now *that* was something I want in my mouth."

"You should have told me you wanted to drink," Adan said, his voice shaky as he recuperated.

"You should have sense that's what I wanted. No need to complain, had you not goaded me so, I wouldn't have needed replenishing in the first place," Kysen remarked.

"Again, what do we do now?" Warren asked.

"We go back home and hope a cure becomes available, until then, I think I can drink your blood and stay alive as long as I can," Natasha said.

"Bullshit, that's not our only option!" Warren argued. "Kysen, what can we do now?" He looked back at the vampire.

Kysen huffed. "As Xavier said, the stronger and more powerful the blood, the better her chances are. When I tasted her blood, the virus seemed to be taking a minimal effect on her system. But it was still there. I propose we go to my Maker the Goddess, Irikara."

"Kysen, are you sure," Darian asked.

"She's far stronger and more powerful than anyone else I can think of. She's the original Fount of our line. However, it's no guarantee that she will help us. We must approach her very carefully. I will speak for us as she does not take too kindly to outspoken underlings as I do," Kysen said.

"You take to us kindly?" asked Warren.

"You're still alive, aren't you?" Kysen looked at him.

Warren nodded.

"Well then, if you think you can get out of line with Irikara, you'd be making your last mistake. She'll kill you instantly, and that's if I don't get to you first. Don't even *think* about anything that would be … Perhaps you two should stay here," Kysen looked at both Xavier and Warren.

"I won't leave Natasha's side," Xavier said.

"Neither will I," Warren added.

Kysen sighed. "You must humble yourselves completely in her presence. She is a Goddess and shall be treated as such, do you understand? If you insult her in any way, I'll kill you without hesitation. Do I make myself perfectly clear?" he asked, looking at all of them.

Darian nodded. He had never met Irikara, and was anxious to meet his Master's Maker.

Warren nodded. "I'll keep my mouth shut, I swear." He did feel a chill run down his spine after being threatened by Kysen. He was sure he wasn't the only one.

"I won't do anything that would ruin Natasha's chances of survival," Xavier said.

Kysen nodded once then looked at his lover. "Adan, you should come," he said.

"Why?" Adan asked, confused and not all that anxious to meet yet another vampire too drunk on their own power as far as he was concerned. Kysen was more than a handful.

"Because, she will want to meet you, as you are my lover and companion, she's told me so," Kysen informed.

"If you think I should, I'll go," Adan said.

"I need to speak with her," Kysen said, and then he closed his eyes, his expression one of concentration. *My Goddess, I request permission to come to you,* he said telepathically.

Have I ever denied you permission, my child? Irikara replied.

No, my Goddess. I will be there shortly.

Do not forget to bring your new lover I have heard so much about.

Yes, my Goddess.

I await your arrival, oh and my dear child...

Yes, my Goddess?

You will pay me Homage.

As you wish, my Goddess.

Their connection ended and Kysen opened his eyes. "She will see us and I was correct, she wanted to meet you, Adan."

"Well, let's not keep her waiting," Xavier said.

"She wants *Homage*," Kysen announced.

"What does that mean for her?" Warren asked.

"She will want a show of some sort, a tribute. I am not sure ... it will be her discretion," Kysen said. "I am most certain it will be sexual in nature."

"If she helps us, she can have whatever she wants," Warren said.

Kysen cocked a brow in mock surprise. "Are you sure? Would

your lover approve?" he asked Warren.

Warren thought about Matthew. "I'll talk to him."

"Perhaps you should, because she will want her *Homage* paid to her *before* she hears what your requests are," Kysen said.

"So basically, we give her what she wants and hope that she'll give us we want?" Xavier asked.

"That is correct," Kysen replied.

"Let's go," Xavier said, rising from the sofa and helping Natasha to her feet as well.

"All right, then," Kysen said, rising. He walked away only to return a few minutes later carrying an ornate suitcase.

"What's that?" Adan asked.

"Something for Irikara," Kysen replied.

"We should go now, it's a long flight," Darian said.

They left Kysen's home climbing into the waiting SUV. On their way to the airport, Kysen made arrangements for his airplane to prepare for travel to Egypt.

While they were on the airplane, Kysen decided to give them instructions. "It will not be sunset when we arrive, so we should stay on the plane until you two rise," he said, settling more comfortably in his seat.

"I want to thank you again for this, Kysen. I won't forget it," Darian said.

"Oh, I won't let you forget it. I've got a good mind to send you cards on a monthly basis, reminding you of my efforts in resolving this situation." Kysen tossed him a look before closing his eyes.

Darian smirked. "I really can't tell if you're joking or not at this point."

"Is that so?" Kysen asked, cocking a brow.

"You may be petty enough to take the time out to send me numerous cards with such a reminder. Then again, you are lazy for one so old, you may not even bother," Darian replied.

"For insulting me, I should follow through … but as you've said, I'm rather relaxed in my refined age. Such trivial things are beneath me." Kysen smiled at his vampire child, showing the whiteness of his teeth.

"How are things going with you and Adan?" Darian asked, curious about his Master's happiness.

Kysen looked at Adan who was watching the two of them. "He's outspoken, and at times obnoxious and stubborn."

"And those are my *good* qualities," Adan retorted.

Darian chuckled, a faint vibration in his chest. "You didn't answer my question."

Kysen looked at him. "You were right. I needed someone new in my life and Adan is perfect."

"You needed someone with a level of patience as strong as *adamantium* to be able to tolerate your personality," Adan said.

"*Adamantium* doesn't exist. You need to separate your comic book world from the real one," Kysen teased.

"As I said, one needs patience as strong as indestructible metal, be it fictional or factual, to deal with this man," Adan retorted.

Kysen snorted. "His Pride on the other hand has taken some getting used to. I'm still thinking about having another home built on my property which they can live in, separate from me."

Adan simply rolled his eyes and shook his head.

"You should all get some rest on this flight," Kysen said. "Darian, why don't you pilot the airplane while I take a nap?"

Darian looked at Kysen, slightly confused. "I can't pilot the plane mentally as you do."

Kysen smirked. "I know. I meant for you to physically pilot the airplane."

Darian snorted. "We should have taken my airplane, I have my own pilots." He rose from his seat.

"And it would take us longer to get to Egypt than it would if I was piloting. Is that what you would have wanted?" Kysen opened one eye, looking at his child.

Darian smirked but refuse to answer Kysen. He didn't want to give him the satisfaction of being right. Somehow being around Kysen always made him feel like his inexperienced fledgling all over again, as if he was still being taught lessons with the ancient vampire always in control. "Very well," he said, walking toward the cockpit.

Natasha, Xavier, Adan, and Warren noticed the dynamics between Kysen and Darian. It never ceased to amaze them how humble Darian was in Kysen's presence as opposed to how he was in his own element. Xavier knew it had everything to do with Kysen being Darian's Master and his Maker. Also, he could see why Darian wanted to be on his own. Kysen rested while Darian flew the plane for the next several hours until the sun rising forced him to rest.

Darian walked over to Kysen, tapping him on the shoulder. "Master, you need to take over."

Kysen stretched his limbs as he smiled. "Go on, rest. I've got it."

Darian nodded and walked over to the sofa.

"You can take my bed if you like," Kysen offered.

"Are you sure you and Adan don't want it?"

"If we do, I'm sure we won't disturb your rest."

"Are you that lackluster in the sheets? Say it isn't so," Darian teased.

"Cute. I only meant two men enjoying each other's bodies wouldn't be disturbing to you," Kysen said.

Darian rolled his eyes. "In any case, I'd rather not wake up with the two of you having sex beside me."

"You know, you're always welcomed to join us."

"He *is*?" Adan asked, with a questioning expression.

"He belongs to me, of course he is. Besides, I say nothing when you play stallion to your fillies, now do I?" Kysen tossed his young shifter lover an expression of his own.

"I'm not the only one playing stallion to them, while you're sitting there complaining about them living with us," Adan shot back.

Kysen chuckled. "Don't be jealous."

Adan smirked. "I'm not having a threesome with you and Darian."

"What if Irikara wants that?" Darian asked.

Adan looked at him. "That'd be the only way."

"Again, there is no need for your jealously, really." Kysen smiled at Adan then he turned back to Darian. "You sure you do not want the bed?"

"I'll rest here." Darian lay down beside Xavier on the sofa, folding the younger vampire in his arms.

Kysen chuckled as he watched the two men lying together. He thought about the times when he would have Darian in his arms that way, for a second he missed their intimacy. He cleared his mind of the memory. Darian was sharing that with Xavier and Natasha now and he had Adan.

His lover yawned. "I'll take the bed then," Adan said, rising to his feet.

Kysen watched him disappear down the hallway leading to the bedroom. He heard the door open and close and decided not to join him. Instead he watched over the others while they slept as he mentally piloted the plane, making the aircraft fly faster than its conventional speed. He thought about their predicament; the virus attacking all of the humans, the civil unrest in the streets the world over. He thought it would come down to something like this happening... well, not the virus part, but he knew supernaturals would one day rise up against the humans. It was only a matter of time and time was always on their side. Hours passed before they landed on Irikara's private airfield. Kysen continued to rest for the next few hours until the sun set.

***

He felt the gentle nudging of his lover, Adan and he opened his eyes. "Did you sleep well?" Kysen asked.

Adan nodded. "Did you?"

"I did." He looked around, noticing Darian and Xavier still resting. He looked out the window and noticed the sun was disappearing behind the horizon turning the sky a golden and ruby hue. "Darian will be up soon." He rose from his seat. "I'll be back." With that, he left the airplane.

Darian rose ten minutes later. "Where's Kysen?" he asked Adan.

"He left saying he'd be back. Didn't tell me where he was going," Adan answered.

"Warren, wake up," Darian called out to the other shifter.

Warren stirred, stretched and then wiped his eyes. "I'm up. I had no idea how tired I actually was."

Natasha woke up right before Kysen returned carrying several shopping bags with him.

"Here, put on these garments," Kysen said, handing each of them a bag.

"Is something wrong with our own clothes?" Warren asked.

Kysen cocked an eyebrow. "I honestly think with your attitude, you should stay on the airplane. You ask far too many questions and

183

may forget yourself in Irikara's presence."

"I wouldn't," Warren said in his defense.

"You would," Kysen stated.

"No, I wouldn't. I can control my temper."

Kysen chortled. "If you spoke to Irikara the way you're speaking to me right now, you would never see you lover again ... speaking of him, have you called him?"

"I did. Matthew wasn't keen on me paying *Homage* to your Master—"

"—As I thought. It is for the best," Kysen said.

"*Although* he wouldn't hold it against me because it would be for Natasha's sake," Warren added.

"How noble of you. I'll help ease your conscious. You will stay here," Kysen said.

Warren thought about everything he knew of himself and what he knew of Kysen and he came to the realization that staying behind would probably be the best decision for him, even if he didn't want to admit it vocally. "You never did answer my question," he reminded Kysen of the question that began their little dialogue.

"I know." Kysen turned, walking into his bedroom, carrying his ornate suitcase.

The others didn't bother to argue and began to dress in the comfortable linen clothing. When Xavier rose, he dressed in the new linens as well.

"This does feel nice," Natasha commented, after putting on her new outfit.

"The temperature is rather cool for this region during this time of year considering its normal weather," Darian said. "The clothes will help keep you comfortable."

"Have you ever been here?" Xavier asked.

"Yes, I lived here for some time when Kysen was grooming me for immortality," Darian said.

"You never met her, right?" Xavier stated.

Darian shook his head. "But from what I've heard, her beauty is said to be unnatural."

"I'm nervous about meeting her," Natasha said.

"In all honesty, so am I," Darian admitted.

They all turned when they heard the bedroom door open and then close. Kysen emerged from the hallway, looking completely stunning leaving them speechless. He was dressed in the style of the ancient Egyptians, wearing a gold and jeweled plated necklace and nothing else to cover his muscular torso. Gold earrings, arm bands and bracelets. His privates were hidden behind a gold and jeweled toga and he wore gold sandals with straps that crisscrossed up his leg to his knees. Even more beautiful were his golden-brown eyes decorated in black eyeliner. His long black, braided hair was pinned behind his ears with the aid of a gold ornate headband in the shape of a serpent. To top off the look, his beautiful dark chocolate complexion was dusted in a light coating of shimmering gold powder. Darian and a few of the others cleared their throats as they fought to regain their composure.

"I've never seen you look this way before," Darian said, as he struggled to fight back his lust.

"I know. This will please Irikara," Kysen said. "We should leave now."

The others had to gather themselves, they were still bewitched by the ancient vampire's appearance. Not only that, but he smelled exquisite and they were pretty sure the fragrance was old in nature. The five of them climbed into the waiting limousine, leaving Warren on the airplane. Fifteen minutes later, they pulled up to an enormous white marble and gold palace.

"Wow, this is just beautiful," Natasha said, in awe.

"Yes, it is," Kysen agreed as he opened the door, climbing out.

The others followed his lead as he walked up to the door, which opened on its own before them.

CHAPTER FIFTEEN

IRIKARA

F ollow me," Kysen said as he led the way to his Maker who was beckoning him. They walked through the palatial home of the Egyptian Fount, spellbound by all of the wondrous things they saw. Ancient furnishings and decorations adorned the halls and spacious rooms. Priceless art and sculptures were everywhere as they made their way into an even larger room which featured an exotic waterfall surrounded by tropical plants and fountains filled with tropical flowers of various shapes and colors adding a certain fragrance to the area. Several large, fluffy, white pillows were placed around the room. There was only one divan in the room that looked almost like a throne and the most gorgeous woman any of them had ever seen was sprawled over its cushions.

Irikara smiled as she looked at Kysen, her golden brown eyes raked over his body, drinking in his beauty. All of his gloriousness she sought to preserve over six-thousand years ago stood before her. She, herself was dressed in a gold-plated and jewel encrusted brassiere. She was also wearing gold arm bands and bracelets as well as gold and jewel encrusted necklaces. Her shimmering thin skirt with the splits up the sides slipped a little when she shifted her position, revealing beautifully shaped legs and feet also adorned in gold sandals. Her dark brown skin was dusted with the same golden powder Kysen was wearing. Her hair was a lovely and intricate sculpture in and of itself—decorated with gold and ruby accessories intertwining her many braids.

Her guests stood in complete and utter awe, they could feel her power rolling over them in waves sending tingles throughout their limbs. Her eyes scanned over her guests, taking in their appearance.

She knew all about Darian, her child's *Chosen One*. Indeed, she thought he was lovely as he stood before her in his own splendid beauty. His stunning forest-green eyes were truly a sight to behold. Had Kysen not turned him, he would have been someone she would have given her blood to, making him a God among men as she'd done with Kysen. It wasn't just his eyes that were captivating; it was his physique and his aura. For one so young, he had such charisma.

She then looked at Adan, the lion King her child had chosen for his new companion. She thought he was unique in his beauty as well with his golden eyes almost the color of a lion. She smiled to herself. For Kysen, his attraction was always in the eyes, and then it was in the defiance of his lovers which seemed to peak his arousal. She looked at the others. Indeed, Xavier was another beauty, deserving to be of her line. Although he looked a bit worse for wear considering the stress he was under. Natasha didn't seem to spark much interest for Irikara. She saw nothing exceptional about the young human besides her pretty green eyes, which seemed rare for her race, as her own eyes were.

Kysen approached first, kneeling to one knee and bowing at the waist. The others did as he did, as instructed. "My Goddess, thank you for granting us entry into your territory."

"My dear Kysen, you are always welcomed into my home," Irikara said, her Egyptian accent was thick as she pronounced each word.

"Thank you, my Goddess. I do come on this day with a favor to ask of you," Kysen said, still kneeling.

"Indeed you have, but I will have my *Homage* first."

"Of course, my Goddess. What is it you ask of me?"

"You do not ask this favor for yourself, and so therefore, your companions must pay me *Homage* as well."

"Of course, my Goddess. What is it you ask of *us*?" Kysen raised his head, waiting for her to respond.

Irikara looked at her guests then very elegantly beckoned to Natasha. "You, come here, sit beside me." She rose slightly, sliding to the side to make room for the human.

Kysen cocked a brow, turning to look at Natasha, who seemed as shocked as the rest of them. She did as she was told; rising to her feet and walking over to the very ancient vampire and sitting were she'd indicated. It felt very odd sitting next to such a powerful being, feeling her power come off of her in waves. It made the hair on the back of Natasha's neck stand on end.

Irikara ran her fingers gently over Natasha cheek, brushing some of her hair over her neck. "Your lovers would do anything to save you. I haven't quite figured out what it is about you that would make two vampires so invested in you. I'm slightly curious about that … only slightly."

Natasha didn't say anything in response to that, not sure if she should or shouldn't. Kysen had been quite detailed about what was acceptable behavior and what wasn't and she wasn't willing to test him when he said he'd kill them if they insulted or angered Irikara in any way.

"Servants," Irikara summoned.

Two humans entered the room, both naked from the waist up, one man and one woman. Natasha was surprised that the woman didn't seem uncomfortable having her breasts exposed. As she watched the woman approach Irikara, she figured she was just used to such nudity.

The servants kneeled. "My Goddess," they said, expectantly.

"Bring us two glasses of wine," Irikara said.

Natasha turned to say something, but then closed her mouth.

Irikara chuckled. "Do not refuse my hospitality, I don't offer it lightly. Besides, it will help settle your stomach."

Natasha didn't argue; she only nodded. When the servants returned with the wine, she took the glass, taking a sip of the sweet liquor.

"I had this vintage shipped in this morning for your arrival," Irikara said, tipping her glass to her lips, smiling. She returned her attention back to Kysen and the other supernaturals. "Kysen, my darling, it has been too long since I've last seen you."

"Yes, my Goddess," Kysen answered.

"Far too long, I am pleased to see that you are over your melancholy. I'm sure your reunion with your own child and your new lover are to be the reason for that."

"Yes, my Goddess."

"This pleases me," Irikara shifted again on her divan. "Have you fed?"

"No, my Goddess, I have not."

"Then we will tend to that after your *Homage* to me. It's been so long since I've seen you lie with another," Irikara's eyes panned over toward Darian. "I can sense the lust flowing from your young one, he desires you, still."

Darian looked up at Irikara, then toward Kysen, but remained silent, he lowered his head again.

"Do you desire him, Kysen?" Irikara asked, purposely putting him in a predicament, as Adan tossed Kysen a glance, but said nothing.

"My Goddess, as you are aware, there will always be a link between Maker and child, I desire him as I desire you," Kysen wisely replied.

Irikara laughed outright at his candor. "You have grown much wiser since we last met, my Kysen. Brilliantly played. Nonetheless, I shall have him take you before me. Seeing you in rapture will please me greatly."

Natasha made a soft sound, her lips tight as she fought the urge to cuss the ancient vampire out.

"Hmph, it would seem that your human female is possessive." Irikara laughed. "It matters not. You belong to me and all that follows you belongs to me. Begin."

Both Darian and Kysen rose and began removing their clothes. Irikara raised her hand, palm exposed, stopping them.

"Entice me, not bore me," she warned, not satisfied thus far with the "show" they were putting on.

"My apologies, my Goddess," Kysen said, nodding a bow in respect. He walked over to one of the large pillows that adorned the room, lying down on the cushion. He supported himself on his elbows as he watched his child approach him. Darian knelt down beside Kysen, allowing his lust to grow, unleashing his pent-up passions. He ran his fingertips along the length of Kysen's leg, running them over the powerful muscles underneath his skin. His hand traveled between his Master's legs, up this thighs and disappeared under the gold toga causing Kysen to gasp. Darian leaned closer, running his tongue in swirls over his Master's chest, along the ridges of his muscular stomach and dipping into his navel eliciting a moan from Kysen.

Irikara smiled as she leaned forward, pleased with what she was now seeing. She watched Xavier become aroused and knew he was used to seeing Darian with other people, but this was probably even more enticing as his Master was making love to his *own* Master. Adan, she noticed was also aroused, but he was also jealous. She chuckled softly to herself, seeing both the lion King and the human woman share the same emotion. Unfortunately for them, Irikara could care less, she would have her *Homage*.

Darian suckled gently on one of Kysen's dark nipples, rolling the tender flesh between his lips, flicking the little nub with his tongue and Kysen flinched. His hand gently stroked his Master's shaft bringing forth beads of wetness on the tip. Without taking away his attention to Kysen's sensitive nipples, he unfastened the clasp that held the toga in place, folding back the flaps exposing Kysen impressive erection.

Both Xavier and Natasha released a soft gasp, but said not a word.

"He is a God in every sense of the word, wouldn't you agree?" Irikara asked Natasha, who squirmed on the cushion beside her.

"Y−Yes, they both are," Natasha said, not wanting to sell Darian short. Although, she did have to admit, Kysen was looking *damn* good.

Irikara chuckled softly as she sipped more wine. "That stands to be seen, now doesn't it?" She was waiting to see Darian's nakedness for the first time, until then, she was withholding judgment.

Again, Darian began to stroke Kysen as he suckled his neck. Slowly he began to maneuver himself between Kysen's legs, kissing and sucking his way downward. His lips parted as he lowered his mouth over the engorged tip of Kysen's erection. The ancient vampire gasped and arched, hands instinctively going for Darian's head, fingers running through the luxurious silky, black locks. Darian's fingers worked over Kysen's nipples as his lips, throat and tongue worked over the hardness in his mouth. He continued to suckle and fondle him until he sensed his climax nearing.

"Do not let him release yet," Irikara ordered.

Darian pulled away just before the point of no return. "I was not going to, my Goddess," he said as he watched Kysen tremble before him. His Master fought to regain composure after the sexual tease and his toned abdomen was constricted as he pushed back his orgasm. Darian rose to his feet and finished undressing, removing his thin linen shirt, then he slid his fingers under the waistband of his pants and pushed them down. Stepping out of them, he shuffled the clothing out of the way with his foot. His own impressive manhood bobbed before him, uncut and ready.

"Mmmm, indeed he is a God among lesser men," Irikara agreed, smiling at Darian's masculine perfection.

One of Irikara's male servants approached Darian holding a jar of lubricant on a gold tray. His eyes were glazed with lust as he took in both vampires' beauty. Darian dipped his hand into the jar, scooping up some of the contents and rubbed it on himself, massaging his erection at the same time. The muscles in his pecs jumped underneath the skin as he brought waves of pleasure throughout his loins. He took another helping of the lubricant and kneeling down, spread the gel in and around Kysen's opening. Both men moaned with pleasure—one in receiving and the other in giving. Once Darian was satisfied, he guided himself inside his Master, moaning as he did. His eyes closed and his mouth opened as he was engulfed in sensual heat and tightness. Kysen arched, driving his hips forward, pushing Darian deeper into him. They began to grind against each other causing their bodies to rock together. Darian stroked inside him with the skillful rhythm of a man who had had centuries of practice and enjoyment in the act of lovemaking. Kysen began to pull him even closer, when Darian seized his arms, pushing them over his head and pressing them to the cushion. Kysen couldn't help but smile at his child who was taking a more aggressive position at the moment.

"You think you're in control," Kysen panted.

"Who's on top," Darian smiled as he drove himself deeper into his Master, causing the other vampire to arch in pleasure, taking them both by surprise. Their lovemaking continued until they both began to feel the familiar sensation of their passion coming to a crest. Darian's pace quickened as Kysen's hips drove forward harder. Suddenly, both men belted out their spent passions as the sensation of the lovemaking seemed to fill the room. Darian's head was thrown back, his eyes closed as he grunted and panted, riding his orgasm at full force. Kysen's body quaked with pleasure as he moaned and panted. Once neither man could give no more, Darian collapsed on top of Kysen, struggling to catch his breath.

"Well, that pleased me greatly," Irikara said. "And from the quickened pulses and the heightened arousal in this room, I sense that I am not the only one pleased by what we just saw."

Natasha's face was as red as it could get as the blood under her skin darkened her cheeks. She had been holding on to her wine glass so tightly, she was surprised it didn't break. Both Xavier and Adan were breathing heavily, but both men stayed in their knelt positions, as Irikara never gave them permission to rise. Finally, Darian rolled over, falling beside Kysen on the cushion.

"Your own lovers are so stimulated after watching the two of you, they looked to be about ready to burst," Irikara said with a wicked laugh.

Kysen rolled over, looking at his Master and Maker. "My Goddess, have we satisfied you?"

"Oh, indeed you have, come here, the both of you … as you are," she said, her eyes glinting as she watched them approach her, the thickness between their legs softening and bouncing with each step they took.

Both vampires knelt at her feet, heads bowed.

"You've done well. I now see why my Kysen chose you as his child, Darian. For giving me such pleasure, I offer you this one time only, a gift so rare, so precious, men have started wars over it."

"Thank you, my Goddess," Darian repeated the title Kysen had called her. It seemed to please her even more.

She gave Natasha a smile as she caressed the side of their faces, running her fingers along their chins, lifting their faces to her. "Drink."

Shocked and trembling with anticipation, both men gently took her proffered hands into theirs, pressing their mouths against the delicate skin. Irikara released a short gasp as their fangs broke through her flesh. Darian moaned loudly as he gripped her wrist all the harder, the sound muffled by her skin as he sucked greedily of her blood, taking in as much as he could. Kysen sucked softly, drinking the ancient blood with sheer pleasure. When he could take no more, he pulled away, regretfully. His body hummed with the new potent power infusing with it and he knew Darian was experiencing the same thing but on a grander scale as it was his first time drinking from their original Fount.

Irikara chuckled as she watched Darian cling harder to her arm. "Young ones always have a hard time releasing, even though they can take no more. Enough," she told him. Darian continued sucking, unable to pull himself free. "Enough." With the slightest flick of her wrist, she sent Darian airborne, crashing into one of the white and gold-laced marble columns before landing with a hard thump onto the marble floor. The pain and shock of the impact helped him ease out of his bloodlust but the room was still spinning as he leaned his back against the column for support. He sat there, dazed, sated and aching waiting for his vision to clear. His entire being vibrated with an energy and power he couldn't possibly define or fathom. He had never in his life felt as powerful as he felt now and he was delirious and giddy with the sensation as he sat there recuperating.

Irikara's skin healed instantly and she beckoned for more wine. Her servant poured her another glass and she settled back onto her divan. "I already know why you've come to my home," she said, getting to the point, finally.

"Will you grant us a small amount of your ancient and powerful blood so that we may cure Darian's human lover?" Kysen asked, still kneeling beside her feet.

"No." Irikara took a sip of her wine.

Xavier wanted to ask her "why not?", he wanted to beg her to help but he didn't want to risk the threat of being killed. He looked at Darian, who still seemed to be getting his bearings after having been thrashed against the thick marble column. Not to mention, he appeared to be drunk from the blood he'd drank. Xavier wondered if Darian would be much help to them at this moment.

"Irikara–" Kysen began, but a stern and intense glare from Irikara quieted him. He lowered his head again.

"Are you challenging me, Kysen?" Irikara asked.

"No, my Goddess," he replied, head still bowed.

"I will not give this insignificant human one drop of my blood."

"I thought you liked me?" Natasha asked, unable to remain silent.

"Whatever gave you that ridiculous impression?" Irikara asked; an amused expression on her face.

"Well, there wasn't much, but you did offer me wine and you wanted me to sit next to you," she answered innocently.

Irikara chuckled. "It gave me pleasure to have you near me as you watched your lover bed his Maker. I could feel your anger and jealousy as well as your lust and I found that entertaining. That's really what humans are for, to serve us."

Natasha's jaw tightened, but she remained silent, which was torture for her in and of itself.

Irikara continued. "You do realize that he enjoyed being able to be free with another person other than Xavier and yourself, do you not? You humans with your restricted pseudo-morality, limiting yourselves and all of the pleasures you could have. Of course, there are some among you who are enlightened, and your fearful little species has the gall to look down on them. It really is a shame that you constrain yourself so." She turned, looking back at Darian with a lustful smile on her face. "He is a caged sexual beast, they both are and you keep them confined, their lusts never fully quenched leaving their desires ever rampant." She took another sip of her drink.

"That's not true!" Xavier said, unable to withstand the heartbreak he saw in Natasha's eyes. Before he could say another word, he was thrown into the corner of the room by what looked to be an invisible force and knocked unconscious.

Everyone looked at Irikara who hadn't moved, she still sipped her wine. "Be thankful I allowed your lover to keep his head attached, vampire," she said, looking at Darian who had finally regain his sense of self and was now gazing at his child's crumpled form lying on the marble floor. He looked back at Irikara with a mixture of lust, wonder and anger. "The next time one of you speaks without me allowing it, I will kill you," she said.

No one spoke. They barely even bothered breathing, except for those who had to.

"Now, as I was saying … your impending death will only free them, I am sure they know this is the other side of that coin—as they say, 'the silver lining in the clouds.' Regardless, I do not know why any vampire would shackle themselves to such a moody, foolish human in the first place, but it is their choice." She made an offhand gesture. "As I have said, you are not worthy of my blood. Seek out another source. Now, leave my home."

Darian rose from the floor and walked over to Xavier's unconscious form, lifting him in his arms. He was angry and disappointed, not to mention unaware of what his next option was. Adan rose to his feet as did Natasha. She wanted to get away from Irikara as fast as she could and walked briskly towards Darian.

Kysen's jaw tightened as he dared to speak out of term. "My Goddess, can you help us in any w–" A delicate hand applied pressure around his neck, cutting off his words.

Darian stepped toward them, but Irikara forced him to stay where he was as if an invisible wall blocked him from moving forward.

She pulled Kysen closer. "You forget yourself, my child."

"Forgive me, my Goddess," Kysen said through strangled gasps. He could feel his larynx slowly being crushed and the pain was intense.

Irikara looked down at her *Chosen One*, seeing the suffering on his face and her grip softened. She exhaled one long sigh before puncturing holes in her tongue with her fangs. Leaning forward, she kissed him, letting her blood flow into him, healing his injury. Their kiss became more passionate, more desperate, as he crushed her to him. It was as if the others in the room were not there as they kissed each other. Irikara pulled away, her hand gripping Kysen's hair, yanking his head to the side right before she plunged her fangs deeply into his vein. He cried out in a mixture of pleasure and pain, then he began to moan and quake as his body was enrapt with the most indescribable pleasure. He felt another powerful orgasm build inside him with an intensity that shook his entire being before it rushed forward, spilling forth in several waves of ecstasy cascading over him until Irikara released him. Weakened and still shaking, he laid on his side at her feet, struggling to lift himself up.

Irikara smiled down at him. "I'm not done with you yet," she said. She lifted his head, staring into his eyes and Kysen smiled in further anticipation as he climbed to his knees. She settled back against the cushions of the divan as his fingers danced up her leg, pushing the fabric of her sheer skirt up her thighs. With the dominance of a man who was used to taking what he wanted, he parted her thighs and leaned forward pressing his face between her legs. She gasped, one hand holding his head closer as her other hand caressed his muscular back and shoulders. Kysen continued to lick and suck at her tender flesh, bringing her to the height of her ecstasy the way he knew he could. Irikara cried out over and over as her orgasm erupted from her, causing her to thrash against the cushions as Kysen continued to stroke her. When her pleasure began to fade, he pulled away with a satisfied smirk.

"Do you want me inside you, my Goddess?" Kysen asked his chest heaving with the lust he felt for his Maker.

"Do what you know that will please me," Irikara replied.

"As you wish." He smiled as he pushed her down on her divan. He mounted her roughly, gliding himself into her with a force that made Natasha wince.

Natasha hadn't thought she could become more embarrassed or uncomfortable than when she'd watched Darian and Kysen make love, but she'd been wrong. Apparently, immortal beings didn't have any hang-ups about modesty. She looked at the others standing around her and not one looked bashful. As a matter of fact, they all seemed to be aroused by what they saw. Irikara, however growled with unbridled desire as she gripped Kysen's forearms. He pounded into her with an animal's abandoned, driving and rocking against her bringing forth more pleasure.

Right when he knew she was reaching her second climax, he paused. "My love, my Goddess ..." he panted. "I beg of you, help us."

She looked up at him, her hips grinding forward. "You play a dangerous game with me, Kysen."

He drove forward, causing her to moan and both their bodies shuddered with ecstasy. "I only ask for Darian's sake," he said through clinched teeth.

"Because he is to you as you are to me?" she panted.

Kysen nodded, driving hard against her again, causing her to cry out. "He is."

"You'll pay for this," Irikara said then she pulled him down on top of her, pressing his face into her neck.

Kysen understood what she wanted and he sank his fangs deeply, catching the first drop of her precious blood. He drank deeply once again as he continued to ride her. With each swallow, he was gaining the information she was giving him, it all ended with a rush of intense pleasure that spilled over them like magma. He rocked hard against her, his mouth still sealed to her neck as he rode her through their orgasms. Afterwards, he pulled away, collapsing on top of her, panting heavily.

"You're very fortunate I love you so. I would have killed another one of my line who dared to do what you have just done," Irikara whispered into his ear so low, only he could hear her.

Kysen chuckled low, the sound of his voice sending tremors over her flesh. "I owe you, My Goddess."

"Leave my home before I have you flayed," Irikara said, without much conviction.

Kysen rose, leaning over her he dipped down, kissing her once again. She allowed it. Then he climbed off of the divan, recovered his gold toga, and fastened it back into place. He joined the others and they left, driving back to his airplane. Once on board and in the air, they began to speak all at once.

"I can't answer you all at the same time, you know this," Kysen said, staring at them.

"Master, did she help us?" Darian asked, hoping everything that happened wasn't in vain.

Kysen nodded. "To tell you the truth, Darian, I'm rather upset with you."

Darian blinked. "Why? I didn't insult her." He hoped his over-zealousness didn't count as an insult. That, he couldn't help. Her blood was electrifying. It pulled him in and refused to let him go. Never in all of his years of existent had he tasted something so robust, so exquisite, and so pure. Even still, he tingled with sensation from his feeding and he could feel his muscles growing even stronger as well as his mental abilities.

Kysen walked into his bedroom, leaving Darian to ponder his last statement. When he returned several minutes later, dressed in a cream linen shirt and pants set. His hair was damp as he toweled it off. He sat down on one of the comfortable seats and looked at his child. "Have you figured out why I'm upset with you?"

Darian exhaled. "I did what I had to do, Kysen," he said, referring to the blood sample he gave the human scientists.

"No, you did what you wanted to do, resulting in the series of unfortunate events that have followed your rash decision. Because of you, I had to endure such humiliation."

Darian raised both eyebrows. "Was all of it 'such humiliation?'" he asked Kysen in Greek.

The others were silent as they watched the two of them converse. Natasha was actually shocked to hear Darian speaking to Kysen in his native tongue.

Kysen smiled, thinking about the pleasure he shared with both Darian and Irikara. He looked at him. "Well, not *all* of it," he responded in kind.

"Oh *really*?" Adan commented, in English. He understood Greek and couldn't help being slightly agitated. "I had to watch you have sex with two people tonight. If anyone has the right to be pissed it's me ..." His voice trailed off as he thought about the real reason they were there. "I take that back. It's Natasha. She's the reason why we are doing what we're doing. Let's stay focused." He was ready to complain about what he'd seen before he realized what was more important. He understood that what was done was done to save Natasha and he wasn't angry anymore.

Kysen cocked a brow. "Regardless of the reason why I bedded my two lovers, I don't see why you're so upset anyway. We've both bedded the women of your Pride and you've never complained."

Adan smirked. "That's because they belong to me and I have my duties I must perform as king. Allowing you to satisfy some of them isn't as easy for me as you think it is. I'm simply sharing what is mine with you, as you share what is yours with us. I'm committed to our relationship, Kysen." He gave an offhanded gesture. "Like I said, it doesn't matter. Let's move on."

Kysen chuckled. "You were still enticed by what you saw, even though you were angry."

"What part of 'let's move on' are you not getting? Besides,

weren't you talking to Darian," Adan said with a sly smile.

Kysen grunted. "Before you rudely interrupted us—yes." He returned his attention to his child. "Natasha is your human, Darian. The only reason I am extending myself this much is because you belong to me. Had these vampires decided to kill you instead of her, it would have dragged me into a war I'd rather not be engaged in."

"I ... I'm sorry," Darian said, understanding Kysen's anger.

"You're still young, and apparently, rediscovering your humanity has weakened your resolve. You make decisions against your better judgment because of it. Had they killed you, I would have sought to kill them and I may have died in the process. What you do doesn't only effect you, please remember that the next time you decide to play hero," Kysen said. "Now, we are going to Australia, where we will meet with another Fount. Irikara, whose love for me was far greater than her distaste for you ..." he nodded in Natasha's direction. "... has told me through her blood that this Fount has sympathy for the humans. I have to contact him to request permission." He picked up the phone.

"Can't you contact him like you contacted, Irikara?" Warren asked. He watched the ancient vampire, waiting for his response. He also wanted to ask what had happened when the others had gone to visit Irikara. Everyone was in such an uproar when they returned and he could smell Darian and Kysen all over each other and knew what had happened between them. But what was even more curious was Xavier lying unconscious on the sofa.

"No," Kysen answered. "I have no mental link with him. Now, if you please." He made a gesture for them to stay silent, and then he dialed the number and waited for an answer.

"Hello?" A male Australian-accented voice greeted.

"Hello, my name is Kysen Mysah, child of Irikara and I beg your permission to enter your territory so that we may speak with you," Kysen replied in a formal request.

"Irikara told me to expect your call. When you arrive, come directly to my home," he gave them the address of his private airport. "See you then." He ended the call.

Kysen brows creased. "That went better than I expected."

"I was thinking the same thing," Darian said.

"I don't feel so good," Natasha said.

Warren placed his hand on her forehead. "You're getting a fever." He frowned.

"I think I'm going to be sick," Natasha said.

Warren helped her up, taking her to the bathroom, and staying with her as she vomited yellowish bile into the toilet. He wet a towel then pressed it to her face, patting her forehead and cheeks. He pulled her to him, holding her as tightly as he could without crushing her. He hated what she was going through, hated that he couldn't help her.

Darian entered the room. "You should drink some more of my blood. That might make you feel better."

Natasha nodded as he opened a vein, giving her his wrist. She closed her mouth over the wound, sucking the blood into her mouth. Immediately, she could taste the difference in his blood from before he drank from Irikara. His blood was much more powerful now with a flavor that was indescribable but absolutely delicious. When he pulled away, Warren held her back as she reached out for Darian, struggling to get closer to him to feed again. They waited a few minutes until she regained her senses. When they were both satisfied, seeing that her pupils were normal and her breathing had slowed to a calmer pace, Warren let her go.

"I hope I don't become an addict if I live through this," Natasha commented, thinking about all of the vampire blood she had ingested since being infected.

Darian chuckled sadly. He reached out, caressing her face. "I promise to keep my blood under crack prices."

Natasha laughed, thinking about the comparison she had made between the two several years ago. She leaned forward, hugging him tightly.

He wrapped his arms around her, kissing the top of her head softly. "Don't give up, we'll figure something out," he whispered.

After a while, the three of them reentered the seating area of the airplane.

"Feeling better?" Kysen asked Natasha.

She nodded. "I still feel a little sick, but not like I was."

"We have another long flight ahead of us, at least sixteen hours with me piloting," Kysen informed.

"I'm glad I've gotten used to flying. I still don't like it much, though," Natasha said, settling down on one of the sofas.

"This is the most traveling you've ever done at one time, isn't it?" Darian asked.

She nodded. "The worst part is, we were in beautiful Egypt, I wanted to see so much and we were their less than a day." She pouted.

"I'll take you back," Darian said, kissing her hand.

"Kysen, I've been meaning to ask you, was there really a great flood?" Adan asked.

Kysen frowned. "Wasn't this question asked of me before?"

Adan shook his head. "Not by me. So was there one?"

Kysen chuckled. "Where one of every animal had to be rounded up and saved?"

"Yeah, like that."

"Not to my knowledge. There was a 'great flood' before I was born, but not of a biblical level."

"How was life during that time?" Natasha asked.

"Your lover over there has asked me these same questions in the past, please ask him what you want to know about me," Kysen said, growing annoyed with the many questions.

"I'm sorry," Natasha said. She had forgotten who he was, how his personality was. He seemed so loving and giving, but then she reminded herself, this was all for Darian, not her.

Darian smiled. "I'll tell you soon, when I'm in a better mood to tell such tales."

Natasha nodded, accepting his response. She turned on the television, tuning to her favorite show. Some of them watched TV, while others napped to pass the time away. When the sun rose, Xavier and Darian rested. Kysen continue to fly the plane, even though he looked to be sleeping.

Warren looked at him. "Kysen?"

"I'm awake, you'll know if I'm not when this aircraft plummets to the ground," Kysen said.

"No talk about plummeting planes, please," Natasha said. She was getting sleepy and had curled up on the sofa. Two hours before, she had contacted her parents, they weren't doing very well. Her mother spoke very slowly on the phone and her father had been sleeping. Miko had told her that even with her blood, they looked to have only a few days left at the most. Heartbroken, Natasha thanked her for her help. She then had called Elise, wanting to talk to her son and check in on them. Elise told her the children were all right, they loved and missed their parents, but she and her Pride were keeping them preoccupied. Elise had wanted to know how things were going for her and she told her. Natasha could hear the pain in her friend's voice as they spoke. Not wanting to hear the tears in Elise's voice anymore, she thanked her most graciously for all of her help before ending the call. Now she sat in the chair, forcing herself to fall asleep.

Warren looked at her. "Do you want to talk?" he asked.

Natasha shook her head and wiped away the tears that streaked her cheeks. "Not really," she said sadly.

"All right, I have questions about what went down in Egypt, but I'll just ask them later."

"That would probably be best," Natasha said, knowing she had a few choice words she wanted to say about her experience in Egypt that she didn't want Kysen to hear. They decided to get some sleep for the rest of the hours they were in the sky. All except Kysen.

CHAPTER SIXTEEN

AKAMA

When they arrived in Sydney, Australia, there was an SUV waiting to pick them up. Already loaded in the SUV were two coffins which Kysen put Darian and Xavier in. Adan, Natasha and Warren climbed into the back seat, while Kysen climbed into the passenger side, he looked at the driver.

"I'm to take you directly to his mansion," the driver informed.

"Very well," Kysen said.

They drove in silence until they pulled up to a beautiful and modern mansion. The lawn was manicured to perfection with beautiful exotic flowers and plants placed around the property giving the landscape a majestic appearance. The mansion itself was a three-story white and silver marble wonder. French windows and doors were covered with beautiful cream curtains and they were large enough to allow a lot of natural light to come through. There was a large angelic fountain carved from marble in front of the mansion which the driveway rounded. The driver pulled up and turned off the engine. They all climbed out and walked toward the back to retrieve the coffins. Kysen carried Darian's while Warren carried Xavier's. The driver led them to a large room with a seventy-two inch screen television, enough seating for twenty people and a very powerful vampire Fount lounging on one of the sofas.

"You may leave us, thank you, Roland," the vampire said, dismissing his servant.

Kysen placed the coffin very gently on the floor, as did Warren.

The ancient vampire rose and turned. Like Irikara, he was unnaturally beautiful, with cheekbones to kill and die for. His brown eyes scanned over the faces of his guests and his perfectly shaped mouth parted in a beautiful smile. He wasn't exceptionally tall, but he wasn't short either, at least five foot eight. His body was well-muscled and his hair was cut short close to his scalp. His beautiful, flawless dark-chocolate skin seemed to shine under the bright lights, which was almost mesmerizing. For all intent and purposes, he dressed very modern and modest, wearing a green pullover t-shirt, blue jeans and black loafers.

"Welcome to my home, please make yourselves comfortable." He gestured to the comfortable brown sofas and chairs adorning the room.

"I thank you for seeing us," Kysen said, still taken aback by the personality of this particular vampire Fount. He had never met one older than himself who seemed so free spirited and friendly.

"Before we get started, why don't we wake up your young ones, shall we?" The Fount walked over to the two coffins.

Kysen, possessively stepped closer to Darian's coffin, standing in front of it.

The Fount smiled. "Protective of him, I see. There are no windows in this room. He will be protected from the sun."

Kysen nodded, and stepped aside, allowing the other vampire access to Darian's coffin.

The Fount opened both coffins, looked at the vampires resting, and he cocked a brow. "Absolutely lovely, indeed."

He rose as both Darian and Xavier's eyes shot open. They blinked knowing they were awakened by another's will and not the sunset. Each climbed out of their coffin.

"I've released you from your resting states because I'd rather not have to repeat myself at sunset which is a few hours from now. Please, have a seat," The Fount said.

Still in shock, Darian sat down on the sofa beside Kysen and Natasha. Kysen was the only one of them who didn't seem to be in complete awe of the power the other vampire possessed. They figured it was because he was used to it, having been turned by Irikara.

"My name is Akama. I don't need to read your minds to know why you are here. I know what you went through and I'm sorry my kind hurt you this way," Akama, the ancient Fount said to Natasha.

"Thank you for saying that," Natasha said, not sure what else to say.

"Will you help us?" Xavier asked.

"You want my blood?"

"Just enough to see if it can cure her," Darian said.

"If it can cure her, it can cure everyone else infected," Akama said.

"We're hoping so. Her parents are also infected and don't have much longer to live," Xavier said.

Natasha winced and lowered her head, trying hard not to cry when she thought about what her parents were going through.

Akama nodded. "Very well, let see if this works."

"You're going to help, just like that?" Adan asked; shocked that he seemed to be so much more down to earth than the other ancient vampires he'd met, present company in Kysen included.

"You're expecting me to demand *Homage* then wait for you to beg and plead for my help?" Akama asked.

"Well … yeah." Adan looked at him.

"I'm not that arrogant. The way I see it, you've been through enough in this past year. Some things should come without struggle, such as help," Akama said as he walked toward Natasha. He leaned down in front of her and with his nail he opened a vein on his wrist. "Hurry now before the wound closes."

Natasha leaned forward, locking her mouth over the flow. The first taste of his blood caused her to moan aloud. She wrapped her arms around his arm, pulling him closer to her. She sucked as hard as she could on the most amazing thing she'd ever tasted. Akama's blood was better than Kysen's, better than Darian's, better than sex. Unfortunately, she was beginning to feel a stirring inside her stomach, and then pain shot through her intestines along with a vicious wave of nausea forcing her to pull away. She gagged and vomited a stream of blood on the floor. Akama had moved out of the way, avoiding the bile. Xavier rubbed her back as her stomach purged the blood from her system.

"I must say that I wasn't expecting that," Akama commented, perplexed by what he was seeing.

"None of us were. It seemed like it should work," Warren said.

Natasha shrank back from the vomit, cuddling closer to Xavier, who held her tenderly. She actually felt worse after having tasted the Fount's blood. Sweat began to seep from her pores and cold chills rippled through her body as her temperature rose.

"Perhaps you should give her your blood now, I'm guessing yours didn't have such an adverse effect," Akama said to Darian, who was still dumbfounded to see that Akama's powerful blood failed to cure her.

Darian nodded, cutting his wrist, he gave her his blood once more. Natasha was almost afraid to drink it, but she had to try anyway. Tentatively, she put her mouth on the wound and sucked very gently. His blood didn't sicken her like Akama's did, but it wasn't as effective as it had been before. She still felt cold chills after he pulled his wrist away, but her fever began to subside a little.

One of Akama's human servants entered the room. "Yes, Master?" answering the ancient vampire mental call.

"Please clean this up," Akama said, pointing to the bloody mess on the floor.

"Yes, Master," the servant said, leaving the room. He returned a few minutes later with a mop and bucket and began cleaning.

Natasha shivered slightly and moaned. Her stomach still ached, but she wasn't feeling as bad as she did when Akama's blood was inside her.

Xavier looked over Natasha. "It's not working as well as it was," he observed, tossing a glance to Darian, who looked to be as concerned as he was.

"We'll wait a few hours and then try again. Kysen …?"

The other vampire looked at him. "Yes?"

"Would you be willing to give her your blood once more?" Darian asked.

Kysen opened his mouth to say something he knew would probably crush his child's heart, so he decided against it. By the look of relief on Darian's face, he knew it was the right decision. "When the time comes, I'll give it to her."

Darian put his hand on Kysen's. "Thank you, Master, for everything you're doing."

Kysen nodded.

"What do we do now?" Warren asked as he watched the human

servant mop up the last puddle of vomit.

"How many times are you going to present that question?" Kysen asked, slightly annoyed with the young shifter, whose presence there seemed unnecessary to him.

"Until we find a cure," Warren replied. "I love Natasha, Kysen. She's one of my best friends and I don't like watching her suffer and I don't want her to die. I'm trying my best to help wherever I can."

Kysen huffed. "I need to rest. I am more irritable than I would like to be right now." That much he was certain of. Even being around Darian was beginning to annoy him at the moment.

The servant finished cleaning and left.

"I want the vampire who did this to her!" Xavier growled as his anger flared. "We find him, we find the others and we can stop them and force them to give us the cure."

"If we're going to go in that direction, we're going to need a lot more supernaturals than just us," Adan said.

Akama nodded. "The vampire who infected you and the one you've vowed revenge on," he gestured to Xavier. "His name is, Roycean... well, just Royce these days. He's over eight-thousand years old and Thallos's *Chosen One* and lover. There isn't a vampire among you who could challenge him ... well, challenge him and win, that is."

Even Kysen cocked his eyebrows when he heard the other vampire's age.

"We have to do something; I won't sit back helplessly and watch her die," Xavier said through gritted teeth as he struggled to contain his rage.

"Are you're willing to risk your lives? You may not survive an encounter with them," Akama said.

"I've never been afraid of death and I've always believed some things are worth fighting and dying for. If I can risk my life to defend my territory, I can do that and more to defend those I love," Xavier answered.

"She is the mother of your children, which I find unique. Not only that, she is the link to your humanity, you love her very much," Akama said, crossing one leg over the other.

"We do," Darian said.

Akama nodded. "At least you know what it's going to take to save your human."

"The way I see it, this is one hell of a virus. I'm willing to bet the cure is in the blood of the one who designed it. He's making sure the ball stays in his court," Warren said. He hated to admit it, but he was actually impressed with the ingenuity of how the virus was created.

"It makes sense, when Thallos said the 'cure was in our blood' I assumed it was in the blood of all vampires. But then you all sought my help and that made me wonder if the cure was in a Fount's blood specifically," Akama said. "However, that assessment was incorrect as well."

"Um, who's Thallos?" Natasha asked. "You've mentioned the name before, I'm just curious."

Akama chuckled. "He is my greatest and oldest friend and the vampire who announced the message. He is the Fount of the European line."

"The blond guy?! That son-of-a-bitch!" Natasha said, and then she looked at Akama, who was looking at her with amusement. "I'm sorry. He's your friend, but ..."

Akama waved his hand dismissively. "No need to apologize. I can't blame you, as you only know him as the *son-of-a-bitch* who infected you with a seemingly incurable disease. I, on the other hand, know him as the *son-of-a-bitch* who still owes me an Anaconda Pavilion SGX."

"Do you agree with what he's doing?" Natasha asked after learning that Akama and Thallos were the best of friends; no doubt the two loved each other very much.

Akama thought about her question and then he answered. "I don't agree with the method in which he's choosing to fight this injustice. However, I do agree that it is time for a drastic change."

"I hate to think of all the humans dying out there, children, babies … I know from my own experience that most vampires don't really regard human life as precious or something worth saving past their own bloodlust, but if we're in a position to help these innocent people, not just me, I think we should," Natasha said, looking at the others.

"Vampires aren't the only creatures who've had a blatant disregard for human life. Humans also seem to lack compassion for one another," Kysen said. "Was it not humans who tested syphilis on other unsuspecting humans? What about the Crusades, slavery, the Trail of Tears ... the Holocaust? Was it not humans who've destroyed whole cities simply for political and financial gain? Is it not humans who strap bombs to their bodies and then walk into a shopping mall filled with hundreds of innocents with hopes of taking as many lives with them into the afterlife as possible? Humans are just as guilty of mass slaughter as anyone else, if not more."

"That's true, Kysen, I can't deny that. But there are still humans who fight even knowing that the odds are stacked up against them. They fight knowing they might die. They fight against injustice and they've been fighting for supernaturals since the exposure. Now they are fighting to survive, who will fight for them?" Natasha asked, looking at the others.

Akama whistled. "I see why they are in love with you. You're a feisty one; a tiny little spitfire even in your current state. I want to help the human race, but I am only one Fount. If Thallos has joined up with others then he'll see my interference as a threat to his plan. He'll try to stop me, of course," he said.

"You think he'll try to kill you even though you're his friend?" Natasha asked.

"He won't go that far and there are reasons why. Nonetheless, he is resolute in this matter, so he may try to stop me by any other means necessary. He will not let anyone, friend, lover or foe get in the way of his mission. He has always been this way. I can't take him on alone or even with your group at my side."

"So what if we can get other Founts to join you?" Natasha suggested.

Akama laughed. "Can you imagine requesting Irikara's assistance in this fight?"

Natasha looked off to the side, and then she frowned. "After meeting her, I don't even want to see Egypt on a postcard right now."

Akama laughed.

Kysen growled. "Watch your words, human."

"Kysen, you have to admit, Irikara wasn't very nice to her," Darian said, hoping to calm his Master down.

"There is no reason for her *to* be. Irikara is a Goddess, be grateful she bothered to help you at all. She *and* you would both do well to remember that," Kysen stated, giving his young child a stern stare, which said he would not abide any negative comments about Irikara.

"My apologies, Kysen. I didn't mean to anger you," Darian said.

"Me neither," Natasha added, hoping to calm him down. She really didn't want to upset Darian's Master. He had been one of the key players in trying to save her life. Besides, if they were going to seek out the creators of the virus, she would need him even more.

Akama smiled at Kysen. "I remember when Irikara first told me about you. Her *Chosen One*, the man who was her physical counterpart. She first discovered you, a merchant trader in Egypt, and a very successful one at that. She said your beauty was remarkable and the very fact that you shared the same eye color enticed her."

"Is that so?" Kysen asked, intrigued.

"We watched you one night. You were sleeping off a full day's drunk, having recently lost your woman and child during the birth. She told me then she would turn you, make you a 'God among gods.' But first she would prepare you for an eternity of pleasure. That's definitely Irikara's way."

Kysen watched the other vampire, complete awe plastered on his face as he had never told another soul about his mate and son, not even Darian. This vampire knew his most intimate details and he wondered just how much more he knew.

"You were married?" Darian asked, equally stunned.

Kysen had to break his gaze from Akama to focus on Darian's words. "What?"

"You were married?" Darian repeated.

Kysen cleared his throat as he gathered his composure. "I was and that was a long time ago," he said, not wanting to elaborate.

"They died?" Darian prodded gently.

Kysen turned away, closing his eyes as if he could shut out the memory. "Darian please ..." he said, not wanting to remember the pain and heartbreak he endured at such a great loss. His hands trembled slightly as he rubbed them together and he looked at them in amazement. After all these years, the memory of his woman and child dying that night still had such an effect on him.

Darian regarded Kysen. "I'm sorry. I will not ask again," he said, seeing the pain in Kysen's expression was painful for him as well and he decided he wouldn't pry anymore for both their sakes.

"Ah, I apologize if I reopened an old wound. I sometimes forget my manners," Akama said. He walked over to Kysen, placing a gentle hand on his shoulder comfortingly. A few seconds later, his servant entered the room, Akama turned to address him. The servant bowed and announced that the lunch was ready then he left.

Surprised, Warren looked Akama. "You had lunch prepared for us?"

"I assumed you'd be hungry when you arrived, especially being shape-shifters. Your kind seems to eat every four hours," Akama joked. "Well, we should eat, while you two rest." He gestured toward Darian and Xavier.

"This is actually amazing to me, as it's been centuries since I've been awake during the day this long," Darian said.

"It's my will that's keeping you awake," Akama said.

"As much as I wish I could stay this way, my body is rebelling. I feel drained and my limbs feel heavy … it's a strange sensation," said Darian as he flexed his fingers in an attempt to eliminate the numbness.

"The sun will set in the next four hours, so I'll let you rest. Why don't you make yourselves comfortable," Akama said.

"Do we have to?" Xavier asked, still as stunned as Darian was that they were awake during the afternoon. That, and the fact that he did not want to leave Natasha's side.

"If you don't, you really will be too exhausted to function even after the sun *has* set. Young vampires need their rest, it's important. I only released you so that you could see if my blood cured your human lover. Please, lay down because I'm going to relinquish my will over you."

Reluctantly, both Darian and Xavier lay on the sofas in the den. Natasha walked over to both of them, kissing each man.

"I wish you could see the sun," she said, pleased to see them up and about so early. She gave them a smile that couldn't hide the sadness she felt as she thought about the things they couldn't enjoy, such as feeling the heat of the sun on their skin.

"One day we will," Darian said, knowing what thought saddened her. He gave her a reassuring smile.

Akama released his will and both Darian and Xavier fell back into their resting state. Natasha backed away, staring at the two men. Now, she couldn't wait until sunset when she could talk and be with them again.

"Shall we?" Akama asked, gesturing toward the door.

Natasha allowed him to guide her out of the room and he led them to his dining room where the meal was spread out. The table was covered with platters of choice cuts of roast, ham and chicken. There were two bowls of chicken and potato soups, various cheeses, crackers, freshly baked bread, French fries, fruit and vegetables.

"This smells great," Warren said.

"Then let's not let it get cold," Akama said. He took a seat followed by the shifters and Natasha. They began to make their plates.

Akama looked at Kysen who stood in the doorway, leaning against the frame. "You don't eat human food?" he asked as he took a bite of his chicken sandwich.

Kysen shook his head. "It is not to my liking, no."

Akama chuckled. "You're still young and I'm sure you don't enjoy the evacuation process, is that it?"

Kysen cocked an eyebrow at being referred to as "young". He tried hard not to scoff at the comment. Akama *was* four-thousand years older than him, as was Irikara. He told himself, to them, he was young.

Akama laughed again, this time, more boisterously. "You're not used to being thought of as *young*, are you?" He sighed. "Well, at six-thousand, I suppose not."

"To answer your question, I *do not* like the process of eliminating food from my body. Not to mention, compared to the taste of blood, human food simply pales. It holds no interest to me."

"I can tell you've recently fed from Irikara, for your age you are extremely powerful. That's the benefits of not only feeding from a Fount, but being turned by one. You automatically had the advantage over any other vampire who wasn't. I'm sure that accounts for a good portion of your blind devotion to Irikara."

Kysen shifted his weight from one foot to the other. His chest swelled with a deep intake of breath. "I would prefer if we do not discuss my feelings regarding Irikara."

"Let's talk about your feelings about Darian, then," Akama began. "He's obviously your favorite. I don't know of many vampire Masters who would go to the length of trouble you've gone through for one they turned that they don't have strong feelings for."

"Your point?" Kysen asked, one eyebrow rising.

"Natasha wants to cure the humans who are suffering and dying from this disease, as do I. I'll need help–"

"–I do not care what happens to the humans dying of this disease," Kysen injected.

Akama's expression grew hard and his jaw tightened as he fought to contain his anger. The others remained silent as they felt the powerful aura of the Fount spread across the room toward Kysen. "Do not take my generosity or my calm demeanor for weakness. I will not tolerate rudeness, don't interrupt me again."

Kysen stiffened, his features contorted in pain as he nodded. "Forgive my insolence," he said in a strained voice. Akama's aura had swirled itself around him, encasing him in heat and intense pressure. It finally dissipated, leaving him cold and gasping for air.

Adan was surprised to see Kysen display any signs of subservience. In the six months that he'd known him, the ancient vampire didn't seem to possess a humble bone in his body. He knew this entire situation was probably enraging Kysen beyond his limits, but he was impressed with how well he was adapting to not being the top vampire in the room.

Akama nodded, accepting the apology. "As I was saying, we need to gather as much power on our side as possible--"

"--I'll support you," Natasha said, and then she closed her mouth tightly, realizing she interrupted him as well. "I'm sorry, go on."

Amused, he continued. "With Natasha wanting to help, Xavier will get involved, Darian will then follow. Where does that leave you, Kysen?"

Kysen focused on the powerful vampire, noticing how he was manipulating the situation. "You believe if I join your crusade that

Irikara would follow, thus giving you her support in the process."

Akama smiled. "I've known her for nine-thousand years, we have been lovers and are friends, but I know she will not lift a finger to help the humans or our cause. She, however, will not let *you* die if she could prevent it. Now I don't know how many supernaturals Thallos has working with him, but I'm willing to bet he has eyes everywhere. How else would he have known that Darian gave the humans the sample in the first place?"

"I was wondering that myself," Warren said.

"If we are to challenge him, we'll need to have the more impressive combination of power on our side in order to force him to back down. With Irikara on our side, we might be able to get other Founts to join us," Akama said.

"Irikara has that much influence?" Adan asked respectfully.

Akama chuckled. "Being the only female Fount, I'm sure you can guess what power she wields."

A few eyebrows rose in contemplation.

"However, if and when we attain this cure, I still want to continue the fight for equality. I don't want things to go back to the way they were. We need new laws that are without bigotry or all of our efforts, good or bad, would have been in vain," Akama said.

"We should contact the Council and see where they stand in all of this?" Adan said, taking another bite of his meal.

"Since they are the ones who represent us, that is a smart move," Akama agreed.

"So does this mean we have to go back to Egypt?" Natasha asked with a hint of disappointment.

"It does. We'll need her most definitely. It's not going to be easy to convince other Founts to join us. Most vampires who are that old are like Irikara or him." Akama pointed toward Kysen, who only smirked.

"Who's going to contact her?" Natasha asked.

The room grew silent. Everyone figured it would be either Akama or Kysen who would make the call.

"I will," Akama said.

"What if she demands you to pay *Homage*?" Warren asked.

The Fount chuckled. "She will not ask that of me, we are of equal power and stature. However, to appease her, it would be in our best interest to present her with a gift."

"Like jewelry or something?" Natasha asked.

"Or something." Akama smiled.

"You're talking about giving her a human servant, aren't you?" Adan asked.

"That would be a gift she'd deem worthy," Akama answered.

"No way, I'd rather pay *Homage* than trade humans like baseball cards," Natasha said. She hadn't enjoyed paying *Homage* to Irikara before, but she surely didn't want to subject a human to her servitude.

Akama smiled. "The human would come from my household, they are already in servitude." He didn't have to read her mind to understand the meaning behind her words.

"Then they should stay with you," Adan said. He was willing to bet Akama was a much kinder Master than Irikara.

"Humans have always served Irikara with pleasure, they worship her. I see nothing wrong with that offering," Kysen said in defense of Irikara.

"I do," Natasha said. She had gotten used to vampires having human servants. She understood it was a part of their world, but she couldn't abide treating these trusting humans in such a callous manner, not when there was another option to choose from. "We pay her *Homage* instead."

"Would you be willing to pay *Homage*, since you've so brazenly opted for that option?" Kysen asked her.

"I would."

"And if Irikara had any interest in you at all, you would be. No, Natasha, it is not you who would be making the sacrifices, it will be those around you," Kysen said.

"I'd do it," Adan said.

"Me too," Warren added.

Kysen scoffed. "Don't you need your lover's permission first before you jump into the deep end of the pool?" he asked, looking at Warren.

Warren's jaw tightened and before he could speak, Akama interjected.

"This is turning ugly," he said and looked at Kysen, "Not to mention it's unproductive."

Kysen turned to leave, when Akama called out to him. He stopped at the mention of his name. "Yes?"

"I really could use your support, a powerful vampire such as yourself," Akama said, hoping to appeal to Kysen's vanity.

Kysen turned. "If they threaten Darian, then I'll extend my support."

"They already have, by hurting me," Natasha said.

"Darian wasn't physically harmed in their attack against you. Emotionally, he's been hurt, but it's nothing he won't recover from if you happen to die in spite of our efforts." Kysen studied her expression; he wanted to make sure she understood that she was not his priority.

Natasha stiffened as if she'd been shot in the heart. His words were harsh and left her speechless.

Adan watched as Natasha's shoulders sank and her eyes moistened. He turned to his lover with a disapproving scowl. "Kysen, that was cruel," he said.

The ancient vampire looked at his lover. "Perhaps it *was* cruel, but it was also true. As much as Darian means to me, if I lose him, the pain I'll experience will be indescribable. However, I will survive it and it will be the same for him."

"But you're going to do whatever is in your power to prevent that, right? Darian's only doing the same thing," Adan said.

"If Darian pursues this endeavor, I will be there to protect him and only him," Kysen replied.

Akama nodded. "Fair enough."

"What about me?" Adan asked.

"I will not let you go with me into battle. I can't be concerned with the safety of both you and him. Besides, your Pride needs you more than I do. The only reason why you are here is because Irikara requested your presence," Kysen said.

"It's nice to know you care," Adan said with a devilish smirk.

Kysen huffed but remained silent.

"Since you're on board, would you contact your Maker for us?" Akama asked.

Kysen sighed. "She may very well refuse me. I have already tested her patience once in gaining assistance to find you."

"I'm willing to bet she has a little more tolerance for you than most," Akama said.

Kysen frowned. "Very well." He turned, leaving the room going back into the den where Darian and Xavier rested. He looked down at his child, his young love ... his *Chosen One.* "If you've got at least one sane cell in your brain, I hope you listen to it and stay out of this feud between the humans and the supernaturals."

Squatting down, he brushed a strand of hair from Darian's beautiful face. He stared at him reflectively. "You will not, though? You will protect Xavier who will protect that foolish woman and I will have to protect you. Sometimes you are more trouble than you are worth ..." He sighed and chuckled. "... I suppose that saying would actually hold some weight if you did not mean the world to me." He kissed Darian's lips then sought out another chair, making himself comfortable. Mentally, he contacted Irikara.

My Goddess, I have another request, he beseeched.

Akama's blood did not work? she asked.

No, my Goddess, it did not. Darian will no doubt take actions that would put him in harm's way in order to save her.

And what will you do?

He is my love, my child ... I will protect him with my life.

I forbid it! If he chooses to pursue fruitless quests, that is of his consequence. I will not risk losing you because of his stubborn foolishness. Humans die. Either on this day or the next, he will lose her eventually because she is mortal. It is high time both he and Xavier accept that truth.

My Goddess, you cannot ask me to stand by and do nothing to protect him, knowing what he means to me?

I do not ask it, I demand it. You will not follow him to his death. Thallos will kill you if you dare to challenge him.

I will not risk losing Darian.

Than perhaps you should confine him until this feud is over.

He will never forgive me if I allow Natasha to die ... and more importantly, Xavier, as he is Darian's Chosen One.

I will confine you, then.

Then I will never forgive you for letting Darian die when you could have helped me save him.

Why now *do you insist on protecting him when he has been without you watching over him for eight-hundred years?*

I have always watched over him as you have watched over me. He was never in any real danger during that time. This is something much more different.

Do not go.

I must.

You enrage me, Kysen.

It is not my intentions, my Goddess. You know my devotion to you, my love has no bounds. I ask you please, help us.

There was a long pause before she responded.

I grant you permission to see me. I will have a promise as well.

A promise?

One that must be accepted on pain of death if it is not kept.

As you wish, my Goddess.

Kysen ended his mental connection and closed his eyes, resting his mind as well as his body.

***

"He's out cold," Adan said, after checking in on Kysen. He returned to his chair.

"I'm actually happy he took his ass to sleep," Warren said. "I haven't been enjoying my time with him, that's for sure."

"He's under a lot of stress and he's not use to it. I admit, he's handling it badly," Adan said.

"You must be seeing another side of him we don't," Natasha said.

"I have. He has his arrogance, most vampires do. But I've also seen his kindness, compassion, gentleness and the measure of his love," Adan answered. "And believe it or not, he has a pretty good sense of humor."

"I don't believe that shit," Warren jested.

"Oh it's true, it's true. He has me laughing a lot," Adan said.

"I know I see it in what he's willing to do for Darian," Natasha stated.

Adan nodded. "It's probably good that he's resting now. He hasn't really rested in nearly two days and when he did manage to catch wink, that's all it was. It's no wonder he's so irritable."

"There is that, but I'm assuming he's used to instant gratification. Vampires, in spite of being immortal beings, really have no patience for the 'hurry-up and wait' moments of life," Akama said, taking a bite of his roast.

"He's probably frustrated that very little progress has been made and only more drama seems to loom ahead," Adan commented as he finished off another sandwich.

The others thought about what they said and couldn't help but agree. Kysen wasn't the only one frustrated by the way things were going. They all wanted Natasha and her parents cured, but nobody wanted it more than Natasha herself. Getting sicker after drinking Akama's blood was a setback that she wasn't prepared for, and she found herself fighting off despair all over again as his blood was the one suspected cure they had all been hoping for.

After finishing his meal, Akama rose from the table. "We should leave but one more thing before we go. I want to prepare you."

"Prepare us for what?" Natasha asked.

"You have already visited Irikara and are aware of her expectations. Please understand that other Founts will be like her in the sense that they will not acknowledge you unless they want to. Do not expect them to engage you in conversation as many feel the offspring of each line is beneath them," Akama warned.

"Well, that's a comforting thought," Warren commented.

"It really isn't. However, vampire society is a hierarchy. The most powerful rule all," Akama said.

"So basically we should expect to be ignored and we shouldn't put up a fuss about it, right?" Adan asked.

"Exactly. There are sayings in America I believe that goes like this: 'Children should stay in a child's place' or 'Children should be seen and not heard.' That is how most Founts and ancient vampires feel," Akama said. "You don't want to demand their attention if they aren't giving it freely."

"All right, I get it. I don't think it will be a problem. As long as they help us, I can stay quiet. I think it will be interesting to see how you all interact with each other," Warren said.

Akama chuckled. "You may be disappointed. Some of us can be quite juvenile in spite of our advanced years."

"Now I *really* want to see how you all are together," Warren said with a little laugh.

"But wait, we don't even know if Irikara will see us yet, Kysen didn't say," Natasha pointed out.

"Telepathically, she has told me she's expecting us. The less time we waste, the faster we can help you," Akama said, walking out of the dining room back into the den where the three vampires were resting.

The others followed him. Warren picked up Xavier's body putting back into the same coffin he was in before. Adan did the same for Darian. Akama picked Kysen up with ease.

"Wow, he must really be tired," Natasha said, referring to the six-thousand year old vampire. "I would have thought he'd wake up by now."

"I'm forcing him to stay in his resting state. He needs it. Let's go, the SUV is waiting," Akama said.

They loaded up the truck and climbed in heading for the airport. When they arrived, there were two vampires waiting outside of the airplane.

"Who are they?" Warren asked.

"They are with me," Akama said as he climbed out of the SUV with Kysen still in his arms.

Warren and Adan retrieved the coffins and then followed Akama toward the plane with Natasha in tow.

"Miaka ... Zaire," Akama greeted, nodding at each vampire.

"Master," they said in unison. Both were very beautiful. The Asian female whose name was Miaka wore her hair cut in a bob style. Her pretty brown, almond-shaped eyes peered over the others with a mild fascination. The male, Zaire, looked to be of African descent, with cheekbones not as prominent as Akama's, but a damn close second. Natasha thought his hazel eyes were remarkable against his beautiful onyx complexion.

Akama addressed Miaka. "I want you to go to Chicago, to Natasha's parents' home." Mentally, he gave her the address.

"They'll need to drink blood stronger than Miko's or they'll surely die. We need to buy them more time. Tell Miko I sent you care of Darian. Go now."

Miaka nodded and flew upward, disappearing into the bright blue sky.

"Thank you so much for that. You don't know how much that means to me," Natasha said, having heard what Akama said to his child.

"You're welcome." Akama smiled.

They all boarded the plane, settling comfortably into the seating. Once in the air, after all introductions were done, they began to chat again.

"I still can't get over how cool you are," Warren said to Akama, who laughed.

"I don't look down on humans or other supernaturals. We all must share this world and I see no reason to oppress another simply because of my status as a vampire," Akama said.

"I've been meaning to ask you, how many Founts are there?" Adan asked.

"There are seven of us, one per continent. As I've said, I am the Fount of the Australian line, Irikara is the Fount of the African line, Thallos—the European line; Maska—North American line; Tenock —South American line; Arsalan—the Asian line; and Semei is the Fount of the Antarctic line."

"Do you ever share continents?" Natasha asked as she folded a blanket around her shoulders to keep warm from the fever chills that were creeping up on her.

"We ask each other's permission if we choose to travel. However, we do not share continents. I control all of Australia, and I will not allow any vampire equal to my power to reside my territory," Akama said and then he looked off to the side. "Well, I take that back, there is one circumstance." He smiled.

"I think I know what that is," Warren said. "Geez, I thought Kysen was territorial having control of an entire state. You have opened my eyes. Having control of an entire continent totally trumps that."

Akama chuckled. "I suppose it does. However, I do allow other supernaturals along with their respective leaders to live freely in my territory as long as they behave themselves. Other Founts have their own rules."

"What's with Irikara?" Natasha asked.

"She allows other supernaturals to live in her territory. However, she is the one leader they must all abide. On a monthly basis, they must travel to her palace and pay her *Homage* to thank her for allowing them residence," Akama answered.

"That's kind of bogus," Natasha remarked.

"It's not unusual for one as powerful as she to demand such from her subordinates. I don't, but I don't look down at those who do. It does serve a purpose and keeps younger, more rambunctious supernaturals in line without being cruel," Akama said.

"Well, since you put it that way ..." Natasha still wasn't sure, but Akama did make a point. *Irikara could be worse.*

"If you don't mind me asking, and let me know if I'm out of line, but how did you become a vampire?" Adan asked.

"You're out of line!" Akama growled, causing the others to shrink in their seats. However, Zaire only laughed.

Natasha looked around, but remained silent, not understanding what was happening.

Finally after staring them down for several seconds, Akama began to smile. "I don't mind telling you. I just wanted to *fuck* with you, as they say."

"That was so wrong," Warren said, giving a nervous chuckle as he calmed himself.

"But it was funny." Akama chuckled.

"If you say so," Warren mumbled. He wasn't ashamed of showing fear when the situation called for it. Remembering what happened to Kysen earlier, he wasn't going to underestimate Akama. There was no telling what a vampire would do if they were pissed, especially one as powerful as this Fount was. However, he was relieved to see the vampire had a sense of humor and can even joke around.

Akama chuckled once more before growing serious; his expression lost all signs of humor. "I was twenty-one years old–"

"I thought you looked young," Natasha interrupted. She thought the same of Irikara when she first laid eyes on her, but didn't want to ask. She then remembered she cut him off ... again. "Oh, I'm sorry, didn't mean to interrupt you."

"I'm starting to think you can't help yourself," Akama teased.

"I do have a big mouth, or so I've been told." She shivered slightly as a cold chill ran down her spine followed by another wave of nausea.

"Let me get you another blanket," Akama said, he walked over to a cabinet and pulled a thick blanket out. He then went to Natasha, draping the blanket over her shoulders.

"Thank you," she said. She was still feeling feverish even though Darian's blood seemed to be keeping her temperature from rising to a dangerous level for the time being.

Akama frowned. "Do you feel nauseous in any way, what are your other symptoms?

"I don't really feel good at all. I don't really have an appetite that's why I didn't eat much. My stomach hurts a little, like mild indigestion or the first onset of the flu, which makes me a little nauseous. My body aches in places, but all of that was way worse after I had your blood."

"I see."

"Can you please finish the story? I need something to take my mind off everything that's going on," Natasha said.

Akama nodded. "All right. I lived in a small village along with the other members of my tribe. One night, I was awakened by a strange noise. It sounded almost like a growl, but I couldn't identify the animal that might make such a noise. Naturally curious, as the world was an amazing place with so many new and interesting things to discover, I left my hut to explore. I searched for a few minutes, using only a torch and the light of the full moon. I saw nothing. When I was on my way back to my hut, that's when it grabbed me, clasping a hand over my mouth. Instinctively, I fought with all my strength to break free from its grasp, but I couldn't, its grip upon me-- unmovable."

"What was it?" Warren asked. He was completely enrapt in the story as were Adan and Natasha. Zaire only looked on with mild interest, as he had heard the same story several times before.

"It turned me around, so that I may look upon it. I can describe it only as a demon. The eyes were red orbs in deep sockets. Its limbs were powerful and thick, very muscular. It had claws for hands, with nails as sharp as knives. The skin was black and thick as leather. I also remember it was taller than any man I'd ever seen. Today, I'd say it was about ten feet. The feature that stood out above all others, however, were its enormous black wings that spread out from its sides so majestically and demonically at the same time," Akama said. He stared forward, as if reliving the moment. His eyebrows were creased and his jaw was tight as he recollected the details.

"You must have been terrified," Natasha commented.

Akama nodded. "I was. It held me still, but then it took its hand from my mouth. I remember wanting to scream, but not being able to. I continued to look at this demon and it smiled down at me, revealing a mouth full of pointed, razor sharp teeth. That's when I tried to break free again, but it held me with ease, escape was impossible. I can tell you today, that the expression on his face wasn't one of malice, the opposite really. The demon looked approvingly at me, its eyes raking over me from head to toe. It smiled wider before leaning downward, closer to my neck. I panicked, thinking it would rip out my throat as I had seen the animals do to each other. Again, I wanted to scream, but couldn't. The demon didn't want me to and the ability wasn't there, though the motivation was. I could feel the heat of its breath upon my skin; it was warmer than the heat of the hottest breeze I had known. Then it bit me, hard, I remember that. There was no rapture at first, only severe pain and the force of its pull. I could feel my life being drained from me into *It*. Then I could feel something else coiling inside me, so pleasurable, so intense."

He paused, running a finger along his bottom lip. The others remained silent, simply waiting for him to continue.

"I was wrapped in complete ecstasy. There was no greater feeling, even today I've never felt anything as wonderful as what I experienced on that fateful night. As a matter of fact, the only thing that has come close to that sensation is sex and feeding from another Fount. Before I could die a happy man, the demon pulled away, and all reality returned to me. I was dying and the thing that had killed me smiled down at me with glee. The demon then pulled me closer to its chest holding me still with one hand. With the other, he bit into its own wrist, making an incision. We both watched the blood flow from the wound; it looked almost black under the light of the moon. A spasm ran through my body as the demon pressed its wrist to my mouth, forcing me to drink. The first drop of blood that hit my tongue sent me into frenzy. I locked on, sucking as hard as I could, swallowing greedily. The fluid flowing into me was simply extraordinary in every sense of the word. It satisfied all of my desires, even those I had no idea existed. As I fed from the demon, I felt its essence enter me, it filled me completely and when I could take in no more, I pulled away."

"What did you see?" Warren asked.

"To this day, I can't fully explain what the demon allowed me to see. I can only describe it as hell. There was pain, torture, fire, hate, and fear."

"Did the demon ever say anything to you?" Adan asked. He had been so enrapt with a childlike innocence with the history of vampire creation that he hadn't realized he was now leaning forward, elbows resting on his knees as he stared at Akama as the Fount told his tale.

Akama nodded. "Not in words. When its blood entered me, a part of its soul entered me. Through the visions, the demon showed me how it escaped what I believe was Hell. But it still wasn't free. A force from Hell was pulling it back. Putting its life and soul into my body, and six others was the only way it could remain free. Again, it smiled, only now its eyes were hollow, empty, the red glow was gone and only black orbs looked down at me. It let me go, stepping back and before my very eyes, the demon caught fire in a flame so fierce only ash remained once the flames died. I stood there in shock, surrounded by darkness and trees and the sounds of my tribe members searching for me."

"How did you know you could make other vampires?" Warren asked.

"When did you drink human blood for the first time, how did it feel?" Adan asked.

"Were you lonely?" Natasha asked.

"Could you go out in the sun even then?" Warren asked.

"When did you meet the other Founts?" Adan asked.

Akama chuckled at the eagerness and interest of his young

companions. "Those are all stories for another day."

Disappointed, they moaned.

"I don't mean to pry, but can you at least tell us when you knew you had to drink blood to live?" Adan asked.

"Very well, I suppose I *could* go on. It's not a story I enjoy reliving. There is a lot of sadness in this tale, but …" Akama looked down at his hands as he rubbed them together as if trying to warm them. He looked up at the pairs of eyes staring back at him and cleared his throat before continuing. "That night, my body hummed with energy, I had run back to my hut telling my tribe what had just happened. Some didn't believe me while others wanted to know more. Of course, I had no wounds or bruising to show as proof and as the sun started to rise, I began to feel weighted down, as if my limbs were too heavy for me. I went to lie down and slept for hours awaking only once the sun had set."

"Did you have to hide from the sun?" Natasha asked.

"No. The sun didn't burn me, but it did put me to sleep. When I rose the next night, I was ravenous and I could smell the blood of my tribe all around me. It called to me, and I was caught by a powerful thirst that demanded to be quenched. I wanted it, needed it. I attacked them that night, unable to control my bloodlust, drinking from several men, women and children. I remember their screams of agony as I crushed them in my embrace because I was unaware of my newfound strength," Akama said. "I can only image the vision they saw in me as I fed from them. Eyes that were once brown, warm and compassionate were now blazing red with a passion for carnage. My smile that was once charming to those around me, now brought them to their knees with fear as it was filled with teeth as sharp and dangerous as a shark's. They saw a demon in me."

"I can't image what you all went through at that time," Adan said. "What you lost … I'm sorry."

Akama nodded, a grim expression on his face. "When the village tried to defend itself from my attack, I fought back, killing many more. They tried to burn me with fire and it didn't work, although it was very painful. It was at that point, I fled into the trees never to return again. I still had no idea what had happened to me, or what my future was to be. I knew I was faster and stronger than the humans of my tribe. Things that would kill them didn't seem to kill me and I had an intense hunger for the blood that flowed through their veins and new teeth in order to get the sustenance I required. I also began to realize as time went on that it was the demon essence inside of my body that needed that human blood in order to survive. Without it, I would die."

"I thought a vampire could live forever without drinking human blood, but they'd just suffer so much until they did," Warren commented.

"Offspring vampires can survive without human blood, this is true. We cannot," Akama answered. "The longest I can go without fresh blood is a year."

"So your thirst was stronger than most newborn vamps these days?" Warren asked.

"It was. It took at least five people a night to sate my hunger and that was with me draining them bone dry," Akama said. He sighed, rising to his feet. "Well, that's enough of that for the time being."

"Is that how other Founts became vampires?" Natasha asked.

"Pretty much, although each person's experience may vary slightly. For me, I was infused with the heart of the demon's soul through its blood." Akama answered.

"How were the others different?" Adan asked.

"For Irikara, I believe, when it happened to her, she received the demon's spirit," Akama said.

"The Ancient cultures believe that the soul has seven parts, some believe in five, like the Egyptians. Could this be where that belief originated?" Adan asked.

"Quite possibly."

"What part of the demon did Thallos get?" Warren asked.

"Its ass," Natasha mumbled. She looked away shyly when the others laughed at her remark.

"Not quite. From what he's told me, he felt the 'mind' of the demon enter him," Akama answered after his laughter died.

"How did this demon's soul break apart into seven different entities?" Natasha asked.

"Through demonic magic, I suppose. It did what it had to do in order to exist. We are its vessels and through those we turn, it *further* secures its survival," Akama said.

"Does that mean vampires are evil?" Natasha asked.

"Vampires are born from something that is evil, this I believe. But to each his or her own as far as what road they travel. I believe it's no harder for a vampire to disconnect from their humanity than it is for a human."

"But how can vampires treat humans the way they do knowing they used to be one?" Natasha asked.

"We need human blood to thrive. Humans need animals, plants, air and water to thrive. The slaughtering of an animal and the harvesting of plants is no more inhumane to most humans than the slaughtering of a human to almost all vampires. We are what our nature makes us. We are all predators. If a human chooses not to slay a cow for sustenance they will opt for fruits and vegetables. What their bodies are denied in their sacrifice, they make up for with vitamins. For vampires, we may choose to feed and not kill, which is a test in and of itself. The desire, or need if you will, to take life is ever present; much like it is with an animal in the wild."

"Then there's Synblood, that's an option." Natasha mentioned.

"I wouldn't go *that* far," Akama smirked.

"Do you know about shape-shifters?" Warren asked, once the chuckles faded.

"How you came into being?"

Warren nodded. "Yeah."

"I can't be sure because I've never met an original. It's suspected that a demon worked it's magic then, too. I believe it was also ten-thousand years ago on the same night I was turned. Irikara knows more about that than I do and she isn't always forthcoming with her knowledge or her secrets." Akama rose from his chair and made his way into the bathroom. The supernaturals on the plane could hear when he relieved himself of his beverage and Warren and Adan were amazed.

"I didn't think I'd ever hear a vampire take a piss," Warren said.

"Crude much, Warren," Natasha said.

"I'm sorry but I'm just not used to it." Warren shrugged.

"Don't feel bad, I was thinking the same thing," Adan said.

"I guess. I don't hear anything. I'm kind of happy about that, I would hate to hear what you all do in the bathroom all of the time," Natasha said.

"You learn to ignore it," Adan said.

"Back to how we came into existence, I wish he knew more about that. I really want to know, but I don't want to ask Irikara," Warren said.

"She seems like the type who won't tell you even if you did," Adan said.

Natasha looked at Zaire. "You have been so quiet, are you all right?"

Zaire smiled exposing his pearly whites and enhancing his cheekbones. "I'm fine. I've heard his tales before. Maybe he'll tell you all more of them. He's been both feared and worshiped in the span of his ten-thousand years, so don't be surprised if he gets talkative. You may find yourselves wishing he'd put himself to rest," he chuckled at his own joke.

Warren and Adam simply smiled, they understood the humor. Natasha watched Zaire carefully. She wondered how old and powerful he was and why Akama had brought him along. She decided to find out.

"Are you here to help us?" she asked.

"I am," Zaire said.

"Mind if I ask how old you are?"

"Didn't anyone ever tell you it's rude to ask a person's age?" Akama said as he exited the bathroom.

"Well, yeah, but I find that your ages are one of the many things that are so impressive about supernaturals. Besides, if we're going to take on Thallos and his crew, you said we needed really kick-ass vampires on our side, right?" Natasha said in her defense.

Akama chuckled. "Zaire is seven thousand and Miaka is over six ... thousand that is."

Natasha was shocked. "Ooookay, that's pretty kick-ass." She winced and curled a bit tighter into a ball on the sofa.

"You should rest," Warren said.

"Maybe you're right," Natasha said, she tried to make herself more comfortable in spite of the way she was feeling.

"Here, take this." Adan gave her two pills. "This should help you sleep."

She took them, swallowing them quickly. Within an hour, she was sleeping soundly.

The others talked, some took naps. When the sun set enough behind the horizon that its rays would cause no harm, Darian rose from his resting state, opening the coffin and climbing out. He took a seat closer to Xavier's coffin, running his fingers lovingly over the lacquer-polished lid. He then looked at the others, his eyes settling on Zaire. "You're new."

"I am," Zaire answered.

"Darian – Zaire, Zaire – Darian."Akama gave the brief introduction. "Natasha and Xavier who is still resting belong to him, Zaire."

Zaire nodded.

After that, Warren approached Darian settling down on the sofa beside him. "Are you hungry?" he asked.

Darian smiled. "Are you offering?"

Warren smirked. "No, of course not. I just wanted to know so I could point and laugh at you."

Darian chuckled. "Oh, in that case …" He grabbed Warren's wrist, biting into the vein before the shifter even realized he was caught in the vampire's grip.

Warren moaned louder as Darian fed from him. He had to admit, the vampire's bite was more intense and pleasurable than it had been in the past, which seemed unbelievable. A very powerful orgasm rolled through him, erupting from him with a force that left him slumping over Darian's chest, his wrist still sealed to the vampire's mouth.

Finally, Darian pulled away, licking the healing wound of the last drops of blood. "That was exquisite, as always," he said, releasing Warren's hand.

Warren shivered as the last remaining tremors of his orgasm faded. "Ass," he mumbled under his breath as he leaned backward on the cushions. His entire body felt more relaxed than he'd ever experienced and he was satisfied in a way he'd never known. He felt almost guilty that he should feel such bliss knowing who gave it to him, not to mention that one of his best friends was suffering so.

Darian gave a quick smile then looked at Kysen, who was still in his resting state. "Are you going to let him rise anytime soon?" he asked Akama.

"He hasn't been resting long. I think he needs the rest. I'll let him rise in the next three or four hours," Akama answered.

Darian nodded, he walked over to Kysen, kneeling beside him. He gazed lovingly at his Master, admiring the long dark lashes and the sensual, yet masculine shape of his mouth, the fullness of his lips. He traced a fingertip along the chiseled edge of Kysen's cheekbone. "He really is beautiful, isn't he?"

"Remarkably so, yes," Akama agreed.

"Is that a vampire thing?" Warren asked.

The others looked at him.

"Is *what* a 'vampire thing'?" Akama asked.

"Turning only pretty people." Warren's gaze shifted from Darian to Akama. "Seems really shallow."

"It could be viewed that way, yes. With shifters, many have been turned by accident or in malice; others by choice and some are born. With vampires, the process is far too intimate to be anything but deliberate. We choose our companions out of lust, love and sometimes loneliness and fear. However, we do manage to get in a good glance at the specimen before doing so. I will say not every vampire judges others simply by how beautiful they appear."

"Really, cause I've never seen a vampire that wasn't considered movie star perfection," Warren said.

Akama smiled. "I suppose you *could* say average-looking vampires are rare. As a group, vampires are vain by nature. I believe it stems from how each of the Founts were chosen."

Warren nodded. "I get what you're saying. Between you, Irikara and Thallos, it seemed as though the demon was targeting only the abnormally gorgeous."

Akama arched a brow. "'Abnormally'?"

Adan chuckled. "Akama, you have to admit, he has a point."

Akama shrugged one shoulder. "Quite possibly." He looked around the airplane toward his own beautiful vampire child and smiled. *So I may very well be as superficial as any other vampire,* he thought.

Darian walked toward the sofa Natasha occupied and sat down.

"Let's turn on the TV. I want to know what's going on," Warren said.

Zaire snapped his fingers, and the large flat screen television sparked to life.

"Okay, that was pretty cool. Shifters can't do that," Warren admitted. "Did you have to snap your fingers, though?"

Zaire smirked. "No, I did that for dramatic effect."

Some of the others snickered before they all turned their full attention to the TV set as the *World News* station was returning from its commercial break. The female anchorwoman reported the current death toll, which had reached over five million humans worldwide who had painfully succumbed to the virus now known as "Vampire Flu." The anchorwoman then went on to explain that the CDC was still trying to come up with a vaccine, but as no vampires had come forward to donate their blood, the process was difficult, at best. Hospitals were now full to the max with the sick and dying and temporary triage centers were now being constructed on hospital parking lots to accommodate the influx of patients. In related news, there's been a rise in human and vampire crime, as several vampires have been killed or kidnapped in the past few days and several humans have been killed in what was suspected as retaliation.

The anchorwoman cut to footage of several reporters who had been speaking to people around the world about the current situation. Several humans and shifters expressed their thoughts on the matter. In London, a reporter stopped a man walking by and asked him how he felt about everything that was happening.

"The S.U.I.T. organization is over-extended and unable to maintain order as they had promised. I guess they shouldn't have fired all of those shifters," one pedestrian said with an English accent.

In Spain another pedestrian said in her native language, "Vampires are evil, this just proves that!" Her message was translated in English subtitles at the bottom of the screen.

In Rome a female said. "This is a cry for equality. We need to all share this world, it's the only one we have. Why can't we live in peace together?"

The scene flipped back to the anchorwoman who sat behind her desk composed as she continued to report the news. There were several floods, some resulting in mudslides, a forest fire in California and one minor earthquake in El Salvador. None of the damage from those natural disasters however could compare to the damage done by the Vampire Flu, the anchorwoman said.

"Damn, this is so fucked up," Warren fussed.

"I suppose after what happened to you, other vampires are taking heed to their warning," Akama said, nodding his head toward Darian.

"It would seem so," Darian replied.

"What is the Council doing about all of this?" Adan asked.

"My guess is they are trying to work with the human government, but without the cure or a donation of their blood and no friendly link to Thallos, they don't have much to negotiate with. At this point, I'm sure they are looking quite inconsequential to the humans … powerless," Zaire said.

"The only reason why the death toll isn't higher is because vampires are giving their blood to humans secretly, the way Darian has been," Akama said.

"If we can't get a cure, those humans are still going to die," Warren said. He cast a look at Natasha sleeping on the sofa beside Darian and lowered his gaze. He didn't want his friend to die and he especially didn't want her to die in the painful, sickly way that she was dying.

"One step at a time, first let's get to Irikara and see what she says. After that, we'll know our next move," Akama said.

"Man, turn this shit off, it's too fucking depressing," Warren said.

Zaire turned the television off the same way he turned it on, with the exception of the snap of his finger.

Xavier's eyes opened with a start and he opened the lid to his coffin, sitting up at the same time. He looked around the airplane, immediately noticing Darian sharing the sofa with Natasha. He climbed out, closing the distance between them with lightning-quick speed. "Is she doing all right?" he asked.

Darian looked at his lover then he rose. "Follow me." He led Xavier into the farthest room on the airplane, which happened to be the bedroom. He knew the others would still hear every word he said to his child, but some privacy was better than none for what he had to discuss.

"Darian, what's wrong?" Xavier asked, growing more anxious.

"She's dying, Xavier, you know that, don't you?" Darian studied his lover's face, seeing the anger and sadness spread across his expression. "Xavier?"

"I'm not blind to what's happening to her, Darian. Our blood isn't working well enough to stave off the sickness. Every second that passes, she's dying and we can't save her."

"If we can't get a cure, have you prepared yourself for her death?"

Xavier looked away.

"Have you?"

"I've asked myself that question many times since I first met her. I could never admit to myself that I would ever be prepared for her death. I couldn't imagine it; even now I still hold out hope that we can save her."

"So you're not prepared."

Xavier looked at Darian, his brows furrowed in anger. "Have you?"

"Yes."

"*How* ... how?"

"She's human, Xavier. I have always expected that her death would come to her, it is her fate as a human."

"Have you ever thought about turning her?"

"Yes, even if it was against her will, but I could never resolve myself to that decision. If she were to hate me afterward, it would all be for not."

Xavier nodded. "I've thought about the same thing."

"It doesn't matter at this point. As it stands, she's too far gone for that."

"Not if we get the cure. She was willing to turn before."

"To save her life when she was desperate enough to hang on. If her life can be saved, do you honestly believe she'll want to live forever as a vampire? She hasn't expressed such desire in the past."

Xavier was silent as he pondered Darian's question, then he spoke. "I can't lose her Darian. If we save her, I can't ..." his voice trailed off.

Darian turned, running his hands over his face. "I fear that you aren't being realistic about this situation and you're going to suffer for it greatly if the worst comes to pass." He turned back around, looking at his young lover. "Over a century old and still so very immature."

Xavier frowned as he thought of Natasha's pending death combined with Darian's disappointment in him.

Darian walked closer to him, wrapping the younger vampire into his embrace. He kissed the silky brown hair on the top of his head. Gently, he caressed Xavier's face, lifting it to his own before planting soft, delicate kisses on his eyes, nose, mouth and both cheeks.

"My love," he whispered passionately once he pulled away. "I too loathe what has happened to our Natasha. I hate that I can't save her. I don't want her to die. But if you are to survive this, you are going to have to accept that her death may be inevitable. She already has."

Xavier lowered his head, a feeling of defeat crept across his subconscious. Darian allowed him time to express his grief, without judgment. He only gently stroked Xavier's back during their intimate moment. After a little time had passed, Xavier nodded in his resolve, taking a deep breath and releasing it. "When the time comes, I'll deal."

Darian studied him for a few seconds and then nodded, deciding not to press the matter. "Let's return."

The two vampires emerged from the bedroom rejoining the others. Xavier sat on the sofa where Darian had been sitting earlier. No one said anything about what they had heard the two vampires discussing. They knew it wasn't their place to comment.

Darian took the chair opposite Akama, looking at the ancient Fount with a keen interest. "What if Irikara refuses to help?"

"We'll cross that bridge once we get to it. For now, let's rely on the hope that she'll want to help Kysen help you," Akama said.

Darian smirked. "I wouldn't be surprised if he charged me for his services after this is all over."

"Kysen?" Akama asked.

"Yes."

"He won't. I'm willing to guess being in your presence is payment enough."

"You think so?"

Akama nodded. "He's already explained to us that he'll go only to protect you. We're going to use that same love he has for you to urge Irikara to help us, because she has that same love for him."

"'Whatever works', as they say," Darian said in agreement. He looked at Kysen again. "Is there any other reason why you're keeping him in his resting state? He really doesn't need these many hours."

Akama chuckled. "I'd be lying if I didn't say the atmosphere is so much more peaceful with him like that."

Darian laughed. "So his charm hasn't worked on you."

"Oh, it has. I understand him very much. However, he's shown so little of his charm as of late, I believe your companions needed him to rest more than he needed it himself."

Darian laughed a bit more boisterously this time. He could only imagine the mood Kysen was in before he was put to rest. "Let's hope he feels invigorated once he awakens."

"Let's hope." Akama knowingly smiled.

Darian looked at Xavier who was pulling away from Adan. The shifter had offered to feed him and Xavier had been grateful. They continued to talk amongst themselves, discussing topics that didn't revolve around death, pain and sickness until they reached their destination. Akama released his power over Kysen and the ancient vampire opened his eyes, looking around. Immediately, he sensed Irikara's power.

"We're in Egypt?" Kysen asked noticing that he was on an airplane that was no longer in flight.

Darian nodded. "Yes."

"I have been resting for at least *ten* hours."

"From what I've been told, you needed the rest."

Kysen tilted his head sideways. "Not *that* much rest."

"Very well then, *they* needed the rest," Darian said, gesturing to the others.

"When this is all over, I don't want you to ask for my help for at least a century." Kysen rose from his chair, stretching his limbs.

Darian chuckled, knowing his Master was joking … well, he

hoped he was joking.

They all departed the plane, climbing into the waiting limousine Irikara had arranged for them. The mood was somber as some of them were filled with anxiety, fear and despair. It was not long before they reached Irikara's beautiful palace. No one knew what awaited them, but they hoped the second meeting would go better than the first one had.

CHAPTER SEVENTEEN

Irikara's human servant led them into another room, different from the first one they'd been in. It was as if they walked into a tropical paradise filled with tranquil waterfalls, lush grass and exotic flowers. The air was cool and fresh and brushed over their skin like soft silk. Tropical birds flew in the air and landed on the trees and stones. Their beautiful singing enhanced the splendor of the room, making it seem all the more like a dream. Warren was amazed at the grandeur of the palace as it was his first time inside and he looked around in wonderment at every beautiful sculpture, every elegant piece of furniture and all of the pretty servants he saw.

Irikara was seated on her throne beside one of the majestic waterfalls surrounded by several gorgeous vampires, both males and females of various races. All were topless and their bodies were lightly covered in gold dust. To Natasha they were dressed very much in the same way Kysen had dressed earlier. The six vampires were lying on fluffy pillows or sitting on divans and they stared back at them with expressions that were passive, curious, envious, or filled with desire.

"It has been a long time, my beautiful Irikara," Akama said, boldly approaching the other Fount and kissing her lightly on the cheek, which she upturned toward him.

"My dear Akama, it has been too long. You should visit more, such fun we can have." Irikara smiled.

"I shall take you up on your offer, indeed. Unfortunately, this visit is not a frivolous one. We come to seek your assistance."

Irikara's jaw tightened. "I know." She turned toward Natasha. "Let the human woman come forward."

Darian nodded at Natasha, releasing her hand so that she could step forward. Natasha came closer to Irikara, standing before her. Irikara glared down at her, making Natasha feel extremely uncomfortable as if her life was in danger … well … immediate danger. She could feel the ancient vampire judging her, resenting her, it made her want to run back into the arms of her vampire lovers, but she stood her ground.

"Your death is all but inevitable if I don't help you, this is true," Irikara said.

Natasha nodded. "It would seem so."

Irikara's eyes scanned over the others there, including her child, Kysen. She then settled her gaze on Xavier. "Young one, step forward."

Xavier obliged, taking the space next to Natasha.

"Before I granted you all access into my territory, I informed my Kysen that I wanted a promise given to me."

Xavier nodded. "Yes, my Goddess, we are prepared to give you whatever you desire."

"Are you?" She looked down at him, one eyebrow rising.

"Yes, My Goddess." Xavier's expression showed that he was prepared to keep his word.

"I will help you only because Kysen has adamantly declared that he will protect Darian, who is here to protect you, Xavier."

"Darian loves Natasha and he's doing this to protect her as well," Xavier said, hoping to enlighten her.

Irikara laughed wickedly. Her high-pitched voice echoed throughout the room. After a few seconds, she began to calm down. "Do you really believe that?"

"Yes."

"Oh my dear young one, it is true. He does love her very much. But that is not why he is here. His motivation is you."

"Forgive me, my Goddess, if I don't agree," Xavier said.

Irikara's expression hardened. "You think because I don't share your bed, that I couldn't possibly know what is hidden in your hearts? Let me explain something to you, young one. Nothing is hidden from me. Even secrets you keep from each other you cannot keep from me. Revelations so unspeakable to you that you dare not entertain them … but I know what they are."

"Then enlighten me, my Goddess," Xavier said. There was no doubt the sole female Fount agitated, unnerved and enchanted him. He was enamored with her, but he was also angry with her. At this point, he wasn't sure he wanted to know her version of the truth, but he knew he had to ask if he was going to save Natasha.

"Darian loves her and he wants to save her, but fact is; the only reason he has gone to this extreme is because he doesn't want *you* to lose her. Your pain is something he doesn't want to bear; his love for you is that great. You are his *Chosen One*, as Kysen is to me. It is why I will help you."

"You believe this?" Xavier asked.

"You do as well. It's one of those revelations that you don't want to admit to yourself. You know that it was you who first desired Natasha. The very sight of her enticed you. Darian wasn't so impressed with her the way you were. Didn't you hope that you could change his mind? It wasn't until Natasha slapped him that she became something exciting to Darian. For you, Natasha was the humanity that you still possessed. For Darian, she was entertainment, ever unpredictable, she quickened him. Oh, it's true, the more time the three of you spent together, the stronger your bond became and the love between you grew. But you know, if Darian ever had to choose between the two of you, without question, he'd choose you." She went on. "In fact, I'm willing to bet Roycean knew that when he decided to attack her and not you. They wanted to teach Darian a lesson and use him as an example to others, but they did not want to take his favorite away from him. Humans are more expendable. They spared him that pain simply out of vampire camaraderie, a decision they'll soon regret, I'm sure."

Natasha lowered her head, Irikara's words cut through her like a knife and for a split second she wanted to flee the room. Fighting back the tears, she began to understand why Irikara's words hurt her so. She knew them to be true. She didn't doubt Darian's love for her, but she knew he'd choose Xavier over her. She remembered how they both courted her before she decided to join them. She knew Xavier wouldn't leave Darian for her, she had to accept them. She looked at Xavier, his jaw tightened and his hands balled into fists. She could tell he was frustrated and enraged, his illusions dashed, the truth exposed. She was about to dip deeper into despair when she realized something else Xavier was. He was standing there right beside her, and so was Darian and that was good enough for her.

She looked up at Irikara. "What you said may be true. I'm all right with that. It's okay if Darian has his favorite. He and Xavier were special to each other long before I showed up on the scene. But understand this, they are still both here trying to save me and that's all that matters."

Irikara lip curled up on the side. "You think so, do you?"

"Yes."

"Very well. As I've said before. Because my *Chosen One*, Kysen is willing to risk his life to help Darian who's helping Xavier who's helping you, I demand this as my promise …" she paused for dramatic effect. It was working. She could see their expressions change in anticipation. "… Once you are cured of the virus, immediately afterward, Xavier is to turn you, to make you his… completely."

There were a few shocked expressions coming from Xavier, Natasha, Warren and Adan. Darian almost seemed relieved, but remained silent. Kysen smiled, lowering his head to hide his expression. Akama remained unreadable.

Irikara went on. "The only reason why we are in this particular situation is because you are mortal."

"That's not true, my parents were ill, that's why Darian tried to save them," Natasha said in her defense.

"No. It's because you are human and because you were infected with the virus. That is why Darian has involved Kysen, who is all *I* care about. Had you been a vampire, you could have dealt with your parents on your own. You could have turned them before this happened or resolved yourself to their inevitable death. Which you must still do, you do realize that, don't you?" Irikara ran a long dainty finger along the bottom of her chin as she gazed at Natasha.

Natasha opened her mouth to protest, but then she closed it knowing the ancient vampire, no matter how annoying she was at the moment, was also right. Even if they managed to save her parents from this virus, they would still die one day unless they were turned into vampires. Could she do that to them? Did she even want it for herself? Immortality was the price she had to pay to save her life and theirs. She thought about how willing she was to turn when she was first infected. At that time she didn't think about what it really meant. All she knew is that she wanted to live.

Now she had to think about it. Living forever, feeding on human blood, quite possibly watching her parents die and maybe even her two children. Could she do that? Or would she turn them and all of their offspring? She never really gave much thought to the price of immortality.

She looked at Xavier who smiled down at her trying to reassure her. She wondered about what he and Darian went though, seeing their family and friends die before them and having to deal with the pain of their loss. Could she put herself through that? As she reflected on Irikara's terms, she realized that this was bigger than her. If their plan worked and she could be cured, countless others could be cured and all it took was her to agree to become a vampire. In the end, the sacrifice was small.

She looked back at Irikara. "I agree. Once I am cured, Xavier will turn me."

"Natasha," Xavier began. "Are you sure?"

Natasha nodded. "I think someday it was going to come down to this. I never had an answer before, now I do. I'm sure."

"Well aren't you a 'throw yourself to the lions' sort of human. I still find you quite unappealing, but we do have an accord," Irikara said in her usual bitchy tone laced with her Egyptian accent. She looked at the others then to the other Fount. "Akama my darling, I have spoken to our good friend Arsalan and *he* told *me* that Thallos is in league with Semei and Tenoch."

Akama's eyebrows arched. "Oh really? I'm surprised Semei and Tenoch can stand each other's company long enough to work as a cohesive unit."

Irikara chuckled. "Apparently, killing humans for their insolence is something they could both agree upon."

"So our target is a triumvirate of Founts. We're going to need more help," Warren said. He couldn't take his eyes off Irikara for one second. She was absolutely beautiful and majestic at the same time. He was beginning to understand just what kind of influence she had over the other Founts. He could see just by Akama's behavior that she was extremely desired.

Xavier had taken Natasha's hand and returned to stand beside Darian. Irikara allowed him to do so. She was preoccupied with Akama at the moment. She would most definitely request a visit from him once this feud was over. She had almost forgotten how delicious the Fount of the Australian line was.

"What do we do now?" Adan asked, hoping he wouldn't get tossed across the room as Xavier had been on their earlier visit.

"Well, if Irikara would accompany us, we may be able to convince Arsalan and Maska to join us. That would give us the much needed advantage we seek," Akama said. He looked at Irikara. "Will you accompany us?"

"Why do you need me to 'accompany' you?" Irikara asked teasingly.

"Because you know as well as I do that if I request their help, they won't oblige. However, if you do so, they will," Akama answered.

Irikara feigned shock. "Oh surely you do not think that I have that much persuasion over them, do you?" she batted her eyes playfully.

Akama chuckled as he approached her throne. "My lovely and beautiful Irikara. I wouldn't ever dream a woman such as yourself could *ever* doubt your powers of persuasion."

"Mmmmm, you do flatter me." Irikara smiled. She threw a glance at the others. "So be it, I will simply have to tolerate your company … well … At least I will have my Kysen with me."

Kysen bowed his head. "Always, my Goddess."

"Aisha will be joining us," Irikara announced. "I have already contacted her and she'll meet us in Japan."

"Perhaps we should leave then," Akama suggested.

"Indeed." Irikara rose from her throne with Akama's aid, though she didn't need it. "Ade, watch over my palace," she said to one of her male vampires.

A male vampire who looked to be of African descent bowed his head. "Of course, my Goddess."

CHAPTER EIGHTEEN
ARSALAN

They were all seated comfortably on Irikara's gigantic airplane, one of those new models that was big enough to carry at least five-hundred people. It had been gutted out and was two levels. There were three bedrooms, two luxury bathrooms complete with steam showers, a gourmet kitchen, living room, dining room, and entertainment room. It was definitely the most extravagant airplane any of them had been on. It was truly a palace in the sky.

"Your airplane is very beautiful, so is your home," Natasha complimented, hoping to break the frigid ice that was ever so present between them.

Irikara tossed Natasha a glance that said she could care less what she thought about her airplane or her home. As far as she was concerned, the human was beneath her and she blamed Natasha for Kysen being put in harm's way. "Try to remain silent for the course of this trip," she advised … or rather warned.

"Maybe we should have taken separate planes," Natasha mumbled under her breath even though she knew they could all hear her.

"I wanted to, remember? But your lover Darian wanted to keep you close to Kysen so that he could give you his blood and I did not want to part with Kysen so that we could travel separately." Irikara was growing ever more annoyed with the human woman. "I must warn you, one more comment like the one you just made will result in your instantaneous death, thus sparing us any more inconvenience."

Natasha didn't dare doubt the conviction behind her words. She knew Irikara would care less than a damn about Darian and Xavier's anger with her and she also knew that Kysen would forgive Irikara for killing her and Darian wouldn't hold Kysen responsible, because all in all, she *had* been warned. She decided to keep her mouth shut, especially whenever she was in Irikara's presence. Also, if she had any negative comments, they could most certainly wait. She laid her head on Xavier's shoulder, relishing the sensation of his warmth as he pulled her closer to him.

The mood on the airplane was tense as the hours passed by. For the most part, many of them slept during the trip. All were happy when they finally landed in Tokyo, Japan. After an hour of traveling in three cars, they arrived at a beautiful mansion. The landscape was covered with trees blossoming pink lotuses and the lawn was decorated with brightly colored flowers. There was a hand-crafted stone bridge expanding over a koi pond filled with beautiful multicolored fish of varying species. There were more ancient sculptures on the property representing the rich Asian and Indian culture that gave the estate a magical aura. The human servant led them inside, taking them to a room that was decorated with ancient Asian furnishing. The color motif was red, black and gold and the sofa, chairs, curtains, tables and carpeting brought out the beauty and rich culture of the room. The servant instructed them to wait there before leaving, closing the door behind him.

"So this is Arsalan's home?" Warren asked as he looked around the room. "It's very beautiful, Xander would be a little jealous, I bet."

"Thank you," A voice on the other side of the room said, startling everyone except Irikara and Akama, both of whom had noticed when Arsalan entered the room. "Irikara, Akama, such a pleasure to have you in my home. Please, have a seat."

The Founts seated themselves in the two comfortable chairs closest to Arsalan. The others remained standing as it seemed Arsalan didn't offer them seats or even acknowledge they were there. Again, they looked at the newest Fount; his beauty was bewitching, holding their gazes captive. His golden brown skin was smooth, flawless. The light from the lamp behind him reflected beautifully on the silky dark hair that crowned his head. His golden, reddish-brown almond-shaped eyes scanned over them, drinking in their appearances and his luscious mouth parted in a smile revealing perfectly white teeth.

"You do travel with pretty company, I see," Arsalan said to his two comrades.

"I wouldn't have it any other way," Irikara said with a coy smile and then she frowned. "Although I have traveled with prettier company who were more tolerable. Not to mention the circumstances were more favorable."

Arsalan chuckled deeply. "Have you grown bored of your *Chosen One* already?"

"Bored, no. Just disappointed," Irikara said.

"On that note, let us get right down to business, shall we," Akama said.

"Well, aren't we impatient? I haven't seen Irikara in over three-thousand years, and I haven't seen you in over two-hundred. Aren't I allowed a few minutes of idle conversation?" Arsalan remarked.

"I wouldn't mind if time wasn't of the essence," Akama replied.

"The human woman isn't dead yet. So, tell me, why haven't you come to visit me in all this time?" Arsalan looked at his old friend and on and off again lover.

"We just don't see eye-to-eye. We argue every time we get together. The sex is great—"

"Just 'great'?" Arsalan asked sarcastically, one eyebrow rising.

Akama smiled. "Fair enough. The sex is amazing, indescribable, the earth rumbles and the heavens smile down upon us."

"That's the way I remember it as well." Arsalan smirked.

With a roll of his eyes, Akama continued. "Nonetheless, this is your territory and you've made quite the habit of reminding me of that fact, especially whenever we are in disagreement. Even eternity is far too short to deal with that kind of bullshit."

Arsalan sneered.

Irikara giggled. "Gentlemen, gentlemen, let us not have such hostility. The only way I want to see you two entangled in the heat of passion is when you're making love. No fighting."

After tossing a knowing smile to Irikara, Arsalan readjusted himself in his chair. "We should get down to business."

"Agreed," Akama said.

"You want my help in challenging Thallos, Semei and Tenoch. This is a confrontation that could end in bloodshed, you are aware of this, aren't you?" Arsalan asked.

"I don't plan on losing my child," Irikara remarked.

"I have thought about this, which is why I hope that both you and Maska will join us. If they see that they are outnumbered, this confrontation may end peacefully," Akama said.

Arsalan scoffed. "I seriously doubt it, and you're lying to yourself if you even considered entertaining such a ridiculous notion. Thallos is as stubborn as a mule and as vicious as they come. He won't take kindly to you or anyone telling him what to do. Besides, do you honestly believe he will give you the cure?"

"You're right. Blood will be shed. But with a greater force on our side, hopefully it won't be us having the most casualties," Akama said.

Arsalan sighed then he looked at Irikara. "Tell me, my beauty. How in the hell did he convince *you* to join him on this ludicrous crusade?"

"I have but one weakness," Irikara began.

Arsalan took her hint and looked over her shoulder at their companions targeting Kysen. "You spoil him, you know."

"And you do not give special care and attention to Bahashiri? If her life was in jeopardy, you would go berserk," Irikara pointed out.

Arsalan nodded. "Point taken. I suppose it's a good thing I don't involve her in this."

"Maybe you should. Because she's so important to you, wouldn't it be wise to have her beside you at this point?" Akama suggested.

"Why?"

"So that she can't be used against you once we challenge Thallos and the others."

"Is that why you have Zaire with you?"

"That's one of my many reasons, yes."

"Well, I haven't decided if I want to help you. I don't see any *reason* why I should risk the life of my *Chosen One*." Arsalan looked at Akama.

"Because you know as well as I do that Thallos is going about this the wrong way," Akama said.

"That's a matter of opinion. Sometimes being a tyrant gets the results you want much faster than being a saint. Wouldn't you agree?" Arsalan smiled.

Akama shook his head. "We don't want to live in a world where we rule by the iron fist of fear. This will only breed more resentment and hate."

"Akama, my friend … that is how people have always ruled. If one thing history has shown us all is that those who would bring peace to this world are not welcomed. Need I bring up the many assassinations committed throughout time? When humans created law enforcement, the military, kingdoms, and other forms of government, it was to rule with fear. How else will you keep your subordinates in line? Vampire politics is very similar, as you are well aware," Arsalan said.

"Call me idealistic if you wish−"

"Akama, you're idealistic and foolishly so," Arsalan interjected.

Akama scoffed. "That may be, however, I am but one of those few who would like to see a world at *some* sort of peace. We need order and this feud between us and the humans can only end badly if we continue on this way. There must be a point in all of this where we can come to an understanding. Humans want no part of this any more than we do."

Arsalan cocked a brow. "Perhaps they should have spoken up before matters escalated to this point. Silence creates chaos."

"So does fear," Akama countered.

Arsalan stared quizzically at his friend for a few seconds before responding. "What do *you* fear?" His eyes narrowed slightly as he waited an answer.

"That when pushed to the brink, the humans will push back. Think you that we are the only ones who can come up with a virus that has a designated target? You speak of what history has proven. We'd be sorely mistaken if we were to underestimate the humans. Mankind is not weak. As a matter of fact, if they feel as though they have nothing to lose, they have been known to pull no punches. Can you imagine this beautiful country being bombed… oh, wait, you can, can't you?"

Arsalan's jaw tightened. "That was uncalled for."

"You lost your entire coven during that time in Hiroshima, didn't you? If fire could kill us, you'd also be dead. Is that the kind of future you're looking forward to? We need humans to survive, not the other way around. If you have any love for the offspring of our lines, you will do what you need to do as a Fount to secure their lives." Akama looked at both Irikara and Arsalan.

"I have just one question," Arsalan said.

"What?" Akama asked.

"How long did you practice that speech?"

Akama's expression gradually changed from serious to humorous and he chuckled. "You're an insufferable son of a bitch, do you know that?"

"You know, there was a much less righteous way to convince me to go with you."

"Oh really, what was that?"

"I'm sure you can guess." Arsalan's gaze drifted over Akama's body lustfully, longingly.

Akama sighed. "Are you serious?"

"Very. I've missed you."

Irikara huffed. "Well now *I* feel very disappointed. I was told that I would be needed to convince you to join us and all this time, all you wanted was Akama. Well, *this* was a shameful waste of my time," she fussed.

"I thought we would need you," Akama said in his defense.

"Apparently, you don't." Irikara settled back into the chair, watching the two men.

"Irikara, my darling, you are many things; *insignificant* is not one of them. Anyone who can pry your lovely ass from that throne of yours has my attention. The very fact that you're here and prepared to fight Thallos has interest me. However, I'm greedy. I'm going to have to demand things go my way this time." Arsalan returned his gaze toward Akama. "I want you so badly, I can taste you! Give us a decade together, that's what I ask of you and I'll join your merry band of misfits."

"I'm no misfit!" Irikara retorted.

"Granted. Misfits and Goddess," Arsalan corrected himself.

Akama sighed once more. "One decade?"

Arsalan rolled his eyes. "My goodness, Akama, am I that horrible to be around? You're acting as if I've asked you to pull the flesh from your bones."

"No, you're not that off-putting. You know how I feel about you. But I'm not looking forward to all of the head-butting that's sure to come."

"Reconciliation sex will be well worth it."

"That's not enough to convince me, besides my territory will be left unguarded."

"Who's going to take it over in your absence? No other Fount would dare. What's your next pathetic excuse going to be now?" Arsalan was losing his patience.

Akama laughed. "Well, I would be lying if I said I didn't miss you."

"Lying through your teeth, yes indeed," Arsalan agreed.

Irikara huffed. "For two ten-thousand year old men, you are both acting like human teenage boys."

Both Founts looked at her, eyebrows cocked.

"Well, you know I am right," Irikara said, placing her hand on her chest for emphasis.

Akama sighed. "Very well, One decade."

"It is but a drop in time for us. I will make it worthwhile, don't worry," Arsalan said. Leaning forward, he kissed Akama passionately, letting his tongue caress his lover, eliciting soft moans of pleasure from him.

Irikara sat silently, smiling at the view she was now witnessing. When the two men broke their kiss, she giggled. "Well, now I really am glad I decided to join you."

"We should leave now, it's going to take us a while to get to Alaska," Akama said.

"I would suggest we just fly there ourselves, but your companions would fry, sizzle and burst into flames before we got there. The sun is almost up anyway. Let's get to the plane," Arsalan said.

"Before we do that, we need to make arrangements for your jet as well," Akama said.

"Why, Irikara's monstrosity is big enough for us all?"

"I now remember why I don't visit you more often, or invite you over as much," Irikara said to Arsalan.

"I only mean that your palace with wings is more than accommodating for us. I see no reason to prepare my jet," Arsalan clarified.

"I just thought it would be easier if we three traveled separately, with Kysen, of course. I'll have Zaire tend to Natasha," Akama said.

"But what if Thallos somehow finds out about your plan and decides to destroy their airplane and we're not there to protect them? Then what?" Arsalan said breathlessly, feigning worry.

"I have been shielding the minds of our companions since we first met just in case Thallos has been keeping track of them. However, you make a valid point, it's better to play this as smart as we can. We should stay together," Akama said.

"I wasn't being serious. You know that, don't you?" Arsalan looked at his now, *on* again lover with one eyebrow lifted.

"Oh, I know. You were being an ass, but you still made a good point. We have no idea what Thallos knows or doesn't know or whose mind he's read. We should remain together. It may be the only reason why he and the others haven't attacked," Akama said.

"Oh Good lord, I expect some compensation once we're on that manmade contraption," Arsalan stalked off, brushing past the rest of them.

"Let's go," Akama said to the others, who seemed more than anxious to get back in the air.

***

On the plane, Zaire did as he was instructed. He gave Natasha some of his blood, letting her take it from his wrist. She had grown more resistant to Darian's blood and Kysen's was following suit. Zaire being stronger, but not a Fount seemed to put some of the symptoms she was experiencing into remission for the time being. As the aircraft carried them over the continents, both Darian and Xavier were beginning to feel the effects of the sun rising and knew they would be resting soon. They continued to talk to Natasha, hoping to keep her mind off of what was happening to her. When the sun rose, both vampires rested comfortably in one of the bedrooms free of windows. Natasha decided to go to sleep as well, she really didn't to want be in Arsalan or Irikara's presence and sleep was the best option to avoid them. Not to mention, it was the only reprieve she had from her sickness. Warren was also sleeping, as was Zaire, but Adan and Kysen were wide awake and watching the three Founts conversing amongst themselves.

"Stop looking at me that way," Akama told Arsalan, who had been staring at him longingly for several long minutes.

"What way?" Arsalan responded slyly, with a slight curl of his lip.

"What are you, *twelve*? I can't believe you're being this immature at *your* age, no less," Akama teased. "You're setting a bad example for the younger ones over there."

Arsalan laughed outright, slapping his knee. "What can I say? You bring out the worst in me."

"This is going to get even more interesting if Maska joins us," Irikara remarked.

"I'm sure it will," Akama said. He looked at Arsalan. "Have you two gotten over your little disagreement?"

Arsalan frowned. "That swine hasn't apologized for breaching my territory uninvited, so I would say we have not."

"Speaking of, is he aware that we're coming?" Akama asked.

Arsalan gave his two comrades a devilish grin. "No."

"If he destroys my airplane because you failed to alert him to our presence, I will personally eat your heart after I rip it from your chest," Irikara warned.

"Such threats! Really Irikara, do you honestly believe that Maska would harm anything that was yours?" Arsalan asked.

"He's still smitten, no doubt," Akama joined in on the tease.

"Of course he is … you all are. Still, my warning stands." She settled more comfortably in her chair.

"So I see." Arsalan said. "Anyway, why is it my responsibility to contact Maska. It's three of us here?"

"Fair enough, Akama, did you contact him?" Irikara inquired.

"No, he wouldn't freely or favorably grant us access anyway simply because Arsalan accompanies us, so why bother with the formalities," Akama answered.

"You do know him well," Arsalan said with a chuckle. "Speaking of things said to one another. I didn't forget about what I said. I want to get started on our renewed relationship … right now." In a movement too fast for the others to see, save the two Founts, Arsalan was atop of Akama, hand cupping his groin.

"You're ten-thousand years old and you have no patience, nor skill for the seduction?" Akama taunted.

"Two hundred years wore down my reserve. Now all that is left is a fire burning within me that desires you more than blood." Arsalan kissed his lover deeply. The two remained sealed as their tongue explored each other's mouths, rekindling the passion between them. "Let's go." Quickly, he led Akama to one of the unoccupied bedrooms on the airplane.

"Men," Irikara whispered to herself as she watched the door close behind the two Founts. She looked at her child, Kysen. "What are you thinking about?"

"Do you not already know?"

"I haven't pried. Besides, I wish to hear your voice. Come sit by me."

He did as she requested, taking the chair once occupied by Akama.

"Now, tell me what is on your mind, my child."

"I thank you for helping Darian, for helping me. I am ever amazed at your wisdom for it was quite wise to demand that Natasha be turned. Sheer brilliance."

Irikara smiled as she reached over, lovingly stroking Kysen's cheek, she ran her fingers gently over his jaw line, before lightly gripping his chin between her finger and thumb. "I will always protect you, my love." She leaned forward, tilting his chin downward and kissed him before letting go. "What else is there?"

"Watching the three of you together, I've never seen you with another Fount … You're different when you're with them."

"We are of equal power so therefore, we can be quite candid around each other, 'tis a rare opportunity. The allure is not lost on me, and although one of us cannot dominate the others, I always get my way." She smiled coyly.

"So I've heard."

"If Darian does not survive this war, what will you do?" Irikara asked, her expression growing serious.

Kysen's jaw tightened as he thought about the unthinkable demise of his child, his Darian. "Honestly, my Goddess, I do not know. This all originated from Thallos."

"This all originated from the humans denying supernaturals equality. Why supernaturals would beg and plead is beyond me, when they can simply take. Thallos is only doing what is necessary to prove a point. Darian and his coven have been caught in the crossfire. It is unfortunate and nothing more."

"So you do not agree with Akama?"

"Do you?"

"I see both sides of the coin, I will say that."

Irikara gazed thoughtfully as her child. "If Darian dies, and you chose to avenge him, I will be by your side. But you must promise me this is only if Darian dies, no one else, regardless of what domino effect may follow."

Kysen laughed. "If Xavier dies, he'll fight and you know what will happen next."

Irikara huffed, showing signs of her frustration. "What is it about Darian that has you so in love with him? He left you for eight-hundred years. He knew where you were and never sought to reunite with you until he needed you. Why do you care so much for him? He is not worthy."

Kysen smiled sadly at his Goddess. "You cast me away from you after being with me for two-thousand years. Do you remember your reasoning?"

Irikara brushed a few braids from her face, tucking them behind her ear. "You are co-dependent and I felt you would not grow stronger clinging to me. You needed to be free to experience eternity with all of the power I had given you. To be what a God was meant to be."

"When Darian left me, I was crestfallen, but I began to understand. Irikara, he left me for the same reason you did. He left me so that we would both become stronger. I needed to know what it felt like to be alone to know that I could survive it. He needed to know he could survive the life I granted him without me by his side. He has your strength, your courage, your exquisite beauty. He has your poise and your charm. I would die if I lost him as I would die if I lost you."

Irikara was silent as she looked at her *Chosen One*. She now understood. She nodded. "You will not lose him, you will not lose me." She leaned forward, kissing him again. "Come." She rose from her chair, taking Kysen's hand. Together, they retreated to her Master bedroom, closing the door behind them.

Adan watched the door close behind his lover and Irikara. He felt a ping of jealousy and anger that *she* would make love to what was *his* in his very presence, but he also understood the bond between a Maker and their child. He couldn't complain that much, Kysen was more than patient when he had to mate with the females of his Pride. It was only to alleviate his guilt that he decided to allow his females the choice between him and Kysen, but even then, it was the rarest of occasions. He looked around the airplane seeing that he was ultimately alone as the others were resting or asleep. After a few hours of watching television he decided to go to sleep.

CHAPTER NINETEEN
THALLOS, SEMEI AND TENOCH

"You shouldn't have asked Arsalan to join us, Semei!" Thallos roared.

"I thought it wise to get him on our side," Semei said in his defense. His hazel eyes glared at his friend.

"Oh did you? What you did was alert him to our plan. Weren't you aware that he still harbors feelings for, Akama?"

"That bleeding heart, sentimentalist," Tenoch remarked.

Thallos rolled his eyes, ignoring the comment about his friend. He couldn't really disagree with the description. For as long as he'd known his friend, Akama, the Fount was sympathetic to human plight, always looking for and at, the better side of humanity.

"Spare me the accusations that I'm the one giving our plan away. I warned you not to expose yourself or any other vampire on television, but your vanity would have it no other way. I also said we should keep our unit small, but you decided to … as they say, outsource." The sunlight shining through the window gleamed off Semei's bald head as he stood there, arguing with Thallos.

"We needed eyes in all places. Vampires who tried to help the humans needed to be punished for betraying their race," Thallos sat down in one of the comfortable chairs adorning Tenoch's living room. "It was a necessary maneuver in order to prove that we could maintain complete control over this situation … and we do."

"Had you simply used another's voice to alert the humans instead of exposing yourself, anyone who dared to oppose us would have nothing to go on," Semei complained.

"The discovery of at least one Fount's involvement in this was inevitable with the concealment of so many minds," Thallos said, crossing one long leg over the other. "That is why I volunteered to be the face of our movement."

"Why are you so concerned about Akama?" Tenoch asked.

"From the moment they landed in Australia, I've lost my mental connection over them. I don't like not knowing what they are doing considering who Kysen is linked to. Three degrees of separation is too close for my comfort," Thallos replied.

"Then perhaps you shouldn't have involved Darian in the first place," Semei chastised.

"That was not an option and you know that. I had to make an example out of them, or we would have been challenged by others. What I will admit to was underestimating his devotion to Xavier and Natasha," Thallos said, running a finger along the width of his bottom lip.

Semei smirked. "Perhaps this will ease your anxiety; Arsalan had no interest in getting involved one way or the other when I contacted him."

"You're underestimating his relationship with Akama," Thallos said. "The two have a strong bond even if Akama chooses to deny it from time-to-time and we'd be remiss to ignore that fact. I'm sure a smile of promise and a wink from Akama would easily persuade Arsalan to side with them."

"So what if he tells Akama about us. What will that bastard do?"

"Watch yourself, Semei," Thallos warned, not wanting to hear any more insults directed at his best friend.

Semei smirked. "My apologies, I'll withhold my sentiments concerning Akama."

"I think that would be best," Thallos said.

"Still, the question remains the same," Semei said, getting back to the point.

"I don't know. I *do* know that I don't like Arsalan knowing about our plan during this crucial time and he's not standing beside us." Thallos ran his fingers through his long blond locks.

Semei walked to the other chair and sat down. "Even so, two against three, I like our odds."

"Well, Irikara turned them down already, even *knowing* the circumstances. As you've said, as long as no harm comes to Kysen, she won't help them," Tenoch said. His large brown eyes looked over his two companions, and he smiled, revealing one dimple on his right cheek.

"Still, I don't like the fact that their minds have been blocked from me and I can't break through Akama's shields," Thallos said, frowning.

"That is one thing I have always found rather disappointing ..." Tenoch said, pausing for suspense and undivided attention.

Semei huffed. "If you're done pausing for the dramatic effect, finish your damned thought please, so we can move on."

"You are in a mood, I see. Very well, I have always found it disappointing that we cannot read each other's minds. That we are of equal power," Tenoch said.

"Would you be the weaker of us if we weren't?" Thallos asked. "Be careful for what you wish for, my friend."

"Who said I wish for such things. I'm simply stating I wouldn't mind having two territories." He smiled wickedly at his companions.

"In the midst of all that's happened, I was actually forgetting the reason why I abhor you ... Gratitude for reminding me," Semei said.

"Likewise," Tenoch retorted with a slight bow of his head.

"Anyway, I think we're concerning ourselves with needless trepidations. Can you even imagine Arsalan going against us?" Semei chuckled. "He's my closest and dearest friend. He'd never risk hurting me."

"Always expect the unexpected. You've been too relaxed in your immortal existences," Thallos said. "Arsalan isn't my only concern. I don't think you fully have a grasp of what is really at risk here."

"I'm fully aware of what's at risk, Thallos," Semei said, giving the other vampire a menacing glare. "You'd do well to remember that we are on your side."

"I *am* aware of that. In regards to Irikara, which is another reason why I'm not at ease. I've tried to read the minds of her human and vampire servants in her palace. Their minds are blocked."

"That's nothing new," Tenoch said. "All Founts block the minds of those who reside with them in their homes."

"That is true, but even the minds of those who reside in her territory are blocked to me," Thallos said. "It was not that way before. I knew they felt her aura there and that confirmed that she was still in Egypt. Now with their minds blocked, I have no way of knowing if that's still true."

The other two Founts finally understood Thallos.

"I see your point," Semei said. "Irikara is the one Fount who sends out waves of her power to all of her subordinates. This *is* cause for concern. Would it be wise for one of us to reach Maska, to see if he would join our cause in case they are forming a movement against us?"

"We'd be making a mistake if we didn't try to get Maska to join us," Thallos said. "Tenoch, you're friends with him, why don't you make the offer."

Tenoch sighed. "I have already contacted Maska about this endeavor before we moved forward with the plan. He was not interested."

Thallos sighed. "Ask again. I'm not willing to take any chances that our plan may fall through because of any possible sympathy for the humans."

"Hmph, Maska could care less about the humans," Tenoch said.

"That's not what I meant," Thallos replied.

Tenoch chuckled. "Akama?"

Thallos nodded. "He's the variable we could never plan for, yes."

A human servant entered the room carrying a tray with three wine glasses filled with fresh human blood. He offered them to the Founts who took a glass each. Once his tray was empty, he left the room.

"I'll go to him, but don't expect his answer to change just because you want it to," Tenoch said then sipped the blood.

"As long as he does not interfere with what we're doing, I'm content," Thallos said before draining his glass.

***

MASKA

Tenoch stepped out onto his front porch, with its beautiful white columns and red brick flooring. He took to the air, flying at speeds only a Fount could master. Within an hour, he landed on the front steps of Maska's luxurious mansion located among the beautiful mountain tops of Alaska. A human servant opened the door and stepped aside to allow him entry. He walked past the servant following the traces of his friend's aura to a large room filled with the visuals and fragrant aromas of exotic flowers and plants. Maska laid face-down on a comfortable massage table and one of his female vampire servants was kneading the muscles in his shoulders and back. He did not bother to look up when he addressed his friend.

"Tenoch, if you are here in supplication, don't waste your effort," Maska said by way of greeting.

"Think that highly of yourself, do you?"

"Of course."

"Why won't you join us? Our cause is just," Tenoch questioned.

"If I were to join you, it would be to rule the humans entirely. To be worshiped as the Gods we are, not to subjugate ourselves to their wills. You do this to demand equality. You three are content to live amongst them as you have been for the past six or seven thousand years. I, on the other hand, remember the days when humans would willingly sacrifice themselves at our feet just for a taste of the power we could offer them," Maska said.

"Those days have long since passed."

"Nonsense, humans are exceptionally susceptible to persuasion. They are always searching for meaning in their lives, something or someone to believe in, be it Allah or Aliens. I see no reason why we cannot be the Gods we once were. At least the power we possess is tangible. We break down their laws, their governments, their way of life, they will have no choice but to follow us … or die."

"You're trapped in your own delusion if you believe the entire world would succumb to our rule."

"You are too much of a coward to challenge my theory, I see. You, Semei and Thallos are too afraid to use your power the way it was meant to be used." Maska laughed harshly.

"Remind me, why are we comrades?"

"Because I am the only one who can tolerate your glib personality and that annoying smile you have."

"I pray that's not true," Tenoch joked before growing serious. "Maska, you may want to rule, but we don't. I like the way this world has evolved, I'm content. We just want to do what is best for those of our lines. The humans need to learn this lesson so the mistakes of the past don't continue to be repeated. Our goal is not to have absolute power over them. Perhaps if you climbed down from this mountain top you live on and experience this world, you'd find the joys it has to offer and lose your taste for dominance."

"Not bloody likely," Maska shot back.

"So you won't join us?"

"No."

"So you'll remain an onlooker?"

Maska grew even more curious. "Why do you ask?"

"No reason. I was just offering you a chance to be a part of history," Tenoch lied, well, sort of. There wasn't a soul alive who would deny that the three of them were creating history with their viral outbreak.

"I *am* a part of history… the better part of it. That is not the reason you are asking me these questions, and you know that," Maska retorted, pressing the issue.

"If you're not going to join us and you're happy where you are, we don't need to discuss this any further."

"You bastard! Speak now, the truth."

"What I am going to tell you must never be repeated or I won't speak to you for a thousand years."

"That is doing me a courtesy," Maska joked.

"That doesn't convince me to be entirely honest with you," Tenoch warned. "Besides you know you'll wither and die if I don't visit you at least once a month."

Maska smiled. "Your companionship has meant much to me over the past ten millennia. Very well, I will not say a word."

"There is concern that Akama may be plotting against us."

"He may have empathy for the humans, but he would not be foolish enough to challenge the three of you for their sake."

"There is *also* concern that Arsalan is with him."

"That filthy, wretched rat," Maska cursed, looking up at his friend for the first time since he'd entered the room. His light brown eyes were lit with a fire that only hate could bring.

"He is that. He may also side with Akama because of their relationship. That is, if Akama is actually planning something against us," Tenoch said with a smile, noticing he'd finally gotten Maska's attention at the mention of Arsalan's name.

"You do not know for certain?" Maska asked.

"We were monitoring Darian and his group's activities, but all contact has been blocked ever since Akama became involved."

"Ahhh." He gazed at his friend thoughtfully. "There is more."

Tenoch smile widened. "There is *concern*–"

Maska huffed. "You have many 'concerns', I see."

Tenoch ignored Maska's snide comment and continued. "There is *concern* that Irikara may be with them." He studied his friend very carefully at the mention of Irikara's name. And yes, that was cause for concern.

Maska's eyes softened and a smile came across his face baring with it a hint of lust and love. He was no doubt recollecting fond memories. "Kysen must be involved," he speculated.

"He is. His *Chosen One*, Darian challenged our rule and his human suffered his punishment."

Maska laughed outright, slapping the massage table. "Oh my! I have not had a hearty laugh like that in a long while. My, my, my, your plate is quite overflowing. It is no wonder you are trying to share some of it with me. I want no part of it."

"So, you'll stay neutral?"

"As far as I am concerned, this is all a waste of time regardless of opposing opinions," Maska said.

"You're always a joy to be with," Tenoch retorted. "I'll visit you later." He vanished, flying back toward his home in Brazil. Once inside, he joined the other two Founts. Royce was now in the room and feeding greedily from Thallos, his mouth sealed to the Fount's left pectoral.

"I take it, he refused?" Thallos asked breathlessly, moaning slightly from the pleasure he was feeling as his lover fed from him.

"Did you really expect him to join us?" Tenoch asked, taking the chair opposite Semei's. The two exchanged *looks* that showed they were just barely tolerating each other's presences for the sake of their mission.

Thallos laughed. "I hope the two of you can keep it together long enough for us to see this through." Even he had been surprised when the two Founts decided to work with him. It was no secret among the seven Founts that Semei and Tenoch hated each other. Both men had Irikara to blame for that. As far as he was concerned, Irikara had all of them bewitched. However, Semei and Tenoch were the only two who fought for her love in a battle that nearly destroyed them both and brought each man no closer to Irikara's heart.

"I don't need for you to watch over me, Thallos," Tenoch said. He remembered the fight he had with Semei, which Irikara provoked with her seduction of them both. Had Maska not reasoned with him, he would have challenged Semei again. In the end, Irikara refused to be claimed by one, especially since she was desired by all. It was a reality they all had to accept. Still, their jealousy was ever present.

Royce pulled away from Thallos, unable to take in any more blood. Thallos, palmed his lover's chin, tilting his face upwards and kissing him passionately. He could taste his own blood on his loved one's tongue as they shared their kiss and it heightened both of their arousal.

"I love you," Royce told Thallos with a passion that was both honest and unbridled.

Thallos ran a finger along the length of Royce's jawline. "I know."

Royce sat on the sofa next to him, relishing the powerful sensation that was flowing through his body and basking in the love and devotion he felt for the Fount.

"Should we release a warning to all vampires who are using their blood to keep humans alive?" Semei asked. "They may not be giving it to the government … however, they are still interfering."

Thallos shook his head. "That was expected and also in our best interest."

Semei was puzzled. "I don't pretend to understand everything that is going on in that mind of yours, but I'm going to need you to explain your reasoning right now."

"At first, I was in agreement with you, but then I gave our predicament more thought. The humans are aware that drinking vampire blood is buying them time, but death by this virus is inevitable," Thallos said. "For the first time since our exposure, humans on a global scale are realizing how much they need us. I think it would be in our best interest to continue to allow vampires the opportunity to help their humans as long as they don't try to be heroes by aiding the world's governments."

"When do we open negotiations?" Tenoch asked.

"When the death toll has reached ten million worldwide," Thallos replied.

"That shouldn't be too long. Currently it's eight million the world over," Royce pointed out.

"At ten million dead, the humans would be foolish to refuse our demands," Thallos said.

Semei chuckled. "What if they tell us that 'they don't negotiate with terrorists'?"

"Then we'll tell them the cure will be withheld until the death toll reaches one-hundred million. Maybe then, they'll be willing to bend their high-handed morals," Thallos answered.

"If the Council can't come to some sort of agreement with the humans after all of this, I plan on killing them. They've proven to be nothing but a disappointment. This is their last chance at redeeming themselves as far as I'm concerned," Tenoch said.

"I believe we actually agree on something," Semei told Tenoch.

The Founts discussed their next move or moves depending on various scenarios. After a while, they fed then went to rest. All except Thallos and Royce who spent a little more time together before resting. They all agreed that in less than three days, they would be able to negotiate with the humans and if the humans were smart, they would be able to come to reasonable agreement. That was the expectation, at least.

CHAPTER TWENTY
A HEATED REUNION

The other three Founts and their companions arrived at Maska's home in Alaska. The human servant wasn't surprised to see them when he opened the door and allowed them entry. They were led through the grandeur of Maska's mansion, passed by all of his beautiful artwork and handmade furniture. The Fount was waiting for them in his den among several of his servants both human and vampire.

"You have a lot of nerve to enter my territory without permission," Maska told his unwelcome guests.

"Come now, Maska. There's no need for friends such as we are to request each other's permission for a visit. You proved that yourself when you visited my territory two centuries ago," Arsalan said, taking a seat on one of Maska's comfortable, handmade chairs. He looked around the room, silently admiring the furniture which was works of art in their own way.

Maska sneered. "We have never been friends, Arsalan."

"And to think, there was once a time when we used to enjoy each other's company." Arsalan said, smiling devilishly.

"Having sex does not mean we had a friendship."

Arsalan laughed. "Don't worry, the feeling is very mutual. However, I didn't come all the way to your retched territory to discuss the endless depth of my distaste for your very existence, no I did not. We're here to ask you to join us against Thallos, Semei and Tenoch."

"If I thought Akama would remove your revolting head from your body, thus ending your miserable life, I'd take on all three Founts willingly simply to show my gratitude. However, we both know that is just wishful thinking on my part," Maska shot back.

Akama couldn't help but laugh. "The both of you are setting such a terrible example for the young ones over there." He pointed to their young companions who were standing in the far corner of the room. "What's disappointing is that I've said that particular phase more than once in the past forty-eight hours."

"Well, I don't recall anyone asking you to play referee or assume the role of a parent," Arsalan retorted.

"You're both ten-thousand years old and look at you." Akama sighed. "For the sake of progression, can we put aside the hostility and talk business?" he asked the two Founts.

Maska huffed. "Very well. I will tell you exactly what I told Tenoch when he asked me; 'No, I will not get involved.'"

"Any reason why you won't?" Akama asked.

"I already know; he wants to rule the humans. Still living in the past, I see," Arsalan remarked.

"Well, I see no reason for us to continue this conversation. Apparently, you have all wasted your time coming here. Please leave," Maska said.

"You're a coward, Maska," Arsalan stated.

Maska sneered, revealing the tips of his fangs. "Get out."

Akama rose, ready to depart. If he wouldn't join Thallos' party or their own, he was satisfied with the other Fount's neutrality. He paused when he noticed that Arsalan and Irikara remained seated.

"You preach on and on about ruling the humans, you've done so for the past four-thousand years, yet you make no attempt to. Have you lost your spine? You have not made even the smallest effort toward what you claim is your goal," Arsalan said. "We will not support you; therefore you will not support us. *Swine!*"

In a fit of blind rage, Maska lunged from his chair striking Arsalan across the jaw. The other Fount regained his bearing and countered with a backhand, knocking Maska back into his chair. Both men rose, poised to attack, their fangs bared as they hissed at each other. Irikara rose from her chair and stepped between them, placing her hand on their heaving chests. The fearsome Founts continued to growl at each other, but they didn't attempt to lunge forward, not with Irikara standing in the way.

"Calm down, the both of you. I did not come on this venture to bear witness to the two of you airing out old issues better left in the past. I would like to get back to my territory at some point, so let us sit down and discuss this like four rational beings," Irikara said as she slowly removed her hands from their chest, but not before letting her fingers brush along their muscular torsos. A tiny smile of satisfaction flashed across her face before her expression went blank.

Both Founts looked at her then back at each other and gave a silent nodded. They stepped away and the three of them settled back into their seats. They began to calm down even though they didn't take their eyes off each other. Akama stood watching the three Founts, shaking his head at their antics, which he had grown accustomed to having known both men for as long as he had. Their younger companions stood silently as they witnessed the feud between the two male Founts. At that moment, some were happy to be on the far corner of the room, seemingly oblivious to the powerful vampires and hopefully away from danger.

"Gentlemen, please give Maska and I a minute so that we may speak … privately," Irikara requested with a sweet honey seduction added to every word. She knew full well what she was doing and the allure she possessed. Men gave in to her every whim and she would be damned if she were rejected. Kysen had been the only man to ever deny her. Had he not been her favorite, she would have surely killed him. She watched as Arsalan finally retracted his fangs. He rose from his chair and left the mansion with Akama, followed by their young companions. She turned back around, meeting Maska face-to-face.

"If I do not see him ever again, it would be a blessing," Maska said under his breath. "Did they use Kysen against you to get you to join them?"

"Kysen asked me to join and I did so, but not without a request of my own. Now I have one I will ask of you and I expect nothing less than a positive response. I want you to join us, Maska. With you on our side, Thallos and the others would be less likely to challenge us."

"Keeping Kysen out of harm's way?"

"As much as I can."

"You do realize having me with you will not dissuade him from what he is doing. If challenged, he will make certain to send as many to the afterlife as he can. Furthermore, what about our solemn oath?"

"I am sure you are well aware that our goal is not to kill Thallos," Irikara said.

"I am sure you are well aware that Thallos will not give up without a fight which may incidentally result in his death or the death of another Fount," Maska replied.

"None of us want that, which is why I am here speaking with you," Irikara said.

"I told Tenoch I would stay out of it … that is my final answer. It was an acceptable answer for him, and it must be acceptable for you as well," Maska said, settling back into his comfortable chair.

"Tenoch is your closest friend, are you not concerned for him?" Irikara ran a delicate finger down the length of Maska's arm, sending an electric current through the surface of his skin and igniting his lust for her.

Maska panted slightly as he struggled to remain calm under her seduction. He cleared his throat before replying. "He does not have Thallos's conviction. I am fairly certain he will not attack me or you for that matter. Neither will Semei. Their feelings for you are too strong. I must admit, Akama persuading you to join him was very smart, indeed." He chuckled under his breath as his eyes lingered lustfully over Irikara's voluptuous breasts.

"That is exactly what I want to hear. Tenoch will not attack you. I am quite certain you are not willing to lose Tenoch after all this time. If we fight, he may not survive. The risks are too great for us all to take such a chance, would you not agree?" Irikara watched Maska, looking for any sign of resignation.

"Then perhaps you should abandon your plans to attack and let this … whatever this is … take its course," Maska said with resolution.

"Hmm." Irikara rose from her chair, walking behind Maska. She placed her hands gently on his shoulders, running her fingers over the firm muscles. "I'm very disappointed to hear you say these things, very disappointed indeed."

Maska began to tense underneath her touch in spite of his inner struggle not to show any signs of apprehension. Irikara was the one Fount none of the men wanted to ever disappoint.

"The humans will come around, they know they are unmatched.

They are beneath us. I feel that for all of your declarations of doom, you are panicking unnecessarily," Maska said in the calmest tone he could muster although the slight quiver to his words betrayed his façade.

Irikara ignored his assumption as she continued to gently message his shoulders. "Perhaps Arsalan was not too harsh in his accusation."

Maska huffed before turning around to face her. "You, yourself care nothing about the human race! The only reason why you are trying to convince me to go with you is to protect Kysen. If he was not involved, you would not be here. Save your judgment for someone else."

Irikara gave him a wicked smile with a slight curve of her lips. "It is true my concern for the human race is minimal at best. However, I do not make declarations about ruling the humans without any conviction behind them, as you do. You are too afraid to try to rule on your own and need the rest of us to join you. Let me tell you, my dear Maska, I do not see that happening any time soon."

Maska looked at Irikara, speechless.

"I will promise you this: If my Kysen is to parish in this confrontation, I will seek to destroy your *Chosen One*, Gabrielle."

"You would not dare!" Maska hissed.

"I will. You know that I will."

"Does our history together mean anything to you?"

"Does it mean anything to *you*? You should not want to see me suffering the loss of my child. If you love me as you say you do, you will help me protect him," Irikara challenged.

"Woman, you work a dark magic. Of that, I am certain."

"What is your answer?" Irikara asked.

Her face was void of all emotion, making her unreadable. A cold chill rippled through Maska but he managed to keep it from showing.

Maska nodded. "Very well, because I do love you and I want to protect Gabrielle, I will join you." He didn't doubt that Irikara wouldn't hold a grudge against him and her vengeance would be cruel. He also knew that the other Founts would not join him if he sought to imprison or punish her. If anything he'd be the one locked away if he attempted retribution.

"Would you happen to know where they are?" Irikara asked.

Maska shook his head. "No. Tenoch would not divulge any information to me unless I joined them."

"Perhaps you can contact them, tell him you changed your mind."

Maska laughed. "He would not believe me. Unlike you, they never threatened to kill one of my own."

Irikara sighed. "We should go."

"I will have Gabrielle at my side. We do not depart until she is with us," Maska said.

"Fair enough. How long before she is able to join us?"

"She will be here within the hour."

"I would hope so. The sooner we can be done with this, the better."

They delayed an hour for Maska's child, Gabrielle to arrive. She entered the mansion, making her way to the room where her Maker and Master waited for her. She entered and looked at both Maska and Irikara and knew something was terribly wrong.

"Hello, Master," Gabrielle said, bowing to Maska. "Goddess Irikara," she gave in greeting to Irikara.

"My child," Maska said as he rose from his chair. "You will accompany me on this foolhardy venture. I will have you by my side if only to protect you."

"Master, what is wrong?" Gabrielle asked, her Spanish accent accentuating each word, making them sound exotic. Her straightened herself and brushed long dark brown bangs from her green eyes to gain a better view of her Master's face.

"We four Founts will confront Thallos, Semei and Tenoch. Hopefully we will be able to come to a reasonable and speedy resolution so that I may return to my territory," Maska informed.

"I thought … Never mind, I will accompany you as you wish," Gabrielle said. Mentally, she communicated with her Maker. *Master, if I may, I thought you said we will stay out of this. Why now are we getting involved?*

In the same fashion, he answered her. *Irikara vowed retribution against me if her child died as a result of me not helping her.*

How is that your fault if Kysen is foolish enough to die? Gabrielle asked.

Because she asked me for my help. If I refused and he died, she would see that as a direct result of my refusal to protect him, Maska replied.

I've never known you to give into anyone's threat. What did she say to you to get you to submit?

She told me she would kill you.

Oh.

Maska gave her a quick nod. "We leave now." They followed Irikara who took to the sky leading the way back to her airplane. Both Founts and Gabrielle rejoined the others who were waiting for them. Having waited an hour for Irikara to give word about Maska, Arsalan was somewhat surprised to see that she had convinced the other Fount to join them. He was sure Maska would be stubborn and stay put, although when he saw Gabrielle enter behind them, he suspected Irikara had pulled the right string. Arsalan wasn't the only one shocked to see Maska and his *Chosen One* climbing aboard; Akama was taken aback as well as the others. No one asked him why he decided to change his mind. They only accepted that he was there.

"We have but one obstacle before us," Irikara began. "We have no idea where they are."

"I was trying to figure out a plan on how to find them myself," Akama said.

"Well?" Irikara looked at him.

"After trying to read the minds of the vampires in their territory only to realize that I was being blocked, I decided our best option is to send in Arsalan."

"This is news to me?" Arsalan said.

"They know that I would never join them. They at least suspect Irikara is working with me if they can't detect her through her subordinates," Akama said.

"I've been shielding myself ever since I joined you. They'll suspect me as well," Arsalan argued.

"Maybe, maybe not. Semei would be willing to accept you, especially if you say I spurned your advances," Akama said.

Arsalan began to think about that plan. "So you're saying I pretend to join them to spite you and perhaps strong-arm you into becoming my lover?"

"It is not farfetched," Maska remarked. "Which only speaks

volumes about your character."

Arsalan smirked. "At least it proves that I have the motivation to achieve my desires. What's your excuse?"

Maska growled, baring his fangs once again. Arsalan hissed, baring his.

"Gentleman ... this is neither the time nor the place to settle old scores. I'll not have my plane ruined because the two of you could not control yourselves," Irikara interrupted.

The two male Founts looked at her, then back at each other. They retracted their fangs and settled back into their seats.

Akama shook his head, but continued. "It's our only recourse. We can't fly around looking for their location, narrowing our search between their three territories. Do we all agree?"

"Tell me again why I'm the best candidate? Why can't we use Maska ... unless your concern is that he will turn belly-up and betray us," Arsalan asked, purposely provoking the other Fount.

"Arsalan, please, stop antagonizing him. The reason why I said you should do it is because of what you've just said, 'you have motivation to achieve your desires.' I have every confidence that you'll be able to convince them to let you in, especially if they find out that Maska joined me and Irikara."

"You want them to know about that?" Zaire asked.

Akama nodded. "If there's one thing we all know is that Maska refused to help them. If we managed to get him on our side, my hope is that they'll be desperate to tip the power scale to their side when Arsalan offers to join them. Four against three, it's what we want; it's what they'll want, too."

"Ah, I see. Makes perfect sense," Zaire agreed.

"Sound plan, but you're missing one aspect," Arsalan said, leaning forward and kissing Akama deeply.

"And that is?" Akama asked once the kiss was broken.

"You didn't take into consideration how serious they are about this mission of theirs. They may not take too kindly to me only wanting to join them for the sake of blackmailing you into my bed. We all have a clear idea of Thallos' character. Even if I can convince Semei and Tenoch to let me in, and that's an unlikely possibility, Thallos will refuse me. The three of them have wholly committed themselves to this attack on the humans. They aren't going to want to accept someone whose agenda isn't theirs," Arsalan said.

Akama frowned. "I understand."

Gabrielle walked over to Maska, placing a hand on his shoulder to gain his attention. "The sun will be rising soon, the young ones will need to rest," she said, referring to Xavier and Darian. At seven thousand years old, she was as resilient and ancient as Zaire and Kysen, so she would not need to rest, at least not at sunrise.

"The differences in the time zones have been putting us in a predicament regarding the younger ones," Arsalan said with a hint of agitation.

"How are we going to find out where they are?" Zaire asked, getting back to the important topic at hand.

"This is also a long shot, but it's worth a try," Warren interjected, gaining everyone's attention. "If you call him using your cell phone, we can track the pings using satellite to see which tower the call bounced off of to connect. This won't give us an exact location, but it will let us know which city they're in at least."

Akama pointed at Warren. "That may be our best option."

"How will you be able to locate them if you're all blocking each other?" Natasha asked.

"We can still feel each others' auras. Each Fount is connected in a mystical way. We know when another Fount is nearby," Akama said. "We can shield our thoughts from each other and we can communicate telepathically with each other. However, we cannot completely mask our presences from another Fount."

"That explains why you all were worried about our plane being destroyed by Maska for entering his territory uninvited," Warren commented.

Maska chuckled softly.

Irikara cocked an eyebrow. "No one was worried, little wolf," she remarked with an air of arrogance so thick you could almost see it.

Warren decided not to say anything else on the matter. He felt he didn't need to—they all remembered the conversation the three Founts had. If they wanted to keep face, he wasn't going to expose them anymore than he already had.

"More or less, yes, you are correct," Akama said, getting back on the subject of locating their targets. "If we can get close enough to the city they're in, we'll be able to feel the echoes of their auras, and zero in on them."

"Well, we should do this tomorrow night," Zaire said.

"Another thing, when we do attack them, I think it's wise if the weakest members of our party aren't there," Arsalan suggested.

"Meaning the human woman and shifters?" Akama asked.

Arsalan nodded. "Especially them."

"Hey wait a minute. I'm not afraid to fight," Warren said in his defense.

"Do you honestly believe that you will have a chance to even lift a finger against them?" Arsalan pointed out. "Do you realize how quickly I could kill you? How easy it would be for any of us to snuff out your life? Even the youngest of us over there …" he pointed toward Xavier. "… can kill you. Shifters have their purpose in this world and fighting vampires isn't one of them. Serving our wills and our … *appetites* is your only worth."

"What the *fuck* did you just say to me?" Warren blurted out in his anger. He had been on the receiving end of a lot of vampire arrogance in his lifetime, but never had he been told that his only usefulness was to serve as a feedbag or servant to a *fucking bloodsucker.*

Arsalan was out of his chair, across the room with his hands wrapped tightly around Warren's neck within an instant. "You are not in a position to question me." He applied more pressure cutting off Warren's air supply.

"Please, don't hurt him, please!" Natasha pleaded for her friend's life. Xavier held her close, keeping her out of harm's way as she struggled in his arms to get free. He wanted to go to Warren's aide as well. He wanted to tell the Fount that Warren didn't mean to anger him. But he knew that Warren meant every word and lying would only incite more rage in the powerful Fount that might result in all of their deaths. Furthermore, his priority was protecting Natasha. He knew she had no idea how powerful these Founts were and how little they cared about killing supernaturals they felt were beneath them.

Kysen held on to Darian and Adan when he felt their bodies tense. He would not risk his child or his lover being killed while trying to defend their friend, who in his opinion didn't know how to adhere to better judgment and remain silent.

Akama rose from his chair, stepping close to Arsalan. "Release him, Arsalan. We don't have time to fight amongst ourselves."

Arsalan released a low growl and tossed Akama a *look* that proved he had no patience for *lower beings* mouthing off. He settled his menacing gaze back on Warren whose face was now turning blue. "Remember your place, dog," he said as he loosened his grip letting Warren fall to the floor gasping desperately for air.

Warren coughed, gagged and choked until he could finally fill his lungs with air. He stayed on the floor on his hands and knees struggling to regain his composure. When his breathing returned to some sort of normalcy, he looked up at Arsalan who still stood over him glaring down. "It is that same arrogance that put us in the predicament we are in now."

Arsalan sneered. "And you still speak out of term even though you were warned." He shook his head in disbelief at the young wolf's stupidity … or was it bravery? He couldn't quite decide which one.

"How can you demand equal rights from the humans if you don't even consider yourselves equal to any species or even each other?" Warren shot back.

"Stupidity it is," Arsalan said as he reached down grabbing Warren by the collar of his shirt.

Akama caught his hand, stopping him. "Let him go, Arsalan. I'll not see any harm come to these young ones. Not by our hands, at least."

Arsalan huffed but released Warren. "You tolerate them far too much, lover." With that, he walked away returning to his chair with a sour expression distorting his otherwise beautiful features.

Akama helped Warren to his feet and sighed as he looked at the young shifter. "You present a good question. Nothing is ever really equal. There will always be the rich versus the poor. There will always be those who have plenty versus those who have none. And where we are concerned, there will always be a divide between the most powerful among our kind and the weakest. As a wolf, I'm sure you are aware and accepting of these levels."

"From the Alpha to our youngest member, however, we all love and respect each other," Warren said in his defense.

"But you are not equal. Feline shifters don't see themselves equal to canine shifters and vice versa. Young one, don't you see that you have accused us of something that we are all guilty of, including humans?" Akama held Warren gaze as he waiting for a response.

Warren thought about what the Fount said, as much as he wanted to deny it, he couldn't refute the truth in what was said. He nodded. "I just want there to be peace. I always have."

Akama smiled. "I can tell; you seem the type. You're like I am, ever the idealist, or so I'm told. What we want is what is fair. In your Pack, you all share one meal, one home, and one family. In this world, we all must share it and everything in it. If there is one lifeboat, let's share it. There is more than enough for everyone to enjoy, wouldn't you agree?" he asked him.

Warren nodded. "It's too bad some wouldn't."

"That is why we must convince them before too many lives are lost," Akama said.

"Why are you even here, if not for sustenance?" Arsalan asked Warren.

"I'm doing this for Natasha," Warren said, feeling more noble than afraid.

"Doing what, marching to your death for her? Don't allow your pride to overpower you common sense. You know you'll only get in the way. Surely, you must be aware that you're no asset to this fight. Your death will be quick and forgettable in the mist of battle. Is that the legacy you want to leave behind?" Arsalan watched Warren from his chair.

Warren wanted to argue, but logic won out. He knew the Fount was right. No matter how painful it was, he had to admit to himself, he was not needed. He shook his head.

"If Darian doesn't go, Kysen won't feel obligated to go," Irikara said.

"We need both him and Darian," Akama pointed out.

"But not Xavier?" Arsalan asked.

"If Kysen goes, I must insist that Xavier go as well. He and his human are the only reason why I have been drawn into this," Irikara fumed.

Xavier tossed Darian a look of annoyance. He didn't too much appreciate being discussed as if he wasn't there. Darian nodded, but remained silent, fully understanding his lover's sentiments. He also knew it would be unwise to interrupt the Founts at this point.

"Very well, we'll take the two youngest along. Therefore, we're going to have to wait until nightfall for sure before we confront them," Akama said. "Arsalan, will Bahashiri be joining us?"

"She will, I've already contacted her," Arsalan said.

"That's good to know. We have no idea how many people Thallos has working with him. We don't want to go in unprepared," Akama said.

"I'll contact one of my own to join us. He can be trusted," Kysen said.

"Who?" Darian asked.

Kysen gave him a mischievous smile that made Darian even more suspicious.

"Who are you contacting, Kysen," Darian asked once more.

"Julius."

Darian snorted. "Why him?"

Kysen chuckled knowing the real reason behind Darian's attitude. "Because he's nearly four-thousand years old, he has drank from Irikara, as you have and he'll fight to the death if I ask him to. That is all you really need to know. Be grateful I'm doing this for you."

"My apologies, Master. I didn't mean to question you," Darian said.

"Yes you did, let that be the last time you do so on this matter," Kysen replied.

Darian nodded.

"Good then," Akama said, noting the conversation between Maker and child had reached its conclusion. He continued. "We'll stay in Maska's territory for the time being. Rejuvenate ourselves. Arsalan make the call from your territory in case they have the same technology we're going to use. We don't want them growing suspicious any more than they already are, no doubt."

"Very well," Arsalan agreed.

"Once you get a general location, contact us and we'll fly there," Akama said.

"I'll meet you, then?" Arsalan asked.

Akama nodded. "You will have to, so don't waste time needlessly."

"What if you lose?" Warren asked.

"That's a very likely possibility. If we do fail, Natasha's fate will be decided. Either the human government will give into the demands of Thallos in a time for the cure to be dispersed ... if that's his plan. Or she'll die if it comes too late, if at all. I suggest you prepare for the worst and wait to see if the best happens," Akama answered.

"Sound advice," Adan murmured.

"That's kind of where I've been all along, actually," Natasha said softly.

Irikara huffed and rolled her eyes upward. The human, her lovers and her friends annoyed her to no end. She almost wanted to kill the woman herself. "Well, I will not be staying in Alaska or Montana. Perhaps we will go to Chicago. I would like to see this little city I hear so much about," she said.

"Maska, is that acceptable?" Akama asked. He knew that Irikara would get her way. Not one of them had ever managed to deny her anything she wanted. He was right.

"If Chicago is where you want to await Arsalan's response, then so be it. I am sure the Master of the state and city would be more than willing to accommodate us," Maska said, turning toward Darian.

They all followed suit, looking at Darian for confirmation.

"But of course," Darian answered. "I'll contact my hotel for arrang–"

"We will stay in your home," Irikara interrupted with another demand.

Finding himself unable to refuse, Darian nodded. "I'll call home and have them make arrangements."

"I will be sleeping in your bedroom, as I assume it is the most luxurious," Irikara said.

"As you wish," Darian replied through tight lips. It was taking all of his reserve not to refuse her.

"Splendid! We leave now," Irikara said, smiling devilishly.

Natasha frowned, thinking about how Irikara was going to be staying in *her* house, sleeping in *her* bed that she shared with *her* men. Then another thought came to her and she mentally kicked herself for not thinking of it earlier. "Wait!"

The others turned toward her some with questioning expressions, some with annoyed ones.

"What is it?" Akama asked.

Natasha cleared her throat. "Arsalan doesn't have to go, well, that's not what I mean—"

"Speak your mind human! Your lovers may have the patience for you, but we do not," Maska said with unwarranted rudeness.

Damn motherfucker, really? Natasha thought to herself as she looked at the North American Fount. So far, the only Fount she liked was Akama and *thank God* for him. "What I'm trying to say is I can use my ability to link to one of them. That way we could spy on them and they may or may not know it. It's worth a shot."

Irikara laughed. "You silly little human, do you think you have the ability to see what we do not want you to see? We all know what you can do and it does not impress."

Akama lowered his head as he rubbed his temples. "Let's be productive, please."

Irikara huffed in agitation and then took a deep breath. "All right, humor me. Arsalan obtains something personal of Semei's, we give it to her and she makes a connection, gods willing. We all wait for her to awake from a nap to tell us fragments of a dream she had only to discover that Semei has his mind blocked and all of the visions she has seen have nothing to do with him."

"Natasha's ability is a lot more powerful than you're giving her credit for," Xavier said.

"I did not give you permission to address me so casually," Irikara growled, her eyes glaring at Xavier.

"My Goddess, please. I want to return to my home as soon as possible. I beg of you for patience," Kysen said to some of their relief. Being around so many powerful vampires, those more powerful than he was did not settle well with him. He couldn't wait until he could get back to his own territory where he ruled. There was only so much belittling he could tolerate.

Irikara turned toward him, she saw the expression on his face and she sighed. "Very well … I suppose."

"Good. Arsalan, I'm sure you can enter Semei's territory with ease, gain something of his and bring it to us. We'll be heading toward Chicago and we'll meet you there," Akama said.

"Be gone then," Maska said "encouraging" Arsalan's departure.

He was in a foul mood and didn't really want to talk to anyone. The only bright side he could see was at least that bastard Arsalan was going to be taking his leave soon. That was one annoyance he could do without.

Arsalan tossed Maska a disdainful glare then turned toward his lover. "I'll see you later." He kissed Akama once more then he opened the airplane door and flew away.

"Let's take off," Akama said. Irikara powered her plane, lifting it off the runway and propelling it through the sky toward Chicago at an astonishing speed.

"How long do you think it's going to take him to get to Semei's home?" Adan asked.

"He should arrive there in about an hour. That's if he traveling as fast as he can. It'd be about three hours if he took the long route and slower pace," Akama answered.

"Wow, that's got to be amazing," Warren said.

"Have you ever been flying?" Akama asked.

"Without the aid of a man-made aircraft, no."

"Maybe when all this is over, you can ask one of your vampire friends to take you for a round." Akama smiled.

"I might just do that." Warren returned the smile.

The tension on the plane was so thick you could cut it with a knife. Gabrielle looked at Irikara from across the plane. She tried hard not to let her dislike of the Fount show in her expression or her thoughts. She reached over, patting Maska hand reassuringly.

Natasha hated being so high in the sky with so much agitation between her and her companions. To her, the hostility grew with each new Fount they picked up. Each one was worse than the last as far as she was concerned. She walked into one of the bedrooms to get away from the other Founts. Darian, Xavier and Warren followed her, lying on the bed beside her.

"How are you feeling?" Xavier asked.

"Weak, tired, scared and, a little hopeless," Natasha said, trying not to cry.

Xavier gathered her into his arms. "I don't know what's going to happen. I can't promise you everything will be all right. I can just promise you that I will do everything in my ability to save you."

"I know. Somehow, I feel like all of this is my fault. That Irikara was right," Natasha said.

"Self-pity doesn't become you," Darian commented. "If this is anyone's fault, I'm to blame. I was the one who made the conscious choice to give blood to those scientists."

Natasha looked at him. "Yeah, but you only did so to save my parents, because I have my human attachment to them."

"That's bullshit, Natasha," Warren said. "Irikara may be ten-thousand years old, but that doesn't make her right."

"Shhh, careful what you say about that woman on her plane. I'm sure she can hear everything we're saying," Natasha said.

"Granted. I don't fancy being tossed out at ten-thousand feet in the air. But still, even if you were a vampire at that time, what were your choices? You couldn't turn your parents into vamps. So all you could have done was given them your blood to try to keep them alive until a cure came along? Same thing that's happening now," Warren pointed out.

"Yeah, but if I was a vampire before the virus was released, don't you think I might be handling this better? Or I might have even turned my parents by now," Natasha speculated.

"They're your parents, Natasha. I don't think you could stand by and let them die whether you're a vampire or not. If Darian hadn't given the scientist the blood, you would have yourself," Warren said.

"I would have never allowed that," Darian said.

"What do you mean?" Natasha asked. "Why not? You did."

Darian looked at her. "Not without some measure of regret. The pain I saw in your expression was difficult to bear. Seeing you in so much turmoil impaired my rationale and I acted impulsively. A rash decision was made that we're still paying for," he said. "You have to understand, being a vampire gives you a broader understanding and acceptance of death where humans are concerned. Having outlived so many and being the cause of that death myself, I know what it means to see life slip away, to have it flow over my fingers … my lips. You have not resolved yourself to you parents' foreseeable death or your own, for that matter. Humans for all their mortality feel as though they are immortal and are always fighting to stave off the inevitable."

"You think if I was a vampire, I would have been calmer about their death and if I couldn't save them, I could give them peace?" Natasha asked, slightly irritated by Darian's words.

"Maybe, maybe not. Watching your parents die won't be easy either way. And if they didn't want to become vampires themselves, you really have no choice but to resolve yourself to their death. It was my foolishness that forced me to protect you from that truth. I should have never interfered," Darian said.

"I can't believe you're saying this," Natasha said, shocked and sadden by Darian's words and a single tear from each eye left a wet trail down her cheeks.

Darian leaned closer, wiping her tears with his thumbs. "I'm not saying this to be cruel, but endangering you and my coven by defying this vampire to save humans was not wise, Natasha. Your parents are still suffering and now you are as well. It is a mistake I will never make again."

Natasha sat up, keeping her gaze locked to his. "You tried to do the right thing. I'm not blaming you for this."

Darian's lips curled slightly giving her the faintest of smiles. "If we could turn back the clock, would you wish me to do the same thing knowing where my action would lead us? Speak honestly."

Natasha thought about her answer carefully before giving it. She thought about how fruitless Darian's sacrifice turned out to be. She also thought about the many sacrifices made by heroes throughout history in which one person made a huge difference when faced with insurmountable odds. She decided to give the best answer she could.

"I would still want you to save lives, but I don't know if I'd want you to risk everything to do it. We got lucky that only I was attacked. He could have killed my children and everyone in the house, all of our friends … and call me selfish, but I'm not willing to risk that. Does that make me a bad person?" she asked.

Both Darian and Xavier shook their heads. "No, it doesn't."

Warren slapped his hand on the bed gaining their attention. "Can we end this pity party, for God's sake? It isn't our fault anyway. We can't be sitting here blaming ourselves for what the hell is happening. I'll tell you who's to blame, that crazy-ass motherfucker, Thallos. He's the one who came up with that fucking virus, him and his psycho trio," he fumed.

Xavier actually chuckled. "If Thallos, Semei and Tenoch are to blame, so are all of the human governments that allowed this injustice to grow, festering such resentment and outrage."

"There you go with the big picture again," Warren said.

"We're simply pawns in this game. This battle is between the Founts and the humans," Darian said.

"When do you think it'll all end?" Warren asked. "I mean, they aren't even trying to negotiate, they are just letting people die."

Akama entered the room. "It's an interesting conversation you are all having in here."

"We're just trying to gather ourselves," Warren said. "Maybe you can give us some perspective."

"I can?" Akama asked with one brow cocked.

"Yeah. Why do you think Thallos hasn't opened negotiations with the governments yet? All the governments have got to be willing to talk by now, the death toll is over eight million." Warren waited for the Fount to give his perspective.

Akama frowned, crossing his hands over his chest. "If I know Thallos, and I believe I do, he's most likely waiting for the human governments to be desperate enough to accept the terms of their negotiation."

"Like what? Half the world's population has to die before he decides to give the cure?" Warren asked. "Isn't that bad news for you vampires?"

"Well in all truth, vampires can feed from shifters if need be. And your blood is far more superior to that of humans," Akama replied.

"I don't know about you, but I don't want to live in a world without humans," Warren said. "Not to mention, I don't want to be the main food source for vampires. Devin might not mind, but I sure as hell do."

"We are in agreement, which is why we're taking certain steps to insure we save the human race," Akama said. "Even if you hadn't come to me, I would still seek to save them. As unfortunate as it is that Natasha and her parents must suffer, having Irikara and Maska with us wouldn't have happened if they weren't involved. Everything, no matter how horrible or delightful, happens for a reason … remember that." He turned, leaving the four of them alone.

"Did he just come in here and drop some of that ancient-ass wisdom?" Natasha couldn't help but joke in spite of her current condition.

"I think he did," Warren agreed.

"Zaire's blood is helping so far, right?" Xavier asked Natasha.

"Yeah, the nausea went away for the time being," she said.

"How many hours before we get to Chicago?" Warren asked.

"I believe we have four more hours," Darian answered.

"I almost want to stay at the hotel, but I know that's not practical," Natasha said, dreading having to have the Founts in her home. Well, not all of them were repulsive. She'd be honored to entertain Akama as a guest, but as far as she was concerned, that bitch Irikara had to go. And the same went for that jerk Maska, too.

"I know, but it is what it is. Hopefully it'll just be for one night," Xavier said.

He, like Darian and Natasha didn't appreciate Irikara's manipulation. He could tell that it was a skill she had perfected over her long, long lifetime. He kept hope that they would save Natasha and be rid of their powerful company within the next twenty-four hours. He looked out the window, the sky was starting to lighten up and soon the sun would rise forcing him and Darian into their resting state. Until then, they talked to pass the time away as they traveled to Chicago. That was a destination they were looking forward to.

CHAPTER TWENTY—ONE

John entered the den where a few of the others were watching the news. He, along with the rest of Darian's coven had been staying with Elise so that they could be watched over during the daylight hours. The first few nights were tolerable, but now he was starting to suffer from a little cabin fever. The huge mansion was beginning to feel a bit cramped with her entire Pride and Darian's coven and human servants. He looked at the news, becoming shocked and dismayed that the death toll had reached nine million in less than twenty-four hours. He knew for those humans who didn't have any vampire connections that this virus was destroying their bodies at an amazing speed.

"Hey guys," he said to get everyone's attention. It worked, they all turned, looking at him. "Darian just contacted me, said he was on his way back—"

"—Is Natasha all right?" Devin asked, hoping they were coming back because they cured her.

"No. I did ask that and she's still sick. Darian couldn't get into detail, but he told us to get his mansion prepared for guests. Apparently we are expecting some very special guests," John informed them.

"So like what, we break out the good dishes?" Christopher asked. "Do you know who's coming?"

"He said four Founts and a few others. I know for sure Kysen is coming."

"Founts?! Do you mean the most ancient vampires alive?!" Gary asked, growing excited as he thought about meeting one.

John nodded enthusiastically. "I know! I'm pretty excited to meet them, too. Although Darian did say to stay reserved. I hope that I can."

"We might not be able to meet them. By the time they get here, the sun will be up," Gary complained.

"Well, we still need to get the house prepared," Christopher said, rising from his chair.

"Some of us should go with you. Besides, I'd like to meet one of these Founts my damn self," Sergio said.

"I'd be lying if I said I wasn't intrigued," Elise said.

"I'm going," Devin jumped up.

"I want to go, too," Carman said, rising from her chair.

"Me, too," said Sebastian and Daniel in unison.

"Now wait a minute. Hold on. That's it … just Devin, Carmen, Sergio and myself. No one else is coming," Elise said, holding her hands out in front of her. "I'll not leave the children without the proper amount of protection."

All of the other shifters who had been ready to join them sat back down, sad, but agreeable.

"Good. Now, we'll be back later," Elise said. Then she gathered her purse, and left with the others heading toward Darian's mansion.

Two hours later, they had the guest bedrooms prepared well enough to accommodate royalty, vampire or otherwise. Unfortunately, the rising sun forced the five members of Darian's coven to rest. Elise and three members of her Pride met the guests in the foyer.

"Hello and welcome," Elise greeted the Founts and other vampires as they entered. Zaire and Kysen carried the two coffins containing Darian and Xavier. They placed them down gently in the foyer before turning to address their host.

Irikara passed through the entryway, her eyes panning over the interior of the mansion. "I must say, I did not expect a Master vampire to live in such a mediocre dwelling," she said as she made her way past Elise, Sergio and Devin who were staring at her wondering who she was. They could sense that she was powerful and they suspected she was one of the Founts they'd heard about.

"Irikara, there's no need to be rude. If you wanted a palace to rest in, we could have stayed in Alaska," Akama remarked as he entered.

"Hello," he greeted Elise and the others.

Irikara giggled. "Even Maska's residence was beneath me. There just is no substitute for my own home." She looked around again. "I suppose this will have to do." She glanced at Elise. "And you will attend to us." It was more of demand than a question.

The tone of the vampire's words didn't escape Elise and she gave her a curt smile. She believed this crude woman standing in front of her was the very "Irikara" Kysen had once spoken about. She decided to be courteous enough to the vampire Fount. "I came to help prepare the mansion for your arrival."

"Very well," Irikara said.

Elise looked past Irikara to see Natasha standing by the doorway. "There you are!" She walked over to her friend, ignoring the other Founts to hug her. The other members of her Pride, did the same, hugging Natasha each. "How are you feeling?" she asked.

Akama only chuckled while Irikara and Maska huffed and scowled. Neither Fount was used to being ignored, least of all, for a human. Kysen simply rolled his eyes at the reunion of friends. He was more than a little anxious to be done with all of it at this point. Adan stood quietly beside him, watching the bittersweet interaction take place.

"Zaire gave me some blood to stave off the symptoms of the virus, but I'm still not feeling one-hundred percent, it's more like forty-five percent," Natasha said, understating what she was really feeling, which was stomach cramps, nausea, chills, head and body ache.

"Do they know how to cure you?" Sergio asked.

"We think the cure is in the blood of the Founts who started this. We're supposed to seek them out tomorrow night," Natasha replied.

"Do you need our help?" Elise asked.

"No," Maska answered, having listened to their conversation. "That would be one more problem we certainly do not need."

"And that is?" Sergio asked in the same haughty tone that laced Maska's words.

"Weakness in our ranks," Maska answered with a sneer.

"Is that so?" Sergio remarked. He inhaled deeply, puffing his chest out a little in his annoyance. Elise noticed his heightened state of agitation and decided to intervene before the matter got out of hand.

She placed her hand on his arm and with a gentle nudge, coaxed him away from the Fount toward the direction of the den. He took her hint and walked away without incident.

Elise looked at Maska, whose presence was a little unnerving to her, though she made certain not to show it. As a queen, showing fear in front of her Pride was never an option. Appearances were always important. "If you're going to have to fight for the cure, we want to hel–"

Elise's was interrupted by Maska's hand taking hold of her throat, cutting off her air as he lifted her several inches from the floor. With the exception of the other two Founts, no one else in the room had even noticed he had moved. Sergio turned in time to see *his* queen and lover attacked. He tried to go to her aide, running toward her, but he was tossed through the wall of the parlor into the living room by an invisible force so powerful it kept him pinned to the floor.

"This is but a small display of my power. Understand, you would both be dead by now if I so wished it," Maska said. "You cannot help us." He released Elise, setting her down gently.

Elise rubbed the soreness on her throat as she adjusted her necklace. She had to admit, what she witnessed what extremely impressive. If all of the other Founts were as powerful as he was, then it was true ... they couldn't help.

Irikara watched Sergio rise to his full height, dusting himself off as he did. She raked her eyes over the physical exquisiteness of his body. "My, my, aren't you magnificent."

"I'm also a one-woman man," Sergio remarked.

Irikara giggled. "As if that means anything to me." She stepped closer to him, running a finger down the length of his chest. She smirked as she noticed Elise's growing irritation—the heaving of her chest, the flaring of her nostrils and the hard glare the Pride queen gave her.

"They are here to help us," Akama said, hoping to ease the animosity that was building between the two women. "We're guests in this home."

Irikara's perfectly arched eyebrows rose in mock surprise. "Oh, and here I was under the impression we are here to help them."

Akama chuckled. "Come now, you know I meant they are here to help us settle in. I'm surprised you're not seeking a bed right now."

Irikara smiled seductively at Sergio. "Who says I am not thinking about a bed at this point."

Elise wanted to rip this woman's eyes from their sockets, but decided to react in a manner befitting a queen and *not* a banshee. She approached Irikara, smiling coyly. "You look positively *worn down*. I'm sure you're probably exhausted. Darian informed us that you would need to replenish your energy for tomorrow night. Billy could show you to your rooms."

Akama lowered his head, smiling to himself. The young shifter Queen was quite the spitfire.

Irikara's eyes narrowed into slits. There was no mistaking the underlying insult in Elise's comment. "You are but a speck to me. Something I can flick away like dust. If I so choose, I could kill you within a blink of an eye and take your king for myself."

"Irikara!" Akama moved between the two women. He was impressed by Elise's demeanor. He could clearly see that, as a queen herself, she would not abide Irikara's insults even if it meant a certain death. "We are guests in Darian's home, these are his friends." He gave the female Fount an expression that told her to calm herself.

"Indeed," Irikara smiled at Akama. "Perhaps I am rather tired. I desire rest."

"Of course," Elise said. It took everything she had to be civil to Irikara. She turned toward Billy. "Please escort her–"

"The Goddess Irikara," Kysen corrected Elise.

Elise gave him her most pleasant smile in place of the middle finger she wanted to give him. "Billy, please escort the *Goddess Irikara* to your Master's bedroom."

Billy nodded and bowed to Irikara and then did as he was told.

Irikara followed the human who led her to a set of double mahogany doors. He opened them, revealing the grandeur of Darian, Natasha and Xavier's bedroom. She looked around at all of the lavish furnishing and pouted. "I suppose this will do," she said as she dismissed the servant with a wave of her hand. He bowed and closed the door behind him.

Turning he saw Natasha walking down the hallway. "I've been so worried for you," Billy told her, hugging her gently.

"I still don't know what's going to happen. I don't want to fear the worse, but I don't know if they are going to be able to save me," Natasha said, allowing herself to confide her true feelings to her human friend.

"You can't give up," Billy said.

"They've been giving me their blood to keep me alive. But even now, I can feel myself dying. I know I don't have much time left. I know I want to see my children before I die. If they don't return with the cure tomorrow night, that's what I want to do," Natasha opened the door to the bedroom she was going to sleep in.

Billy watched her walk in, wanting to say something comforting to her but he couldn't find the words. In reality, he didn't believe there were any words he could say that hadn't already been said. He tapped on the now closed door. "Call me if you need anything, Tasha." With that, he left, returning to the den.

Downstairs, the others began to make themselves more comfortable in their new surroundings. Maska who was still in a very sour mood, remained silent. His aura was masked, however, his sheer presence did little to put the others at ease. Some wished he'd simply retire for the time being as Irikara had. But no such luck, at least not yet.

"… We'll do what we can to save her." Akama finished updating Elise on what was going on. He could tell by the expression on her face that she was concerned for her friend.

"She's sicker than she claims to be," Sergio said, frowning. He had been very worried for Natasha and had grown increasingly frustrated every time they spoke with her over the telephone only to realize she was still suffering from the virus.

"The virus is growing immune to our blood, this is true. But she's not dead yet and there's still time," Akama said reassuringly.

There was a silence that filled the room as the others continue to gaze at the powerful vampires sitting before them.

"I can smell your fear and you needn't be afraid," Akama said to Devin.

"Are you sure about that?" Devin asked as his eyes darted over to Maska.

Akama chuckled. "My friend here won't harm you, will you Maska?"

All eyes were on the other Fount now, awaiting his answer.

Maska released a heavy sigh. "Your fear of us simply punctuates the point I made earlier when I said you were weak."

"Just because I'm scared as hell of you doesn't mean I won't fight back. Besides, your point was proven when you 'displayed' your power," Devin replied.

One of Maska's eyebrows twitched and a pleasant smile crept across his face which seemed to throw the others in the room off balance. Many didn't think he knew how to smile. "I finally found one among you whom I like. To answer your question, I will not harm you. Although, I could kill Thallos for his actions. Had he not started this chain of unfortunate events, I would be at my home relaxing right now."

Akama shrugged. "It isn't just one person responsible for this, but many."

Maska rolled his eyes. "As they say in this day and age, 'whatever'. I'm still here and not at home."

Akama chuckled then returned his attention back to Devin. "Are you more at ease now?"

"I'm sorry, it's just … I don't know what to say or if I should say anything at all," Devin replied.

"You can ask me questions, I'm sure you have plenty," Akama said.

"Are you really ten-thousand years old?" Devin asked, he looked at Akama with eyes as big and round as saucers.

Akama chuckled. "I am, give or take a few decades."

"Holy shit! That's so amazing! Don't you ever get bored with life?"

Akama seemed to reflect on the question. "Sometimes, I do."

"What happens then?"

Before Akama could answer them, Maska interrupted him, rising to his feet. "Ah, these are the sort of questions that bore me. I will take my leave now," he said, looking at Billy to escort him to his room.

"Maska, thank you for helping us," Akama said.

"I really had no choice," Maska replied. He left the room; following Billy to another guest bedroom.

"He's kind of scary," Carmen commented about Maska.

Devin cleared his throat. "If I may ask… if you don't think I'm out of line… if it's okay–"

"Ask the damn question already," Sergio blurted out.

Akama chuckled and waited for the younger shifter to gather his thoughts and obviously his courage.

"All right. Um, how come you're not like them?" Devin asked. Having met Maska and Irikara, he had an even higher opinion of Kysen who was the only other ancient vampire he'd ever met. At least with Kysen, they were never attacked.

"I find myself giving this explanation quite often," Akama said. "I don't look down upon those younger than myself or other humans. Before I was a ten-thousand year old vampire, I was also a one year old vampire and before that, I was human. I've been where you are. So keep in mind when you're older, how to treat those younger than yourselves."

A few of them nodded in agreement.

"Another thing you all need to realize is keep whatever opinions you have to yourself as best you can. You don't want to piss any of these guys off," Warren said.

The others looked at him and nodded. They didn't want to doubt the warning behind his message.

"We should all get some rest," Akama said. He turned toward his child. "Zaire, watch over them and await Arsalan's arrival."

"Yes, Akama," Zaire replied.

"I'll show you to your room," Devin said and he led the final Fount to Miko's room which was the third nicest room in the mansion.

"Thank you," Akama said before closing the door.

Devin returned back into the den. "They're so gorgeous, I swear, I want one."

"Suit yourself; they're more high-maintenance than they're worth, trust me. *Especially* Irikara," Warren remarked.

"I could do without her being here," Elise said, brushing her long brown hair over one shoulder.

"I was so worried you two were going to go at it," Carmen said. "I couldn't believe she just flirted with Sergio like that."

"Ugh! I don't want to speak about that woman right now," Elise said.

"Well, I really liked Akama. As a matter of fact, I hope I can convince Akama to bite me later," Devin said almost as an afterthought.

Zaire laughed outright. "You're funny." He had been observing their conversation and couldn't help but laugh.

"Do you think he would?" Devin asked.

"Really Devin, is that what's on your fucking mind right now? Getting off?" Sergio asked, inadvertently cutting in.

"The thought crossed my mind. I didn't mean anything by it. Jeez!" Devin fussed. "It's not every day I meet the most powerful vampires in the world."

Sergio sighed. "Look, I get it, you love being bit and I'm sure that's probably your biggest wet dream, but there are way more important things that we should be focused on."

"Okay, let's discuss them," Devin said with a little more attitude than normal. "There's the rising death count that we can't do shit about. There's the shortage of water supply we can't shit about. There's Natasha's illness we can't do shit about which is the most frustrating of all and on top of that, there's the impending battle we're told we're not needed in. So forgive me for wanting to engage in something to take my mind off of my helplessness right now!"

Sergio cocked an eyebrow. "Feisty when you want to be, aren't you?"

"This is me being nice, but don't label me shallow again, or you'll see *feisty*," Devin shot back. "And fuck you for calling me 'feisty'!" He rolled his eyes and turned away, but not fast enough to hide the smile that he couldn't restrain.

"Fine, you made your points. Gutter mind, you better hope he doesn't drain you dry," Sergio said in his own way of dropping the subject.

"I'm willing to bet that's one awesome way to go, though. But yeah, let's hope." Devin offered him a charming smile and Sergio just shook his head.

Kysen sat in silence as he watched the other vampires and shifters talk amongst themselves. The banter between the two leopards wasn't particularly interesting, but he did find it slightly humorous. He looked at the other ancient vampires, noting that Gabrielle wasn't as talkative as Zaire, but she also didn't seem as stand-offish as Maska was.

His lover, Adan sat down next to him, claiming is attention. "How are you doing at this point?" he asked.

"I cannot recall a time when I have been this exhausted, infuriated and disappointed in my entire existence," Kysen replied.

"Want to go to our bedroom?" Adan asked, imploringly.

Kysen smiled. "I do believe that would ease some of my anger. I do not think it would help my exhaustion, though."

"At least you won't be disappointed."

"No, I do not think so," Kysen said, smiling lushly. "But what about my exhaustion?"

"Oh, you can't be too sure. You may discover some energy you didn't think you had," Adan whispered as he rose from his chair.

Kysen winked as he stood up. He turned toward Elise and Sergio. "I have contacted a child of mine who will assist us. He will be arriving shortly."

"What is his name?" Elise asked.

"Julius," Kysen replied.

Elise nodded.

Adan led the way and Kysen followed him to the bedroom Darian had assigned them.

"Looks like they are getting along wonderfully," Elise commented.

"I guess so, he does seem a little less of an ass," Sergio said.

"Shhhhhh!" Devin shushed. "Dude! He can hear you. Do you want him coming back down here and kicking your ass?"

"I'm just saying he seems to be more at peace," Sergio stated.

Warren chuckled. "You're just seeing the exhausted version of him. He hasn't changed much, although I do agree that having Adan in his life has changed him a bit."

"He still seems a bit happier," Elise noted.

"Then I guess Adan's been taming him, like he said he would,"

Devin said.

There were a few chuckles from some of them at that comment.

"I'm going to rest now, I need to replenish my energy," Gabrielle said.

"You'll be sleeping in the guest bedroom," Elise said. "Billy, if you could."

Billy nodded and escorted Gabrielle to her room.

All of the vampires with the exception of Zaire who was given instructions to watch over them, were now resting. Warren sat looking at him, still curious as to why he was Akama's *Chosen One*. He liked him well enough and he seemed nice, but he still knew little to nothing about him. He felt sort of guilty that he was now involved. He was still amazed by how fast this horrible situation of theirs had snowballed.

Zaire felt the attention he was suddenly getting. He looked up from the book he had just started reading to see several pairs of eyes looking back at him. "What is it?" he asked.

"Are you afraid of facing the other Founts?" Devin asked him.

He thought about his reply before he gave it. "Yes, but I will follow my Master into death if need be. Although, I don't think it would escalate that far ... but who's to tell?"

"How do you feel about what's going on?" Elise asked.

Zaire answered. "I blame the Council for not demanding equal rights. I blame the humans who've allowed this injustice to go on for this long. I blame the most powerful of our kind for ignoring the suffering of others. And as much as I love and admire Thallos, I blame him for deciding to use this virus as a weapon."

"You *love* him?" Devin asked.

Zaire nodded. "Of course, I do. You have to understand, he and Akama have been best friends for over nine-thousand years. I don't agree with what he's doing, but I'm willing to bet he'll get the results he wants."

"I'm sure he will," Sergio said rather grimly.

"If you don't mind me asking, how old are you?" Devin asked.

Zaire smiled. "Seven-thousand, six-hundred and forty-eight years old."

"Shit!" Devin and Sergio said in unison.

"That is one thing I admire about vampires. You have eternity ahead of you," Elise said.

"Sometimes, it gets tiring," Zaire said.

"Yeah about that, what do you do when you get bored with life?" Devin asked once again. His earlier attempt to get an answer had been thwarted by Maska.

Zaire shrugged. "When it gets to the point when you need a break from the mundane, you can entomb yourself for a few years, or centuries. It's best to let someone know beforehand what you plan on doing. After taking a *Reprieve*, you're very weak, starved, you'll need someone to help you rise and feed."

"I take it you've had a *Reprieve*?" Sergio asked. "For how long?"

"Hmmmm … I think I must have slept for fifty years one time. Another time, I slept for two-hundred," Zaire answered.

"What about Akama?" Devin asked.

"Unfortunately being a Fount, he can't take a *Reprieve* as the offspring can," Zaire said. "He needs blood regularly. I hope that shares some light as to why some of them are the way they are."

"Jaded, arrogant and obnoxious," Elise commented. "Well, with the exception of Akama."

Zaire chuckled. "He's different. He enjoys watching people evolve … he enjoys people. He loves watching history in the making and even though what's going on now is unfortunate, it's also a good thing, too. Changes will be made."

"What kind, though? That's the question," Warren said.

Zaire nodded. "Thallos doesn't want to rule humans, that won't be in his list of demands."

"Yeah, but that guy Maska does. He said so."

"Maska will not be getting his wish. If he could have it his way, he would have many years before now."

"Do you think Thallos will give us the cure?" Warren asked on a more serious note.

"He will if the odds are properly stacked against him. That much I'm certain of," Zaire replied.

"That's good to know," Warren said. "We should go check on Natasha."

They all agreed and went upstairs to do just that. Warren opened the door and they stepped into the room.

"She doesn't look good," Devin said grimly. "Maybe we should call the others to come here."

"The others?" Zaire asked.

Devin nodded. "Xander and his Pack, Richard and his Pack, I think they'd want to be here."

"That's a good idea, I'll do that," Billy said. Then he walked to a corner of the bedroom to make his calls.

Elise emerged from the bathroom carrying a cool damp towel. She began wiping sweat from Natasha's face. "Her fever's getting worse."

"Not to mention her skin is starting to break out," Sergio said, pointing to a new open wound on Natasha's right arm that was weeping blood and puss.

"Jesus." Elise gave a silent prayer. She couldn't believe her eyes. Here was one of her best friends, dying and she could do nothing to save her. She thought about what a great loss it would be for them all, but especially for Natasha's children. For them to grow up without their mother was something Elise didn't want to imagine.

Billy stepped up to them. "They said they're on their way."

"Good," Elise said.

"We should wake her up," Zaire said.

"Should we? I mean at least she's sleeping through the worst of her suffering," Devin said.

"She needs to drink some more of my blood, or she'll be in worse shape when she does finally wake up, if she'll even wake up at all," Zaire said.

Elise looked at Sergio and Devin then back down at Natasha. "Very well." She began to shake Natasha gently, then a little more forcefully until her eyes opened.

"Are we there yet?" Natasha asked weakly, her eyes were barely open. She ran her pale tongue over her dried and cracked lips trying to moisten them.

Elise frowned but managed to keep her tears from flowing. "No, darling, you need to drink more blood to help heal you," she said. She slipped several pillows underneath Natasha's torso to prop her up.

"Here," Zaire offered Natasha his wrist. Blood poured freely from the wound he'd made and now Natasha was gently sucking, taking as much as she could.

Warren reluctantly pulled his gaze from them to look at his watch. "I wonder what's taking Arsalan so long?"

"He'll be here, don't worry," Zaire said, his eyes still locked on Natasha. He frowned seeing that his blood was having very little effect on her. "Her illness has gotten worse."

Warren and the others saw how pale and slick with sweat Natasha's skin was, they noticed the wound on her arm did not heal completely and they knew the time had come to accept that they might not be able to save their friend.

***

Arsalan made it home an hour before, showered and fed. He had to wait for his *Chosen One*, Bahashiri to join him with the technology he would need to trace the telephone call before he could make it. He wasn't one to put all of his eggs in one basket, so to speak. He'd use both Warren's idea as well as Natasha's ability. He made the decision before going home, to go to Semei's mansion and retrieved a personal item that was dear to his friend. The benefit of doing that eliminated one location they needed to search. He didn't want to try the other Fount territories; that would draw too much suspicion. Thallos and the others were not in Antarctica and that was good enough for him. His child, Bahashiri sat next to him on his lush sofa, watching and waiting for him to make his call. Setting the system in place, he sat down to call his good friend, Semei, dialing his cell number.

"I didn't expect to hear from you so soon since we last spoke," Semei said upon answering.

"I didn't think we'd be speaking this soon either," Arsalan replied. "So why are we?"

"I've had time to think about your proposition and I'd like to take you up on your offer."

There was a few seconds of silence on the other end, Semei was curious as to why his friend had changed his mind. He was curious *and* suspicious.

"Are you still there?" Arsalan asked, breaking the silence,

knowing he was still on the line.

"Why now?" Semei finally asked.

"Does it matter?"

"You know that it does. This is a very sensitive time and we cannot afford any sort of interference."

"So I've been told before," Arsalan said. "Akama asked me to join him, Irikara and Maska–"

"Irikara and *Maska*! They are both with him?" Semei asked, shocked to hear that Maska had joined with Akama. He was quite certain that the Fount of the North American line would stay neutral.

"They are both with him. They wanted me to joined them–"

"Why didn't you?" Semei asked, now even more suspicious than before.

"How many times are you going to continue to interrupt me?" Arsalan gritted out.

"I hadn't realized, please continue."

"As I was saying, they wanted me to join them, but Akama was unwilling to adhere to my request."

"And that was?"

"What else could he possibly give me that I would want?"

"Ah, with such a small request, it's surprising that he'd turn you down. Perhaps your skill isn't as good as you've credited yourself," Semei teased his best friend.

Arsalan huffed. "I'm not even going to dignify that with a response … Besides, my skills are all that I've said they are and then some. He's just playing hard to get. You know how stubborn Akama can be."

"So much for not 'dignifying that with a response.'"

"Are you going to accept me or not?" Arsalan pressed.

"That depends. What were you doing in my territory earlier today?" Semei asked with a hint of suspicion. He had read the minds of several humans in his land and learned that Arsalan had been sighted. It annoyed him even more to know that the mind of his bed servant had been tampered with. He knew Arsalan was hiding something. "So, are you going to answer me?"

"I have nothing to hide. I visited upon your territory to see if you were home, I wanted to speak with you face-to-face. I didn't think it

would incite so much mistrust in you for me to see my best friend,"
Arsalan replied rather angrily. He wanted to make sure his friend was
aware that he'd hurt his feelings ... *well, not that much, but still.*
Although, he couldn't blame him. He knew he was taking a huge risk
by going to Semei's territory. No doubt the powerful Fount would
have been monitoring his land as they all were. He hadn't anticipated
the fact that Semei had assigned a shifter to his bed chamber and he
had to mentally compel the servant to leave. That made it all the
more difficult for him to lie. Semei would have detected his
handiwork on the servant.

Semei sighed and ignored Arsalan's reply knowing he was lying.
"Why do you want to join us now? If you're looking to pay him
back, I don't think enraging him is the road you should travel."

"It's leverage, my dear friend."

"I see. So you really aren't interested in what we're doing. You're
just hoping to blackmail him into your bed." Semei sighed in
agitation. "Arsalan, you're my oldest and dearest friend, but you
have crossed the line with this insult."

"Have I?" Arsalan asked, he had expected some form of
antagonism from his friend, he just didn't know how much he was
going to receive.

"Yes, you do realize how serious we are."

"At nine million dead worldwide and counting. Trust me, Semei, I
realize."

"I'm afraid you don't. We don't need a member on this team who
isn't as dedicated as we are. Point of fact, you'd be willing to betray
us as soon as Akama spreads his legs for you."

"Oh, now that was just crude. Besides, I'd be more than willing to
be the one who does the spreading."

"Beside the point, what I said is true. You've just told me that you
only want to join us to gain leverage. We don't need, and we don't
want someone to join us with their own agenda. I'm sorry," Semei
said. He suspected there was something more to Arsalan's request
and he did not trust him, not at this point, at least.

"You're the one who contacted me, trying to convince me to join
you," Arsalan shot back.

"That was a mistake that I don't plan repeating."

"You don't trust my intention?"

"No, I do not. I suspect you've taken something from my home to let that human who is with Akama use her ability on. I tell you now, it won't work. If she tries to link with me, I will make sure she suffers so much so, the death from the virus would be far more merciful."

"Well, since we have done away with pretenses; save me the trouble and tell me where you are."

"So you're not denying it?"

"Why bother with lies."

"Indeed. Well, whatever you've stolen from me, I expect it returned."

Arsalan chuckled. "Of course. Now, back to my question … where are you?"

This time is was Semei's turn to laugh. "Are you serious?"

"Very."

"Well, in that case, I'm insulted. It's good to know whose side you're on. You chose Akama's bed over your best friend."

Arsalan groaned. "Oh, come now. That isn't the reason why I joined him."

"Oh really? Enlighten me."

"He was very convincing and made quite a few sound points."

"Was this before or after you fucked him?"

"My, my, you're in a mood. Jealous?"

"Disappointed. I always knew you had a soft spot for Akama, but I held out hope that you'd see what we're doing is the right thing," Semei said.

"I see what you're doing is a means to an end …"

"Exactly."

"Whose end is the question?"

Semei laughed. "Do you think the humans can stand against us? You give them far too much credit."

"And perhaps you give them far too little. My friend, I don't want to hurt you or those you love, but I have made my decision to stand with Akama," Arsalan said, laying down the gauntlet, so to speak.

"And I have made mine. Remember my warning, if the human woman tries to use her ability to connect to me, I will end her."

"Duly noted."

With that, both Founts ended their conversation.

Bahashiri cocked both brows. "That went well."

Arsalan rolled his eyes. "About as well as a stake in my heart. It was quite unpleasant to hear the pain in his voice at my betrayal."

"Think he'll ever forgive you?" she asked. Her light brown, almond-shaped eyes gazed affectionately at him. She hated to see him fight with those he loved.

Arsalan nodded. "He will, but he's been known to hold grudges *longer* than necessary." He ran his fingers through his dark locks. "Were you able to gauge their location with that device?"

Bahashiri nodded. "They are in Brazil, I'm sure they're residing in Tenoch's mansion."

"I don't know whether to be surprised or insulted by the fact that they aren't even attempting to hide," Arsalan mused.

"I could care less. At least we know exactly where to go. Less time I am forced to spend with Irikara and Maska is a blessing, indeed," she remarked.

"Very well." Arsalan said with an amused snort. He rose, stretching out his limbs. "We should meet with the others."

"Do you think they'll leave that location knowing what they know now?" Bahashiri asked.

"I don't know. Regardless, it's where we'll go."

Bahashiri nodded and followed her Maker and Master as he left the mansion and flew toward Chicago.

CHAPTER TWENTY–TWO

W e may have a problem ..." Semei said as he entered the
spa where Thallos was getting a massage.

"And that is?" Thallos asked without looking up. He groaned
slightly as Roycean pressed firmly on his back massaging the
muscles underneath his smooth, alabaster skin.

"I've just spoken with Arsalan, he requested to join us."

Thallos looked up finally. "Did he?" he asked, an eyebrow rising
in suspicion.

"He did. His reason for wanting to join us, at least the lie he told
me, was because he wanted to use us as leverage against Akama."

"You think he wanted to know our location ... to spy?"

"Yes. He had no intention of joining us. To say that I am angry that
my friend betrayed me is an understatement. He had the sheer
audacity to enter my territory and steal my possessions to give to
their human woman!" Semei gritted out.

Thallos chuckled. "I don't care if they know our location.
Eventually they'd find us anyway, it was inevitable. I won't stop
until the world's governments give in to my demands."

"Don't you mean *our* demands?" Semei corrected with a cocked
brow.

"They were *my* demands originally and the two of you agreed; that
is how we ended up here. I will not flee from Akama or anyone else
he has with him," Thallos said as he sat up on the massage table,
gently brushing Roycean's hands from his shoulders.

"Maska is with them."

Thallos looked at him sharply, his mind obviously putting all of
the pieces together and it was evident he didn't like the results.

"I just thought you should know," Semei said with a cocky tone.

Thallos heaved a sigh. "This changes nothing."

"Do you really want to have Roycean here when they arrive?"

"I'm not leaving his side," Roycean said.

"This isn't a matter of you proving your unfailing loyalty to him, Roycean," Semei said.

"It's better to have him here with me in this territory, than out of the range of my power where I cannot protect him," Thallos said. "You be wise to gather Sade to you now that we know they are close to finding us, if they don't already know exactly where we are. I suspect that phone call alone had its own hidden purpose."

"I have here who I want here. My *Chosen One* will remain uninvolved. They won't attack her if she's innocent. It's not Akama or Arsalan's way," Semei said.

"But it is Irikara's way. Are you willing to take those chances?"

"Yes. As for you, do what you like." With that, Semei walked away.

"Do you think he's right?" Roycean asked his lover.

"There's really no way of knowing. I won't be risking your life." Thallos turned to Roycean, taking him by his shoulders. "Listen to me very carefully. They will try to use you against me, we cannot let that happen. You must hide yourself and I will mask your presence."

"I want to fight with you—"

"No! I have told you how you can help me."

Roycean wanted to protest, but he knew when to remain silent. More importantly, he knew when Thallos was resolved on a matter. "As you wish. Where should I ... *hide*." He said that last word as if it was something foul, disgraceful.

Thallos grunted, having noted the scorn in his *Chosen One's* tone. "You *will* bury yourself in the forest nearby." He leaned forward, kissing his child passionately before releasing him. "Go now."

Without saying another word to each other, Roycean walked away to do as he was commanded. Thallos slid off the massage bench and began to dress. He went to his guest bedroom, turning on the television. He could tell from the mental images and thoughts he gathered from the humans and supernaturals in the area that the death toll had people the world over terrified and hopeless. It's wasn't something that he wanted to do, but he felt drastic measures had to be taken for people to do the right thing. He sat down and waited for the latest news report.

***

Ten minutes prior, Xander and several members of his Pack and Richard along with the members of his Pack had arrived at Darian's mansion. Tatiana was now at Natasha's bedside, assisting Elise in trying to bring down her fever. They were all distraught to learn that nothing seemed to be working. Zaire and the others had to watch Natasha get sicker from the virus. Her body having adjusted to Zaire's blood was no longer repairing her damaged cells.

"Fuck, when is Arsalan going to get here?!" Warren asked to no one in particular. He was wondering why it was taking the Fount so long to join them. He wanted to find out where those other Founts were hiding, so they could kick ass and get Natasha a cure. The time delay was really taking its toll on everyone.

"I don't know. He should have been here hours ago," Zaire said as he held the waste basket for Natasha as she vomited.

Elisa helped her lie back onto the bed and she wiped the sickly sweat from her face with the cool cloth. "It's going to be all right, Natasha."

Natasha coughed and grimaced as her body shook with pain. Her bones felt brittle, so brittle that the slightest movement caused them to ache. The fever she was suffering from had not abated and what blood she had taken from Zaire was now inside the wastebasket. She didn't want to admit it to herself, but she knew it was true. She was going to die, just like that woman in the video. She looked up at Elise. "I want to see my children one last time before I die. I have to."

"Of course," Elise said, nodding.

"At least the virus isn't airborne, you can hold them," Devin said as he left to get her children.

He returned a few minutes later carrying the infant Aria and toddler Matthew in his arms. Elise helped Natasha sit up on the sofa so that she could receive her babies. Very gently, Devin placed Aria into her waiting arms. Natasha smiled down at her beautiful daughter and silently memorized every tiny detail from her soft, curly, brown hair to her tiny fingers with the tiny nails that would scratch so viciously to be so small. She began to cry knowing that she would never see her first birthday. Never see her little girl grow up and find love and happiness that every mother wished for their children.

Without needing to be asked, Devin sat little Matthew down on the bed beside Natasha and she leaned over kissing his tiny forehead. She ran her fingers over his hair down the length of his face and brushed along his chubby cheeks. He looked so much like his father. She held both or her children, savoring the moment for all it was worth. She looked up at all of her friends who had gathered near her in her time of need. People she trusted with her life. They were more than friends, they were family. It was her only comfort; she knew that she would be leaving her most precious gifts in the most trusting and loving hands she could.

She looked back at her son. "Now, Matthew, you take really good care of your sister, be a good big brother, all right?" she told her son. He looked up at his mother with the most innocent expression, not really understanding or even knowing that this one moment would be the last time he'd see his mother smile back at him. Natasha chuckled through her tears and her pain and sickness and despair as her little boy wrapped his tiny arms around her giving her the biggest hug he could as if he truly understood her words. "Mommy loves you so much, so, so, much! Always remember that. Please always remember that I loved you both with all my heart." She kissed both of them once more before nodding for Elise to take him. Her strength was failing and it was becoming more difficult for her to hold them.

As Elise reached down, taking Aria from her grasp Natasha cried, long mournful wails poured freely from her as she said her final farewell. The room filled with her anguish, Warren had to walk away; it was too much for him. Billy followed shortly after. Tears flowed freely from Devin's eyes as he could no longer hold back. He took Natasha into his arms, holding her not wanting to let go. Sergio picked little Matthew up and held him close to his chest. The toddler had begun to cry having seen the tears in his mother's eyes run down her cheeks.

"I'll take him back to his room," Sergio offered, he stood still waiting for a confirmation from Natasha.

Natasha nodded. It was one of the hardest decisions she ever had to make. One part of her wanted to hold her children until the last dying breath left her lungs. The other part of her didn't want to further expose her children to her sickness and her suffering. That wasn't the last memory she wanted to leave them with.

Sergio took Aria from Elise and left to put the children in their rooms and to calm down little Matthew. He sat in the rocking chair in Matthew's room, holding the child close to his chest. He spoke to him in a soft, soothing voice, telling him of how wonderful and strong his mother was. How sweet and kind and how loved she was. He gave the child promises of protection and love for all of his life. As he sat in the chair with the toddler in his arms, he couldn't imagine giving the same speech to his own children. He couldn't imagine having to live life without Elise and he began to cry for the pain Darian and Xavier would have to endure. He cried for his blessing and what they might all lose.

***

Finally, Zaire had put Natasha to sleep. It was the most humane thing he could think of to do. He never enjoyed witnessing human despair or pain, but he understood why Akama said it was important that he did. It kept him alive inside and it made him appreciate life. He wasn't detached from humanity like a lot of vampires were, he held on to his compassion. To him, it was a gift.

They all left Natasha to rest and after some time had passed the others were able to regain their composure. Sergio rejoined them in the den, announcing that the children were sleeping and as they sat, discussing their situation the doorbell chimed.

"I'll get it," Billy said, rising to answer it. He returned to the den with another vampire in tow. "He said Kysen sent for him."

The other vampire stepped forward into the room. He was quite beautiful. Short, dark, wavy hair covered his head; his blue eyes scanned the faces in the room. He smiled with a mouth that was as sensual as it was masculine. He stood five-feet, ten inches and his muscular build was tastefully dressed in a beautiful designer suit.

Elise rose from the sofa, walking toward the handsome vampire.

"You must be Julius," she greeted as pleasantly as she could considering the mood she was in.

"I am," Julius said, smiling at Elise, his eyes drinking in her beauty.

Sergio's growl was low and menacing as he leaned forward.

Julius looked over Elise's shoulder to see Sergio still sitting on the sofa, but looking very alert. "I see you're already spoken for."

Elise nodded. "I am."

"Pity ... for me." Julius kissed her hand.

As far as flirtatious vampires went, Elise felt this one wasn't too bad. Sergio on the other hand was in no mood for ogling eyes and he had had his fill of vampires for the day *and* there so-called "charms". He did give Julius credit for the fact that he backed off once he realized that the beautiful female leopard belonged to him. Elise sat down and gestured for Julius to do the same. He did, taking the chair opposite Devin.

"So Kysen is your Maker?" Sergio asked.

Julius nodded.

"So in vampire terms, does that make you Darian's brother?" Sergio asked.

Julius rolled his eyes. "We share the same Master, but he's no 'brother' of mine."

"O-kay," Sergio said, leaving it at that. He could tell there was bad blood between Darian and this new vampire. The last thing he wanted now was more animosity in their group.

Julius looked around the room, frowning. "So, this is Darian's mansion ... it's exactly what I expected from a Spartan."

"What do you all have against this place, I think it's beautiful," Devin asked. He was extremely curious why older immortals seemed to dislike Darian's home.

"The home itself is rather contemporary. I supposed that's to appease the younger vampires of his coven. It lacks elegance and class in many respects," Julius replied.

"More importantly, what does Darian have against you?" Warren asked, remembering the annoyance Darian exhibited at the mention of Julius's name. He knew he was probably being rude in asking the question, but at that point, he didn't care.

"You'll have to ask Darian," Julius said, feeling the younger shifter was brash in his questioning. He looked at Elise. "Where's Kysen?"

"He's upstairs with Adan, I believe they're resting," Elise said.

"Resting?" Julius arched a brow. "Is that what they call it these days?"

"Well, I'm sure they'll be resting when they are done," Elise said. She, like Julius could still hear Kysen and Adan in their room and she had no interest in their love life.

"Ahhh, I'm anxious to meet this, Adan," Julius said.

"You will," Sergio said.

Julius looked at him, staring silently for a few seconds then he turned his gaze to Elise. "I see the Grecian is still too weak to rise, even at this time of day."

"You mean, Darian?" Justin asked.

Julius nodded. "What I find amazing is that he's able to claim this territory and he's not even two millennia. I'll give him credit for that. But as I look around, I can tell that he has a lot of help from the shifter community."

"You're wrong there. Darian had control of this territory before we even knew him," Devin said.

"These days, we're friends and we all work together to keep what's ours. Unlike other vampires I've met, he's willing to share. Do you share your territory?" Elise asked.

"Ah, defensive, I see. I suppose he does have a way with women …" Julius looked at Devin. "… and men," he teased.

"So, where is your territory?" Sergio asked, changing the subject of Darian and Elise's prior relationship and the Master vampire's bisexuality. Neither topic something Sergio wanted to think about.

Julius smiled at the shifter king. "Greece. I reside in Sparta."

"Is that where you're from?" Justin asked. He couldn't help but be curious, this was a vampire who'd known Darian and Kysen for centuries.

"Heavens, no," Julius replied. "Troy was once my home."

"'Ah, defensive, I see.'" Elise mocked. She wasn't in the mood to hear insults about Darian from some vampire she's never met. "I suppose you *would* have a grudge against a Grecian," she retorted,

310

knowing the history the two countries shared.

Julius couldn't help but smile at the beautiful woman before him.

"If so, why on Earth would you want to live in Greece?" Elise asked.

"Why not, it's beautiful and so very close to my former home."

"You like having all the supernaturals there under your control, don't you?" Adrian stated.

Julius' smile widened.

"Yeah, I thought so." Adrian shook his head. It never ceased to amaze him that the older the vampire was, the pettier they seem to be *and* arrogant.

"Was it really a huge wooden horse filled with Greek soldiers?" Devin asked.

"It was. I of course was among the few council members who were against accepting the 'gift' from the Greeks. That night would prove our ending," Julius said, reflectively.

"What happened then?" Xander asked. The Greek war with Troy was always a topic of interest for him. Darian had told him what he knew, but it was nothing compared to someone who was actually there. With Julius, he could get first-hand accounts. Not to mention, he welcomed the distraction the conversation provided. At this point, he wanted to think about something other than the hell they were all in.

Julius looked around the room. He could smell the sickened woman sleeping somewhere in the mansion and the pained and weary expressions of others. He read some of their minds and knew that they had been through a lot and still had a way to go. He decided to beguile them with ancient tales if only to let them focus their minds on something other than their pain.

"Well, there was a celebration, as most of Troy assumed we'd defeated the Greeks who could not breech our walls. After most of the celebration was over and many had returned to their homes to rest for the night, we were attacked. The city was set afire, the people--slaughtered in the streets and in their homes while still in their beds. I had been fighting the Greeks, killing as many soldiers as I could when one bested me. Have you ever been run through with a jagged blade?" Julius asked the others.

"Yes, I have," Xander answered.

"Well, then, you know how painful that can be. As I lay there dying, watching my once beautiful and powerful city burn before me, Kysen came. He offered me life everlasting and power beyond my imagination. He was beautiful and exotic as he stood over me. I could feel the power emanating from him and knew him to be a God. I wanted what he offered so I accepted his gift … not that I had much choice," Julius said.

Before anyone could ask him any more questions with the hope that he'd be willing to elaborate, Zaire turned on the news, which manage to capture their attention. The anchorman was giving information on the new death toll, which had just reached ten million worldwide and the locations with less resources took the biggest toll.

"This shit is fucked up on so many levels," Devin said after hearing the report.

"Shhh!" Elise quieted him as she continued to listen to the news.

The anchorman went on with his report. Apparently the Center for Disease Control was still unsuccessful in finding a cure, but new developments were coming in daily. According to a survey, that news gave little to no hope to those already suffering or to those who feared that a cure would never come before their water supply diminished. The Supernatural Council spokesperson, Cynthia Meadows met again with the United Nations to discuss the state of the world. Ms. Meadows urged the UN to cease their harassment of supernatural-owned businesses and properties and to negotiate for equal rights for supernaturals. There was much criticism directed at both parties as neither side could come to an agreement. The Council spokesperson blamed the world governments for denying supernaturals the same rights as humans which was the reason for the sudden viral attack. The UN refused to give into the demands of the vampire terrorist group. They announced that if a cure has not been given within twenty-four hours, they would have no choice but to 'fight fire with fire'. The anchorman added that a war between supernaturals and worldwide human military force seemed 'inevitable'.

"This is what we're trying to avoid happening," Zaire said. "This is what Akama was warning us about. If the humans decide to attack, it's not going to end well for anyone. There are going to be a lot more casualties on both sides."

"Tell me about it," Adrian said. "I'm willing to bet the few rights supernatural have now are about to be revoked."

"That's a sure bet. The next thing they're going to do is kill vampires who're registered. As good as I am at my job, I can't take on the United States military forces to protect Darian and the others while they rest," Billy said.

Julius laughed and the others turn toward him.

"I fail to see the humor in this situation," Xander said.

"You have to forgive me, I envisioned Darian getting shot with one of those crafty ultraviolet bullets the humans have while he lay helpless one morning," Julius said.

"Can we not talk about Darian getting killed? You may have an age-old grudge against him for some shit that happened to your hometown three-thousand years ago that didn't even have shit to do with Darian, but to us, he's our friend," Devin said with a tone that was so serious the other shifters in the room were a little taken aback, not that they didn't agree. "Besides it's more than enough real death going on, we don't need to wish for more; hypothetical or otherwise?"

"Hmmph ... fair enough," Julius studied the young shifter. He could rip his heart out in less than a second, but that didn't stop the leopard from speaking up. He respected that. "For the record, I do not wish Darian death ... just a thorough beating." He sighed. "So according to the news, we have less than twenty-four hours to convince these other vampires to give up the cure ... what's the plan?"

"That's the problem, I'm not even sure we have one," Warren said. "Arsalan hasn't made it back−"

The front door opening and closing interrupted him. They all turned toward the doorway to see who was coming into the living room. Arsalan stepped into view with Bahashiri following behind him.

"I was just talking about you," Warren said. He wasn't surprised the Fount had let *himself* inside Darian's home, bypassing doorbells or invitations. He was beginning to meet his quota on conceited vampires for the year.

"I heard … and you were saying?" Arsalan sat down on one of the chairs with Bahashiri standing beside him.

"Just wanting to know if you were able to get their location?" Warren asked.

Arsalan nodded. "But I doubt they'll still be there. Semei knows about Natasha as well. He's threatened to kill her if she tries to link with him."

"Shit!" Sergio, Adrian, Ignacio, and Warren said in unison. They all looked at each other in surprise, but then returned their attention to Arsalan.

"The last known location was Brazil. They'll either be in Thallos' territory or Semei's if they decide to leave Tenoch's." Arsalan looked around at all the new faces settling on Julius open-mouth expression. "Calm yourself, young one."

Julius blinked then closed his mouth realizing that the ancient Fount was talking to him. "I'm sorry, but I've never met a male Fount before."

"It's underwhelming to say the least," Warren mumbled.

Arsalan shot the wolf a look. "Be mindful of what you say and especially how you say it."

Remembering the very physical discussion he had with Arsalan on the airplane, Warren decided he'd play it smart by taking his own advice and keep his opinions to himself.

Arsalan smirked then returned his attention to Julius. He looked him over, his eyes roaming his body from head to toe approvingly. "I must say that Kysen has wonderful taste, you are positively *exquisite*."

Julius smiled. "As are you."

"All right, at the risk of getting killed, I have to ask … what are we going to do?" Warren looked at the others. The last thing he wanted to see were these two vampires flirting with each other. As far as he could tell, some vampires seem to have short attention spans when lust was in the air.

Both vampires caught the hint. Zaire lowered his head to hide his smile. He liked Warren and admired his fearlessness.

Arsalan nodded. "We have to–"

"We're not going anywhere until Kysen's child rises," Maska said as he reentered the den.

"Which should be within the hour," Warren said.

"That's what I was going to say. When we are all together, then we'll discuss our plan. Until then, one of us should contact the Council and see what they are doing on behalf of supernaturals," Arsalan said.

"I agree, so why don't you make that call," Maska told Arsalan.

The two Founts shared glaring looks before Zaire interrupted. "I'll contact the Council."

Akama walked into the den, running his hand over his hair. "No, you should go to Natasha's parents' home. Since we haven't been informed of their deaths, it's safe to assume they are still alive, but barely. If Natasha is in the condition she's in, then they'll be in a worse state. Zaire, your blood is more powerful than Miaka's, it will sustain them. Besides, you can do no more for Natasha," he said.

"Do you want me to bring them here?" Zaire asked.

"Yes. They should see their daughter one last time if this is to be their end," Akama said.

"Wait, that's if you don't get a cure, right?" Warren asked.

"Correct."

"Isn't there another one of you who's stronger than Zaire who can give Natasha blood?" Tatiana asked.

"Zaire is the second strongest among us who isn't a Fount. For now, she's on borrowed time. If we can't get the cure before she dies … well, I would suggest you all say your peace now," Akama said as sincerely as he could.

Natasha's friends grew quiet, their expressions becoming more solemn. Not one among them wanted say good-bye to her.

"I understand how difficult this must be for you," Akama began. "But you'll feel even worse if you never got the chance to say your final words."

"Question, are we taking her with us?" Julius asked.

"I don't think Darian would want Natasha traveling now … you know, in her condition," Devin said sadly.

"But if we can get the cure and if she is with us, she can be cured right then and there. As it is now, time is of the essence. And hour or more of travel could make the difference between life and death," Julius clarified.

The others thought about what he said and not one could disagree.

"And smart too," Arsalan said with a wink toward Julius.

Akama rolled his eyes, but decided to refrain from commenting on the blatant flirting. "We'll just have to make her as comfortable as possible."

Kysen, Irikara and Adan entered the room. Irikara found herself a comfortable chair while Kysen and Adan remained standing.

"Are we leaving now?" Adan asked.

"This is how it's going to go," Arsalan said, gaining everyone's attention. "We leave now; take Darian and Xavier along with us. Their current location is Brazil–"

"But you said they might not be there," Devin interjected.

Arsalan inhaled deeply, his chest broadening as he released a sample of his powerful aura which washed over the others like a frigid mist. The effect left everyone who wasn't a Fount frozen, unable to move or speak and their bodies tingled and burned with an inner fire that frightened them. "I do not appreciate being interrupted." He released his hold over the younger vampires, shifters and Billy, the one human who felt his aura more keenly than the others. Needless to say, he'd like to avoid another burst of power if ever possible. They all exhaled and panted as they struggled to regain their senses. "Now, as I was saying, Brazil is the location I tracked them to. If I know Thallos, and I think I do, he won't run even if Semei thinks it would be wise to."

Akama nodded. "He'll stand his ground, but he still thinks he has the upper hand."

"Why would he think that?" Devin asked, he hoped he wouldn't get another aura attack for his inquiry. "I mean, now that it's four of you against three of them, you can kill him can't you."

Kysen laughed sardonically.

"What's so funny?" Devin asked him.

"Because the Founts aren't trying to kill each other," Darian said as he entered the room. He looked at Akama. "Isn't that right?"

"Yes. Our goal isn't to kill Thallos, Semei or Tenoch, it is to out-muscle them, if you will," Akama answered.

"But if you can kill him, why won't you? He's a threat," Sergio asked, he was just as confused as Devin was.

"It's not because you're best friends is it?" Warren asked.

Akama shook his head. "As much as it would pain me to kill my best friend that is not the reason why not one of us could ever die."

"Tell them already, I am growing annoyed with the guileless expressions on their faces," Maska said. "That is if you are not too ashamed to share your story."

Akama tossed Maska an annoyed expression of his own. "Very well, we have time to kill while we wait for Zaire and Miaka to return with Natasha's parents. While we're in transit to Brazil, I'll contact the Council and see where they're at with negotiations. If I know Thallos, he'll be doing the same. At ten million deaths, the governments can't be that steadfast in their opposition."

"You'd be surprise, the humans are declaring war on all supernaturals if a cure isn't made available in, oh ..." Warren looked at his watch. "... Nineteen hours."

"That's unfortunate, but not unexpected," Akama said. "We have to get the Council to convince them to work with us. We have to ..." he trailed off as another idea came to mind. "The Council needs to be *our* face, the face of the supernatural race. No longer can they send a human representative to be their spokesperson. I believe that is one of the reasons why the humans have not wanted to give supernaturals equal rights in the first place."

"Olendale is not going to like that idea," Julius said.

"I'm far past caring what Olendale would like," Akama said. "I will contact him in a few minutes and demand that he hold a press conference himself and address the people of the world."

"What do you want him to say?" Arsalan asked.

"I'll let his people write his script for him as long as he explains to the humans that a cure is coming, but the demands are still the same. If they want to avoid a full-scale war between our two races, then we must come to an agreement, preferably peacefully. If they want to work with us and the Council, we can create new laws that would be beneficial to us all. The alternative is to deal with Thallos who will not stop hurting humans until the same demands are met," Akama said.

317

"Non-violent vs. violent ... this reminds me of the civil rights movement," Devin pointed out.

"It is a civil rights movement," Akama confirmed. "Only the roles are reversed. The side demanding equal rights has taken much drastic measures and there are no attack dogs, lynches and fire-hoses, instead, it's a killer virus. We have to stop this injustice on both sides."

"What's going on?" Xavier asked as he entered.

"Just listen and you'll find out." Warren said.

Julius leaned over to gain a better view of Darian's *Chosen One*. He cocked a brow as he gazed lustfully at Xavier. His eyes scanned over every delectable inch of the younger vampire and the moan he released held all of his sexual intentions. Darian noticed Julius' lecherous appraisal of his lover and growled low in his chest as a warning. The others turned toward him then followed his gaze to Julius.

"Not now, Darian. I need to know what's going on," Xavier said, urging his lover to put aside his territorial nature.

"Yes, of course," Darian said as he leaned forward, kissing Xavier's temple in an apology.

Julius settled back against the cushions with a wicked satisfied smile plastered on his face. "Yes, Darian, stay focused on what's important."

"Julius." Kysen gave his child a warning look.

Julius looked at his Maker and nodded stubbornly.

"I still want to know why you can't kill another Fount," Sergio said, bringing up the topic of conversation to their earlier question.

"Because we don't want to risk all of the vampires of his line or Semei's or Tenoch's perishing. We're not sure if killing even *one* Fount would kill all vampires," Akama said.

"Can you elaborate?" Xavier asked. He had stepped closer to Akama getting his attention.

"As I've said, we seven Founts were made into vampires at the same time on the seven different continents. Each one of us representing a group of ancient people, our souls are linked and we feel each other at all times. I've already explained that the demon that created us divided its soul into each of us. We don't know what would happen if one of us were to die."

"What if nothing happens?" Devin asked.

"When I was about two-hundred years old, I wanted to end my life," Akama said. "It isn't something I'm proud to admit, but at that time, I was overcome with grief and the guilt of my actions. I had slaughtered everyone I'd ever loved the night I was turned, family ... friends, and it didn't stop there. For years, my bloodlust raged on and I had killed countless others. It was only by accident that I learned I could make others like me. So because I didn't want to be alone, I turned many humans and watched as they slaughtered innocents just as I did." He paused as he rubbed a finger over his left brow.

They all waited for him to continue and he did.

"I grew melancholy and wanted to end my reign, so to speak. I commanded one of my children to decapitate me. I knew that fire would not affect me, nor did the sun's rays as it had destroyed some of those whom I'd turned. So my only guess would be to remove my head from my shoulders. When he sliced into my neck with the blade, stopping at the bone, I felt such pain, but so did he. I knew then why he hadn't finished me completely. He began to bleed from a wound identical to my own. It weakened him severely, nearly onto death. Of course, having seen what happened to him, I couldn't follow through. I healed a few seconds later from my near death experience and was able to tend to him."

"Not only did every vampire in his line suffer the wound, but we all felt it as well," Arsalan said.

"It was Semei who came to me, I believe it was because he sensed my pain and turmoil more keenly, because he was closest to me, location-wise," Akama said. "He helped me through my immortality and to accept what I'd become. He taught me another perspective, I will forever be grateful to him for that."

"Funny how the two of you became enemies," Arsalan said.

Akama looked at him. "It's more like 'frenemies', as they say. And now you two are best friends, but that's beside the point." He turned back toward the others. "Fact is we can't risk even one Fount being killed, or we may risk the existence of vampires everywhere."

"Well, I'm convinced," John said. He and the others had risen and were able to catch the most important part of Akama's tale.

"Okay, with that in mind, how are we going to convince Thallos and the others to give up the cure?" Ignacio asked. "Do we beat it out of him?"

"I was going to ask the same thing. I was under the impression that we were gathering forces so that we can overpower them," Xavier said.

Akama sighed heavily. "We are, but this is a very tricky situation. We want to limit how many people we involve. I don't want anyone to get hurt or killed. However–"

"We are your pawns," Kysen said, purposely interrupting the Fount.

Akama turned to him. "Yes."

Kysen scoffed as he tossed a glance toward his child, Darian. "The things I do for you …"

"Kysen …" Darian began, getting his Master's attention. "I don't know what to say."

"We knew it was going to come down to this, me fighting for you, maybe even dying for you," Kysen said.

Darian came toward him. "I can't ask this of you."

"Ah, but you have." Kysen took Darian's face into his hands, tilting his face upward. He kissed him gently then he pressed his forehead to his. "Say no more. I love you, my beautiful child. Never forget that and never forget the sacrifices I've made for you or the lessons I've taught you. Do you understand?"

Darian nodded.

"Good." Kysen released him then turned toward the others. "What is our strategy?"

"Semei's *Chosen One* resides in Antarctica. We should retrieve her," Irikara said.

"She has nothing to do with this," Arsalan said.

"And neither does Kysen, but I will not have my child engaged in battle while his sits safely in his territory," Irikara pointed out.

"But–"

"Irikara's right," Akama said, cutting off Arsalan. "We need leverage. Irikara, go get her, we'll meet you in Brazil."

"Why must I do the errand," Irikara fussed.

Akama huffed in frustration. "We're running out of time." He turned toward the entry way, they all did when they heard the front door opened. He sensed his children, Zaire and Miaka approaching with the humans. "Good, now that Natasha's parents are here, we may leave." He turned back to Irikara. "Please Goddess, just this once can you get off your high horse and do this one task?"

Irikara's eyes widened, then narrowed to slits and if looks could kill, Akama would have been speared by a thousand daggers. He stared at her, not willing to change his mind.

"Who made you the leader of us?" Irikara asked.

"Oh, for heaven's sake! I'll go!" Arsalan said. He didn't wait to hear any objections. He vanished from their sight moving faster than any other being who wasn't a Fount could see.

Akama gestured to the others. "Let's go. We'll need at least two shifters to join us for sustenance, who will accompany us?"

"I'll go," Warren said.

"I will, too," Devin said.

"Hell, you might need my help, so I'll go," Ignacio said.

"Well, that will do," Akama said.

"I'll get Natasha," Xavier said, and then he walked away.

"Is my daughter all right?" Mrs. Hemingway asked. She looked a bit worse for wear. Her skin had taken on a pale, sickly color. Both she and her husband had lost weight, as Natasha had. They smelled like death to those whose senses were keen.

It's now or never, Warren thought as he looked at Natasha's parents.

"No, she's not," Zaire said, approaching both parents. He took the mother's hand into his own. "I managed to put her to sleep to ease her suffering, but she doesn't have much time left."

She began to cry as she nodded. She could tell by her own condition that they didn't have long to go either. She hated knowing that her daughter was suffering as she was and it saddened her even more that her daughter had been attacked. She wanted justice for her child.

"We do not have time for this sentimentality, we need to leave," Maska said.

Zaire nodded in agreement. "We need you to come with us," he told the parents.

"We figured as much," the mother said, not wanting to argue. Her husband, Franklin held her hand, squeezing it slightly. Marian looked at him and the two shared a moment of silence that spoke volumes for the love and trust they had for each other.

Xavier came back down stairs with Natasha still sleeping in his arms. The others said their farewells to their loved ones then the three remaining Founts and all their *Chosen Ones*, Darian, Xavier, Warren, Ignacio, Devin, Julius and the three infected humans left the mansion. Xavier drove, transporting the humans who were too weak to fly with the vampires. Natasha's parents had fallen asleep on the ride over and once they arrived at the airport, they all boarded Irikara's airplane. Xavier, Darian and the three shifters laid Natasha and her parents on the bed in what could only be considered the master bedroom on the aircraft. Xavier climbed in beside Natasha and Darian took the chair closest to the bed. The others sat in other chairs still available or on the floor.

They were quiet for a long time. Devin was the first to break the silence. "I'm not his biggest fan, but I don't want Kysen to die."

"Neither do I," Darian said. He couldn't help but be humbled when he reflected on what his Maker was willing to give up for him. Kysen didn't have to help, especially not when he'd finally found happiness with Adan, and yet, he was there with them … possibly going to his death.

"Well, hopefully Akama and the others can work this shit out so that no one gets hurt or dies, like he said," Ignacio stated.

"We still don't know what the damn plan is," Warren said.

"In all honestly, I don't think they even know what the damn plan is. I'm willing to bet they've never found themselves in this kind of predicament. If they were dealing with any other supernatural, they'd just kill them, but they can't do that now," Xavier said. "They're just as confused and unprepared as we are."

"Yeah, but because they're ten-thousand years old, they don't want to admit that," Devin said.

"Shit, would you, if you were that age? Would you want to admit you had no fucking idea what you were doing?" Ignacio asked.

Devin thought about what he asked, then chuckled sadly. "No, I guess not. But I'm me now, only twenty-something years old. I have no problems admitting I don't have a fucking clue."

The others chuckled. Natasha stirred in Xavier's arms and he readjusted himself so that she was more comfortable. He gazed down into her face, his eyes traveled over her body, noting all of her open and festering sores. He wanted to kill the vampire who did this to her, but he knew it was out of his hands at this moment.

Darian saw the tightness in Xavier's jaw, and sensed his anger and sadness. He placed a hand on Xavier's thigh. "Don't give up," he told him.

"I don't want to give up, but I don't want to be unprepared if we can't save her," Xavier said.

"There's nothing you can do. There's nothing any of us can do that we aren't already doing," Darian said.

Xavier nodded even though there were no words that could comfort him at this point. He wanted to get to Brazil and put a *hurting* on everyone there, Fount or not.

"You two should feed from us. I know you've got to be hungry by now, Xavier," Devin said.

Xavier nodded. "You're right." He slid off the bed and walked toward Devin, who offered his wrist. He bent toward the exposed flesh and bit.

Warren gave himself to Darian and the two vampires feasted to regain their strength. Once it was over, they all returned to their seats. Xavier settled back into his place beside Natasha on the bed. They continued to talk about lighter subjects, topics that brought smiles to their faces. That was enough for them to pass the time away.

***

"They suspect we have no clue as to what we're doing," Akama said with a slight chuckle.

"Well, do we?" Maska asked.

"Yes and no," Akama said. "We know it's going to come down to whose *Chosen One* is more valuable to them. For Thallos and Semei, is the life of their *Chosen One* more valuable than their mission. If so, they will be forced to give us the cure. If not, then I'm not sure what to do from there. Perhaps, we take the blood by force, and then try to figure out just how in the world did Thallos create this virus and its cure before there aren't any more humans left to save."

"You are putting a lot of faith in that plan," Maska said.

"Well, there's not much on this earth we can treasure. Life is fleeting, times change but remain the same and if we manage to find one person in our lives that complete us, wouldn't you want to hang on to them?" Akama asked.

"Fair enough," Maska said.

"I'm surprised you did not decide to start killing off the vampires of their lines," Irikara said. "If Thallos wants to make the world more supernatural friendly, I seriously doubt he would allow you to destroy his line."

"The point is to preserve as much life as possible, sacrificing the few for the many. Granted, what we are doing is the hardest decision I've made in a long time, but it's a means to an end … hopefully," Akama said.

"Besides, throwing down that kind of gauntlet would just encourage their retribution. Your entire line would fall victim as well as ours," Maska said to Irikara. "I think what we are doing now is our best option."

"If Kysen dies, I will kill all of your *Chosen Ones* regardless of the outcome," Irikara threatened.

"Irikara, be reasonable," Akama said.

"I am. If I lose the one person who means so much to me, I will not hesitate to deliver the same pain to all of you." Irikara stared at the other two Founts, the truth of her words was quite evident in her expression.

"Well then …" Maska turned toward Akama. "Just when things were starting to get boring and our situation was not stressful enough, you came through once again, Irikara. What would we do without you?" he said sarcastically as he rolled his eyes in utter annoyance.

"Suffer eternity without ever knowing the sensual embrace of a woman as powerful as you are," Irikara retorted with a smile that was as seductive as it was menacing.

Maska sneered, but remained silent. It was true. No woman could truly survive the full force of their passion. He knew if he wanted to share his 'passion' with her again in the same century, he had to stay on her good side.

Julius chuckled from across the plane. He sat, composed with one leg draped lazily over the other. He'd been watching the Founts, listening to their conversation. It amazed him how they were amongst themselves compared to how they were among their subjects. Irikara mesmerized him most of all. He'd met Irikara twice in his lifetime, even bedded her, so he knew full well how special she was. But like the others, he wanted to have a back-up plan in case things went wrong. He loved Kysen and didn't want his Maker to die … especially not for Darian or any human.

"I don't want anyone to lose their life, Irikara, diplomacy is a must, right now," Akama said.

"That is all fine and well. My warning still stands," Irikara said.

Julius cleared his throat to get their attention. "How do you know Thallos won't try to kill you? You may not want to hurt him or his line, that doesn't mean he won't try to see what would happen to vampires if a Fount dies."

Akama gave Irikara one more look before addressing Julian. "The very fact that they are fighting for the equality of all supernaturals and that they haven't tried to destroy themselves in ten-thousand years allows me to have faith in my plan."

Irikara giggled. "Touché."

"Let us hope that they love their *Chosen Ones* as much as you do," Maska said.

Akama sighed. "I need to contact Olendale." He picked up the airplane's phone and dialed.

Olendale answered after five rings. "Yes?"

Akama shook his head. The arrogance of some--be them human or supernatural--annoyed him. He put it aside; there were more important things at hand than giving the vampire an attitude readjustment. "Olendale, this is Akama."

Olendale perked up. Immediately he grew nervous wondering what the powerful Fount wanted with him. "Akama, to what do I owe the pleasure?"

Akama rolled his eyes. He didn't much care for the president of the Supernatural Council, but he had to put his personal feelings aside for the greater cause. Besides, Olendale was of Thallos' line.

"I'll say this only once. I want you to address the public and reassure them that everything is being done on our part to insure that we acquire a cure."

"The Council has already addressed the public with such a claim," Olendale said dryly.

"The Council's *spokesperson* addressed the public. I want *you* to do it," Akama said.

"Sir, the humans wanted it that way, to have a human representative for the Council," Olendale said.

"And that was the first battle we lost, making it easier to lose the others. You should have insisted on being treated equally from the very beginning."

Olendale grunted slightly and Akama knew he'd struck a chord. It was as he suspected, as long as the Supernatural Council got their kickbacks, they didn't put forth much effort into their agenda. Well, that was going to change.

"The humans need to be able to see a friendly supernatural face during this time of peril." Akama's tone was direct and leveled, leaving no room for negotiation.

"What would you have me say to them?" Olendale asked, catching the hint that he didn't have a choice in the matter.

"You will tell them that the acts and opinions of some does not represent the entire supernatural community. Tell them that there are supernaturals working very hard to obtain a cure and that we would like to live alongside humans without discrimination and hostility. Inform them that they must want the same things or there will be more attacks from rebel groups who will refuse to allow things to continue as they have … are you getting all of this?" Akama asked.

"Yes, sir." Olendale replied.

"Very good. Tell them that the humans must work side by side with the Council in order to establish laws that are just and that would benefit both humans and supernaturals."

"The Council has tried on many occasions to do just that, sir. But the humans have refused to collaborate," Olendale said.

"I'm aware of that and look where their repudiation has gotten them? Make sure you remind them that refusal to work willingly with the supernatural race would not be a wise idea. Fact of the matter is, they can either work with us, or deal with the rebels who apparently aren't asking as nicely as we are," Akama said. He felt that he would be remiss if he didn't use this situation to their advantage. Though it was unfortunate many lives had been loss, more would continue if they didn't come to an agreement and soon. Ten-million deaths were both an opportunity and a tragedy. He didn't want it to be in vain.

"Is that all, sir?" Olen asked. He wasn't too thrilled about being Akama's errand boy, but he knew well enough that when a Fount gave you an order, you followed it.

"Yes. I expect to see you on television addressing the public within the hour, not a minute more," Akama said.

There was a moment of silence and then Olendale answered. "Yes, sir."

"Good," Akama ended the call. "If the humans are smart, they'll listen when he speaks."

"We can only hope," Maska said sarcastically.

"We should feed," Irikara said, looking toward the bedroom door where the three shifters were with Natasha and her parents.

"Are you even thirsting?" Akama asked.

"Well, I am not suffering from hunger if that is what you are implying. But still, if we are to face off with Thallos one way or the other, we should be in peak condition, would you not agree?" Irikara shot back.

Akama snorted. "You're ever the cunning beauty, Irikara."

"I believe I will feed from the coyote. He is powerful enough to sate my ... need," Irikara said with a sultry undertone.

"Just what *need* are you referring to," Maska asked with an implicating rise of his brow.

"Whatever I *need* him for," Irikara said as a matter of fact. She sent a mental call to Ignacio, commanding him to come to her.

They all heard a bedroom door open and a few seconds later, Ignacio stepped into the room, approaching Irikara. He knelt beside her chair exposing his neck. Warren and Devin entered the room in time to see Ignacio give himself to Irikara.

They knew that their friend was not in control of his actions. They didn't like that the sole female Fount had taken such liberties with their willpower.

"You know, we all volunteered for this, you don't have to turn us into your little puppets," Warren said.

"I did not give you permission to speak, and you and yours are whatever I want you to be," Irikara said.

She leaned forward now and with the speed and precision unmatched by any being, bit into Ignacio's tender vein. He gasped and arched forward, his muscular chest pressing firmly against her breast. Seductively, she wrapped an arms around his torso, holding him close as she fed. His body shook uncontrollably as orgasm after orgasm rippled through him. Warren and Devin watched transfixed, their anger slowly melted into fascination and strangely enough, lust and envy that their friend should experience such primal and sexual bliss.

Akama rose, approaching both shifters. "You don't have to feel that way."

Warren blinked as the sound of Akama voice pulled him from his trance. "Huh? What? What way?"

Akama chuckled. "Never mind, are you ready?" he asked imploringly.

"Ah … yeah, sure." Warren said, still trying to gather his thoughts together. His eyes were still fixed on Ignacio as the last tremor shook him and Irikara pulled back. He watched as Ignacio slumped to the floor, still panting. "Um, can we go into another room?"

"Funny, you don't strike me as the easily embarrassed type," Akama said.

"Yeah, normally I'm not. But current company makes me want to keep this little interaction private," Warren said.

Akama smiled. "I understand." He gestured to the bathroom door. "Shall we?"

Warren nodded and led the way. The two men closed the door after they entered.

"Are you as shy as he is?" Julian asked Devin.

Devin turned to him. "No, not nearly. So which one of you will it b–"

"Oh, God! Don't stop!" they heard Warren belt out from behind the closed bathroom door.

Devin's head shot toward the door and he stared at it for a second or two and then he turned back toward the others, his eyes settling on Maska. "You! I think you will be next and then Arsalan when he catches up with us. I'll feed him, too."

Maska chuckled in spite of himself. "Please, calm yourself, my young shifter. My bite may be too much for one as young as you to handle," he teased, knowing full well the reason why Devin picked him.

"No, no, I can handle it just fine. Well, I'm ready whenever you are … you're ready, right?" Devin asked as he chewed expectantly on his lower lip.

Maska smiled and nodded as he beckoned for Devin to come closer. Devin obliged, kneeling beside the Fount's chair with his head tilted. Maska struck, burying his fangs deeply into Devin's pulsating vein. Devin cried out, his hands instinctively gripped Maska's arms as his body ignited with intense waves of pleasure. Maska's feeding was the most extraordinary thing Devin had ever experienced. He was no longer bound to his body, but had become a sensation. He was sex, the most unbridled sex he'd ever had. He had never known such pleasure even as the Fount's pull began to fade. He felt a sinful sense of remorse that he may never again feel the way he was feeling now. Maska pulled back, licking his lips as he held Devin still.

"Are you able to balance yourself?" Maska asked.

Dazed and panting, Devin nodded. "Yeah … I'm cool … told you I could … handle it."

Maska chuckled then released him. Devin fell limply to his side where he drifted blissfully to sleep.

"Hmmm, he wears denial well," Julius said.

Akama exited the bathroom with Warren in his arms. He took one look at Devin and Ignacio sleeping on the floor and laughed. "I've got a feeling we'll be pestered to feed from them again before we return home."

"Especially that one," Julius said, pointing to Devin.

Zaire looked at his watch, "We'll be landing soon."

"Excellent. The sooner we can end this the better. I am eager to return to my home," Maska said as he shifted uncomfortably in his seat.

"I would have to agree. I have grown quite bored and annoyed with my present company. I think when this is over, I may even ban Kysen from visiting me for at least a century," Irikara said. Her tone was so matter-of-fact, the others really couldn't tell if she was joking or not. They didn't bother to ask her, either.

Akama turned on the television, going directly to a reliable news station. Just as he had requested and expected, the president of the Supernatural Council was getting ready to address the world. He turned the volume up.

"…We are now going to go to the president of the Supernatural Council, Olendale Cantilia via satellite," the anchorman said.

The camera then switched to Olendale, who was a handsome blonde with sparkling blue eyes that conveyed depth as well as knowledge. Those penetrating eyes stared forward through the camera ready to address the world. "Thank you, Michael … We the Council are working quite diligently to create a cure that we hope we can distribute very soon. We want humankind to know that we are doing everything within our power to make sure no more lives are lost. However, in order to insure that this and nothing like this will ever happen again in the future, we ask that the world's governments work with us to establish laws that will govern all of us equally and fairly. As unfortunate as this situation is, it came about because rebel supernaturals felt that the laws were unjust. The recent handling of the S.U.I.T. organization was a clear indicator that matters would get far worse–"

"–Excuse me, Mr. Cantilia, I'm sorry to cut you off there, but is seems as though the Council is using this terrorist assault as some sort of stepping stone to persuade the world's government to agree to your terms. Who's to say that the Council isn't behind these attacks? I'm sure that is a question on peoples' minds now," the anchorman said.

Olendale shifted in his chair in a manner that meant he was getting more comfortable. There wasn't any hint of anxiety or anger in his expression as his gaze sharpened. "The Council in no way endorses the actions of these rebels, however we are open-minded and understanding enough to comprehend the expressed concerns of this group. We understand that if a person believes they are backed into a corner, then their only recourse is to come out fighting. Sometimes, they don't look for other, less violent alternatives. Unfortunately, that is the stand this group has taken. We, however, want the same things: equality and peace among our two species. That is all that we have ever asked for. The Council and supernaturals around the world want to work towards a future where a war between our two species can be avoided."

"Let me ask this: is the Council saying that the world's governments can either deal with you, or continue to be at the mercy of these vicious rebels?"

"Hardly. The Council and I, as its president, believe I speak for the world's supernatural populace when I say that hate, stubbornness and bigotry have lead us all to this point. If this pattern continues, the open war will remain upon us. Fact is there are some of us who will stop at nothing to force the hand of your governments to simply do the right thing. We, the Council want to work together to bring about negotiations that are just and we want to do so in a manner that is without bloodshed. The choice, which is undeniably clear, is yours." Olendale leaned forward, peering even deeper into the camera. "Work with us, or war with us, that is the option you have been given, whether you protest it or not." He sat back into his chair. "As I've stated, we are working toward finding a cure, however, that cure would come a lot faster if certain demands are met. These demands are the same as our requests. Please reconsider your position on retaliation and let us all end this with negotiations."

The anchorman frowned, but nodded when the camera switched back to him, disconnecting from Olendale's satellite link. "Well, you heard from the president of the Supernatural Council and if I'm not mistaken, it was his first time making a public appearance. What are we going to do? We have to trust our government to do what is in our best interests during this difficult time. We're going to go live now, to see what the people think about what we all just saw and heard. We're going now to Rosa Velasquez who's in New York City's Time Square. Rosa?"

A few seconds past before Rosa received the signal. "Hi, Michael, yes we all watched on the big screen here in the back, that very monumental address from the President of the Supernatural Council. I have here a few people with some very interesting opinions. Sir, would you mind sharing your thoughts?" She pointed her microphone toward the mouth of a black man standing to her right.

"What's happening could have been avoided like that guy said. We need the government to just be fair. We all have to share this world and no one should be discriminated against," the man said before taking a step back.

"Thank you, sir. And ma'am, would you like to share your opinion?" Rosa asked an older lady that stood on her left.

"Right now, my daughter-in-law is fighting for her life. She doesn't have time left to wait for these politicians to put their egos aside and do the right thing. People are dying and when the history books are written, how do they want to be remembered? As heroes who did the right thing under pressure or as egomaniacs who boasted about not bowing down to terrorists? The world is waiting for our leaders to protect us … by any means necessary, the sooner the better. The question they need to ask themselves is: will war save lives? Because at this rate, we won't have many lives left to save."

Rosa pulled the microphone from the elderly lady with a grim expression. "That testimony you heard is the collective opinion of the majority of people here and I would assume the world over. Only time will tell what happens next. Back to you in the studio, Michael."

The camera switched back to the anchorman who vowed to keep the people updated whenever new developments came in. He did mention the death toll was now a little over ten million. As they continued to look at the stats of the death toll in various cities all over the world, the news program was interrupted first by static, and then Thallos's beautiful face appeared from the haze.

"Oh, what's this now?" Akama mumbled as his gaze stood affixed on the screen as did the others.

"Ten million dead. That's an impressive number, don't you think?" Thallos's piercing blue eyes stared forward, demanding attention. He went on. "And it will only grow until our demands are met. It would be wise for the human race to heed our warning. Take the opportunity extended to you from the Council or the next number you will see on the death toll will be one-hundred million." With that the screen went black then clicked back to the anchorman who had been speaking before the interruption. He was unable to conceal the fear and uncertainty in his expression as he nervously sifted through the papers in front of him. His cleared his throat and stuttered slightly as he struggled for the right words to say after such an announcement.

"Ah … l-ladies and gentlemen, we have just heard from who we presume to be the leader, or at least spokesperson for the supernatural terrorist group responsible for the recent viral outbreak and the substantial rising death toll," the anchorman said. "We will keep you posted with up-to-the-minute updates as soon as they come in." With that, the news went back to the television program that was playing before their interruption. Like all TV shows that were playing for the past few days, it was a rerun. The only "live" or "new" show that was on *was* the news. Akama muted the television and tossed the remote on the table. With a heavy sigh, he looked at the others.

"Do you think the humans will negotiate or risk more lives?" Julius asked.

Maska shrugged. "Humans are anything but predictable. Some are, but some will surprise you and often times, not for the better."

"Well, that is a grim outlook," Akama said.

"It is true. Who knew so many would follow the leadership of that insane German dictator in World War Two, or the Mongol Warlord who slayed over a million people?" Maska pointed out.

"Even they met their end. Regardless, fear will play a huge part in whatever decisions the human race will make, as it always has. Fortunately, there are always those willing to do the right thing at all costs. We have to believe in that," Akama said.

"*You* have to believe in that," Maska retorted.

"Whatever the case, if we don't get the cure to the humans within the next few hours, I believe war will be declared on us. It's the only recourse the humans have left. To kill as many of us they can. To use fire against fire," Zaire said. "In fact, the only reason I think they haven't already is for fear that they might lose. One vampire, even the youngest of our kind can destroy a number of humans. But when push comes to shove …"

"It is a fight I believe the human race would eventually lose, but not without our side taking on considerable damage and loss. I'm not willing to risk that," Akama said.

"You were always weak that way, Akama." Maska sneered at the other Fount with a mixture on pity and contempt in his expression.

Akama didn't bother to respond. Instead, he turned to stare out of the window at the clouds as they flew by. For the remainder of the flight, they sat in silence, which was more a torment for Julius than anyone else. He was used to talking, but whenever he attempted to start a random conversation, the others either didn't have much to say, or didn't say anything at all. Akama seemed to be in a state of contemplation, while Irikara and Maska were just agitated almost to the point where he found their company intolerable. But he knew one thing … he didn't want to go into the bedroom with Darian and the others, so he sat there and looked out the window.

CHAPTER TWENTY-THREE

Olendale sat in the backseat of his limousine at the UN headquarters for the World Supernatural Organization as the gate security verified his information. The guard returned with his ID and forms, handing both to him through the half-rolled down window.

"You may enter," the guard stepped back while another pressed a button to open the gate. The sleek black limousine drove smoothly past the armed men and made its way to the main building. Olendale's assistant, Courtney Preston straightened out his burgundy and black tie, making sure he was pristine for his presentation. Her loyalty held no bounds, as he was her maker, saving her from certain death by brain tumor. She knew how important it was for supernaturals and humans to find common ground and was hoping for all of their sakes that this meeting would result in a positive direction.

"I'm surprised they finally invited you to one of these meetings," Courtney said.

"They're desperate," Olendale said.

"You would think they wouldn't want you here for fear that you'd compel them, wasn't that their reason for requesting a human representative in the first place?"

"It was, though I really should have insisted on attending. I never did and they took the upper hand. This virus is a curse and a blessing."

"Do you think they'll finally negotiate, or do you think they are requesting your presence simply to declare war?" she asked Olendale.

Olendale chuckled softly. "I have a little more faith in the human race to be smart enough not to issue a declaration of war … But if my faith is misplaced, I'll simply have to do my best to convince them of the error of that decision."

Courtney nodded and looked out the window. "We're here."

Olendale sighed as he glanced at the double doors to the United Nations building. "Let's get this over with, shall we?"

The driver opened the door and stepped to the side as Olendale climbed out with his assistant following. He adjusted his clothing as he made his way up the stairs and into the building. Once he checked in with security, he was led by the UN representative to the conference room where the other delegates were waiting. He took his seat and his assistant took her place behind his chair.

"It's very nice to have you join us in person during this difficult time, Mr. Cantillia," The Security-General addressed the president of the Supernatural Council.

Olendale gave a curt smile as he noted the undertone of sarcasm in the man's voice. He decided to refrain from reminding them that they were the ones who decided he wasn't invited because he was a vampire. "I felt it was time I attended one of these meetings, especially considering what's at stake."

"Indeed. Let's begin, shall we?" The Security-General, Soon-yun Lee gave his opening statements, addressing all of the representatives, media and attendees; then he went into his speech highlighting the urgency of their current predicament and their solutions. "I propose we bring to the table the possibility of retaliation for these attacks so that we may prevent this happening in the future," he concluded.

"Excellences, ladies and gentlemen, I cannot stress what a terrible outcome that decision would create. I am the representative for supernaturals and I speak for the entire race so allow me to draw you a mental picture. If you declare war on us, the millions of innocents dying now would pale in comparison. Conversions would increase exponentially and our armies would grow to an unimaginable number. We would overtake every village, town, city, state, and country; killing or enslaving the humans who refused to submit. If you're still not convinced, I'll give you another scenario. My assistant who is only fifty years old in both her human and vampire years combined could terminate every single man and woman in this room in less than a minute's time."

There were several gasps, grumbles and groans collectively around the room as each of the fifteen delegates and thirty-five media agents looked at each other; then back to Olendale and Courtney who smiled sweetly. Somehow they knew that she would no doubt prove Olendale's point if he so wished it. Needless to say, if gave them something to think about … and fear.

The Security-General tried very hard to keep his posture so that the two vampires didn't notice the chill that ran down his spine. He cleared his throat before speaking. "Surely you would agree that we must punish those responsible for releasing this virus. They've caused millions of deaths, they've terrorized the world and we cannot ignore this simply because you advise against it."

Olendale stared at the man for several seconds making him and the others uncomfortable. "The two men you saw on television cannot be pursued. You do not have a force strong enough to track them, let alone capture and execute them. You cannot possibly comprehend the true power of an ancient vampire. You saw only a glimpse of it several months ago with the murder spree in Chicago. Your entire S.U.I.T. organization was rendered utterly useless and it took several groups of supernaturals to take out four vampires and one shifter."

"So we are to do nothing? The people will not stand for that," Security-General Lee said.

"You have no choice. I don't say this as a threat, but more of a forewarning if war were to be declared. Excellences, ladies and gentlemen, I do not wish to see more suffering, nor does the supernatural race. We want to live among you all peacefully, but the only way this can be done is if our request were agreed upon. I fear the cure, that will no doubt save countless lives, will only be relinquished if a treaty is made. I cannot leave this table tonight without coming to a compromise at the very least; one that would be beneficial to both of our races."

Olendale made eye contact with every person in the room. He wanted them to know that he was sincere in his words and in his intentions.

"I believe the last thing we want is to put more lives in jeopardy.

However, please understand that we cannot be at the whim and/or mercy, or lack thereof, of supernaturals that choose to attack the people of the world in order to push their own agenda," Security-General, Soon-yun Lee stated.

"Coincidentally, you would not be giving into *their* demands, but *our* requests, as I've mention before on numerous occasions. We are at this crossroads now because collectively, you've refused to compromise in the past. Now, you have no choice. You really don't. The people of the world will not tolerate a stalemate, nor will they accept a war that would cost more lives with no favorable resolution. Let us make a wise decision on this night, please." Olendale beseeched.

"I've heard enough," United Nations President, Ava Paxton began. "If there are no objections, I'd like to ask President Cantillia to please list your resolutions."

There were a few whispers around the room as several people conversed with each other, but in the end, there were no objections.

Taking that as a sign, Olendale began to give his proposal. "In respect to the urgency of the situation at hand, I'm going to go through this list informally as time is of the essence. We the supernatural race would like: the opportunity to pursue public, federal, state and city employment free from prosecution and discrimination. The opportunity for the children of supernatural parents, particularly those born of shape-shifters to be able to attend both publicly and privately funded schools, colleges and universities. Several amendments to the Laws of Co-existence, Law Number One: the criminal and judicial process be extended to a period of up to six months for a proper investigation to be implemented before declaring a supernatural guilty of any crime."

"Excuse me, I'm sorry to interrupt, but are you asking us to hold a vampire or shape-shifter for up to six months?" the Security-General asked. "Wouldn't that promote overcrowding and make for a very dangerous situation in our prisons? We don't have jails constructed to hold that many supernaturals nor the man power."

"A period of seven days isn't nearly enough time to give the accused a fair investigation before deciding their fate, which resulted in many unjustified deaths. As you've said, each S.U.I.T. division simply doesn't have the manpower. In order to insure that they do and that more holding facilities can be constructed for this purpose, we propose a fund financially backed by supernaturals. These funds would be allocated for the hiring and training of more S.U.I.T. officers and staff. The construction of more S.U.I.T. departments per state to alleviate the strain on the current ones. Funding to hire more legal representation for supernaturals that cannot provide their own. In addition, this fund would require the hiring of supernaturals to fill positions."

"I don't think that's a good idea, how can we know these supernatural employees won't go through great lengths to free other supernatural prisoners?" the Ambassador of Foreign Supernatural Affairs said.

"Despite popular belief, supernaturals do have a sense of right and wrong. There are many of us who want to see justice served. In fact, if it weren't for shape-shifters infiltrating the S.U.I.T. organization and vampires assisting them, your arrest numbers would have been significantly lower. To further prove my point, if you look at the records of every S.U.I.T. precinct in the US, Japan and England, the top cops were the shape-shifters or those with shape-shifter partners," Olendale pointed out.

There were more whispers around the room as they discussed amongst themselves the undeniable truth.

Olendale continued. "In addition to that, only in the most extreme cases where the lives of innocents and officers are in jeopardy should a supernatural suspect be executed without Due Process. With the hiring of supernaturals within the S.U.I.T. division, we feel that better judgment would be implied in making the decision to kill a supernatural suspect, especially those who happened to be stressed. In the past we know that a lot of executions were done simply in fear of the supernatural or for pleasure by officers seeking the thrill of the hunt."

"That's an accusation, Mr. Cantilia," the President of the UN stated.

"I'm afraid that it is the truth. It is the reason why so many shape-shifters joined the S.U.I.T., they wanted justice for all and many reported back the crimes they witnessed or heard their human partners and co-workers commit. It is the reason why we've pushed so hard to pass this amendment in the past. That is why I mentioned it now," Olendale said. "There's more."

"Go on," President Paxton said.

"We would like a new process for how supernaturals are tried in court. There should be levels of degrees based on the severity of the crime, if you will. There have been many supernaturals sentenced to death simply because they were caught slaughtering livestock or stray animals. This is not a just ruling. There have been accidental killings as well where the supernatural has shown immense remorse, but was still sentenced to death as if it were premeditated murder. This must end. If humans have a chance for corrective behavior, then so should supernaturals," Olendale said. "And these new changes can be agreed upon by both the Council and the UN. I think this is a very reasonable request."

There was a discussion among them all and within a half-hour, a two-thirds majority vote ruled to approve the amendment to Law Number One.

Olendale moved on to the next thing on his list. "We would like an amendment of Law Number Two concerning willing mortals requesting to be turned into a supernatural. The original wording of this law states that for one to be turned into a vampire is to commit suicide which is against the law. Human morality does not apply here. For us, to bring one into our world is to give life-everlasting to that human. They become our child for we have given them a rebirth. We do not see it as killing them and those humans seeking to become vampires do not see it as suicide. In regards to humans becoming shape-shifters, death is not a part of that process. It is a pact made between human and the shifter community be it a Pack or Pride they are going to join. That human becomes the sole responsibility of that group and human laws should have no governance over that decision, that bond." Olendale shifted in his chair to get more comfortable then he went on. "Conversions happen every day whether you approve them or not, so this law isn't preventing anything. However, it does put supernatural Makers at risk of violating Laws Number One and Two, and this is not acceptable."

Again, there was discussion on the amendment presented and a decision was made to accept it. Pleased with the progress they were making, Olendale continued.

"We would like to add an amendment to Law Number Three, in which a shape-shifter is found hunting in their animal form off sanctioned grounds that they be held until a shape-shifter community can claim them. As it states now, these individuals are contained, charged and then declared a danger to society and are executed. This is not always the case, accidents have happened. The shape-shifter should have a chance to find someplace to belong. To be safe and free on full moon nights."

There was a lengthy and heated discussion among them as they debated to amend Law Number Three. If a favorable decision could be made, then that was the last step towards ending the terror and gaining equality.

***

The airplane landed smoothly at a private airstrip close to Tenoch's residence. Zaire went to get Darian and Xavier from the bedroom. They looked up at him when he opened the door. "We're here," he announced.

"So we are," Darian said, thoughtfully. He didn't know what to expect or how their situation was going to turn out, but he was ready to take some kind of action either way. He looked at the humans lying on the bed. "We should leave them here."

Zaire's gaze followed the vampires. "We need to wake up the shifters, they can stay to look after them," he said.

Darian nodded. "We need to leave now, Xavier."

Xavier climbed off the bed without any more hesitation. The three vampires left the bedroom and walked toward the sleeping shifters. Each approached one and shook them awake.

When Warren looked up at Darian, the Master vampire spoke. "It's time for us to go, we need you three to stay here and watch over Natasha and her parents."

Warren nodded and rose to his feet with a little assistance from Darian.

"Are you going to be all right?" Darian asked.

"Yeah, I'm fine now… just a bit stiff is all. Go on, I'll take care of them, just get them the cure," Warren said.

Darian nodded and followed the others as they exited the airplane.

"They're definitely here," Xavier said as he felt the vibrations of the Founts auras.

"Yes," Akama said.

"They aren't even trying to mask their auras," Julian commented.

"What would be the point?" Maska replied.

"They were expecting us, I'm sure," Irikara said.

"Let's not keep them waiting, then," Maska added before taking flight.

The others followed him toward Tenoch's home. They landed silently on the front lawn. They were accompanied a second later by Arsalan who held Semei's *Chosen One*, Sade, in his arms.

"Semei hid her well, just in case we were looking for her," Arsalan said.

"Of course he did. But he endangered his *Chosen One* when he decided to side with Thallos," Akama said. "Let us get this over with, shall we?"

"Lead the way," Maska said with a sweeping hand gesture toward the mansion.

The group walked through the double doors, which Akama opened telekinetically. They could sense where the others waited and they made their way to the grand ballroom where Thallos, Semei and Tenoch sat at a large, polished marble table. Several scantily-clad humans, both male and female sat on the table as if they were the main course. Semei growled low as he looked at his child in Arsalan's arms. Thallos placed his hand on Semei's arm to keep him calm. The other Fount's growling subsided, but his fierce stare remained fixed on Arsalan and his *Chosen One*.

"We were expecting you. Really, Akama, you have become quite predictable over the millennia," Thallos said addressing the group and his best friend.

"Coming from you, I'll take that as a compliment. We're here for a reason, let's not waste any more time with pleasantries and insults," Akama said.

Thallos chuckled. "Very well then. I'm not giving you the cure."

"I think you will. Besides, you've made your point, terrorized the world and you've cost a lot of our kind their humans. This needs to end," Akama said.

"It will end when I hear an announcement that the humans will give in to our demands or the Council's amendments. Whichever road they take, our goals will be met." Thallos shifted in his chair, crossing one leg over the other. "I have to admit, it was a smart move on your part having Olendale step forward and address the public. So, I'll meet you halfway. When Olendale reports back to us that the humans have met at least ninety percent of our demands, then and only then will I give you or the humans the cure."

"You call that 'halfway'?" Akama remarked.

"It's all you're going to get, 'take it or leave it', as they say," Thallos replied with a conceited smirk.

"That's not good enough. We need the cure now," Xavier said.

The Founts turn toward him, and by the expressions on their faces, not one was pleased that he interrupted them.

"The inevitable death of your human is of no concern to me. Had you not took it upon yourself to defy me, she would not be infected. Apparently, you don't understand your place in all of this," Thallos said to both Darian and Xavier.

"Young Masters oftentimes forget their place. They believe that because I allow them to control territories within my domain, that they somehow are significant in the grand scheme of things," Maska commented.

"I do not have that dilemma," Irikara remarked.

"We only ask that you give us the cure for the humans under my protection," Darian said. "The decision to give my blood was mine alone; she shouldn't have to suffer for my choices. Your quarrel is with me."

"Ah, but her death will be the consequence that you will have to endure for your insolence. This is how I dole out punishment, accept it," Thallos said.

Darian's jaw tightened, he opened his mouth to protest, but the stern stare from Akama and the firm press of Kysen's hand on his arm silenced him.

This conversation is now out of both your control and my own. Be silent, my child or I fear he will kill you and that I cannot bear, were Kysen's telepathic words to him.

Darian didn't respond, but only watched the Founts converse before him.

"I agree with your demands, Thallos, but I don't agree with your methods. Please release your hold on the world before we suffer a consequence of our own," Akama tried to reason with his friend.

Thallos and his cohorts laughed. "Think you that I fear the humans' retribution?"

"I think you have forgotten that just because one has the strongest force, doesn't automatically make him the victor," Arsalan interjected.

"And I believe you're under the foolish impression, no doubt Akama's influence, that somehow if one is most patient, that eventually justice will be served," Semei said. His cold blue eyes were fiercely focused on Arsalan and Sade.

"How many people are lying in their graves now that waited patiently for a time to pass that never came for them?" Tenoch said. "Humans, for all of their boasting about how enlightened they are, really are stubborn, hateful and selfish creatures who want everything for themselves. Even among their own kind, they've shown that they do not want equality or peace. Face the facts, Akama … a firm stand is the only thing they will understand. It's the only thing that will force them to change."

"I don't disagree. I just don't see how killing millions of innocent people can be a positive thing," Akama said.

Thallos smirked. "You will, especially when Olendale gives us the news that they've submitted to us."

"And if they don't?" Arsalan asked.

"What if they declare war on us?" Akama said. "The shifters may side with them; that will leave our kind vulnerable."

Thallos's brow furrowed as he thought about Akama's point. He hadn't factored that the shifters would betray them in order to gain favor with the humans. They had the most to lose; their children were very susceptible to the virus. It was no doubt that some had already passed away due to the virus.

Akama huffed. "I can tell by your wrinkled brow, my good friend, that you never thought about a split between or own race. Have you forgotten that the shifters' offspring are susceptible to your virus?

There's no telling how many of them are dying right now. Do you think they'll view you as their hero? Their white knight?"

A slight rise in Thallos's chest was proof that he was annoyed by his own shortsightedness and Akama's righteousness.

Irikara sighed. "Gentlemen, I came a very long way for this conversation and I am ready to return to my own territory. Let us get on with this. If you do not give us the cure, Thallos, then we are left with no choice but to force it from your hand."

Thallos sneered. "You won't kill me, Irikara and I doubt if you want to see me rip the still-beating heart from your child's chest. What we have here is a stalemate, and you know it. You humor me with idle threats."

"Is that why you have hidden Roycean? I assure you, I will find him," Irikara said. "And then we will see whose child's heart is separated from their body."

"Not bloodly likely!" Thallos growled.

"What about you, Semei? Are you willing to lose Sade for your cause?" Arsalan asked. He let the unconscious vampire in his arms fall to her knees, but he made sure to hold her head in his hands.

Semei leaned forward, scooting inches toward the edge of his chair. His entire body was ridged with rage and alertness. "If you harm her … you know what I'll do."

"I know what you'll attempt to do. But you're out-numbered, surely you know when the odds are not in your favor," Arsalan said.

"Arsalan, if you were ever my friend, you will not harm her," Semei pleaded.

"It's because I'm your friend that I give you the option to work with us," Arsalan said. "Your methods are putting us all in danger, my friend."

"I told you it would have been best to keep Sade close to you. I will not give into them because of your weakness and stupidity," Thallos said to Semei.

"Ah, a Mexican Stand-off. This is exciting," Tenoch said. "Enter."

Upon hearing that word, the ballroom filled with ancient vampires and shifters of various animal species. Fifty-three supernaturals stood before Akama and his group, their power flowed over them in electrifying waves, one after the other.

"Still feel that the odds are in your favor?" Thallos asked their guests.

"The youngest among us is nine hundred, but that's in shifter years," Tenoch said with a chuckle.

"If they chose to risk their lives for your ego, then they'll die without any regret from me," Akama said.

"My friend, the pacifist," Thallos remarked. In an instant, far too fast for anyone who wasn't a Fount to see, he bolted from his chair, advancing toward Akama.

Akama braced himself for the impact. The two collided and skidded across the floor. The other Founts took Thallos's lead and advanced on their friends and vampires. Arsalan saw Semei coming toward him; he twisted Sade's neck, snapping the bones into splinters. Semei grabbed hold of his wrist and applied pressure forcing him to release his grip on Sade. With his foot, Arsalan kicked Sade's unconscious body aside and using his own weight advantage, hip tossed Semei to the floor. The two men gripped each other, clawing and snarling as they tussled and rolled on the floor. Each one trying to gain the advantage over the other while staying on the defense.

Kysen, Julius, Zaire, Bahashiri, Miaka, Gabrielle, Darian and Xavier fought off the other supernaturals as best as they could. Darian advanced on the tiger shifter who had embedded his teeth in Xavier shoulder. Without wasting time, he punched through the shifter's chest, grabbing her heart and snatching back. Blood splattered over the three of them as the shifter shrieked in pain then fell to the floor, lifeless. Another female shifter charged toward them, claws bloody and poised to shred flesh. Darian's arm shot out before her, severing hear head from her neck with a swift and forceful slice of his razor-sharp nails. He kicked the body to the side and helped his child to his feet. Xavier didn't waste any time before getting back into the fight, fending off another shifter who was almost as strong as the one before. Xavier slipped around the shifter, plunging his fangs deeply into the nape of the shifter's neck. He bit down hard, cracking the spinal cord and rendering the shifter motionless. With both hands he drove his claws into the shifter's throat and yanked upward, ripping the head from the body. Blood splattered his face and shirt as he pulled the tendons and muscles apart. He tossed the head to the floor and ran toward a vampire from Tenoch's line who had Darian pinned to the floor as he fed from him. His fangs were buried painfully and deeply into Darian's neck, draining him with lightning speed and vicious precision. Darian's body shook and danced in his arms uncontrollably as his attacker feasted, exhausting all of his strength and power. The vampire pulled away and rearing back, punched through Darian's chest breaking through flesh, muscle and bone. Xavier jumped onto his back, digging his claws into the vampire's neck, but suddenly he was tossed into the air by a powerful invisible energy. He was thrown through the window, shattering glass before he sailed across the lawn, crashing into a tree, splintering it before he splashed face first into the man-made lake. The force of the blow rendered him unconscious and he floated motionless on the surface of the water.

The ancient vampire leaned over Darian's weakened body and grinned. He bent downward, and lapped the blood that stained Darian's chest before taking another bite. A long, satisfied moan rolled from his chest as he drained Darian dry. Finally, he pulled back, smiling, revealing bloody teeth and lips.

"Too bad you have to die, I'd like to keep you," the vampire said with a wicked laugh. Then he punched through Darian's chest cavity, smashing into his heart.

Kysen felt the tremendously painful near-death blow to his *Chosen One* before he saw it. Unfortunately, the vampire he was grappling with made it impossible for him to go to his child's aide. His heart sank when he saw Darian lying helpless with a vampire's fist protruded through his chest. Before the vampire could pull his arm free with Darian's heart in his hands, Julius came up behind him, gripping his arm holding it in place with one hand and ripping his throat open with his other. Blood sprayed from the torn wound, splattering over Darian's face and chest as he lay there, unmoving. Julius tossed the body aside; then he stood over Darian, protecting him as the battle raged, fending off another shifter attacker.

Kysen managed to gain the upper hand with his opponent. He held the vampire in his powerful grip with both hands and combined with a leg sweep he slammed the vampire into the marble floor. The marble cracked and crumbled under the force and weight of the vampire causing the vampire to cry out in pain. Taking complete advantage, Kysen slashed his nails through the vampire's neck, slicing through flesh and bone until the head separated from the vampire's body and rolled away.

Before he could climb to his feet, he was attacked by another powerful vampire. The blow landed with such force, he knocked him down and sent him skidding across the floor. His body smashed into the table leg, breaking it. The vampire was on him again before he could regain his footing, growling and hissing, his fangs glistening with blood. The vampire was merciless, slashing and ripping Kysen's flesh with each blow causing intense pain. The vampire was far too fast for Kysen to counter and when he felt the claws sever his jugular, he knew his death had come. The vampire reared back then slashed his hand downward toward Kysen's throat. But before the fatal blow could land, the vampire jerked forward as his chest exploded spraying Kysen in blood, bone and pieces of his internal organs. The vampire was then yanked back, his body crashing against the wall with a thunderous clatter. He fell like a sack of rocks to the floor and then crumpled to the ground, dead.

As his wounds healed, Kysen looked up to see Irikara coming toward him and he saw again the magnitude of her power.

"On your feet, stay by my side," Irikara said.

Kysen followed her order, rising quickly. He tossed a glance at Darian and saw that he was still lying unconscious from the severe blood-loss, but he knew he was still alive. He was pleased to see that Julius protected Darian from other attackers.

Don't let anything happen to him, Kysen commanded.

I'll protect him with my life, Master, Julius replied. He looked down at the younger vampire, his Master's *favorite* and couldn't help but feel the twinge of jealousy. He let it go for the time being.

Maska and Tenoch were locked in battle as were Thallos and Akama and Semei and Arsalan. The other six Founts fought, dealing equal damage to each other, neither man gaining the advantage over the other for the time being. Irikara worked her way around the room as the power of her aura ripped the heart out of several shifters and vampires who made the unfortunate mistake to take her on. Her beautiful silk cream and golden gown was drenched in blood as was the rest of her body as several bodies exploded around her. Beside her, Kysen killed off the remaining supernaturals that were strong enough to survive the power of Irikara's aura, but were still gravely injured.

The vampire Zaire was grappling with cried out, his body convulsing before it twisted in an unnatural way. Bones cracked and splintered as blood poured from the newly open gashes. The vampire fell to his knees, unable to move as he waited for his body to heal. He knew Irikara had attacked him with the power of her aura and he hoped she wouldn't finish the job. Nine-thousand years was a lot to sacrifice. He looked up to see Kysen walking up to him, arm poised to strike.

"No, please, I beg of you, show mercy!" the ancient vampire pleaded through pain-filled pants. He had never known such agony as he waited for his bones to reformed and skin to heal.

"And what will you offer me for my mercy?" Kysen asked.

"I will be in your debt, whatever you ask of me, I will owe to you," the vampire said. He grimaced as another jolt of pain ripped through his limbs as his breast plate mended itself.

"Remember your promise to me," Kysen said then he walked away. It was always good business, he thought, to have a powerful supernatural indebted to you.

Having been freed from his opponent, Zaire saw the opportunity to help his Maker and he took it. Thallos back was turned and he was locked in a powerful struggle with Akama. With lightning-quick speed he rushed toward the two Founts and plunged his fangs deeply into Thallos' neck drawing as fast as he could. Thallos roared in rage and with a powerful heave, he threw Zaire from his back sending the ancient vampire through the stone wall into the next room. Akama took the advantage, landing several punches to Thallos face. One of the blows managed to crush the bones in Thallos nose and the Fount grunted in pain. Thallos twisted in Akama's grasp, breaking his grip and then he kneed Akama in the groin as hard as he could. Akama screamed his pain through gritted teeth, but regained his grip on Thallos, grabbing the vampire by his long blond hair. Akama wrapped his legs around Thallos's waist and yanked his head to the side by his hair, baring his neck. Quickly, he struck, burying his fangs into the succulent blue vein. Thallos tried to push away, but couldn't. He was held in place by Akama's powerful legs as his strength waned with his swallow of his blood. He fell to his side and his friend continued to feed. It was the only way one could get the advantage over the other and a rare opportunity it was.

Tenoch slowly rose to his feet having finally defeated his best friend. His body ached and his wounds bled after the vicious brawl with the North American Fount. Still, his warrior background had sustained him through many battles and he put each skill learned and taught over the millennia to good use. Maska lay at his feet bloodied, as he also was, but unconscious as well. Tenoch looked around and noticed that Irikara was nowhere to be seen and he knew that wasn't a good sign. Turning to his left, he saw that Akama had managed to gain the upper hand on Thallos. Not wanting to lose ground, he advanced on the two Founts, yanking Akama away. He attempted to bite the other Fount, but Akama gripped a handful of his long, black silky hair, pulling his head back preventing him from leaning forward.

"You fight like a woman!" Tenoch roared.

"Whatever works!" Akama shot back. With that, he gave Tenoch a mule kick between the legs, making sure the heel of his boot smashed into the Founts most sensitive area.

"Arg! You son-of-a-bitch!" Tenoch growled.

Pain shot through his body from the base of his groin. He still couldn't get his hair free from Akama's grip, so he gave up trying to bite the other Fount. Instead he raked his claws across Akama's chest, splitting the skin open.

Akama cried out, but he kept his grip pulling forward and bucking at the same time. Tenoch catapulted over his back landing at his feet with his hair still in the other man's grip. Before Akama could advance, Tenoch kicked upward several times, connecting with Akama's face and torso. With both hands, he clawed Akama's face, slicing open the skin on his cheeks. Finally, Akama lost control of his grip and Tenoch rolled onto his feet and speared the other Fount in the midsection sending them both crashing to the floor.

Tenoch flipped upward and wrapped his legs around Akama's

neck while painfully twisting Akama's other arm at the shoulder joint keeping it pinned. He applied pressure with his thighs in an attempt to force the Fount to submit. He looked at the other Founts around the room, Semei and Arsalan seemed evenly matched, but they were also wearing each other down. Thallos managed to prop himself up on one elbow as he watched the battle, but was still too weak to move let alone assist. The remaining vampires and shifters were still fighting, but the battle was leaning toward Akama's side. Tenoch knew that taking Akama down was their only chance to keep the ball in their court.

Akama couldn't free his head from Tenoch's grip and the pain was unbearable as Tenoch wrenched his arm even harder grinding his bone inside the socket as if he was attempting to rip it from his body. Akama made a note to himself to increase his hand-to-hand combat skills so that he didn't find himself in this situation again. He looked at Tenoch's positioning and saw an opening. He took it. In a last ditch effort he stabbed his clawed hand through Tenoch's side, slicing through the Fount's intestines.

Tenoch screamed and shifted his body to alleviate some of the pain. But Akama continued to rip and tear at his insides. In retaliation, Tenoch plunged his nails into Akama's wrist and forearm tearing back the flesh and muscle. Both Founts screamed and struggled in each other's hold.

"Enough!" Irikara said, gaining everyone's attention.

"Release him!" Thallos demanded and he struggled to move forward.

Irikara pulled Roycean forward, dragging him by his beautiful blond hair. "Either you end this, or he dies," she warned.

"I'll kill Kysen," Thallos countered.

"No, you will not," Maska said. "I'll know the moment you enter my territory, you will never get close to him or my Gabrielle."

"Let go of me," Akama told Tenoch.

"Thallos?" Tenoch looked at the other Fount for confirmation.

Thallos looked around at the massacre and frowned. Supernaturals were strewn about either dead or gravely injured. Semei and Arsalan lay next to each other bloodied and battered and far too exhausted to move as they looked on. Maska was still unconscious as he lay among the bodies. It was quite apparent that he'd loss the upper hand.

"We need to end this, Thallos, you're out of options and you know it," Akama said as he struggled in Tenoch's unyielding grip.

"The cure now, or lose your *Chosen One* and lover of over eight-thousand years. Tick-tock, darling," Irikara said.

Thallos looked into Roycean's panicked and pleading expression. There were only a select few immortals who truly didn't fear death, Roycean was not one of them and he could see the plea in his child's eyes to save him. His one true weakness was his love for his *Chosen One*.

"Release him, Irikara, you'll have your cure," Thallos said. He looked at Tenoch. "Let him go."

Tenoch loosened his grip and Akama pulled his hand from the other Founts abdomen. Both men panted and exchanged angry glances at each other as they recovered from their injuries.

"The cure first, then she'll release him," Arsalan said.

Thallos shot him a heated look. "Think you that I'd risk his life on a betrayal?"

"I think you are selfish and stubborn. I think it took you too long to submit. I think you went through a great deal of trouble to get your way these past few days regardless of whose life was being lost or risked. Therefore, I think you might betray us," Arsalan replied.

"As if I care what you think, Arsalan," Thallos said. He turned toward Irikara. "Let Roycean take to you the cure, and then release him or I swear-"

"Spare me your threats, darling," Irikara shot back. "Come." She dragged Roycean to his feet by his hair ignoring his yelp of pain and curses. He led her out of the room as Zaire walked back through the hole his body had made in the wall.

"I take it we've come to a resolution?" he asked as he stumbled over the scattered stone debris.

"Still a little out of it, I see," Akama teased, but not without concern for his *Chosen One* s wellbeing.

"Yeah, but at least I had a nice nap," Zaire replied.

Akama nodded. "I'm relieved that you're all right. Now when they give us the cure, I want you to deliver it to Warren immediately. I only hope that we're not too late."

Zaire nodded. "Yes, Master."

Irikara returned with Roycean still held helplessly by the nape of his neck in her iron grip. He handed five vials filled with a thick dark red substance to Zaire.

"Do I just feed it to them?" Zaire asked.

"Yes, no more than a teaspoon," Roycean answered.

"Good," Zaire said.

Xavier walked back into the mansion using the same window he was tossed out of. His clothes were dripping wet and he was pale and weak from his blood loss. He could tell that the battle was over, for that, he was grateful. He looked at Roycean held captive in Irikara's iron grip, and it took every ounce of strength he had left not to lunge at the ancient vampire. He knew that attacking Roycean, even at full health would probably result in his death, and besides getting to Natasha was more important than his wish for revenge.

"I want to go with you," Xavier said to Zaire. He staggered a bit but Zaire advanced toward him, catching him before he fell. He hadn't realized just how much blood he'd lost during the battle. However, he was starting to feel the effects more keenly as the gnawing in his stomach grew fierce and his thirst demanded quenching. His wounds were healing, but not as fast as they could and he still felt lightheaded.

"You need blood," Zaire said.

"That can wait," Xavier replied.

"Aren't you going to wait for Darian?" Zaire asked him.

"Darian is alive, he is fine. Go, I'll tend to him," Kysen said.

"Thank you, Kysen," Xavier said, giving a nod to the ancient vampire who nodded in return.

With that, Zaire took Xavier into his embrace left the mansion, taking to the skies.

Kysen went to Darian, lifting him slightly as he bit into his own wrist. He pressed the open wound to Darian's parted lips and waited until he felt the pull of his child sucking the nourishment and power his blood provided.

"That's it, drink deeply," Kysen whispered into his ear. He turned toward Julius, "heal who you can, on both sides."

Julius nodded and walked over to those who were injured doing as he was told. Meanwhile, Darian's limbs gathered strength and he gripped Kysen's arm with both hands as his feeding became more urgent. Kysen began to pant as he felt a powerful orgasm building deep within him. He threw his head back, groaning heavily as both he and Darian shared the peak of their ecstasy. Their bodies rocked together as waves and waves of pleasure coursed through them as his child fed from him. Finally, Kysen could give no more and he pulled his wrist free from Darian's grip. Weaken, he fell back against the wall, gasping.

Darian sat up and turned toward him. He smiled. "Once again, you have saved me. Thank you."

Kysen smirked. "And it's becoming quite taxing. Do try to refrain from getting yourself into trouble, will you?"

Darian chuckled. "I'll try." He looked around for Xavier.

"He went to your human woman," Kysen informed.

"All right." Darian turned toward the others in the room, looking at the horrendous sight before him. One he knew all too well even as a human witnessing the grim aftermath of a battle. Bodies and more bodies spread about, lives sacrificed for one cause or another. Some were moaning as others came to their aid, giving blood. Female shifters, Matrons of their respective communities who survived the worst of the battle, gave their blood to the injured shifters as they licked their wounds. Miaka, Bahashiri, Gabrielle and Sade tended to the other ancient vampires.

"This is a site I could do without," Darian said. "I have never been one who sought the 'glory of battle' as many soldiers phrased it."

Kysen smiled. "No, you sought the glory of the Games."

Darian nodded. "And it wasn't because I was afraid of war. I just didn't see the need to sacrifice myself for another man's gain. Why should I seek the afterlife, while another prospers from my life lost? During those times, I saw no cause great enough."

"And now?" Kysen looked at his child. Darian never ceased to impress or charm him.

"This was a cause worth fighting for. Not just for Natasha's life, but for my children who must grow up in this world," Darian said.

"I see," Kysen said. "Well, in your moment of self-reflection do not forget that you owe your life to Julius as well. He saved you when I could not."

Darian couldn't suppress his frown before it flashed across his face.

Kysen laughed. "This feud between the two of you is just getting ridiculous."

"I suppose I owe him ... my life," Darian conceded.

"Yes, you do," Julius said as strutted over to them. "I'm sure I can find some way you can return the favor." He chuckled.

"I'm sure you will," Darian remarked and turned toward Kysen. "What's happening now?"

"Right now, I do not know. I do believe the physical part of this *discussion* has concluded, one can only hope. Now we'll have to see what's next," Kysen said.

Darian noticed the vampire who had assaulted Natasha still being held by Irikara as the other Founts argued with Thallos for enough blood to save the millions suffering. He looked at the blond vampire who had dared to harm what was his. The vampire who all but condemned Natasha to death. The *rat bastard* who entered his territory without permission and he saw red ... blood red. A low growl emanated from him.

"Calm yourself, my child. If you were to take him on, he would kill you. This fight you cannot win," Kysen said. "And I will not lose you after all we've went through. I will not allow you to challenge him."

Darian looked at Kysen, his expression distorted with the intense rage he felt. "You cannot ask me to do nothing–"

"I am not asking, I am telling you, let it be. Go to your human, she needs you now. What good will your death be to her, or Xavier?" Kysen said.

Darian looked back at Roycean, fighting his urge to strike the ancient vampire who was more than three times his age. In spite of his rage, he knew that Kysen was right. He also knew that Kysen would restrain him if need be. He decided it would be best for everyone if he took his Maker's advice and removed himself from Roycean's presence.

"Very well, I'm going to Xavier and Natasha," he said as he rose to his feet. "Are you sure you will not need me?"

"He has me," Julius said as he stood rather protectively beside Kysen. "Go to your human, Darian. She needs you more than we do."

"Enough," Kysen said, silencing Julius.

"Apologies, Master." Julius bowed his head.

"Darian, I'll be all right. Go," Kysen said.

Darian tossed Julius another scornful look, but thanked his Maker and left, flying toward the airplane.

***

Xavier held Natasha very gently in his arms as he waited for the cure to take effect. Zaire had given the cure to both of Natasha's parents and now he was sitting beside them waiting for them to heal as well. Warren sat in a chair beside the bed, his eyes firmly on Natasha as he monitored the slow rise of her chest with each breath she took.

"Do you think it's working?" he asked Xavier.

"I don't know yet, I don't see any change," Xavier replied.

"Do you think she needs more, maybe one teaspoon wasn't enough," Warren said.

"We were warned not to give more than a teaspoon," Zaire said.

"What if he was lying," Xavier asked. "It's not as if he had incentive to tell the truth."

"Yeah, he could have said any old bullshit just because he's pissed they lost," Warren added.

"No. If she were to die because of his lie, that would enrage you into battle again. No doubt Darian would follow your lead, then Kysen and again, Irikara. He would not wish to cross Irikara, none of them do. Not to mention, we have the upper hand," Zaire said. "Give it time, she was deathly ill, it may take a while for her … for all three of them to recover."

Xavier shook his head. "I swear it took everything I had not to attack him."

Zaire gave him a sad smile. "It's good that you didn't. Roycean would have ripped you to shreds in less than a second, and that's if you're even able to reach him. He's powerful enough to have the ability to create psychic barriers."

"No shit," Warren said.

"No shit." Zaire said.

"Can you do that?" Warren asked.

Zaire nodded. "But mine aren't nearly as strong as his."

They all heard the opening of the airplane door and a second later, Darian entered the bedroom. "How is she?" he asked.

Xavier looked down at her and smiled. "I think you're right, Zaire, her heart rate is increasing and her fever is breaking."

"Her parents are faring better as well," Zaire said. "I can hear their heart rate return to a healthy rhythm."

Darian sat on the bed next to Natasha. Immediately, he could see the physical changes and knew she would be all right. "The cure is working faster now. Soon she'll be completely healed."

"We got to get that cure to the rest of the world and fast as hell, too," Devin said.

"I don't disagree, but I'm not making any moves until Akama tells me," Zaire said.

"Well, I'm sure he'll give you the go ahead soon. Why else would he even bother getting involved if he didn't want to get that cure out to the masses?" Ignacio speculated.

"I hope he hurries up then, no disrespect to him and all," Devin said, catching himself.

"None taken. I understand," Zaire said.

Natasha stirred in Xavier's arms but remained asleep. Her fever had dissipated completely and her skin had returned to its usual healthy complexion and texture. Both of her parents were also healing well as they slumbered.

"Looks like we're out of the woods," Warren said with a sigh of relief.

"For now," Darian stated.

***

"Are there any more vials of the cure? What is it made from besides your blood, Thallos?" Akama asked. He was now fully healed thanks to Miaka.

Thallos on the other hand was still thirsting for blood. The other

Founts refused to let him feed until he complied completely.

"It's a rather complex compound that's simple to make if you have the right ingredients. My blood being the base for the compound," Thallos said.

"We're going to need more, you know that," Akama said.

"You have what you're going to get until Olendale reports back. Unless you plan on taking it by force," Thallos replied.

"Four Founts against three and your army isn't what it once was. Add to the fact that you're too weak to even stand, do you still want to be this difficult?" Arsalan said.

"Thallos, it's over. Trust that Olendale was persuasive enough to get the job done," Akama said. "My friend, please."

"Ah, the bitter taste of defeat, I had forgotten how much you detest it," Maska teased Thallos.

"To be rid of you and your lot ... *so be it*," Thallos relented. "Roycean, give them all of the vials we have in storage."

Irikara released Roycean and he left the room; returning a few minutes later with two large locked containers. He handed it to Akama.

"You have what you need to cure at least sixty-five million humans. That should be enough if they disperse it properly. That is all and I do mean all you're getting from me," Thallos said. "Now leave."

"I'll visit you soon once this is over," Akama said.

Thallos grunted. "Don't bother ..." He wrapped his arm around Roycean's shoulder and allowed his child to help him to his feet. They walked toward the doorway and Thallos stopped, looking over his shoulder at Akama. "... At least not for a few weeks. I'm still very disappointed with you."

"Fair enough," Akama said with a slight chuckle.

Thallos nodded and left the room.

"That goes for you as well, Arsalan. But I'll come to you when I'm ready to speak to you again. I still can't believe you betrayed me this way," Semei said.

"You do that," Arsalan said. He decided to not say anything further. He knew how much his involvement hurt his best friend. But in spite of his earlier protest, he knew what they did was the right thing to do.

"Are you preparing to hold a grudge as well?" Maska asked Tenoch.

"Why should I? I defeated you in battle," Tenoch boasted.

"You swine," Maska cursed.

"Not to mention, I had the advantage over you as well, Akama." Tenoch pointed at him.

Akama snorted. "I'd like to think that we were evenly matched."

Tenoch laughed. "I'm sure you would. But we weren't."

"Oh, I beg to differ. I remember having a good advantage on you." Akama pointed to the Fount's side where he'd stabbed him.

Tenoch laughed. "Had Thallos not submitted first, you would have."

"You talk too much," Maska remarked.

Tenoch laughed again, but more boisterously. "Maybe next time I request a sparring match, you won't decline. You need the practice, my friend." He winked at Maska.

Maska frowned. "I'm leaving. Gabrielle, let us go." With that, he left the mansion in a blink of an eye with his *Chosen One* in tow.

"What about the dead?" Arsalan asked.

"Leave them," Irikara said. "They are not our concern."

Akama tossed her a look that showed his dismay and shock at her lack of compassion.

"Ugh, do not look at me that way. Surely you do not expect us to dig graves for each and every one. They are not of my line or your own. They are their responsibility," Irikara said, pointing a dainty finger at Tenoch. "It is his home, his territory and his to deal with. I am leaving." She turned and walked out of the mansion.

Tenoch looked causally at the bodies strewn about his parlor. Some were from his line even though he hadn't turned them himself. All but one vampire there was one his children and he survived the battle. For Tenoch, even though he didn't have a *Chosen One*, per se ... Raphael was one of his children and he loved him. He was happy to know that Kysen had spared him.

The shifters there owed him allegiance for allowing them residency. The Founts made certain to gather supernaturals for their army that they didn't have a direct connection with—those whose inevitable deaths wouldn't deal them a blow they'd have difficulty recovering from. These select few were ordered there to aid his cause simply because they resided in his territory.

Tenoch nodded. "She's right. Go, I'll deal with this. Their deaths would be in vain on your part, if more people died while waiting for a cure, wouldn't you agree?"

Akama nodded. "Let's go."

He and the others left, flying back to the airplane. Once on board they checked in with Natasha and were pleased to see that the cure was successful. A few minutes later, they were airborne heading for Chicago.

***

Olendale had managed to convince the UN to amend Law Number Three when his cell phone buzzed.

"Excellences, ladies and gentlemen, if you would excuse me. This may be the telephone call we've been waiting for," Olendale announced.

"Please, by all means, answer it," Security-General Lee said.

Olendale answered his cell phone. "Cantillia."

"How are negotiations going?" Akama asked.

"There was a bit of protest on Law Number Three, but it passed, sir," Olendale answered.

"Everything has been accepted?"

"Yes, sir."

The other men and women in the room exchanged glances as they wondered who Olendale could be talking to that held such a commanding presence over him even through the telephone.

"Excellent. We are heading toward Chicago now. I've scent Zaire to the CDC headquarters in Washington with the cure. He'll be making trips to various countries dispensing the cure to their medical centers and research labs. I was not given the compound ingredients, so they must take care with how they dole out the portions, no more than a teaspoon per person who is at the most risk. You may inform the UN of this new development and then I want you to address the public once again. Have your public relations writer draft you a speech to apologize and to reassure the people of the world. Do I make myself clear?"

"Yes, sir." Olendale said.

"Good. You've done well," Akama said.

"Thank you, sir." They ended the call and Olendale slipped his cellular back into his pocket. He looked around the room. "There is good news; the cure is on its way to the Center for Disease Control in Washington D.C. It is also being transferred around the world to other locations so that medical facilities can start administering it."

"That's a relief," UN president Ava Paxton said as she released another sigh. "We have to get that cure to every major medical facility in the country first. We have to get to the big cities with the sickest patients then branch out to every town in every state."

"Shouldn't we test it first?" Security-General Lee asked.

"There is no need. The cure is what it is. You're going to spend enough time rationing it out. There's no need to waste more money and time testing something that is a sure thing, pardon my candor," Olendale said.

"I agree, with the life expectancy of someone infected with this disease varying from one day to a week, we have to move on this now," World Health Organization representative Nancy Marksmith said. "If it saves lives, get it out to the hospitals and clinics ASAP."

"Should there be a charge for this vaccine?" World Health Organization President Henry Wayne asked.

Olendale couldn't contain the chuckle that erupted from him. "My, my and you call us bloodsuckers," he commented offhandedly. "I'm sure you could look at this as a very lucrative opportunity. No doubt you could probably charge a thousand dollars for one drop of the cure and people would pay ... well, those who could afford to, that is. But is that really the right decision?"

"I would think not," Ava said. "It should be given to the public freely as are flu vaccinations." She was appalled that the question was even presented and by the president of the World Health Organization, no less.

The meeting was concluded and adjourned. Olendale left, climbing back into his limousine with his assistant. He was more than thrilled to be free of the human bureaucracy for the moment. It was one of the reasons why he'd been more than happy to appoint a human representative for the Council when requested by the UN several years ago. Even now, it angered him that he had to contact his PR person to create a speech that would put him back into the mainstream human world. His face would once again be broadcast on every television, tablet, computer, and cell phone around the world. And to top it off, he had to be humble and apologize for his race. He was not pleased, not one little bit.

"Where to now?" Courtney asked.

"To the hotel. I have to contact Gerald and have him draft a speech for me to release to the public," Olendale said.

"No need, I've already contacted him and he'll have one available for you shortly."

Olendale looked at her and smiled. "What would I have done without you in my life for all these years?"

Courtney giggled. "I dread to even think about it." She leaned forward, kissing him passionately as she ran her fingers through his luxurious blond locks.

"You're lovely," Olendale said once their lips parted. He kissed her once more on her forehead. "Will our cuisine be waiting for us at our hotel?"

"Yes. I contacted the Master of the city, Cecily, she's made the arrangement to have a tiger shifter service us during our stay," Courtney said.

"Ah, a fine showing indeed. Quite the delicacy. I can hardly wait to feed now," Olendale said with a slight chuckle.

"I thought that would cheer you up."

"Well, as you know, tiger blood is my favorite." He smiled.

Courtney nodded. "I know."

They discussed the meeting and what they thought of it as they headed for their hotel.

CHAPTER TWENTY-FOUR

Natasha awoke on the airplane and looked around. The first thing she noticed was her state of health. She no longer felt sick and weak. Her muscles no longer throbbed and ached. She felt healthier than she ever had.

"How are you feeling?" Xavier asked her.

"I'm feeling great! Am I cured?" she asked with a bit of contained excitement. She didn't want to get her hopes yet until she knew for certain.

Xavier nodded. "You are." He smiled as he embraced her, kissing her passionately.

"Oh my God, thank you all so much!" she said to everyone on the airplane once her lips parted from Xavier's.

"You're welcome," Akama said with a smile and nod.

"You'll be happy to know that your parents survived as well," Darian said as he settled down on the sofa next to her. He kissed her as passionately as Xavier did then he release her.

"Where are they?" Natasha asked, looking around.

"They're still asleep in the bedroom. We didn't wake them because they need the rest," Warren said. He took his turn, hugging and kissing Natasha albeit not as passionately as Darian and Xavier had.

"You better not have died on me," Devin said as he hugged Natasha, squeezing her a bit too hard.

"Ow!" she exclaimed.

"Oh, I'm sorry. You okay?" Devin asked, giving her a once over.

"Yeah, I'm fine. Trust me, no one wanted me to live more than I did," Natasha said, giving a relieved chortle.

"We missed your vibrant spirit," Ignacio said as he hugged her.

Irikara watched the reunion, after a few more minutes she grew bored. "This is all lovely, quite touching, really," she said sarcastically. "Now if we can move on to the bargain that was made."

"Now?" Xavier asked. He was angered that Irikara wouldn't even allow him and Darian the time to prepare Natasha for her change in a more private and intimate environment. Of all the times he'd imagined bringing Natasha to him, he never had an audience watching, save Darian. Another thing that pissed him off was Irikara's blatant disregard for Nataha's feelings regarding everything that had happened.

"Yes, you will do it now. I believe my words were 'as soon as she is healed' to which you readily agreed" Irikara reminded. "I want to see it with my own eyes. When I leave Chicago, I want to know that pesky human woman of yours will not be this much trouble in the future."

"Irikara, perhaps you want to give them time for her to be prepared," Kysen beseeched on their behalf. One didn't need to read Xavier's mind to know what the younger vampire was thinking.

"She has her life, she is prepared. Get on with it," Irikara demanded, her intense gaze never leaving Natasha, Xavier and Darian.

Xavier turned to Darian, who nodded.

"Natasha, Xavier is going to be very gentle; it's going to feel a bit differently than it does when we've drank from you for sexual pleasure," Darian said. "It will feel a bit more intense, but soon you will enjoy it. But afterwards, once his blood is inside you and the transformation process begins, you will feel a lot of pain, mainly abdominal, but it will spread throughout. The pain only lasts for a few moments and once it's gone, it will be gone forever."

Natasha nodded. That was one thing she wasn't looking forward to. She'd seen a vampire be made a few years ago, and she'd heard the stories. She and pain just did not get along. She hated pain and pain hated her. But a deal was a deal and after what she went through, she was actually looking forward to living forever and seeing her children grow up. Having almost been denied that blessing put a lot of things in perspective for her.

"It's all right, I'm ready. I want this," she said.

"All right," Xavier said.

He brushed her hair from her shoulder revealing the pulsating vein in her neck that would soon flow her precious blood into him. He leaned forward, fangs bared and bit deeply, puncturing the vein. Natasha gasped and yelped as his teeth pierced her skin. It was as Darian had described; intense and extremely sexual once the familiar pain faded. She'd never felt anything like it before. Every nerve in her body vibrated with the power of Xavier's pull. Her body grew hot as pleasure coursed through her, growing stronger and stronger until it erupted giving her one of the most powerful orgasms she'd ever had. Her body twitched uncontrollably in Xavier's arms, it was all she could do in her weakened state and she didn't want it to end.

A second later, it did end to her utter disappointment, but then that pleasure was replaced by a different one. Thick, warm liquid flowed into her mouth, delicious and potent. Her body electrified with energy, power and strength as she drew harder and harder on the blood. Once again, she was caught in the whirlwind of ecstasy so magnificent, she could have died just then and would have been happy.

Xavier grimaced in intense pain as he let Natasha nearly drain him dry. He wanted her to be as powerful as she could be and he ignored the agony that throbbed through every fiber of his being. It was something he'd never experienced before; Natasha would be his first child. But as he fed her, giving her life everlasting, he knew firsthand what Darian had spoken about. The bond between Maker and child, it was forming with every swallow she took. They were becoming one and at that moment, he'd never felt as close to her, his *Chosen One.*

"You've given her enough, Xavier," Darian said as he pulled Xavier's wrist from Natasha's greedy mouth.

In her desperation to keep the sensation going, Natasha reached out for Xavier's wrist, but Darian wrapped his other arm around her, pressing her to his chest until she calmed down. It didn't take long because the pain that he had described earlier was making itself known. Natasha cried out as her insides began to burn and constrict. Darian held her as he whispered reassuring words into her ear in hopes to keep her focused and calm during the transition. It seemed like time stood still has her body readjusted itself for a life of vampirism. Finally, it was over. The pain has subsided and all that was left now was hunger. A new hunger, something more savage and merciless than anything she could have ever imagined.

"Drink." Darian said, exposing his wrist. "It will sate your thirst and increase your strength and abilities."

Natasha nodded and took Darian's wrist into her hands. She hadn't even realized that her teeth had formed fangs for this particular feeding ritual. It didn't become clear to her until she drove them through the soft flesh of Darian's wrist. But all of that vanished the moment his powerful blood hit her tongue. Greedily, she sucked the delicious life source into her mouth with an animal's abandon. Darian panted breathlessly as he savored the sensation of her suckling. The thirst of a newborn always brought with it a special kind of urge that made the sharing of blood that much more passionate. He felt his orgasm building and could sense Natasha's cresting at the same time. They climaxed together, gasping and moaning in pleasure until Natasha could take no more and she regretfully pulled away.

Darian fell back breathlessly against the cushions of the sofa. He was completely drained and his body tingled with the aftermath of their union. The others on the airplane had watched the trio with varying degrees of interest and arousal. Irikara, for one had viewed the show with a keen interest. For all of her lofty behavior, she couldn't deny enjoying the turning process—the embracing of a human by a truly spectacular being such as a vampire. Arsalan and Akama were both aroused and needless to say, Akama was satisfied that Natasha was one of them now, more so than Arsalan who was mostly indifferent.

"Are you all right?" Warren asked Natasha once she appeared to have some control over herself. He had watched the transformation and was in awe. He could see the supernatural changes taking over her physical form. She was more radiant than ever before. Her hair was more luxurious, her skin even softer with a healthier glow as he ran his fingers along her jawline.

"Yeah, I'm fine. Man, that was a rush!" Natasha said, her eyes bulging from their sockets. "Wow, is that what I sound like now?"

"Yeah, I noticed that, too," Warren said, noting the slight different in Natasha's voice. Her words seem to have taken on a kind of alluring tone, seductive almost even though she wasn't trying to be.

"So, I guess that *is* a vampire thing. I've always wondered that about you guys. How everything you said sounded so sexy," Natasha said with a giggle as she pointed to Darian then Xavier.

Darian chuckled. "Well, for me, I didn't really notice any difference between my human or vampire voice. Did you Kysen?" he looked at his Maker.

"Do not talk to me," Kysen grumbled.

"Are you serious?" Darian asked. "I thought we were past this. Are you planning on holding a grudge?"

"I am thrilled that you survived this chaos of your own making. However, that doesn't mean I'm still not annoyed by all of the past events." Kysen sighed. "Besides, I am about due to hold a grudge against you. I have spoiled you far too much, that is the problem."

"So true," Julius remarked.

Darian snorted rather uncharacteristically. "With you being silent over there, Julius, I had almost forgotten you were on board. It was a pleasant notion."

"Be happy that I was on board, or you'd be a pile of ash by now. Defeated in battle and tossed out with the rest of the bodies too weak to sustain the heat of the sun," Julius shot back.

"Is there some way I can expedite the repayment of debt owed to you?" Darian asked. "The last thing I want is to be bothered with you in the future."

"Just knowing you owe me your life is repayment enough. There's nothing you could do or give me that would be equal to that, wouldn't you agree?" Julius looked at him with his smuggest expression.

Darian wanted to claw it from his face, but he refrained from giving in to Julius' taunt. "Thank you, Julius, for saving me."

"You're most welcome. But now that you've mentioned repayment … mind if I have a hot tumble with your *Chosen One*?" he asked, flashing a seductive glance at Xavier.

"*I* would," Xavier said. "For one, I'm not in the mood. For another reason, I won't be some pawn in your childish rivalry with Darian."

"He's a lively one, isn't he?" Julius commented before laughing.

"Very well, but if you ever plan on visiting Greece again, that's my demand for *Homage*, just so you know."

Darian couldn't help but shake his head. Julius was one vampire that brought out the worst in him. He never liked him, but one thing he hated to admit, he owed him his life. He was grateful to him for that, despite their eternal feud.

Devin looked at Natasha. "So you're a vampire now, what do you think about that?"

"I'm not sure yet, haven't had much time to process it. I'm still kind of freaking out because I can see, hear, smell and sense things I couldn't before. It's really weird, but not in a good or bad way … just weird," she said.

"You'll get used to it soon, and it won't seem so unusual then," Xavier said reassuringly.

"So is there anyone who is going to show any gratitude to me?" Irikara asked. "All of you owe your lives to me. As a matter of fact, the entire world owes me an immeasurable debt. Had it not been for me, you would have all been outnumbered and overcome by Thallos' army. Had it not been for me, both Darian and Xavier would have lost their human woman to some tragic, tawdry mortal death while they debated and waited around for the moment she would come to her senses and ask to be turned. I made all of the hard decisions and saved everyone so much unnecessary grief and yet not one single word of gratitude."

"I have shown my gratitude to you, my Goddess," Kysen reminded.

Irikara turned to him and smiled. "Yes, you have, my dear child. Of course, it was because of you why I was coerced into this little excursion to begin with."

Kysen sat back in his chair, exasperated. He tossed Darian a look that said: *See, this is why I am upset with you.*

Darian nodded with a sly smile, but didn't bother to comment. However, he did address Irikara. "My Goddess, you were right, and I thank you for what you've done for us."

"It's because you are Kysen's favorite child-" She was intentionally interrupted by Julius annoyed grumble. She turned toward him. "-Yes, his *favorite* child that I even bothered to help you at all. Your happiness means so much to him and his to me. That is why I took the decision away from you. Some humans, regardless of the love they feel for our kind, oftentimes resent being turned and blame their Makers."

"I wouldn't blame them. Even if they asked me on their own, I still wouldn't have blamed them," Natasha said in her defense.

"You do not know that. In the beginning, for some, the experience is wonderful. The freedom, the power, the ecstasy, it is everything the fledgling could have ever hoped for. But then, some grow bitter, hateful and unappreciative of the gift they've been given. It was because Kysen loved Darian so, that I did not wish to see him suffer that fate with one he loves as much as you."

The others were shocked by Irikara's seemingly uncharacteristic display of compassion. During this expedition, many had decided she had no knowledge of what the word *compassion* meant. It would seem they were wrong in their judgment.

"Thank you," Natasha said.

"I did not do it for you," Irikara replied.

Natasha fought the urge to give her the middle finger and a good eye roll to boot. Instead, she opted for a more dignified response. "I know that you didn't. But I still want to show my gratitude."

"Very well," Irikara said.

Akama chuckled softly at Natasha. He didn't need to know what she was thinking to know what she wished she could have said to Irikara. Even he had to admit his fellow Founts were weighing on people's nerves.

"I'm going to turn on the television to see if Olendale has released the statement I requested," Akama said. He pressed a button on the remote control and the flat screen television came to life.

The anchorman was announcing how many hospitals and clinics around the world were nearly overrun with people seeking the cure. Many who were the most in need were being treated while others who were in the first stages of the sickness were treated and released. The news looked hopeful as many people treated recovered at remarkable speeds. In some cases, even before leaving the medical facilities, they were cured. In other news, the United Nations announced that they came to an agreement during negotiations with the Supernatural Council to make new laws and amendments on the current ones.

The anchorman at that point decided to play a taping of Olendale's speech that was released live ten minutes ago. In the video, Olendale apologized to the people of the world for the criminal acts of a few supernaturals. He reassured the people that the Council would work tirelessly alongside the human governments of the world to create a peaceful and fair society where humans and supernaturals shouldn't have to live in fear of the other.

Akama was pleased with the speech and with the progress that was made during this time. It was sad that so many had to die in order for two races to come to an understanding. But at least things looked better for the future and future generations. They watched the news a bit longer until it began to replay. At that point, he turned off the television.

"I'm so happy we were able to cure all of those people," Natasha said.

"It still sucks that so many people have already died," Devin said. "I still can't believe all of this happened."

"I know. It seems so surreal, but then you see all of the death and carnage. People crying and terrified and just feeling lost as they watch their loved ones die." Natasha shook her head in dismay. "I hope this never happens again."

"Well, their demands were met. So hopefully it won't," Warren said.

The bedroom door opened and Natasha's parents stepped into view.

"Mom! Dad!" Natasha said and she rushed toward them. She had to be careful when embracing them so not to crush their fragile bones with her new found strength. "Oh thank God you're all right."

"We prayed and prayed that you would survive this virus," her mother said as she hugged her daughter as tightly as she could.

"Me too," Natasha said. "If it weren't for Darian, Xavier, Miko, Akama and Zaire, we wouldn't have. Their blood kept us alive."

"My heart goes out to the families who've lost loved ones because they didn't have any vampire help," her father said. "Is this nightmare over with?"

Natasha nodded. "Yes. People all around the world are being treated and the laws are being changed to make everything fair for both humans and supernaturals."

"Good. Lord knows I never want to go through that again," her mother said. She turned to face Darian and Xavier. "What is the government going to do to those vampires who caused this? Who tortured my baby on worldwide television?"

"What can they do? Thallos is ten-thousand years old, there isn't a damn thing the government can do against a vampire that damn old," Warren said. "We're just going to have to lick our wounds on this one and hope he doesn't get an attitude again."

"What about what he did to Natasha?" her mother, Marian asked.

"Trust me, there's no one who wants to see him suffer more than Darian and I. But to attack him would result in our certain death. Right now, Natasha, our children and our friends are more important than seeking revenge that will never come," Xavier said.

Finally overcome with a multitude of emotions, her mother began to cry.

"Mom, it's okay. What's important is that we're all here. I wouldn't want anyone else I love to die trying to get revenge for me. I'd rather have you all here with me," Natasha said as she held her mom.

"You feel different, are you sure you're all right?" her mom asked as she ran her hands along Natasha's arms.

"Ah, yeah, about that. Mom, there's no easy way to say this, so I'm just going to come on out with it. I'm a vampire now," Natasha said. "But before you get upset about that. I'm okay with it."

"Did you want to be a vampire?" her mother asked.

Natasha snorted. "I would have chosen to become a troll if it would have saved my life."

"You didn't answer my question."

"When they first asked me, yes."

"Are you sure you're all right with that?" her mother just wanted to make sure her daughter was happy.

"Yes, Mom," Natasha said. She wanted to tell her mom that whether or not she wanted to become a vampire was now a moot point. It was done. Lucky for her, she was going to look at the brighter side of it.

"As long as you're happy and alive, I'm happy," her mother said. She wasn't completely thrilled that her daughter was going to have to drink blood for eternity. Nonetheless, she'd rather be satisfied that they saved her daughter than complain about them turning her.

"Well, I can't say that I'm completely fond of the idea that you're a vampire. I never wanted that for you, but somehow, deep inside… I knew it may come to this," her dad added with another hug. He was so happy that they had lived through their ordeal when so many had perished. But the fact that his daughter was going to live forever was going to take some getting used to on his part. "Are you sure you're happy with that decision?"

"I get to protect my children and be with those I love. I'm happy," Natasha reaffirmed.

They comforted each other some more before settling down. The Founts and other vampires simply looked on. Irikara and Arsalan appeared nonchalant, but Akama and Zaire were intrigued. Julius had grown bored of the human interactions and had taken to reading a magazine, while Bahashiri turn her gaze to the passing clouds and stars.

"How much longer till we reach Chicago?" Devin asked.

"About a half hour," Akama said.

"Good, I can't wait to get home."

"I can't wait to see my children and friends again," Natasha said.

"I bet." Akama gave her a sweet smile.

"I'll call someone to pick us up," Warren said.

"Good idea," Devin agreed.

"Are you going to Darian's airport?" Warren asked.

"That was the plan," Akama replied.

As promised, their airplane landed on the tarmac at Darian's hangar a half hour later and Adan, Elise, Sergio, Adrian and Matthew were there waiting for them. They ran over to them hugging each one in greeting.

Elise pulled away from Natasha. "Who turned you?" she asked; the high-pitch tone in her voice conveying her shock.

"Xavier."

"Are you all right?" Elise asked.

Natasha nodded. "I'm better than all right, I'm alive!"

"Well, I'll take you any way I can get you." Elise smiled and gave her friend another heartfelt embrace.

Akama smiled as he watched the friends kiss and hug. He waited a little while longer before giving a discreet cough. They looked up at him. "I'm happy you're all together again. But I'm exhausted. I can't recall the last time I was this engaged … it's been invigorating. Nonetheless, I speak for my companions when I say, 'we're ready to go home'. So we won't be staying, but if you ever want to visit Australia, give me a call."

"For sure," Natasha said. He was the one Fount she thought was the coolest of them all. "I'd love to visit when I can actually enjoy myself."

Akama chuckled and waved goodbye before closing the door. A few minutes later, the airplane taxied down the runway and lifted off.

Kysen watched the airplane take off. "I should have demanded they take me to my home first before coming here. My own jet is in Egypt and yours is in Montana."

Darian chuckled. "Don't worry. You won't have to hitchhike home."

Kysen tossed him a menacing glare. He was in no mood for jokes.

Adan laughed, but then he thought about Kysen's statement. "Hey, wait a minute, so you were just going to go home and leave me to get there on my own after making me come with you?"

Kysen shrugged.

Adan shook his head. "You're unbelievable at times."

"Kysen, don't worry. I'll have my pilot take you home when you're ready," Elise offered.

"I am ready now," Kysen replied.

"Kysen, let's do it this way. Just fly us there but make sure you go slowly enough so that I can breathe," Adan said.

Kysen chuckled remembering the first time he'd taken Adan flying. He'd traveled at a speed so fast, the shifter nearly suffocated.

"Very well. Come now." He gathered Adan into his arms. "Darian, please give me at least a year's reprieve before you need my help again."

Darian huffed. "Take care, Kysen … you too, Adan."

They all watched as Kysen ascended into the sky with his lover then quickly vanished from their sights.

"Let's get the hell out of here," Warren said.

"Hell yeah," Devin agreed.

They all climbed into the three Sidewinder SUVs and drove back to Darian's home where everyone else was waiting to welcome them back. Natasha had never been so happy to see all of them the way she was now. She hugged and kissed every last person she could get her hands on. Many of them were shocked to see that she was a vampire. And some weren't surprised at all, considering that Xavier and Darian had almost lost her. Turning her into a vampire seemed to be the logical decision. After a while, Natasha parted from the boisterous crowd to spend private time with her children. She held them both in her arms as she went upstairs. She could smell their freshness and sense their innocence more keenly. How fragile and precious they looked in her powerful embrace. She would have to be extra careful to handle them gently. She'd never forgive herself if she were to harm them in any way due to her new vampire strength. Little Matthew hugged her and gave her a semi-wet kiss. He had been quite talkative since she came home and listening to him ramble on was the highlight of her night. Her daughter, Aria just stared at her with the most beautiful brown eyes, so full of wonder. She wanted nothing more than to hold them forever. Xavier entered the nursery and leaned against the door frame.

"You look so perfectly satisfied with them in your arms. You live for them, I can see that," Xavier said as he stepped further into the room.

"They're a part of me. I see bits and pieces of me when I look at them. Even their little personalities show signs of me. I can't believe I came so close to losing them, to them losing me," Natasha said.

"I can't believe how close *we* came to losing you," Xavier said. He leaned down kissing her first and then he planted soft kisses on his two children.

Darian entered the nursery. "I'm not surprised to find both of you here."

"Is everyone else all right downstairs? They're not looking for me, are they?" Natasha asked.

Darian shook his head. "No. They understand. You need time to adjust to everything and everyone around you. There is a matter of your training we need to discuss."

Natasha jumped in her chair. "Whoa! What was that?" she asked as she shivered.

"What?" Both men asked in unison.

"That electricity in the air," Natasha said.

"Oh that," Darian said.

"Did that come from you?" she asked him.

"Unintentionally, yes," Darian answered with a chuckle.

"Wait a minute; did you just assert yourself with Tasha?" Xavier asked him.

"I think he did. He threw a little Master Mojo vibe my way." Natasha shivered again from the tingle left behind by Darian's aura.

"I can't help it, she's a new vampire in my lair, in my territory, and it's natural for me to lay down *some* ground rules. But this is more so for Natasha's benefit than my need to control," Darian clarified.

"Don't you go bossing me around, now," Natasha said.

"Ah, Natasha, things have changed a bit. The dynamic of our relationship has changed because you are a vampire of Darian's line, made by me," Xavier said.

"So, like what … I have to bow and call you Master, or something?" Natasha asked apprehensively.

"I don't always require those in my coven to bow. As for addressing me as 'Master', I think we'll pass on that. For you and Xavier, I've made exceptions," Darian said. "However, I am the Master vampire of this city. There are going to be certain things I ask of you. For one, you mustn't defy me in front of others. My ability to retain control over this territory relies strongly on my ability to control the vampires residing in it, especially those in my own home."

Natasha nodded. "I understand. I guess I didn't really think about that at all. Will I be required to fight in territory battles?"

"You may very well have to," Darian answered.

"That's not something I'm looking forward to, I'll tell you that," Natasha said.

"I'll protect you as long as I can, as I did with Gary. However, eventually, a time may come when you will have to fight. When it does …"

"Don't worry, I'll do my best," Natasha said.

Darian smiled. "I know you will." He walked over and kissed her gently. Then he kissed their two children. "Going back to what I was saying, you'll need proper training. Xavier is your Maker, he's going to train you. I know you'll want to learn control so that you do not hurt innocent people."

Natasha nodded. "I definitely want to learn that."

"We'll start tomorrow," Xavier said.

"Can't I just drink Synblood?" Natasha asked.

Darian frowned. "You're joking, right? … You *are* joking."

"If it's my decision, would you allow it?" Now she was just curious.

"It's a foolish choice, one that will lead to you losing control eventually and feeding on the first human whose blood entices you. Furthermore, you won't have the ability to resist the urge to kill them for lack of practice. It's unnatural for a vampire to force themselves to sustain on synthetic blood. What they don't tell you in the propaganda videos and advertising is that those vampires grow weak and helpless. They are miserable in their existence and many face the sun. The ones who don't commit suicide are often destroyed by their Makers or me. And you can rest assured, other Master vampires dispatching of these pathetic souls is quite common."

"Wow, way to bring in the gloom and doom," Natasha said.

"I think she was joking, Darian … I think," Xavier said.

"I was," Natasha confirmed.

"In case she wasn't, she needed to know the truth," Darian said. "Tomorrow night, she begins her training."

Xavier nodded.

"I'm going to rejoin our friends. When and if you're ready, feel free to come downstairs," Darian said.

"I will," Natasha said.

"Are you going to be all right?" Darian asked.

"I'm fine, babe, just tired. Even though I slept a lot, I never really got rest. I still had visions of people crying, praying, dying and I was too weak to block any of it," Natasha said rather sadly.

"In that case, I'll ask that our friends retire for the night. You need your rest and we really should have time together before the sun rises," Darian said. He turned and left.

"I love that man," Natasha said.

"I love him, too," Xavier agreed.

Natasha rose from the chair and left the nursery heading toward her bedroom with Xavier following. She placed both of their children in the bed and climbed in beside them. Xavier climbed in behind her and held her close.

"I thought I was going to lose you," he whispered into her ear.

"I did too. If it weren't for both of you and all of those ancient vampires, I would be dead," Natasha repeated, thinking about how close she came. "So many more would be dead. You are all heroes, Knights in shining armor … or rather designer suits."

Xavier laughed. "Well, these aren't my clothes. I borrowed them from Irikara."

"Details, details." Natasha giggled and then her laughter faded. "Xavier …"

"Yes?"

"I'm nervous about tomorrow."

"Don't be. Everything will come to you very naturally. Eventually, you won't think anything of it. It will be like eating a hamburger," Xavier said; then he winced. "I probably shouldn't have used a hamburger as an example." He laughed.

"Yeah, you shouldn't. I still think of them as people," Natasha said.

"I do as well. I was trying to make it easier for you." He laughed again.

"I want to talk about something else. A happier subject, I need that right now," Nastasha said as she rocked her son to sleep.

"Very well." He changed the subject to something funny to take her mind off everything that had happened.

A little while later, Darian entered the bedroom and immediately undressed. Going to his dresser drawer, he pulled out a pair of black satin pajama bottoms and slipped them on. Approaching the bed, he slid under the sheets beside his children kissing their tiny foreheads and nuzzling their tiny necks. "They smell so sweet. I've grown to love that scent."

"Everyone does," Natasha said. She yawned and wiped her eyes.

"Get some rest, darling," Darian said. "You and Xavier will soon succumb to the sun and so will I."

Natasha reached out and caressed his cheek. "Sweet dreams."

"I don't dream."

"Do you think I will?"

"I don't know."

Natasha sat up. "How will I be able to help people if I can't get visions in my sleep?"

"You can still take naps at night," Xavier said.

"Yeah, but what about during the day?" Natasha asked. Losing her visions was something she hadn't thought about. It was something she valued, no matter how much sleep they deprived her of. Lives were saved because she could see the present and future. It was a gift, just like her immortality.

"Don't worry about that now," Darian said.

"He's right. Your mental capabilities have increased dramatically. We will test your abilities in the coming nights," Xavier said.

"I hope I will be ab-" The rising son forced Natasha into her resting state.

Xavier chuckled. "That was funny."

"How are you? You became a Maker tonight. How do you feel about that?" Darian asked.

"I feel as though my life has taken on a whole new meaning."

"It has. You now have a life linked to yours. You will feel her very keenly until the strength of the bond fades. But the link will remain for all time," Darian said. "You did well, she's strong … powerful."

"I did as you taught me." Xavier smiled, and then he grew serious. "I thought I was going to lose you tonight, too. When you were injured …"

"A thing of the past," Darian said, sighing heavily. "Although, I've had my fill of battling ancient vampires and abnormally powerful shifters." He chuckled.

"Haven't we all." Xavier said before closing his eyes to rest.

Darian leaned over, kissing both him and Natasha. He scooped up the sleeping children and placed them back into their nursery. After giving instructions to Billy to care for them during the day, he returned to his bedroom and allowed himself to rest for the day.

CHAPTER TWENTY-FIVE
TWO WEEKS LATER

Warren reached over Matthew and snatched up his ringing cellular, sliding his thumb over his touchscreen. "Hello?" he greeted in a gruff voice.

"Good morning, Detective Davis," Michelle Lawrence cheerfully responded.

"Michelle?" Warren asked, perking up a bit.

"That's Captain Lawrence to you, buddy," she said with glee.

"You got your job back?"

"Yes, and thanks to the new legislation, you two have your jobs back if you want them. Fact is we need you."

Warren sat up straight in the bed, slapping Matthew on the chest at the same time.

"Ow, what?" Matthew asked as he rubbed the sore spot.

"Matt, it's the Captain. She wants to know if we want our old jobs back." Warren said.

Matthew sat up. "What? Really?"

"Yeah, listen." Warren placed his telephone on speaker. "You're talking to both of us now, Cap."

"I was reinstated two days ago by a very disgruntled Milton Cunningham." She paused to allow herself a satisfied giggle then continued. "I was given the incentive to rehire all S.U.I.T. officers formally terminated, including those that were incarcerated. Since the laws changed, it's no longer illegal for a supernatural to work for the government or state and city. So your arrest records are being expunged," Michelle informed. "In the aftermath of what happened, people are demanding that supernaturals join the S.U.I.T."

"I can't tell you how happy I am to hear that," Warren said. "I'd love to have my old job back with Matt as my partner, of course."

"Can that be arranged?" Matthew asked.

"That was my plan. You two are excellent together. And now, I can hire more supernaturals, even vampires, although, I'm slightly apprehensive about that," Michelle said.

"I might know a few who would make good candidates who you can trust. They can take the course, I'm sure they'd pass," Warren said.

"I'll look into that. I plan on partnering my human officers with supernatural ones. I'm sure that will save the lives of the citizens as well as my officers," Michelle said. "So, I expect to see you two here this afternoon."

"We'll be there," Warren said, before ending the call. "Can you believe that?"

"I guess some good finally came out of what happened. You know, truth be told, I don't think it would have happened this soon if it weren't for what Thallos did," Matthew said.

"I hate to admit that, but I think you're right. It's a shame that it takes a tragedy for people to do the right thing," Warren said.

"Not always, but when a tragedy does strike, at least something good does come from it," Matthew said as he climbed out the bed. "Let's get ready. We've got to get to work."

Warren smiled and followed him into the shower. They bathed and quickly got dressed and then headed to the precinct. Several officers walked up to them, welcoming them back. Some only looked on, not happy that those *freaks* got what they wanted and now they had to work with them. Warren and Matt made their way to the captain's office and knocked on the door.

"Come in," she called out.

Warren opened the door and they entered. Kyle and Barry were standing by her desk. Neither man looked happy at the moment.

Barry gave a nod to Warren and Matthew. "Nice to see you," he said.

"Same to you," Warren said. "Do you want us to wait outside?" he asked, pointing back toward the door.

"No, we're done here," Michelle said. "Welcome back Detective

Weinstein."

"Thank you, Captain." Barry strapped his guns back into his holsters and both he and the newly promoted Detective Kyle Ronen left.

"What was that all about?" Warren asked.

Michelle chuckled. "Well, Gabriel decided to stay in Montana and join the S.U.I.T. division there, so Barry needed a new partner. Regrettably, Lance passed away during the recent virus epidemic so Kyle needed a new partner. A human paired with a supernatural is my agenda, so it was a perfect match."

"'A perfect match' might be stretching it a bit, Captain," Warren joked. "Kyle hates supernaturals and Barry … well … Barry hates bigots."

"All the more reason for the two to learn to work together. A lot of barriers are going to have to come down and people are going to have to overcome their differences," Michelle said.

"By the way, when did Kyle make detective?" Warren asked.

"Three months ago, the former captain promoted both Kyle and Lance under Milton's orders," Michelle said. "And as long as he plays nice and by the rules, he'll get to keep that shiny new shield."

"Do we keep our old shift?" Matthew asked, getting back on track.

"Yes, but the one exception is that you no longer have to make a showing on full moon days," Michelle said. "I still can't figure out how you two managed as well as you did."

"It wasn't easy. I mostly made sure to pull double shifts the day before so that I could have an excuse to have the *Lunar* night off," Warren said. "I taught Matthew to do the same when he became one of us."

"Smart," Michelle said. "The *Lunar*, is that what you all call it?"

Warren nodded. "It takes control over us and we give into our animal instincts."

"Interesting." She smiled. "All right, let's get you two back into your old routine, shall we." She reached into her drawer and pulled out their badges.

"Ah, look at those beauties," Warren said as he reached for his.

"Feels like I never took it off," Matthew commented as he slipped his back on.

"You have to go down a see O'Reilly and give him this for your weapons," Michelle handed them separate sheets of paper.

They both took the forms.

"Do we still have our old desks?" Warren asked.

"Yes, now go. The sooner you guys get back to work, the more crimes can be stopped," Michelle said.

"Hell yeah," Warren said. "Thanks Captain."

"Don't mention it."

They went to get their weapons and then they returned to their old desks. They made themselves comfortable, rearranging things the way they liked it. They sat down and looked at each other across their desks.

"It's good to be back," Warren said.

"I couldn't agree more." Matthew smiled.

***

Natasha opened her eyes and blinked twice. She looked around the room, Xavier was coming out of the bathroom, towel around his waist and another he used to dry his hair.

"Hey there, luscious," Xavier said.

"Hi, sexy," Natasha replied. "Are we going to *Desires Unleashed*, tonight?"

Xavier chuckled. "No. I still don't think you're quite ready for that."

"I remember John took Christopher there to train. It seemed to work wonders for him," she said.

"You and Christopher are two different beings. I also recall Christopher losing his virginity the first time he fed there. *Desires Unleashed* is a place where your inhibitions are left at the door," Xavier said. "There aren't any taboos, or restraints, or fear, or shame. That back room is intense, Tasha. The sexual arousal alone is enough to make you lose control when feeding. Another thing, they'll want to have sex with you and won't care about having an audience. I know you're not ready for that."

"Since you put it that way, I guess not. I don't know if I ever will be," Natasha said as she climbed out of bed. She was starting to feel her thirst growing. She knew she needed to feed.

"We'll keep it simple. Hunt the dregs of society and take only what you need. You're doing better maintaining your control, but this will continue until I can be certain you can hunt on your own." Xavier pulled the towel free from his waist and caught Natasha's attention.

"Mmmmm, if I weren't so damn hungry right now, I'd lick you up and down," she said.

"Little girls shouldn't say such things to big bad wolves," Xavier teased seductively.

"Big bad wolves shouldn't have such tasty treats," Natasha shot back.

"I must say you've grown more randy since becoming a vampire. I *like* it," Xavier said with a throaty growl as he made his way closer to her. He kissed her deeply, his tongue and lips seducing her completely.

Natasha wanted to surrender to him. She wanted to throw him on the bed and have her way, but the gnawing in her gut was letting her know it would not be ignored. Reluctantly, she pulled away. "I'm starving."

Xavier smiled wolfishly. "I can tell."

"Yeah, I'm hungry for that, too, but I need something else more," she said as she made her way into the bathroom to get ready.

Xavier got dressed and then waited for her to dress as well.

"Are you ready?"

"Yeah, let's go."

They left the mansion in Xavier's new Boa XLS. He drove to a nearby park, pulling into the lot.

"All right, you go, I'll watch you. Take only what you need from one and then erase their memory," Xavier instructed.

Natasha nodded. She was about to climb out of the car when her cell phone rang. She answered it. "Hey Warren, what's up?"

"I'm glad I caught you. I just wanted to tell you that Matt and I got our jobs back."

"Really? That's great," Natasha said, genuinely happy for her two friends.

"Yeah, we've already told everyone, I just wanted to let you know, too," Warren said.

"I'm glad you told me, I'm really happy for you."

"Thanks, listen, I've got to go, just got a call in, but I'll catch up with you later, okay?" Warren said.

"Sure, okay, be careful," Natasha said goodbye and ended the call.

"I'm glad they're back where they belong," Xavier said.

"Me too."

"All right, now go on, I'll be close by."

Natasha climbed out of the car and began walking. She found her target a few minutes later, a nice-looking young man wearing dark jeans and a black coat and hat combo. She started to use the tricks Xavier had taught her, coaxing the man to come closer to her. When he did, she took him by the shoulders very gently and bit into his neck. She was beginning to look forward to this nightly ritual. The blood was indescribable. It was everything—sex, food, happiness and adrenaline. Nothing could compare. The first night she fed, she couldn't maintain control and she was grateful that Xavier was there.

Even now she wanted to drain this man until he had nothing left to give, but that would destroy them both. The guilt would be too much to bear … she never wanted to kill to feed her hunger. She forced herself to pull back from the delicious flow which took more willpower than she wanted to admit. She licked her lips and peered into the man's eyes.

"You won't remember me or this happening to you. Go home," she said and then she released the man. They guy walked away a bit woozy at first, but then he managed to make his way.

Xavier came up behind her. "That was good. One thing, you forgot to heal his bite wounds."

"Oh shit!" Natasha said.

Xavier chuckled. "There's still time, you can catch up to him."

Natasha smirked but did as she was told. She ran up behind the man, grabbing him by the arm. He turned and she put him into another trance long enough to heal his wounds, then she released her mental hold over him and ran away.

"How was that?" she asked Xavier.

"Much better than last week. It will get easier and easier as time goes on. Come on, let's go home," Xavier put his arm around her as they walked back to their car. He opened the door for her and walked around to the driver's side and climbed in. before he could start the engine a man came up to his window, tapping the barrel of a gun against the glass. Xavier looked at the gun, then the man and shook his head.

"Get out the fucking car, motherfucker!" the man demanded. "You *and* that skinny-ass bitch."

Natasha frowned. She considered herself to be voluptuous. Apparently, this guy didn't know what they hell he was talking about or who the hell he was 'fucking' with.

Xavier looked at Natasha. "I think we better do what he says." He climbed out of his car and Natasha did the same. The moment his feet hit the pavement, Xavier grabbed the man with lightning-quick speed. He wrapped his fingers around the hand that held the gun and applied pressure, crushing the delicate bones in the would-be carjacker's hand. The man tried to scream, but Xavier took hold of his mind and silenced him.

"You picked the wrong couple to jack tonight. Or, you picked the right one, it's really up to interpretation," Xavier said.

"Are you going to kill him?" Natasha asked a bit nervously.

Xavier kept his grip on the man. "Do you want me to?" He looked at her.

"No, we can just make him turn himself in," Natasha suggested.

"Not before sating my thirst," Xavier said before plunging his fangs into the man's jugular.

Xavier continued to muffle the man's screams with his hand as he drained him with lethal precision. The would-be car jacker's body shivered and twitched in Xavier's hands as his blood was painfully taken from him. Natasha watched transfixed as Xavier fed. She had always enjoyed watching him or Darian feed from each other for pleasure. But now she found herself enjoying watching them feed for food. Xavier pulled away with a slight tremor. He ran his tongue along his lips, savoring every drop.

"Okay, now he can turn himself in." Xavier planted the desire into the man's mind to immediately turn himself into the nearest police station and confess his crimes. He healed the bite marks and released him. He watched him walk away. "He's killed three people, you know."

Natasha looked at the man and frowned. "Then he'll get what he deserves in prison."

"*I* would have given him what he deserved tonight," Xavier pointed out.

Natasha looked at him. "He didn't deserve to die by ecstasy."

"He wasn't going to. You can make the bite extremely painful if you want to, as I just demonstrated. I'll teach you that, later. Right now, let's go home." He turned looking at her lustfully. He ran the tip of his tongue along his kissable bottom lip and moaned. "There are things I want to do to you that should be a crime."

"Ohh, careful now. You might be biting off more than you can chew," Natasha teased with a bat of her eyes.

"We'll see." Xavier flashed his signature smile as he climbed back into the car.

They drove to their mansion and Natasha pulled Xavier back to their bedroom. She slammed him against the door, closing it as she ripped open his shirt.

"Well, someone's excited," Xavier commented; noting the buttons of his shirt clattering to the floor.

"I can't help it, since becoming a vampire, I feel like I'm always horny," Natasha said as she began planting hungry kissing over Xavier's chest, paying special attention to his erect nipples. Natasha worked her way down, her fingers quickly undoing his belt, button and zipper.

Darian came out of the bathroom, toweling his hair. He stopped and smiled. "I'm glad I came home when I did."

Xavier looked at his growing erection and smiled. "I can see that."

"The more the merrier." Natasha stood up and began undressing. "Come on," she beckoned both men as she backed-up toward the bed.

Like snakes dancing to a charmer's flute, they followed her. Both men smiling with lusty thoughts as they shed whatever articles of fabric still covered them. Xavier climbed on the bed first, taking Natasha into his arms and kissing her passionately. His hand found her plump breast and he moaned as his fingers gently began to massage the tender flesh. He played with her firm nipples between his forefinger and thumb. Natasha gasped and arched on the bed as

Darian slid in beside her. His tongue sought the tiny nipple between Xavier's fingers; he sucked and licked the sensitive flesh sending her into a sexual frenzy.

Natasha ran her fingers through their hair as she squirmed beneath them. Their expert tongues, lips and fingers working her over until she thought she'd orgasm simply from their foreplay. Darian opened his eyes, watching her as he trailed his tongue between her breasts, past her stomach toward the moist heat between her legs. When his mouth covered Natasha, she cried out, arching even higher off the bed. Darian held onto her hips as his lips and tongue sucked and lapped at the delicate folds of her sex. In a movement too fast for Natasha to prepare herself for, he switched positions, pulling her on top of him. His face pressed firmly between her legs as he continued to bring her closer to orgasm.

Xavier growled low in his chest as he moved closer. He slid his hand up Natasha's back gently pushing her forward, exposing the round firmness of her voluptuous ass. His tongue found her other opening, sending a jolt of indescribable pleasure through her body. Together both men brought Natasha to her highest peak. Her body rocked and shuddered between them as they continued to stroke her. She collapsed on top of Darian, breathless and still shaking from her massive orgasm. Xavier pulled her back, sliding her off Darian until he balanced her on his lap. Darian sat up, licking his lips, savoring the taste of her and hungering for more.

"Still think you can handle us?" Xavier whispered seductively into her ear.

"I may have underestimated you," Natasha said with a giggle.

Darian leaned forward, taking her nipple into his mouth once more, working his tongue over the tender flesh causing Natasha to quake with each stroke. With his other hand, he reached between her legs taking hold of Xavier's erection. With expert precision and began to massage the hardening flesh, smiling when the tip began to glisten with Xavier's desire. He knelt before them, taking Xavier into his mouth. Xavier gasped as Darian's tongue swirled around his sensitive tip, dipping into the opening and lapping at the moisture there.

"Ahhh!" Xavier gasped again as Darian worked him over. His

hand found Natasha's tender nub between her legs, each stroke of his fingers brought her closer and closer to another climax. Darian pulled away, smiling as he guided Xavier's hardness into Natasha. She moaned and shivered as she slid down over him completely, encasing him in her heat and wetness. Slowly she began to grind her hips, dragging out both of their pleasures as long as she could. Xavier braced her hips before laying her on the bed. He drove into her deeply and with each thrust; he rubbed against her most sensitive core. She panted and moaned with unrestrained passion as her fingers gripped the sheets. At some point, Xavier flipped her around laying her flat on her back as he drove into again with an animal's abandon.

Darian watched them as he stoked himself, massaging his shaft with centuries-old skill. He moaned as the pleasure he was creating, along with the sight before him, enhanced his desire for release. Finally, he could restrain himself no longer. Positioning himself behind Xavier, he pressed both him and Natasha onto the bed, exposing his lover's opening. Xavier groaned as Darian entered him, pushing deeper and deeper. He pulled back, making sure to caress Xavier's sensitive spot. Then he drove in again, hitting that spot on each thrust. They rocked, kissed and stroked one another bringing each other to their brink.

Natasha was the first to cry out in release as her hand pressed on Xavier's ass, pulling him closer to her. Xavier smiled as he extended his fangs, sinking them into her jugular. Natasha was brought to a brand new height of ecstasy—one she had never before felt. Her body pulsated with a sensation that was indescribable. Every part of her was enrapt in pleasure and heat and she thought she would pass out from the intensity of her orgasm. Darian reached over Xavier, pressing Natasha's face towards his Xavier's neck.

"Drink," he commanded.

She did, biting into Xavier's neck and swallowing deeply. Darian smiled and followed suit, sinking his fangs into Xavier's shoulder as he continue to thrust into him. A thunderous orgasm rolled between them, building and building with each swallow they took until it burst forth in a tremendous tidal wave of one of the most exquisite pleasure they've ever felt.

Darian's screams were muffled by Xavier's flesh as his was muffled by Natasha's. Together, they rode the orgasm over and over again until it finally began to subside. Natasha pulled away, lying limply on the bed. Xavier collapsed on top of her and Darian fell over onto his side. All three were winded and drained, but completely satisfied. Several minutes passed before either of them could form words. It was Natasha who spoke first.

"A girl has to have her energy drinks before she takes you two on," she said with a girlish giggle.

"Not just you," Xavier said, patting Darian's thigh.

Darian's head shot up and he looked at him. "Are you implying that my stamina is waning?"

"Well, I'm still awake," Xavier teased.

"And you look as if you can barely keep your eyes open. I seriously doubt you have another go in you," Darian retorted.

Xavier just laughed because he couldn't deny it. His body was overstimulated and even though he joked about being awake. He was starting to feel the exhaustion creep over him.

"Well, I'm not about to put up pretenses, you two wore me out," Natasha said then she yawned. "At least when I take a nap, I'll get some visions."

"Does it bother you that you don't see them during the day?" Xavier asked.

She shrugged. "Yes and no. On one hand, I feel rested when I wake up. More rested than I've felt in years. On the other, I just hope I'm not too late to help Warren and the S.U.I.T. out when they need me."

"Overall, was it a small sacrifice to make for all that you've gained?" Darian inquired.

Natasha nodded. "The good thing is I can control my visions even more, dig deeper into what I see. Not to mention my clairvoyance is more powerful. I can see present and future events when I touch items now, so it's all good as far as I'm concerned."

"No regrets?" Xavier asked.

"You know, before I got sick, I was really struggling to lose those last fifteen pounds of my baby weight. But thanks to me suffering a slow, sickly, agonizing death, it just took the weight clean off me. So, no … no regrets," Natasha said. She smiled to let them know her words were not just to make them feel better, but for her as well.

"What about the sun, or food?" Darian asked.

Natasha shook her head. "Like I said, I'll take the good with the bad. Do I wish I could spend the day with my children more? Yes. When I had the opportunity, I still missed not being able to spend as much time with you two. The scales are never going to be balanced, but I'm here. And as long as I'm alive, I will enjoy whatever life I have."

Both of her men smiled and took turns kissing her. They cuddled up on the bed, getting more comfortable. Xavier was overjoyed that he had both of his *Chosen Ones* with him. He loved Darian more than words could express and Natasha was his heart as well. He didn't want to lose either of them. He looked at Natasha fall asleep and smiled. He kissed her forehead then turned and kissed Darian.

"My beautiful *inamorato*," Darian said, and then he kissed Xavier again. "I love you."

"I love you, too," Xavier replied before turning back around and closing his eyes.

Darian looked at both of his lovers and smiled. He had his children who he'd help raise for generations to come. He had two people in his life who loved him unconditionally. And he had his coven and friends who were loyal and loved and respected him. He had his Maker back into his life who loved him even till death.

He thought about all of his good fortune and he was content.

ABOUT THE AUTHOR

D. N. Simmons lives in Chicago IL., with a rambunctious German Shepherd that's too big for his own good and mischievous kitten that she affectionately calls "Itty-bitty". Her hobbies include; games, reading, watching television and going to the movies. She has been nominated at Love Romances and More, winning honorable mention for best paranormal book of 2006. She has won "Author of the Month" at Warrior of Words. She was voted "New Voice of Today" at Romance Reviews and "Rising Star" at Love Romance and More. To learn more, and have the opportunity to speak with the author personally, please visit the official website and forum at www.dnsimmons.com . D.N. is always interesting in meeting new and wonderful people.

Facebook: http://www.facebook.com/profile.php?id=100000552496587

Twitter:@DNSimmonsKOTD